The Last Immortal

RETURN TO THRAE

A NOVEL

KEITH W. MICHON

First Printing, October 2019
Second Printing, February 2022
Third Printing, December 2023

ISBN-13: 978-0-578-58344-0

www.keithmichonauthor.com
www.thelastimmortal.net

Dedicated to my wife — my anchor, my role model and my best friend.

Sincere thanks to my publishing coordinator and final review editor Jan Marie Combs.

Be Yourself

CONTENTS

The Last Immortal

RETURN TO THRAE

CHAPTER ONE – THE RESCUE

Approximately two hundred miles above Earth, Chad Stone's small translucent blue enclosure circled the planet. Weeks earlier, just before Chad lost consciousness, he wrapped himself in a thick protective plasma shield to protect his body from the enormous antimatter detonation that he had intentionally triggered. The annihilation event represented a desperate final attempt to stop the attacking Mitel space fleet. The formidable armada had followed Chad, his father Janus Stone and Janus's lifelong friend Markus Kilmar, six hundred light years across the universe. Their goal: secure the secrets of immortality and human hybrid transformation technology for the ruthless, but aging, Mitel Leadership. After the Leadership discovered that Chad was both immortal *and* a human hybrid, they would do anything to capture him.

Once Chad realized the Mitel space fleet would decimate Earth even after his capture, he made the brave and difficult decision to self-destruct his damaged human hybrid mechanical war machine. By increasing his plasma core to almost the speed of light, Chad caused high energy electrons to generate huge quantities of positrons. That initiated a scattering process which quickly produced significant quantities of antimatter. Chad was temporarily able to contain the particles with two spherical plasma shields and the enormous magnetic field being generated by the Mitel armada's corkscrew gravity control beams.

After Chad lost consciousness, the shields dissipated, releasing the antimatter. The instantaneous detonation was the largest the world had seen in over sixty-five million years, obliterating the Mitel fleet along with the majority of Earth's orbiting satellites.

Fortunately for Earth, Chad projected a temporary plasma shield around the planet twenty minutes before the detonation event, sparing the world's population from further harm. He also placed a small shield around the International Space Station to protect it.

Chad's blue translucent enclosure had retained and stored large quantities of oxygen, hydrogen and nitrogen released during the final stages of Chad's reverse transformation from his former human hybrid mechanical appearance. And now, a breathable mixture was slowly being discharged into the shield enclosure; while combining with the hydrogen to form small pockets of water for him to drink.

As the plasma shelter circled the planet fifteen times a day at over 17,000 miles per hour, it absorbed and attenuated the scorching heat of the sun; keeping Chad comfortable when temperatures plummeted to minus 250 degrees Fahrenheit during the nights.

Back on Earth, Janus, working closely with NASA and several other organizations, scrambled to put together a rescue plan but time was running out. Chad was not only weak and exhausted; the enclosure's orbit was starting to decay at an alarming rate. He was slowly falling toward Earth as he circled the planet. It was only a matter of time before the shield plummeted through Earth's upper atmosphere. Chad, having transformed back to flesh and blood from his prior mechanical appearance, had little chance of surviving re-entry.

"We don't have much time," concluded Janus, glancing toward the sky, "and it appears that we only have one chance at this."

Janus stood an impressive six feet eight inches tall, with broad shoulders and hazel eyes, his short salt and pepper hair a stark contrast to his thick black eyebrows and eyelashes. For the first 1,201 years of his life, Janus had been immortal. Fifteen years ago, he transformed into a living hologram to accompany Chad across the universe in a small, cramped Universal Speed Escape Pod (USEP). He returned to human form during Chad's instantaneous annihilation explosion, which triggered the hologram transformation process *in reverse*; a process referred to by living holograms as the *miracle of life event*. Janus no longer knew whether he was still an immortal, but part of him no longer cared.

"Understood," nodded General Michael Talbot.

The general was a career military and family man who took equal pride in protecting his country and raising his four children. Talbot, at 41 years of age, stood six feet three inches tall, with short blond hair, hazel eyes and a muscularly lean and trim physique. Until recently, he had overseen the investigation and cover up of UFO incidents in the name of national security. Working out of the U.S. Naval Space Surveillance System Command headquarters in Dahlgren, Virginia, then *Major* Talbot and his support team raced around the Country in response to credible UFO incidents. The crash landing of Janus's USEP in upstate New York fifteen years ago set in motion a chain reaction of events that changed his life forever. Now that Thraens were living on Earth, General Talbot was assigned to assist and protect them. No more UFO cover-ups. And with a shared passion for the universe and outer space propulsion technology, Janus and General Talbot had become close friends.

The two men stood side by side on the tarmac of the refurbished Kennedy Space Center Launch Complex.

"Crews worked around the clock to attach a prototype USEP to the Falcon Heavy-lift launch vehicle," explained Major Talbot. "Hopefully all the hard work and dedication will enable us to bring Chad back to Earth."

"I hope so," replied Janus. "I'm surprised his orbit decayed so rapidly. The Sun's activity during Earth's current eleven-year solar cycle should not have caused the atmospheric density at Chad's altitude to rise as much as it did. In doing so, it significantly increased the drag forces on his enclosure."

"Our scientists concluded that Chad's annihilation event triggered an unprecedented spike in the Sun's solar flare activity. While recent studies confirm the Sun's solar flares contain antimatter, Chad's sudden production of unprecedented levels of the rare material temporarily attracted increased quantities from the sun."

"In the form of increased solar activity . . ."

"Correct. So even if Chad had been able to shield the world's satellites with his plasma shield, we'd be having a tough time trying to keep all of them up in space. As it stands now, we are constantly adjusting the orbit of the International Space Station to compensate for the increased atmospheric density and drag."

General Talbot glanced at his watch. "Hey, it's time to get ready for launch."

Janus's orb, which had been circling the pad's perimeter, suddenly appeared next to him.

"Is your orb ready to go Janus?"

"Yes. Hopefully it will perform as expected."

"We're counting on it," nodded General Talbot.

After his own transformation back to human form, Janus realized he had retained control over his basketball sized monitoring orb. He concluded that during his fifteen-year long hologram state, some of his electrically charged brain particles, and probably his brain patterns *themselves*, had become integrated into his monitoring orb during their cohabitation and back and forth data sharing.

This ability was a key component in Chad's rescue. Once the USEP reached Chad, the plan was to release the orb and instruct it to use its levitation feature to push Chad's enclosure tightly against the USEP's outer entry door. Janus would wait in the pod's small entrance chamber and once the USEP's outer door slid open, Chad would reach through the outwardly permeable shield allowing Janus to drag him safely into the chamber.

As soon as the outer door closed and the inner door reopened, the astronauts would quickly pull Janus and Chad safely inside the spacecraft. Janus would then instruct the orb to release the shield and re-enter the chamber once it had been depressurized and the outer door reopened.

Out in space, Chad's orbit decay accelerated, and he knew it. He was now less than one hundred miles above the Earth's surface. At sixty-two miles above the planet, he would cross the *Karman line*, commonly known as the boundary between outer space and Earth's atmosphere. Once there, things would get very bumpy.

C'mon guys, he thought.

Denton Millas contacted Chad via the audio feed in a tiny emergency beacon installed behind Chad's left ear. Denton was energetic Thraen who stood six feet four inches tall. He was muscular with gray eyes and light brown skin. His most distinctive features were his infectious smile, thick black eyebrows although the remainder of his head and face were void of any facial hair.

"Chad!" said Denton, "I'm sure you've noticed that your orbit is starting to decay faster than expected. Hang in there. We're on our way."

There was no response.

"Are you getting nervous?"

Although Chad could not respond directly, Denton had worked it out so that one flash meant yes, and two flashes meant no. Chad slowly reached for his emergency beacon. The beacon light flashed once.

"I would be too. But don't worry, Janus will get you. Just hang in there, OK?"

The beacon light flashed once again.

The International Space Station, or ISS, had intentionally allowed its own orbit to decay substantially to remain near Chad's orbiting shield. After Chad's rescue, the USEP would rendezvous and dock with the ISS to evaluate Chad's health. Chad's accelerated orbiting decay had caused the ISS to cease its own decay out of fear of getting too close to Earth's upper atmosphere. A grim sense of urgency had descended upon the mission.

A day earlier, NASA had rolled out the USEP and Falcon Heavy-lift launch vehicle from the Vehicle Assembly Building in front of record crowds. All pre-takeoff flight checks had successfully been completed. It was now or never.

Janus was rushed over to the Medical Quarantine Facility to put on his launch and entry suit before being transported to Launch Pad 39A. When he arrived, he met the three astronauts who would be accompanying him into space.

"It's truly an honor to meet you Janus," said Colonel David Lindsey.

"Same here," added Commander Peter Fossum and Lieutenant Colonel Robert Kelly in unison.

"Thank you, gentlemen," replied Janus. "Now let's go get my son."

The group climbed into a silver shuttle bus. They were driven down to the Launch Pad via the three and a half-mile long crawlerway, a one-hundred-and-thirty-foot double wide cement pathway. The large circular fenced off Launch Pad was also made of cement, with a grass boarder surrounded by marshy wetlands. The pad itself located only fifty feet above sea level, was located adjacent to the Atlantic Ocean. As they drove along, Janus stared out his van window at the dense brush that covered the flat terrain.

Some five billion people worldwide were expected to watch the launch online. When they arrived at Pad 39A, several technicians, called *pad rats*, could be seen completing their final foreign debris check (FOD). The skies were mostly cloudy with rain and possible thunderstorms in the forecast.

We can't delay this launch, Janus thought as he stepped out of the shuttle bus.

Due to the enormous plumes generated by the launch itself, the threat of a grounded lighting strike was a serious concern. Lightning hitting either the launch vehicle or USEP and migrating down the launch plume represented a potentially catastrophic situation that typically canceled a launch until the weather cleared.

We've got to get up there quickly, Janus concluded.

The crew was rushed to the makeshift launch tower. An improvised elevator brought them one hundred and sixty feet up to a temporary spacecraft access arm. The crew scrambled along the arm's walkway to the USEP's cabin door.

Four recently built USEPs had been painstakingly reverse engineered in three scaled versions from the wreckage discovered after Janus's crash landing in upstate New York fifteen years ago. This pod, along with its twin, had been specifically designed to dock with the ISS.

The silver and white wedge-shaped pod had a curved nose that expanded on either side toward the rear of the craft before transitioning into trapezoidal shaped wings. In the back, the pod contained a triangular vertical stabilizer on each corner and a propulsion slot that extended rearward, its opening located just beyond the rear surface of the wing tips. Stored tightly underneath the pod and wings, beginning at its midpoint, sat four large quarter circle ring sections curving rearwards, two on each side. The ring sections were arranged in an alternating pattern since they extended beyond the centerline of the pod, due to their size. Just before the pod accelerated at normal speed, four large ring components extended from underneath the pod via powerful positioning bars. The four curving cylindrical sections turned, rotated, and locked together to form the ring itself; the ring drive shaft extending from each side of the pod's midpoint before being clamped down on by two of the assembling ring sections. Once activated, the spinning ring would immediately cause the pod to accelerate faster than the speed of light.

The craft and ring system were surrounded by interconnected plasma shields to help protect it. The plasma shields also temporarily gathered and stored kinetic energy used to power recharge both the shields themselves and the lower-than-light speed engines. The faster than light speed propulsion system bent both space and time by contracting space in front of the bubble and expanding space behind it, instantly hurtling the pod forward at speeds much greater than the speed of light.

Once the ring system was in place and its magnetic field fully activated, the negative vacuum void accelerated faster than the speed of light; akin to an insanely fast horizontal escalator traveling across a long structure that had just been folded together like a paper fan. The pod's negative vacuum bubble insulated the craft, occupants, and its contents by absorbing, attenuating, and filtering the tremendous g-forces generated by the high-speed travel. Anything inside the void experienced *actual* passage of time as light speed space-time changes occurring outside the pod's void bubble had no effect.

The pod could reach speeds over ten times the speed of light. But that was not the best part. Once the USEP reached approximately twelve times the speed of light, its intense gravitational field caused the craft and ring system to resonate at the exact same frequency as deep space. This allowed the pod's bubble to slip through space for light years at a time *in mere seconds,* analogous to electric current running through a wire. The sudden slip would then cause the pod and ring system to resonate at a slightly different frequency, decelerating the craft to twice the speed of light. The propulsion system would readjust, steadily build up speed to twelve times the speed of light and the process would repeat. Extensive testing had confirmed that the instantaneous travel or *slip speed* (as it was referred to by the development team) would end when enough energy resistance caused the pod's resonating frequency to change as compared to its natural surroundings.

A complex series of magnetic charges imbedded in several locations within the inner layers of the pod's inner skin surface that fined tuned the bubble's magnetic field *inside* the small craft; producing a self-adjusting magnetic field almost identically matched to the gravity on Thrae of 31.931 feet per second squared.

Using hand and footholds, Janus and the three astronauts climbed into the small, vertically mounted spacecraft and strapped themselves into their seats. As Janus scanned the instrumentation panel inside the pod, his mind was flooded with memories of his years spent developing Thrae's faster than speed of light travel program.

Not bad, he thought. *Not bad at all.*

"Welcome gentlemen," said a voice over the command and control communications system. We've completed all preflight checks and are preparing for launch."

"Roger that," replied Commander Fossum.

The inner and outer airlock doors automatically closed while the three astronauts quickly ran through final flight checks. Colonel Lindsey turned to look at Janus.

"Are you ready?" he asked.

"Yes," nodded Janus.

Colonel Lindsey gave Janus the thumbs up signal before speaking.

"Mission Control, pod systems fully functional and ready to go."

"Affirmative," replied the voice. "The launch tower has been retracted from the pad. Commencing final launch sequence now. Prepare to launch."

"Roger Mission Control."

"T minus 2 minutes to launch . . ."

Janus looked around the pod again.

It doesn't have our advanced materials, he thought. *But given the scope of this mission, everything should be fine.*

Janus's thoughts then drifted to Chad.

He must be feeling vulnerable and alone. Hang in there my son.

"T minus 1 minute to launch . . ."

Thirty seconds before launch, the on-board computers assumed control of the launch sequence.

"Ten, nine, eight, seven, six . . ."

The Falcon's main engines ignited, building up to over 90 percent of their maximum thrust. The USEP shook noticeably.

"Five, four three, two, one . . ."

The Falcon Heavy-lift launch vehicle lifted off the pad and streaked towards the sky, its engines now at maximum throttle. Ten minutes later, having separated from the launch vehicle, the USEP entered a low Earth's orbit.

Commander Fossum instructed the computer to scan for Chad.

Nothing.

He pushed the second of four propulsion buttons causing the USEP to shudder and lurch forward under the power of its twin high output plasma thrust engines. The small pod was now cruising over four hundred miles above the Planet. Commander Fossum instructed the computer to perform a second scan. A small object appeared on the three-dimensional display.

"We found him," confirmed Commander Fossum.

"Where is he?" asked Janus.

"Just under ten thousand miles ahead at an altitude of ninety miles."

"We need to get to him quickly."

"Understood."

Commander Fossum pushed the third button initiating maximum normal speed. The USEP lurched once again as it accelerated towards Chad and then gradually descended as it bore down on Chad's enclosure. At eighty miles above the surface, Commander Fossum cut the engines, initiated the reverse thrusters, slowing the USEP to 18,000 miles per hour. Seconds later, Chad's blue enclosure came into view.

"There he is," confirmed Colonel Lindsey.

"He's dropped down to 70 miles," said Lieutenant Colonel Kelly.

Just then, the USEP vibrated substantially.

"We're starting to hit the upper atmosphere," said Commander Fossum.

Janus knew the mission was in serious trouble.

"We can't launch the orb under these conditions," said Janus. "And we can't risk Chad going through re-entry and a crash landing."

"What do you suggest we do?" asked Commander Fossum. Janus thought for a few seconds.

"The slip ring," he replied.

"What?"

"Sixty-five miles above the planet and dropping," confirmed Lieutenant Colonel Kelly.

The vibrations increased dramatically.

Janus unbuckled himself and jumped from his seat. He quickly scanned the controls as he approached the console.

Looks the same, he thought.

From his enclosure, Chad watched anxiously as the USEP bore down on him. He was weak and exhausted and wanted to get out of his shield enclosure which shuddered considerably.

Come on Janus, he thought.

Janus pushed the first propulsion button initiating the deployment of the slip ring cylinder components and driveshaft from either side of the USEP. He quickly hit another button activating cameras imbedded into the lower surface of the pod. Janus then glanced at Commander Fossum.

"Steer us over Chad's enclosure," he instructed.

"But —"

"Do as I ask."

Janus stared back and forth at the camera monitor and three-dimensional displays located just above the center console. He then tapped the slip ring deployment button while holding down another button.

"What are you doing?" asked Colonel Lindsey.

"Over-riding the slip ring deployment . . ."

Just then, the cameras caught Chad's blue enclosure as the USEP slowly passed over it.

"Slow us down to 17,400 miles per hour," instructed Janus. "And bank a few degrees to the left."

By now the USEP was shaking severely.

Chad's pod suddenly reappeared on the middle of the screen.

"OK," said Janus tapping the slip ring deployment button repeatedly. "Increase our speed to 17,500 miles per hour, and lower us down gently."

Janus stared intently at the monitor as Chad's enclosure grew larger and larger. He then tapped the slip ring retraction button several times causing the ring to retract ever so slightly, pinching Chad's enclosure against the bottom of the pod.

"*Got you.*" said Janus.

He turned toward Commander Fossum.

"Get us above the outer atmosphere as quickly as possible. We're almost out of time. From the looks of things, Chad's enclosure is going to dissipate any moment."

Commander Fossum expertly guided the USEP to one hundred miles above the planet. By now, the vibrations had ceased.

Janus quickly approached the pod door.

"What's the code?"

"2247"

Janus pushed the black button to the left of the inside door, entered the keypad security code, pressurizing the chamber. Seconds later, the inner door slid open. He instructed his orb to enter the Chamber. After closing the door and performing a manual depressurization, Janus opened the outer door. He then rushed back to the console.

As Janus stared at the monitors, his shiny metallic orb appeared. Janus instructed it to activate its levitation beam while he tapped the slip ring deployment button several times, gently releasing the enclosure. The orb quickly directed Chad's blue plasma shelter up to the pod's outer door.

Closing his eyes to concentrate, Janus confirmed that the shield enclosure was positioned tightly against the door. He hurried to the inner door and entered the code into the keypad, pressurizing the chamber before the door slid open.

"When I give the word, open the outer door," he instructed.

Colonel Lindsey and Lieutenant Colonel Kelly quickly unbuckled themselves and jumped from their seats.

"Janus, you need to put on your helmet," instructed Colonel Lindsey.

"There isn't time," replied Janus.

The inner door slid open, and Janus scrambled inside the chamber. The astronauts quickly entered the access code, closing the door behind him.

This is it, Janus thought.

"Open the outer door," he instructed.

As the door slid open, Chad's blue shield enclosure was squeezed tightly up against the chamber, sparkling brightly. Janus knew what that meant. The shield was on the verge of dissipating. If that happened, he would be sucked out into space.

Janus could see Chad, in human form, lying in the enclosure. Janus reached towards Chad, only to be repelled by the enclosure wall.

"Come on Chad," he encouraged, "you can do it."

Chad tried to turn towards the door opening.

"He's very weak," muttered Janus.

Chad tried a second, and a third time, without success. The shield was now sparkling so brightly, Janus could no longer see into it.

"Chad!" shouted Janus, his heart beating rapidly.

Chad's hand suddenly appeared through the shield. Janus grabbed it and pulled him into the chamber.

"Close the outer door, *now*."

The door quickly slid closed. Soon thereafter, the orb confirmed that the enclosure had destabilized into sparkling blue sections. Less than a minute later, it was gone altogether.

Once the inner door slid open, the astronauts pulled Chad and Janus to safety. Lying on the USEP deck, Janus hugged Chad tightly.

"Thanks, Janus," said Chad weakly. "Thank you all."

Colonel Lindsey closed the inner door and depressurized the chamber.

Soon thereafter, the inner door to the re-pressurized chamber slid open and the monitoring orb sped into the cabin. By now, Janus was gently rubbing Chad's head.

"Thank you, gentlemen," said Janus.

"How'd you know to do all of that?" asked Colonel Lindsey.

"I directed the USEP development program on Thrae. I probably know this vehicle better than I know myself."

"Wow. I bet."

"Are we ready to rendezvous with the ISS?" grinned Commander Fossum.

"That sounds awesome," replied Chad wearily.

In two weeks, Zan Liss's two multi-seat USEPs had raced back across deep space six hundred light years along Earth's spiral arm. The Mitel armada, sent to Earth in search of the young Thraen immortal hybrid, had failed. The fleet had been sent by the Mitel Leadership, a group of cunning and ruthless old men who ruled Mitel with an iron fist.

Although the USEP's faster than light speed technology had been scaled up and applied to the much larger Mitel space fleet, the huge vessels simply could not attain the same speeds as their much smaller counterpart. Distances that took the USEP weeks to travel required several months for the Mitel fleet to traverse.

At the end of the armada's six-month voyage to Earth, Zan abandoned his position as Mitel Emperor and did what he could to prevent genocide of countless men, women and children. He used his own Mitel space cruiser to disrupt the plans of the attacking outer space armada. He eventually abandoned his badly damaged cruiser and headed toward home. It was a decision he didn't regret. He just wished he had made it sooner. Zan's parents, both Mitel resistance commanders, were killed in front of him when he was only 6 years old by Mitel Embedded Special Forces. He was told at the time that his parents were nothing more than common thieves. Zan was subsequently raised by foster parents on the Arman Matrix, Mitel's largest military base, also called the Hub. In time, the vivid memories of his parents' violent death faded. Zan's insatiable curiosity led him to become an expert mechanic, computer troubleshooter, and eventually a pilot. He also displayed a keen interest in military strategy, technology, programs and innovation. Base personnel would often shake their heads and laugh, saying that Zan could run the entire base all by himself. At twenty-one, he was a Mitel cruiser commander. At thirty-three, he was appointed Emperor of Mitel by the Mitel Leadership. Not until after Zan was appointed Emperor did he learn the truth about his parents. Once he did, Zan meticulously plotted his exit strategy.

The USEPs were surrounded by interconnected plasma shields to protect them. The pods were propelled to speeds over twelve times the speed of light by a large cylindrical graphene ring. The pod's plasma shields insulated the craft, occupants, and its contents by absorbing, attenuating, and filtering the tremendous g-forces generated by the high-speed travel. The plasma shields also temporarily stored kinetic energy used to power the craft's slip ring drive, plasma shields and lower-than-light speed engines.

Once the USEP reached approximately twelve times the speed of light, its gravitational field caused the craft to resonate at the exact same frequency as deep space. This allowed the pod to slip through space for light years at a time *in mere seconds*, analogous to electric current running through a wire. The slip would then trigger the spinning cylindrical ring to slow down and decelerate the craft to less than the speed of light. Once the ring came back up to speed, the process would repeat. The instantaneous travel or *slip speed* would end when enough energy resistance caused the pod's resonating frequency to change as compared to its natural surroundings.

In addition, every USEP contained an artificial gravity system that integrated complex magnetic charges imbedded in several locations within the inner layers of the pod's plasma shields; producing a self-adjusting magnetic field that almost identically matched the gravity on Thrae of 31.931 feet per second squared. The magnetic field also shielded the craft from the damaging effects of cosmic radiation as it hurtled through deep space.

A few years earlier, Zan, aided by his top-notch mechanics, had secretly reverse engineered one of the two small faster-than-speed-of-light pods he had confiscated from an old Thraen defense fortress. He gave the other pod to the Mitel Leadership to distract them from his questionable actions during the mission to Thrae. The Leadership had sent Zan there to eradicate the Thraen resistance once and for all. After being captured in the old defense fortress, Zan made a deal with the resistance in exchange for his life. The gamble paid off. Instead of being punished, Zan was put in charge of the enormous task of reverse engineering the propulsion technology to boost the entire Mitel fleet. During the retrofitting program, Zan secretly had the back end of his own cruiser reconfigured to store and launch his own two USEP pods. That contingency allowed Zan and several of his crew to escape Earth just before Chad's annihilation event. Once the retrofit program was successfully completed, Zan was appointed Emperor, and sent on the ill-fated mission in search of the young immortal.

As Zan's multi-seat USEP entered Thrae's solar system, he disabled the slip departure mode, causing the spacecraft to return to maximum normal power. The pod gradually banked toward its final destination. Along the way, the slip ring unlocked, retracted and rotated the four large curved sections into their storage location beneath the pod. Not far behind, the second USEP followed suit.

Muscular and almost seven feet tall, Zan was an awe-inspiring individual even as Mitel soldiers go. At age 36, he was completely bald, with thick black eyebrows and a matching mustache and goatee. Despite his imposing appearance, his best attributes were his intelligence, leadership and practical understanding of a wide range of Mitel military technologies and tactics.

"Can't wait to stretch my legs," said Ard Lindar, Zan's trusted best friend. With a love for history, Ard was a deep thinker who possessed a quick wit. Like Zan, he was tall, but much leaner, with short brown hair and charcoal black eyes that helped him hide his emotions. Ard's father had also been killed by Embedded Special Forces when he was 3 years old. But unlike Zan, Ard was adopted by a Mitel Leadership member and eventually sent off to the prestigious Mitel Military Academy. Also a cruiser commander, Ard always questioned the circumstances surrounding his father's death. Observing his stepfather growing up, he developed a healthy mistrust for the Mitel Leadership. When Zan told him the truth about his father, the news was not a surprise.

"It feels like forever since we walked on a planet surface and breathed fresh air," pondered Ard.

"It may not be that easy," replied Zan.

"I know. Hopefully the Mitel military has withdrawn its blockade."

"I wouldn't count on it."

Zan let out a long deep sigh before continuing.

"It would've been so much easier had we gotten the high-speed invisibility shields to work. We just couldn't get them to operate effectively on the larger craft."

The two pods propelled their way past the orbits of the four outermost planets in its solar system.

"We're quickly approaching Thrae," announced Zan. "I'm reducing speed to minimum normal."

The pod slowed down as it quietly passed Thrae's two moons. The group peered out of the forward facing trapezoidal windows. Directly in front was a large blue and green marble surrounded by a bluish-gray nebula, the blackness of space and countless stars. Small patches of white clouds dotted the planet high above the green interlocking land masses.

"Now there's a sight for sore eyes," said Ard.

Suddenly, the three-dimensional displays detected a large object approaching.

"We've got company," said Zan.

"What is it?" asked Lia Saar, Zan's former communications specialist. Standing a little over six feet tall with long curly brown hair and pale green eyes, Lia was stunningly beautiful.

"A Mitel cruiser —"

The communications light flashed. Zan reached over and pushed a button, activating the channel.

"Do you register the approaching object?" asked Rad Aarden, Zan's former Chief Medical Officer, from the second USEP. At eight feet four inches tall and almost four hundred pounds, Rad was a giant. The extensive black hair that covered most of his face and body made him look more animal than human. Although thought to be merely folklore, Rad was originally from the advanced but reclusive *Nomas* civilization located deep below the inhospitable Mitel Stone Forest. He was also one of a few Nomas who had ventured out into the world to make a difference.

"Yes," replied Zan. "A Mitel cruiser is closing in on us pretty fast."

"That's not good," replied Rad.

"No, it isn't."

"What are we going to do?"

"Trying to figure that out now," replied Zan, scanning the console data.

"Why don't I like that answer?" replied Ard.

"I'm with him," grunted Rad.

"Picking up another, much larger object behind the cruiser," confirmed Ard.

"A Mitel Transport vessel," Zan frowned.

"Yes. And you know what *that* means."

"Mitel Strike fighters are in the area."

"Should we re-energize the slip rings and make a run for it?"

"There isn't time. Where would we go anyway?"

"Maybe we could — "

"The distress signal."

"*What?*"

"These pods contain a Thraen emergency distress beacon. We uploaded it from the pods we found at the old defense fortress. With a little luck, maybe the Thraen resistance will send help."

"What do we do in the meantime?"

"Try and outrun them," replied Zan. He switched on the beacon. "Rad: tell Dru to follow our lead, OK?"

"I heard you," replied Dru Aldar, his lead mechanic, before signing off. Dru, short, stocky and bald with a gray goatee. He was the closest thing to a father Zan had ever known.

In the Mitel cruiser's Integrated Command Center, or ICC, the scanning specialist detected two small objects. He quickly ran a more detailed scan.

"Commander! My scans show two small crafts headed towards the planet."

"From where?" asked the Commander.

"Deep space. But it's as if they appeared out of nowhere."

"What else do the scans show?"

"The size and configuration of the crafts don't match anything in our known database. Wait, they just sent out a Thraen distress signal."

"They've detected us. Navigator, intercept them. Accelerate this vessel to full closing speed!"

"Yes, Sir."

"Order the transport vessel to launch twenty strike fighters to assist in the intercept. We mustn't let these craft get past our blockade."

"Doing it now," replied the communications specialist.

In the command center of a huge underground Thraen defense base constructed under Lake Victoria, a large lake outside the old population center of Bagan, a hologram technician picked up the distress beacon.

"Commander, you need to see this."

Thraen resistance Commander Arius Court made his way across the command center. A seasoned military man, Arius stood six feet five inches tall, with short gray hair, charcoal eyes and thick gray eyebrows.

"What is it?" he asked.

"I'm receiving an urgent distress signal from one of our craft beyond the outer atmosphere."

"*Where?*"

"Space tracking antennae indicate they are above the old population center of Kotor. Wait, there are two of them."

"But we don't have any craft out there."

"None that I'm aware of and Sir, there is something really odd about the distress signal," frowned the technician.

"What do you mean?"

"We haven't used that type of distress signal in almost *twenty years*. Wait. Tracking antennae now confirm two large objects are moving to intercept them."

Arius stiffened.

"A Mitel cruiser and Transport Vessel," he opined.

"Yes," nodded the technician.

Arias had a hunch there was something very unusual about the two crafts.

"Send six of our new fighters to provide cover fire and safe escort back to the base," he ordered.

"Yes, Sir!"

In less than a minute, Thraen tactical fighters raced up underground flight ramps, exiting through heavily concealed access slots on several of the lake's larger islands, and streaked skyward. The forty-two-foot-long V shaped silver and black multi-purpose fighters had trapezoidal winglets and forward swept wings on each side; two angled vertical stabilizers in the rear above and forward of its large rectangular propulsion slot. Like their Mitel counterparts, the Thraen fighters contained thrust vectoring and gyroscopic directional systems allowing the agile and durable Fighters to operate effectively in both outer space and atmospheric conditions. With four inline high output plasma thrust engines, and six superheated high energy hydrogen plasma burst laser cannons, they represented the next generation multi-role fighter. The Thraen craft were more than a match even when up against a dozen Mitel Strike Fighters.

"The cruiser just initiated a gravity control beam!" announced Ard.

"Time for some evasive maneuvers," replied Zan over the communication system.

"We'll follow your lead," responded Dru.

As the pods weaved to the left, the gravity control beam narrowly missed the second USEP.

"Here comes another one," confirmed Ard as the Mitel cruiser bore down on them.

This time, Zan jerked his pod to the right.

On the Mitel cruiser's ICC, the scanning specialist tracked the progress of the gravity control beams.

"They're successfully evading our gravity beams Sir," he announced.

"What *are* those craft?" grumbled the Commander. "What difference does it make? Order the strike fighters to *destroy them*."

"Yes, Sir."

"Twenty strike fighters bearing down on us," said Ard anxiously.

"Let's see if we can put some distance between us at full speed," said Zan. "Everybody, hold on."

Zan pushed the third propulsion button causing the pod to lurch forward under maximum normal power.

"They're opening fire!" confirmed Ard.

The lead fighters unleashed a barrage of lethal high energy lasers at the pods. Zan zigzagged back and forth to avoid them, shadowed by the second USEP.

It's only a matter of time before they hit us, he thought.

The lead Mitel strike fighter mimicked the movement of the second USEP. Confirming a target lock the pilot prepared to squeeze the trigger before suddenly disintegrating.

"What the . . . !" shouted Ard.

"Reinforcements have arrived!" shouted Rad as the Thraen fighters streaked past them in the opposite direction. Their high energy plasma cannons made short work of the Mitel fighters before turning their attention towards the Mitel cruiser and Transport vessel.

"Whoo-hoo!" shouted Ard.

"OK," Zan sighed with relief. "Let's slow down and head for the surface."

As the cruiser and transport vessel retreated deeper into space, the Thraen fighters quickly turned and headed back towards their base.

Nearing the planet's surface, the USEPs suddenly found themselves surrounded by the Thraen fighters. Two quickly pulled in front of Zan's pod.

"I think they want us to follow them," said Ard.

As the fighters descended directly at Lake Victoria, Zan became alarmed.

"*What* are they *doing*?" he asked just before the first one disappeared into an island entrance slot, followed by the second fighter.

"Hold on tight," cautioned Zan as he approached the entrance. He grimaced slightly as the USEP entered a rectangular tunnel which curved downward. Bright white ceiling and side lights illuminated the passageway. Several seconds later, repeating flashing yellow light strips along the bottom and sides of the tunnel caused Zan to slow his pod to minimum forward speed and deploy his landing gear. Rad's pod followed.

The tunnel opened into an enormous underground cavern. Zan's pod was instantly grabbed by a landing-assist gravity control beam which quickly decelerated and gently landed the spacecraft. Zan steered the USEP as it rolled to a stop behind the fighters. As he powered down the pod's engines, Rad's USEP stopped next to him.

On the ICC, the commander walked over to the scanning specialist.

"Where are the Thraen craft now?" he asked.

The specialist stared at his computer screen before typing quickly. He then stared again.

"Well?" asked the commander impatiently.

"I can't locate them. They've disappeared."

"They must have a large hidden base. We know from the last invasion that they have an extensive underground network. We *must* find it."

"Yes, Sir."

"What was their last known location?"

"Over a large lake . . . then they were gone."

"That makes no sense whatsoever. Useless scanners."

Zan and Ard stared out the pod's trapezoidal windows. The underground base was a technical marvel. Exit tunnels were visible in all directions. A large control center and several enormous air vents hung down from the ceiling. Dozens of Thraen advanced tactical fighters were parked tightly around the perimeter and hundreds of interior windows dotted the vertical surfaces. Bright white lights were everywhere.

"This is unbelievable," whispered Ard.

"I'll say," nodded Zan.

They watched as several hover craft approached from all directions.

"We have company," said Ard.

By now, the remaining Thraen fighters had landed behind them. As the hover craft touched down, hologram soldiers jumped onto the tarmac and pointed their electro laser long weapons directly at the pods. A minute later, one final hover craft approached, landing ten feet behind the others. Led by Arius, several Thraen officers walked past the circle of soldiers. Approaching the pods, Arius motioned them to exit their spacecraft.

Once the outside airlock doors opened, Zan and the others climbed down using hand and footholds. As they gathered between the two pods, Arius and his team cautiously approached.

"Identify yourselves!" he ordered. Arius surveyed the Thraen markings on the surfaces of the pod.

"My Name is Zan Liss."

"*Emperor Liss?*"

"No, just Zan Liss now."

"I'm Arius Court, Commander of the Thraen resistance. What about your armada and its mission?"

"We believe the armada was destroyed. We may be all that's left."

"That's impossible."

"He's telling you the truth," replied Lia.

"Who's she?"

"Lia Saar, Communications Specialist, and a member of the Mitel resistance. As are Dax Bann and Mat Wall," explained Zan. "Without their help, I wouldn't be alive. They hid their true allegiances until things started to get out of hand. They saved my life on the ICC. They are brave and dedicated."

At twenty-one, Dax had been an assistant navigator on Zan's cruiser and a fourth-generation resistance fighter. Mat, only nineteen, was the cruiser's assistant scanning specialist, and a third generation Mitel resistance fighter.

"They're so young," nodded Arius respectfully.

"They are," acknowledged Zan. "But in my opinion, they are the future of Mitel. And to my left is Ard Lindar, previously a top-notch Mitel cruiser commander, not to mention a graduate *with honors* from the prestigious Mitel Military Academy."

Ard rolled his eyes at Zan before waving.

"Standing next to him is Rad Aarden, Chief Medical Officer and his team."

"I must say, you are the largest person I've ever met."

Rad nodded quietly.

"To my right, Dru Aldar and his team of expert mechanics," motioned Zan. "When it comes to space propulsion technology, he and his team are the best."

"Greetings to you all," replied Arius. "But why did you come *here*?"

"To help the Thraen resistance. We tried to stop the Mitel armada from committing genocide on a distant planet. We couldn't go home, at least not yet. Our thought was if we can help you free your people, *maybe* Thrae would consider helping us free ours."

"We welcome any assistance from anyone loyal to our cause," answered Arius. "We heard that you were the architect that upgraded the Mitel fleet. Unfortunately, those efforts have significantly hampered our resistance efforts. To this point, we have been unable to break the Mitel blockade. We have lost many good people trying."

"I am truly sorry," replied Zan sincerely. "But I didn't upgrade the Mitel fleet all by myself. My mechanics were the real brains behind our fleet's transformation. If it's any consolation, we can help Thrae at least achieve the same results and probably better."

"That is a very enticing offer Zan Liss," nodded Arius, "but your armada, what happened to it?"

"It was wiped out by a young Thraen Battle Sphere named Chad Stone who regrettably reversed his energy core."

"So, it's true then. We heard that your armada went looking for him. We had also heard that an infant Battle Sphere escaped our planet during the second Mitel invasion fifteen years ago."

"Yes, he did. Along with his father."

"His *father*? Who?"

"Janus Stone," replied Ard. "But you may know him by another name."

"A name that is more famous than *Janus Stone*?"

"Yes, Zebulon Park."

"*What?* The Battle Sphere that repulsed the first Mitel Invasion? But Park is dead."

"Evidently not. He accompanied his son in hologram form," replied Zan. "I presume he trained him to help defeat our fleet, along with the help of the Mitel resistance, that is," he added.

"The Mitel resistance? *How?*"

"We successfully imbedded our people into the Mitel military," smiled Lia proudly. "Our brave and selfless suicide bombers destroyed several of their craft during the armada's long voyage through deep space."

"That was very courageous. But the boy, the young Battle Sphere, he is *no more?*"

"He had the ability to project protective plasma shields. We sent him a last-minute message to try to place one around himself. We never confirmed that he received it, but even if he had, the cosmic explosion was immense. I don't know how anything could have survived."

"That is regrettable. We could certainly use him here."

"You mean to end the Mitel blockade?"

"Well yes that, but more importantly, to oppose the young Mitel Battle Sphere."

"*What?*" Ard blurted.

"It's a long story," Arius began. "However, suffice to say a young Thraen girl and her family were captured and taken prisoner a few years ago as part of a daring Mitel commando raid. Our intelligence received a tip from the medical community that she was exhibiting early transformation characteristics. A review of her medical records confirmed that her body possessed the classic indicators:

abnormally high levels of titanium, aluminum, beryllium, cobalt, manganese and cadmium. We were waiting for her to grow older. We still don't know how the Mitels found out about her and her whereabouts. At this point, we believe she is being trained to attack our planet, with the Mitel Leadership holding her family hostage to force her to do their bidding."

"That sounds like the Mitel Leadership," grunted Ard. "And to think they sent an armada across the universe."

"We're very disappointed she was taken from us but we're also glad the Mitel Leadership didn't send that armada here. If they'd done that, I don't know if we'd be standing here now."

"You may be right," replied Zan.

"What's the story behind the pods you arrived in?"

"We recovered two smaller ones from inside your old defense fortress several years ago. They formed the basis of our fleet upgrade."

"You reverse engineered them?"

"Correct."

"But how did you know where to find them?"

"I was a young Mitel cruiser commander during the second invasion. We were patrolling around the planet and stumbled upon a small pod. Scans revealed that it contained what turned out to be Chad Stone. Before we could grab his pod with our gravity control beams, it escaped into deep space at incredible speeds. I eventually concluded someone was leading a secret development program. That *someone* was Janus Stone. We spoke briefly during the Mitel attack on Earth. He had no idea that Thrae survived the rolling energy wave."

"Understandable. *Is he still alive?*" asked Arius.

"We don't know," replied Zan.

"I see. We too located a few of the small pods in the old defense fortress, but with the Mitel blockade, there wasn't much we could do with them."

"We *must* get rid of the blockade. That's where Lia, Dax, Mat and the Mitel resistance can help."

"*How?*"

"I'll explain later."

"Here we go again," grunted Ard.

"Well," said Arius, "if the Mitel armada is no more, then the rest of the Mitel fleet could be vulnerable. Maybe there's still hope."

"That's our expectation as well."

"I was told by Zi Liss," added Lia, "Zan's uncle and a Mitel resistance commander that things have a way of working out."

"Let's hope he's right for our sake," replied Arius. "If the Mitel Battle Sphere returns to oppose us, I don't see how we can prevail."

"It wouldn't be easy," said Zan. "But it sounds like we have some time. Before she arrives, we have a lot of work to do. First, we need to eliminate the blockade. Second, we need to start retrofitting your entire fleet. *Then* we'll figure out a plan to deal with her."

"A plan to deal with a *Battle Sphere?*" grunted Arius. "With all due respect — "

"I know what you're going to say, but before the young Battle Sphere reversed his core and facilitated the annihilation, the Mitel armada *almost* captured it."

"Really? But *how?*"

"Using the Mitel fleet's upgraded corkscrew antigravity control beams in conjunction with swarming strike fighters. The fighters lured the Battle Sphere into outer space which allowed the cruisers and transport vessels to attach their gravity beams from all directions. The Battle Sphere was effectively incapacitated. "

"Those enhanced gravity beams," groaned Arius.

"I'm sorry about that too . . ."

"Don't tell me you were also behind that upgrade."

"Yes."

"You possess many talents Zan Liss," mused Arius. "But what if this Battle Sphere also reverses its core?"

"Good question. My hunch is that she won't know about that ability. Remember, she won't have Zebulon Park there to train her."

"True. Tell me then, are you currently a member of the Mitel resistance?"

"In time I guess," replied Zan. "But first, we would like to become members of the Thraen resistance. That is, if you'd have us. As I said, if we can help Thrae free itself from Mitel's repression, maybe Thrae would consider helping us free our people from the oppressive Mitel Leadership."

"Deal," smiled Arius. "From what you're telling me, you and your crew would be of great assistance here." He stepped forward and reached out his hand.

"Great," grinned Zan. The two men shook hands tightly. "I must say, this is an impressive underground facility."

"Thank you. It's one of many."

"*Many*?"

"Yes. It's all part of our underground bunker system. After the first Mitel invasion, we took steps to protect ourselves in the event of another attack. The extensive underground shelters are one reason why so many people survived the rolling energy wave triggered during the second assault."

"I see."

"Yes, you will."

"What do you mean?"

"I will give you a tour. We have two adjacent underground chambers larger than this. In each one, we are building three state of the art space cruisers. The timing of your arrival is perfect."

"Hey! Another development program for you to sink your teeth into Zan," laughed Ard.

"I welcome the opportunity," smiled Zan.

"Excellent," replied Arius. "We'll talk more. For now, you all must all be very tired. Come with us. We'll see to it that you receive some well-deserved rest and relaxation."

"That sounds like music to my ears," clapped Ard.

"Don't get too comfortable Ard," stated Zan. "As I said, we've got a *lot* of work to do."

CHAPTER THREE – BACK TO EARTH

Commander Fossum piloted the USEP towards the ISS while Janus and the other astronauts helped Chad into a launch and entry suit. Due to Chad's weakened condition, he would be evaluated before returning to Earth.

Chad rested comfortably while Janus peered out the small trapezoidal shaped front windows. Commander Fossum had slowed the pod to minimum forward speed. The ISS came into view directly ahead. Commander Fossum shut down the pod's main engines and steered the USEP underneath the space station before turning up slightly in front of it. NASA Command Center assumed control of the propulsion system and initiated the pod's thrust vectoring rockets. The spacecraft slowly turned left ninety degrees before rotating another ninety degrees. The Command Center then reduced the pod's velocity ever so slightly, allowing it to approach the ISS'S IDA-2 international docking adapter attached to the top of the PMA-3 pressurized mating adapter.

In a separate compartment at the back of the USEP, two large exterior doors at the top-center slowly opened to reveal the pod's Orbital Docking System or ODS. The system allowed the pod to connect to the ISS.

NASA personnel monitored the approach closely. To avoid dangerous oscillation from a non-symmetrical docking, the pod's ODS contained a base ring and a guide ring. Three torsion spring-mounted capture latches on the guide ring allowed for the pod's initial soft capture before twelve pairs of structural hooks on the base ring established a rigid air tight connection.

Janus watched intently as the pod drew closer and closer to the ISS. Without a sound, the ODS mated with the IDA-2.

"Docking has been completed," announced the Command Center.

"Roger," replied Colonel Lindsey.

"OK Chad, are you up to making your way inside the space station," asked Commander Fossum.

"I'll try," replied Chad weakly.

The astronauts helped Chad walk to the rear of the USEP. Commander Fossum entered a keypad code pressurizing the small rear bay. After inserting another keypad code, the door slid open and using hand and footholds they climbed one by one into the ODS tube; the three astronauts helping Chad make his way up. As they passed beyond the USEP's magnetic gravity field, they suddenly became weightless.

"Whoa," said Chad before being grabbed by Commander Fossum.

The group slowly made their way towards the docking adapter. The hatch door to the PMA-3 was pulled open as they approached. One by one, they entered the Harmony Module which housed the American Crew. Chad, Janus and the astronauts were warmly greeted by the six astronauts stationed on the ISS. Chief Medical Officer Vladimir Kotov moved forward and patted Chad on the shoulder before he and ISS Commander John Williams helped him towards the makeshift medical area. Chad was placed in a hanging sleeping bag temporarily secured against the side wall.

Vladimir quickly hooked up the ISS's lightweight ultrasound device and ran a scan of Chad's body, the results transmitted down to NASA's Marshall Space Flight Center in Huntsville, Alabama for review. Next he attached both a portable Holter monitor to measure Chad's heart rate, and a Continuous Blood Pressure Device or CBPD to Chad's finger using a finger cuff. That data was also transmitted down to NASA. During launch preparations, Jim and Molly had arranged for Chad's medical history to be forwarded to NASA's expert medical personnel for comparison. An hour later, the results came back: Chad's vital signs were normal, and the ultrasound disclosed nothing unusual. Their recommendation: feed him *a lot*.

Over the next two days, Chad ate almost non-stop while Janus spent most of his time huddled with the astronauts discussing advanced travel technology. NASA teased the ISS crew, saying nothing else was getting done. On the third and fourth days, Chad walked on the COLBERT, the ISS treadmill. He was held in place by bungee cords due to the lack of gravity. With food and exercise, his strength continued to return. Chad's biggest adventure on the ISS was learning to use the Tranquility Module's space toilet.

"Now you're a real spaceman Chad," laughed Commander Williams before turning serious, "and by the way, thanks for saving all of us. You're one *very* special human being, you know that?"

Chad grinned from ear to ear.

On the fifth day, NASA medical personnel decided it was time for Chad to return to Earth. After taking group pictures, Janus, Chad and the ISS astronauts hugged goodbye. Once the adapter hatch was pulled open, Commander Fossum led the way back down the ODS to the USEP's rear door. He entered the keypad code causing the door to slide open. The group climbed into the spacecraft and began to re-acclimate themselves to the pod's artificial gravity. By the time they landed, the crew would be ready to walk on their own.

Mission Control carefully undocked the pod and closed the two large doors in the rear bay. Once the pod moved away from the ISS, everyone strapped themselves in before Commander Fossum activated the first propulsion button. The USEP moved ahead under minimum normal power. The NASA computers calculated and programmed the flight path into the pod's computer. Commander Fossum was instructed to bank left and slowly descend toward Earth.

The NASA computers took full control of the pod's navigation system as it approached Earth's outer atmosphere. Helped by the pod's enhanced outer plasma shields, the USEP passed through the outer atmosphere with only moderate vibration. Looking out the front trapezoidal windows, the crew watched the Sun rise along the horizon. After the plasma shields were intentionally disabled, the pod shuddered slightly, as two triangular shaped forward wings deployed from its lower section.

The computers continued to manage the spacecraft's descent toward NASA's Kennedy Space Center Shuttle Landing Facility on Merritt Island, Florida. Billions of people around the world watched on-line as the spacecraft descended toward the runway.

Molly and Jim Johnson, Chad's adoptive parents, watched from the air traffic control tower as the pod came into view. Jim, a tall and lanky outdoorsman, was a physics professor at the local community college just outside of Coopers Falls, upstate New York. Molly, an avid runner and health enthusiast, was a first-grade teacher at Bickford Street Elementary in Coopers Falls.

Standing next to them were Mayla Tallis and Teri Anton, Chad's former Battle Hologram commander and scanning and logistics specialist. Mayla stood five feet eight inches tall, was athletic and exceedingly attractive. She had shoulder length dark brown hair, charcoal colored eyes and a bronze complexion. Teri, much taller at six feet five inches tall, had wavy dirty blond hair, hazel eyes and a nose that was large but still looked normal in proportion to his long face and wiry figure.

Waiting anxiously behind them was Melissica Erickson, Chad's girlfriend. Melissica stood five feet nine with an athletic build, shoulder length thick brown hair, a light complexion with freckles on her cheeks.

"There it is," smiled Molly anxiously.

Having dropped below two-hundred feet, the USEP had deployed its tricycle style landing gear as it approached the three-hundred-foot-wide runway. At fifteen thousand feet long, it is one of the longest runways in the world.

NASA personnel closely monitored the pod from the adjacent Landing Aids Control Building. Once the spacecraft touched down at approximately 220 miles per hour, it deployed a large rear parachute to slow it down. Without traditional jet engines that use reverse thrusters, the pod needed something else to help it decelerate. And since Earth scientists had not yet invented landing-assist gravity control beams, the parachute would have to do for now.

The USEP touched down at the beginning of the high friction runway, eventually rolling to a stop near the other end. As it cooled down, safety crews raced towards the pod from the access roads. Portable stairs were driven out onto the runway and placed below the entrance door.

Molly, Jim, Mayla, Terry and Melissica were taken onto the runway followed by General Talbot and his assistant, Captain Jason Miller.

After the pod's exterior door slid open, Commander Fossum slowly exited the craft followed by Chad, Janus and the other two astronauts. It was easy to pick Chad out in a crowd. At 16 years old, he was already six feet five inches tall with a muscular, lean build, a light complexion and long black hair and thick black eyebrows and eyelashes like his father.

"He looks so frail," whispered Molly.

Chad shielded his eyes as he was slowly helped down the stairs. General Talbot greeted him with a huge smile and pat on the arm.

"Thank you very much Chad," he said. "You did a really brave thing up there."

"I just did what I had to do," replied Chad modestly.

"We have some people here to see you," motioned General Talbot.

Molly ran towards Chad, followed by Jim and Melissica, while Mayla and Teri watched. Molly hugged Chad tightly before being joined by Jim.

"We love you so much and we're so happy you're OK," whispered Molly. She then stepped back to look at him. "We were so scared . . ." she added, wiping tears from her eyes.

"Thanks Mom," Chad grinned, "I love you too."

Chad then hugged Melissica tightly.

"Welcome back stranger," she said.

"What do you have to say for yourself, young man?" asked Jim.

Chad thought for a moment as he glanced toward the sky.

"I want to go home," he replied eventually.

"*Home?*" asked Molly nervously.

"Yes. Home to Coopers Falls," smiled Chad.

"Not before NASA doctors check you out here and give you a clean bill of health," said General Talbot.

"Groan . . ." Chad sighed.

CHAPTER FOUR – THE MEETING

A 15-year-old girl walked across the heavily fortified Mitel Leadership Complex toward the imposing stone and glass Leadership Building. Glancing up toward the twenty-foot high, twelve foot thick reinforced stone walls, she glimpsed an elite Mitel Special Forces Sniper duck from view.

Several huge security guards surrounded her as she entered the building. Standing six foot, two inches high, she was taller than the average Thraen woman.

"Are you Falon Ross?" asked one guard.

"Yes," she replied hesitantly, "but that's not my —"

"The Mitel Leadership is expecting you," interrupted a second guard.

A third guard pointed a handheld scanning device at Ana, before motioning her to confirm her identity on the retinal scanner. She pulled her long black hair to one side and stared intently at the machine. A light on the left side of the device flashed green.

"Follow me, please," said the first guard.

Ana complied, walking up the wide marble staircase. Two more guards followed behind her, their footsteps echoing loudly. Reaching the second floor, the first guard motioned Ana toward a set of massive stone doors which opened slowly to reveal the Mitel Leadership Forum Hall. Entering the Hall, Ana saw ten old men across the room, seated behind a curved stone bench located five feet above the forum floor. Standing in front of the bench were three more huge security guards.

Approaching the bench, the guards motioned for Ana to stop. The two guards who had followed her up the stairs took positions behind her.

"Falon Ross, we have eagerly awaited your arrival," said the first member directly across from her.

"My name is Ana —"

"Your *Mitel* name is Falon Ross. Do you understand?"

Ana nodded yes.

"Good. Now then, the time has come for you to begin your training."

"But how?" asked Ana somewhat confused.

"It's very simple. You will transform into Battle Sphere mode, which in turn, will activate your Battle Hologram. Your Battle Hologram team will guide you from there."

"OK," replied Ana.

"But first, we are going to send you to the stone formations in Hako. We think it will be an excellent place for you to practice flight maneuvers and test out your laser cannons."

"From there," a second member began, "she could take advantage of the close proximity of Thraen and Mitel solar systems which share the asteroid belt that forms a figure eight. Falon could hone her agility and weapons skills on the large quantities of rock, stone and ice as they swap back and forth between our solar systems."

"A wonderful idea," nodded the first member.

"Once you become a proficient fighting machine," interjected a third member, "You shall return to Thrae and help us *crush* the rebellion once and for all."

"What?" Ana exclaimed. "You want me to kill my *own* people?"

"Not your own people, the Thraen military."

"But I can't —"

"You can and you *must*," interrupted a fourth member. "If you value the lives of your mother and two sisters, you will do *exactly* as we ask."

Ana stood stoically, her hazel eyes darting back and forth as she tried to control her emotions.

"Do I sense some hesitation?" asked the first member.

"No . . . I mean yes! This is all so confusing."

"Why is that?"

"I've been measured, analyzed, poked and prodded," explained Ana indignantly. "My blood has been drawn more times than I can remember. I have been forced to partially transform over and over in a cramped underground bunker, and then scanned again and again" she continued, her eyes welling up in tears. "I haven't seen or heard from my mother and sisters for over a year. I don't even know if they're still alive."

"Your family is safe and in good health."

"Prove it!"

"Very well . . ."

On a black wall monitor, the face of Ana's mother suddenly appeared.

"Mom, is that *you*?"

"Yes, my love, it's me," replied Adria. Her mother's face looked haggard and tired. Her brown hair was now turning gray.

"Are you OK? Are they treating you well?"

"Yes."

"And Caron and Jaida?

"They're OK. We miss you so much and hope that — "

The screen suddenly went blank.

"Why did you do that?" asked Ana angrily.

"You wanted proof that your family is alive and well. We gave it to you," explained the first member.

"But — "

"It's time for you to do what we ask."

"And if I *can't*?

"Don't think in terms of failure."

Ana didn't respond.

"I promise you that your family will remain safe and be released unharmed and you will all be allowed to return to Thrae. That is, as long as you do what you are told. Our quarrel is not with the people of Thrae. Rather, it is with its leadership and the Thraen resistance. Do you understand Falon?"

"Yes," nodded Ana quietly.

"Good. Prepare to leave by morning."

"But — "

"That is all for now."

"But, what if — "

"I said *that is all!*"

One guard stepped towards Ana. She glanced at him, her eyes now bright white. He instantly froze in fear knowing that a quick energy burst would eviscerate him. Ana then stared defiantly at the Leadership. Several members fidgeted noticeably in their seats. Seconds later, her eyes returned to normal. She quickly turned and walked out of the chamber all by herself. There was a long silence.

"Do you think she can be trusted?" asked the second member eventually.

"As long as we retain custody of her family," replied the first member. "That is the only thing that prevents her from killing us like she could have done just now."

"And when she does what we ask? What then?"

"Everything is proceeding as planned. The concrete and aluminum bunker allowed us to prevent her Battle Hologram from materializing. It also blocked her psycho-kinetic ability to summon heavy metal trace elements and helium-4 from the surrounding ground and atmosphere. That kept her from fully transforming despite our count-less triggering events. Quite frankly, I'm surprised she survived.

"Understood, but — "

"All of the extensive testing, scanning and mapping of her hybrid form during her partial transformations al-lowed us to reverse engineer our own *mechanical* Battle Sphere."

"But the fabrication and testing will take time."

"We are already making great progress. Granted, it won't be as fast and agile, nor will its weaponry be as formidable. But with a thousand of them at our disposal, they will ultimately overwhelm and destroy any Battle Sphere. We also won't have to worry about the human element of loyalty."

"I concur," nodded the third member.

"More importantly, our scientists are feverishly work-ing to develop the immortality serum from her blood samples. Once the serum is perfected, we can rule Mitel indefinitely."

"After all this time, immortality is finally within our reach."

"Yes."

"And then what?" asked a fourth member. "*What do we do about the girl?*"

"What then?" the first member smiled. "When she transforms back to human form, we kill her *and* her family. After that, we reduce Thrae to a smoldering lifeless planet once and for all."

Ana woke up early the next morning and was taken to the Hub. From there, she boarded a hover craft which carried her to a military transport shuttle. She was met by Kai Lind, a Mitel military doctor and trained psychologist. At 38, Kai looked young for her age. She stood five feet five inches tall, with jet black hair, light brown skin and deep blue eyes.

"Hi Ana," smiled Kai. "My name is Kai. I'm here to accompany you to Hako."

"Why?" asked Ana.

"To monitor your vital signs and just look after you in general."

"I don't need anyone to look after me."

"You say that now. Have you ever been to Hako? It's a pretty desolate place."

Ana didn't respond.

They boarded the shuttle along with three heavily armed elite Mitel Special Forces soldiers. They all wore *chameleon* uniforms, vests, helmets, boots, and gloves. The equipment automatically changed color based on the surrounding environment; from black to three shades of camouflage: sand/tan, green/brown and blue/gray although the patterns could be overridden to a fixed pattern at any time. The uniform quickly became standard Special Forces combat attire and was also readily available on the black market.

The shuttle took off vertically before it turned and streaked across the sky toward Hako. Ana slept most of the way there. Several hours later, the shuttle slowed down awakening her. The shuttle hovered over a large circular opening before completing its vertical landing. The pilot activated an exit door and retractable stairway located at the bottom of the craft.

The soldiers tossed out their large duffle bags onto the ground below before exiting the craft. Carrying their electro laser long weapons across their chests, they performed a quick sweep of the area. Minutes later, one of the soldiers reappeared and motioned Ana and Kai to exit the shuttle. They climbed down the stairway and placed their smaller duffle bags on the ground. Countless tall stone structures stood along one side of the circular opening. Solid stone formations rose vertically into the air around the rest of the manmade cavity. It looked to Ana like a combination of Stone Forest and art museum. Off in the distance, tall mountains reached toward the sky.

"What *is* this place?" asked Ana.

"That's a good question," replied Kai. "At one time it was a geological research facility. Much of the stone that once filled this opening was used to build the Mitel Leadership complex. It's incredibly dense and durable. I'm not sure what this place is used for now if anything."

Kai picked up her duffle bag, flung it over her left shoulder and walked towards the structure.

"That's our home," she pointed. "The Mitel military supposedly powered up the facility and restocked the food supplies last week." She explained. "If you haven't figured it out by now, they can be pretty unreliable. We should take an inventory of what's here, OK?"

Just then, the shuttle lifted off with a high-pitched screech before turning to head back to the Hub. As Kai and Ana watched it disappear over the stone formations, two of the soldiers grabbed the remaining duffle bags and silently headed towards the buildings. The third soldier continued to survey the area.

As they walked toward the buildings, Ana looked around.

"It's eerily peaceful," she said.

"That's one way to describe it," laughed Kai.

Once inside the living quarters building, they spent the rest of the day cleaning and organizing the food supplies.

"On a positive note," announced Kai, "they left us enough food to last about a year."

I have no intention of staying here a year, thought Ana.

As Kai and Ana kept organizing, the soldiers mostly kept to themselves, rotating every few hours to keep watch outside the facility.

"What are they afraid of?" asked Ana eventually.

"Afraid? These guys aren't afraid of anything," she replied.

"You know what I mean."

Kai studied Ana's face for a moment before responding.

"We are in the middle of nowhere," she began. "I presume this location was chosen to discourage the Mitel resistance from following us here. It's very difficult to get to on foot *or* by hover craft. But as the resistance continues to grow and strengthen, anything is possible, I guess. I'm told that large, dangerous creatures roam these stone formations and mountain regions."

"Like what?"

"There have been multiple sightings of Gugu, Gorg and Onai."

"What are those?"

"Various forms of incredibly large human-like creatures. All of them completely covered in hair. I've been told that some are almost ten feet tall."

"Oh."

"Yeah. And during the excavation of this site, I heard that several enslaved workers mysteriously disappeared."

"Maybe they escaped?"

"As I said, this place is almost impossible to get in and out of on foot. They were probably killed and eaten by the creatures."

Ana didn't respond. By now, she was realizing that another reason for coming to this place was to make sure she couldn't escape if she couldn't transform.

It was getting late, and Ana retired to her sleeping quarters for the night. Unable to sleep, she spent the next several hours sitting in the dark. She stared out her small windows at the stone formations in the moonlight. Ana wondered how her mom and sisters were doing.

The next morning, Ana awoke to bright sunshine streaming through her small windows. She was eager to transform and test her abilities.

My only partial transformations were under closely monitored lab conditions in small test compartments, she thought. *They shocked my body with electricity until I became upset enough to trigger my transformation. And when I was home, I never transformed. No matter, I've got to figure out how to do it. I've got to do whatever it takes to free my family. There's no other way.*

Ana snuck outside dressed only in a towel. She made her way to the center of the opening, glancing back now and then to see if anyone was watching her. Reaching the center she stopped and stood erect, trying to clear her mind.

Nothing.

She tried again and again. Still nothing.

I've got to do this! She thought.

Ana stood motionless for a few more minutes. Then it suddenly occurred to her.

Anger, that's what always triggers my transformation, she concluded.

She focused her thoughts. In her mind's eye, she thought about the surprise Mitel military raid on her family. She vividly remembered being grabbed and forced to the ground by men dressed in black while their bright helmet lights blinded her. She remembered hearing the frightened screams of her mother and sisters just before something was placed over her nose, causing her to black out. Since then, life has never been the same. No joy or happiness. Only loneliness and captivity.

Those memories, and the complete lack of control she now faced, made Ana angry. Her eyes suddenly turned metallic silver. Ana's arms involuntarily swung up above her shoulders. She moved her legs apart to maintain her balance. She felt her whole-body tingle as the silver metallic mesh, resembling shards of glass, quickly spread from her eyes to cover the rest of her body before hardening.

Her Battle Sphere transformation had begun.

From the doorway Kai and two of the soldiers watched in silent amazement as Ana's transformation unfolded.

Metallic elements and other additives imbedded in her bloodstream reversibly interacted with every aspect of her physical being. Ana felt bloated as her stomach filled with electromagnetically charged plasma fluid. Her stomach quickly morphed into the initial stage of the oblong plasma core chamber, encasing her gall bladder. Once encased, it quickly hardened into a magnesium-based superconductor sphere, the combination of which supported her antigravity propulsion system.

Ana's eyes turned bright white as she levitated fifteen feet up into the air. Her body generated a powerful spherical electromagnetic field twenty feet in diameter. Ana suddenly felt very nauseous, like she would throw up. Seconds later, she opened her mouth and expelled a large stream of highly charged blue translucent plasma energy. This was captured by the electromagnetic field and distributed in all directions, forming a bright blue translucent plasma bubble.

As the transformation progressed, Ana's magnetic field grew stronger. She subconsciously activated her latent but powerful psychokinetic ability. The phenomena summoned heavy metal trace elements and helium-4 from the surrounding atmosphere and ground areas. Swirls of shiny particles of titanium, aluminum, magnesium, cadmium, iron and beryllium entered the opening from all directions and whirled around Ana's blue plasma sphere.

As Kai and the soldiers watched from a distance, two new beams of white light streamed from Ana's eyes toward the ground across the opening. The same shiny particles swirled at that location. Seconds later, a three-dimensional hologram appeared in the center of the whirlwind; propagating from the ground up to form a hologram cube matrix three squares high, three squares wide and ten squares deep. The squares, each ten feet high, shined brightly with the same blue translucent plasma light that surrounded Ana. Human-like creatures quickly appeared inside the squares.

Staring at the Hologram Matrix, Ana noticed a small silver rectangular metallic strip float past her. She followed its path until it molded itself to the surface of the plasma bubble. Then a second strip floated by and then another and another as the process quickly accelerated. Glancing down at her body, Ana realized that the shard-like strips were *peeling off* her silver skin mesh in every direction. The floating strips quickly molded to the translucent bubble. As they peeled off, more layers of the hardened silver skin were exposed, only to peel off again. The strips eventually formed the same intricate shard-like pattern against the outer plasma sphere. Once the blue bubble was covered several times over, the peeling stopped.

Ana once again felt bloated and feared she might burst from the inside out. *The final and most critical phase of her hybrid transformation was underway.* In a millisecond, like a controlled demolition, Ana's body expanded in all directions. Her metallic bloodstream additives interacted with the swirling trace elements now being absorbed through her permeable silver skin. Ana's arm and leg bones, combining with the absorbed trace elements as they transformed, expanded, extended and bowed outward to form the vertical metallic support structure inside her silver mesh outer skin. Next, 11 of her 12 pairs of ribs expanded and bowed horizontally to form a secondary support structure that interlocked seamlessly with her vertical supports. This new metallic skeleton not only strengthened and supported the exterior surface of her Battle Sphere; it protected Ana's mutating inner system architecture.

The trace elements continued to be absorbed at a frenzied pace. The two longest pairs of Ana's ribs curved toward each other until they connected and morphed into an internal variable speed flywheel that spun inside her support structure. The flywheel assisted Ana's antigravity propulsion system by coupling and uncoupling with what used to be Ana's sternum, causing the sphere to spin.

When engaged, the flywheel used zero energy as it spun effortlessly in a thin bed of plasma fluid analogous to frictionless ball bearings. When disengaged, the flywheel recharged Ana's plasma energy reserves.

As the transformation continued to unfold at lightning speed, Ana's lymphatic nodules, nodes vessels and ducts transformed into a complex monitoring system which controlled her internal operating systems.

Her nervous system morphed into a sophisticated, plasma based outer defense shield. Her muscles and clusters of nerve cells mutated into two hundred laser cannons that fired superheated high energy hydrogen plasma bursts fed from Ana's former intestines. The plasma pulses themselves were contained by two layers of cross magnetic sheathing. The plasma pulses could be fired continuously at speeds over six thousand miles per hour. Their destructive power was formidable. The plasma was excreted through mechanical pores in her outer skin surface. Her new metallic nerve cells received and processed positioning, tracking, and firing information from her Battle Hologram.

Ana's respiratory system converted into her Sphere's plasma energy generation and delivery system which also produced her laser cannon hydrogen-based energy pulses. Her cardiovascular system hardened to form a complex combination of wire like conductors.

During the transformation, Ana's head, including her brain, eyes and ears, remained largely intact to varying degrees, although they were now fueled by liquid plasma rather than blood. As she surveyed the stone formation opening, she thought she was still encircled by her initial translucent bubble, even though she had become an infinitely more complex and formidable Battle Sphere. Her eyes had been mechanically copied, multiplied and positioned to six locations on the outer edge of her spin surface to form a distributed aperture viewing system that acted like x-ray vision. This allowed her to look in any direction, during any conditions, day, or night.

As she focused her gaze, a faint translucent square outlined in yellow formed. Beyond the square were several semitransparent "mini" screens displaying messages, data, and pictures. They constantly changed and updated as she looked around.

A squat metallic cylinder extended a foot above the top and bottom of Ana's sphere. The sides of the cylinders were encased by glass arranged in a mosaic pattern that matched her silver outer spin surface. The cylinders changed colors based on Ana's emotional state and represented the remnants of her outward facial expression. The glass contained random patterns that pulsated back and forth around the perimeter like a multicolored wave. The yellows and oranges confirmed that Ana was agitated.

By now, the shiny particles swirling around Ana's sphere had all but disappeared. The silver metallic strip seams that made up her outer skin were visible. The transformation was now complete. At over sixteen tons, Ana had successfully transformed into a Battle Sphere, *the most advanced and intricate fighting machine in the universe*.

Without notice, her Battle Hologram initiated coupling of the variable speed flywheel to its sphere architecture, causing Ana's outer spin surface to rotate around the two interconnected cylinders. Ana studied the screens and displays in her view, noticing a screen reading on her lower right that displayed an rpm reading of one thousand.

Ana then noticed team Commander Hayden Colten standing just inside the main entrance. Hayden stood six feet four inches tall, and muscular with broad sloping shoulders. He had short black hair, a dark ebony complexion and charcoal-colored eyes. He was surrounded by the same blue translucent haze as the hologram itself.

Stepping outside the Battle Hologram, Hayden glanced in all directions before walking toward Ana.

"Hologram Team Commander Hayden Colten," said Hayden as he studied Ana's Battle Sphere hovering fifteen feet above the ground.

"Hi," replied Ana.

"Why are we on Mitel?" asked Hayden cautiously.

Ana's mind raced as she tried to decide how to respond. In the background, several voices spoke back and forth over the secure communications network.

"Ana? Can you hear me?"

Ana stared at the Hologram Matrix as several team members moved about the hologram structure.

"If you can hear me, please answer me Ana."

"We're here because I was taken prisoner by the Mitel Military," blurted Ana, "so was my mother and sisters."

"*What?*"

"And if we don't do what they ask, the Mitel Leadership will kill my family."

Hayden paused for a moment to look across the opening at Kai and the soldiers standing in the doorway.

"Ana, the Leadership will kill them anyway," he responded.

"They promised me —"

"The Mitel Leadership is a group of ruthless, lying, self-serving old men. They will say and do anything to achieve their goals."

Ana paused for a moment before responding.

"What other choice do I have then?" she asked.

"Your stated *mission* or hybrid function is to serve and protect the people of Thrae."

Ana did not respond.

"OK, listen," said Hayden softly, "what are they asking you to do?"

"Train here and become a skilled fighting machine."

"That's our job. We also monitor all your Battle Sphere systems including shield strength and energy reserves. We track and prioritize up to one thousand incoming targets at any given time. Our weapons specialists operate two hundred plasma laser cannons imbedded underneath your outer spin surface. We also initiate and cease your *all-out* speed and override your free flight mode in case of emergencies."

"That's great," replied Ana. "Wait. Are you saying I have the ability to fire *plasma laser cannons*?"

"Yes."

"And you guys help me do all of that?"

"Yes, and —"

"Listen. After I'm trained, The Mitel Leadership has instructed me to return to Thrae and destroy the resistance forces once and for all."

Hayden stepped back. The glass shard patterns on her cylinders were still yellow and orange.

"Ana, we could *never* do that."

"But it's the *only way* I can save my family."

"But what about the lives of all the Thraen people?"

"Look, I have no choice!"

"Ana, we *all* have choices. Many of them aren't easy. But we still must make them, and do what's right."

Ana grew angrier, her glass shard patterns now red and orange.

"Where were *my people* when my family was abducted by force in the middle of the night? Where were they when I needed them?" she demanded. "We are now prisoners of the Mitel Leadership with only one way out!"

"Listen Ana —"

"No, you listen. We must do what they're telling us to do! I must free my family!"

"I'm truly sorry, but as I said, attacking our own people is something we can *never* do."

"But you serve me! You must do as I ask!"

"As members of the Hologram Protective Force, we serve the Thraen people Ana. We do this for the greater good of our entire planet. As living holograms, we've dedicated our entire existence to that."

"But —"

"Ana, I'm sorry for what happened to you. I'm also sorry your family was taken from Thrae. It was a surprise attack that caught our forces off guard. We were waiting for you to get older, when you would be mentally prepared to take on your incredible responsibilities."

"What difference does that make now?"

"It makes all the difference *in the world*. Look, if we fly back to Thrae now, we can train you and then return to free your family."

"That's not an option. They'll all be killed. I'm certain of that."

"Unfortunately, *and I don't say this lightly*, but that's a risk you must take."

"I can't."

"We can help rescue them after we train you."

Ana thought for a moment.

"I don't know where they are. And besides, once the Leadership finds out I've turned against them, they'll kill them."

"Then I'm afraid this is where we part ways, at least for now."

"What do you mean?"

Hayden didn't respond.

"You *must* do as I ask —"

"Ana, when you are ready to protect your own people rather than attacking them, we will be there for you, until the very end. But until then . . ."

"Wait! Don't go!"

Hayden and the Battle Hologram slowly faded away until they were gone altogether, replaced by a large dust devil that released its shiny metallic particles back into the ground and atmosphere in all directions.

As she hovered in place, Ana became both furious and despondent, her glass shard patterns now flashing deep red. In her anger, and by thought alone, she initiated free flight mode which sped up her variable speed fly-wheel. That caused Ana's Battle Sphere to spin faster and faster until the ground dust swirled all around her. She tracked her rpm surge on the diagnostic mini screen until it leveled off at one hundred twenty thousand.

"I'll figure everything out on my own!" she shouted. Ana then streaked toward the sky.

CHAPTER FIVE – DISCOVERY

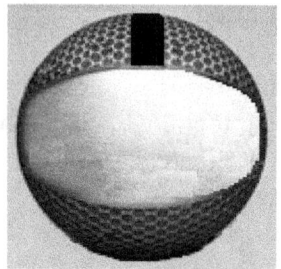

Chad's planned return to Coopers Falls was greeted with mixed results. Thousands of people had died during the short but intense Mitel invasion. The downtown area had been leveled. It would take a long time for the region to recover. Some locals considered Chad an outcast who was directly responsible for all the carnage since he was the stated reason the Mitels came to Earth.

On his first day back, people constantly stopped to look and point toward him.

"We don't want aliens here," shouted one local resident. "You've done enough damage already!"

Some people were much blunter, shouting "Get the Hell out of here!"

A small but vocal underground movement quickly developed with the hashtag #noalienshere. The movement eventually spread across the country, and then the planet.

Chad's girlfriend, Melissica, thought back to the argument she had with Chad inside the large tree grove at the Davis Farm just before the Mitel Armada arrived. She remembered how she tried to explain to him that many people simply won't appreciate what he would do. After his brave actions, it was hard for Melissica to watch Chad listen to all the vocal protesters. But she didn't dare tell Chad *I told you so*.

Janus remained mostly silent. He reminded Chad that what he did was extraordinarily brave and to never believe otherwise.

As the backlash grew, Chad decided not to return to high school. Instead, he spent his time at the quasi-military base site at the Davis Farm, renamed the Davis Advanced Aeronautics Facility, commonly called DAAF. The secure facility quickly became an economic boom for the region as infrastructure and housing construction exploded. In time, the government's construction mandate spilled over into the downtown area, silencing some critics.

After receiving several death threats, Jim and Molly reluctantly relocated to the DAAF. The move prompted conversations about how they wanted to spend the rest of their lives. With Chad's encouragement, they researched how to become astronauts. Basic criteria included a background in math or the sciences and being in good health. Jim, tall and lanky, was a physically fit outdoorsman who also held a master's degree in physics, and Molly, an avid runner and teacher, had an undergraduate degree in mathematics.

They ultimately applied to NASA's astronaut program. Successfully raising a human hybrid son born six hundred light years away with references that included both Janus and General Talbot prompted their special consideration. Despite the typical intense competition, they were immediately accepted into the Astronaut Candidate Program. Given their current living situation, General Talbot arranged for a program instructor to travel to the DAAF to start their study classes. They were also scheduled to begin zero gravity training in a KC-135 aircraft, also known as the *vomit comet*.

"I can hardly wait," said Jim sarcastically.

Janus remained in Florida to help NASA scientists upgrade the USEP pods. While he was very impressed with NASA's reverse engineering efforts, he felt that certain improvements and added safety features were needed to make the small pods more flight worthy.

At the DAAF, Chad assisted Denton in what used to be his Hologram Matrix control room. They tracked space satellites being launched and placed into orbit. They also monitored deep space activity using the *Fort's* surveillance equipment relocated to the DAAF along with several structures from Janus's former observatory hidden next to a pond deep within Randall Park.

"We've got to keep looking Chad, just in case," said Denton more than once.

A few weeks later, Chad stumbled upon Markus' badly damaged orb sitting in a box behind a rack of electronics equipment in the Diagnostics Cube. Although heavy, he picked it up, placed it on a computer shelf and studied it for awhile. The silver monitoring orb was about a foot and a half in diameter with its three blue stripes, one along the top and on each side which met in the back to form an oversized arrow. Directly in the front was its shiny, but now badly scratched oblong screen. Chad turned to Jalen Longen, his Battle Hologram's lead technician, who was sitting across the room staring at his computer screen.

"Hey Jalen," said Chad. "Is there anything else we can do to try to fix Markus?"

Jalen stopped what he was doing and looked over toward Chad.

"Sorry, I forgot all about that orb Chad. It was beat up pretty bad and we didn't register any life form. We tried several fixes, but nothing seemed to work. I don't think there is anything else we can do."

"Please Jalen? I could help you? *Please?*"

"Chad, I . . . OK, fine."

Jalen moved the orb to the large table in the center of the Diagnostics Cube. Over the next six hours, the two re-inspected the orb and prepared a detailed repair plan. They then contacted NASA's Advanced Materials and Processing Branch, who contacted several contractors for assistance. A few days later, overnight packages poured into DAAF with Chad's name on them. Chad organized, cataloged, and stored the materials and connectors in various compartments and storage bins located all around the Diagnostics Cube.

Jalen pulled two technicians off other projects and the group painstakingly repaired and replaced damaged areas. Chad helped provide lighting, tools, materials and connectors to the team as needed. After four grueling days, Jalen turned to Chad.

"I'm sorry Chad," he began. "We've done as much as we can, but we don't have the necessary splicing tool and specific interface connectors to complete the repairs," he explained.

"Where could I find them?" asked Chad.

"On Thrae, unfortunately . . ."

Disappointed and exhausted, Chad slumped into one several swivel chairs. Then it suddenly occurred to him.

"Wait here!" he said.

Chad jumped up from his chair and ran out the doorway. Chad dashed down to Teri's cube now used as a temporary storage room. He began searching through dozens of boxes stacked all around the room. In a large box under Teri's desk, he found the tool case Janus had taken from the USEP the night they crash landed in Coopers Falls over fifteen years ago. It was eventually taken to the Fort, and finally to the DAAF. Chad opened the tool case. Inside was a fusion splicing tool and dozens of interface and splicing connectors of various sizes and shapes.

Chad closed the case and quickly brought it back to the Diagnostic's cube.

"Could this help?" he asked anxiously.

Jalen opened the case. He then stared incredulously at Chad.

"Chad, do you have a time dilation space travel machine hidden back there somewhere?" he asked.

"No why?"

"This is *exactly* what we need. I mean where did —"

"It's the tool case from our USEP."

"*Ohhhh,*" said Jalen, "I get it now. Way to go Chad."

After preparing a final repair plan, the group got back to work. Four hours later, Jalen sealed the final section of the pod's outer skin, took a deep breath and looked at Chad.

"Everything's back together," he said.

"Now what?" Chad asked.

"Time to power it up and see what happens," replied Jalen. He sat down at his computer, entered a few commands and looked back toward the orb.

Nothing.

He typed another set of instructions.

Still nothing.

Jalen let out a deep sigh and thought for a moment.

"Let me try one last thing," he said while he typed.

The pod lifted off the table and hovered silently. Almost immediately, a bright beam of light projected down to the floor from a small lens located just below the horizontal blue stripe on the left side of the orb. From the ground up rose a life size three-dimensional hologram of Markus. The opaque hologram glowed brightly, surrounded by a light blue hue. Standing six feet five inches tall, Markus had smooth skin, pale blue eyes and thick, long, flowing gray hair reaching below his shoulders; and a neatly cropped matching beard and mustache that covered his large square chin.

"Well, it's about time!" boomed Markus in his unmistakable rough voice. "I thought I was going to be stuck in that metal bowling ball for the rest of eternity!"

"Markus!" shouted Chad.

He rushed over and hugged Markus tightly. Markus's focused energy lit up the entire cube.

"Hello, my boy," said Markus tenderly. "That was an incredibly brave thing you did, reversing your energy core to eliminate the Mitel threat."

"Thanks Markus."

"And thank you gentlemen," said Markus. "Last time when the technicians said there was nothing more they could do, I wanted to scream *I'm still in here!*"

"I'm glad you're finally free," smiled Jalen.

"I had thought that Chad's *miracle of life* event would have set me free, but I guess that by being imbedded in the monitoring orb, I was beyond its reach."

"We need to tell Janus!" said Chad excitedly. He called the number at NASA, asked for Janus Stone before handing the phone over to Markus.

"Janus Stone here," said Janus.

"Hello my friend," replied Markus.

There was a brief silence.

"*Markus*?"

"Indeed, it is!"

"What . . . ? How . . . ?"

"That boy of yours, he wouldn't give up. He had the technicians working on my orb for about a week straight. He ordered all the parts and even found the old USEP tool case somewhere here in the Battle Hologram!"

"It's great to hear your voice Markus!"

"Same here. Where are you?"

"In Florida helping to fine tune the reverse engineered USEP pods."

"*Pods*? How many?"

"There are four of them. Two larger ones and two smaller ones. We took one up to get Chad —"

"I know about that part. The communications system here was going non-stop with updates."

"Well good. How do you feel?"

"About the same. Although I hear that you are not."

"That's right. The *miracle of life* event turned out to be true after all."

"Simply amazing. I'm sorry I missed it. Maybe next time."

"Listen, I'm close to finishing up here. They did an incredible job reverse engineering the pods. I've tinkered with them here and there, mostly for safety and reliability. I'm going to head up there to see you as soon as possible, OK?"

"Sounds good my friend. In the meantime, I'll catch up with Chad, Jim, and Molly."

"OK great."

A few days later, Janus was flown back to Albany by a U.S. government jet before being driven to the DAAF facility. He was bracing himself for the reception he expected to receive from the local population as their resentment continued to grow.

I seem to keep repeating my mistakes, he thought.

Janus stared out the limousine window which headed north along Route 87.

Is it poor planning, poor judgment, or both?

At the DAAF entrance, about fifty protesters stood on either side of temporary fencing recently installed to keep them from blocking the entrance. Janus noticed the angry looks on their faces as they pointed and waved their signs. His mood perked up after he saw Markus, Chad, Mayla, Teri and Melissica waiting outside the temporary headquarters building to greet him. He jumped out of the car and hugged Markus tightly before kissing Mayla and then hugging Chad and Melissica.

"Hi Teri," smiled Janus, shaking his hand tightly.

"Good to have you back here Janus," grinned Teri.

Jim and Molly joined the group for dinner at the base's new cafeteria. Janus spent much of the time describing NASA's USEP technology while Jim and Molly talked about the astronaut program. Markus was ecstatic just to be outside his orb, which hovered silently nearby. After dinner, everyone retired for the night except Markus, who hung around the Battle Hologram structure and chatted with the night shift staff until 3:00 a.m.

The next morning, Markus suggested that Janus coax Chad to transform into his hybrid Battle Sphere. Although the tree grove was still there, several buildings were now situated all around it. Not far behind them, several larger structures were under construction. It was a sunny and unusually warm January day and the region had yet to see its first snowfall. Given all the construction activity and associated noise, Janus took Chad to a far corner of the Davis farm. They drove by jeep along the dirt road that eventually crossed a narrow bridge that spanned a rocky brook. Several rows of pine trees stood on the near side of the creek to form a natural barrier. Janus turned off the dirt road next to an old cement pad.

"This seems like a good place to try," he smiled.

"What is that thing?" asked Chad.

"It was probably the base of a storage garage. From the looks of things, the structure fell into disrepair a long time ago and was taken down."

Janus pulled a couple of mats from the back of the jeep and headed towards the pad.

"OK Chad, time for some serious meditation. Are you ready?" he asked.

Chad shrugged his shoulders. "I guess so."

"Good."

Janus placed his mat on the cement pad and sat down. Chad placed his mat next to Janus and did the same and the two sat in silence for a time. A gentle breeze blew through the air and the brook could be heard off in the distance. As they sat there, they could feel the warmth emanating from the pad as it sat under the sun.

"Hey Janus," said Chad eventually.

"What?"

"What would we do if the Mitels decided to return?"

"Given what you accomplished, I don't think that's a realistic possibility. But I want to be ready just in case, which is one reason why we are doing this."

"OK."

They sat for a while longer.

"Janus?"

"What?"

"What would we do if another hostile alien force came to Earth? One that was even *more* powerful than the Mitels?"

"I think that's pretty remote, at least in the short term. But I certainly want Earth to start taking meaningful steps to be ready just in case. Again, that's why we're sitting here."

"OK."

They meditated a while longer.

"Janus?"

"*What* Chad?

"I was thinking. What if two worlds got together and attacked Earth? What would we do then?"

"First of all, I'd make sure you had meditated long enough to transform into Battle Sphere mode. We'd go from there."

"But —"

"Chad, I'm getting the impression that you aren't into this today."

"I'm hungry. I'm also not sure I'm ready yet, given everything that's happened."

"But don't you want to know?"

"Know what?"

"That you can *transform.*"

Chad didn't answer right away.

"I guess."

"You *guess*?"

"I mean yes, of course. But if the Mitels aren't returning, and the chances of us getting attacked by somebody else right now are pretty slim, what's the rush?"

"No rush Chad."

They sat in silence for a while.

"Chad?"

"What?"

"Are you afraid to find out that you can no longer transform?"

"Maybe a little, I guess."

"That's only normal. Listen, let's go back. When you feel like you want to try, you let me know, OK?"

"OK," smiled Chad, "and Janus?"

"What?"

"I'm *really* hungry."

"OK, *let's go,*" chuckled Janus.

Over the next few months, Chad continued to help Denton, Jalen, Teri and the other technicians in the Matrix building. He also enjoyed spending long hours hanging out with Melissica. At the same time, Janus shuttled back and forth to Florida to oversee the design and implementation of several USEP upgrades. Most important, he caused the materials used to produce the four large ring components that extended from underneath the pod via powerful positioning bars to be modified and upgraded. Janus also reconfigured the pod's plasma shields to better insulate the craft, occupants, and its contents which absorbed, attenuated, and filtered the tremendous g-forces generated by the high-speed travel. In addition, he upgraded the efficiency of the plasma shields that temporarily store kinetic energy used to power the craft's slip ring drive, plasma shields and lower-than-light speed engines.

"It's getting there," he told Markus upon returning from his latest trip. "The one thing I can't figure out is how to apply the invisibility shields to the larger craft. I need more time on that one."

As spring arrived, many of the large permanent structures opened. Janus received his own spacious office fitted with a state-of-the-art conferencing system. It allowed him to speak more effectively with NASA scientists in Florida as retrofit and repair issues arose.

The next morning, Chad walked into his office and flopped onto a couch along the windows. A few minutes later, Markus appeared in the doorway.

"Good morning lad," said Markus.

"Hi Markus," smiled Chad.

"Isn't there something you want to tell your father?"

Janus turned his swivel chair toward Chad.

"*Chad*?" asked Janus expectantly.

"I'm ready to try now," replied Chad.

"Are you *sure*?"

"Yes," nodded Chad.

"OK, Great," grinned Janus. "When?"

"How about right now?"

"Sounds good to me," replied Janus. "It's a beautiful day. See you down by the Jeep in twenty minutes?"

"OK."

They drove by jeep along the dirt road and across the narrow bridge to the old cement pad. Sitting down, Janus felt the warmth of the sun being radiated back up from the cement.

"That feels good," he said.

They meditated in silence for several minutes while Markus observed from a distance. After a while, Janus got up.

"Are you ready to try?"

"Yes," nodded Chad before standing up.

Janus walked across the pad and turned around. He raised his arms and moved his feet apart.

"Let's get started," said Janus. "Do as I did."

Chad raised his arms, closed his eyes tightly and tried to relax. He then moved his feet apart.

"Don't force it, Chad. Relax. Take long deep breaths."

Chad reopened his eyes and breathed deeply.

"That's it Chad. Keep breathing. Now I want you to focus on something very important to you. Focus your thoughts on something positive that you love very much."

Chad closed his eyes and thought about Melissica and her beautiful smile.

"Concentrate," said Janus soothingly. "Channel your thoughts but also continue to breathe. Continue to relax. That's it."

Janus slowly approached Chad.

"I want you to try to focus everything on becoming one with your mechanical self. Concentrate."

Chad concentrated and held his position.

Nothing.

He shook his arms, took several deep breaths and tried again.

Still nothing.

He tried repeatedly. The result was the same.

"OK, let's take a break," said Janus eventually.

Chad lowered his arms and walked off into the field beyond the pad. Janus watched Chad as he was joined by Markus.

"What do you think?" asked Markus.

"I don't know. We're in uncharted territory."

"Are you referring to his cosmic annihilation event during the final battle with the Mitels in outer space?"

"There's that, yes. But his Battle Sphere's energy core was also altered. I don't know how that will affect his abilities going forward."

"Then we should take things very slowly, no?"

"Perhaps you're right Markus."

They watched Chad walk across the field to an old stone wall. Chad studied the fieldstone construction for a few minutes before walking back toward the cement pad.

"Hey Chad," shouted Janus. "Let's call it a day, OK? We can try again tomorrow."

Chad waved OK before looking up at the sky.

Over the next few weeks, Janus, Chad and Markus got up early each morning and drove over to the cement pad. They meditated for increasingly longer periods of time before Chad tried to transform. Still nothing. On the third week, Mayla and Melissica followed them over to watch and also do some yoga. During the fourth week, Molly, Jim and Teri also came along to study, stretch and meditate.

"I have a great idea," said Markus as the group piled out of their jeeps. "We should build a gym here."

This time, Chad sat in the field beyond the pad. After a while, he stood up and turned towards Janus standing nearly at the pad.

"OK Chad let's give it a go," he instructed. Janus walked several feet to Chad's left before turning around to face the group. Janus raised his arms, followed by Chad. Janus then moved his legs apart. Chad did the same.

"Concentrate and breathe," coached Janus.

Chad did what he was told.

Jim put down his astronaut study materials, stood up and looked around the field. He loved this area of the Davis farm. It was so peaceful and quiet. When he glanced toward Janus, he noticed that his eyes were now metallic silver. Jim watched as the silver metallic mesh pattern, resembling shards of glass, quickly spread from his eyes to cover the rest of his body.

"Markus, look!" he pointed.

Markus turned around.

"I *don't* believe it," he mumbled.

Janus's eyes turned bright white just before he levitated fifteen feet up into the air.

"Janus, you're transforming!" shouted Chad excitedly.

Suddenly, Chad's eyes turned silver before his arms involuntarily reached up into the air. A short time later, he was levitating adjacent to Janus.

"Well, that finally did the trick," said Markus.

"This is incredible," whispered Mayla.

"*Two* Battle Spheres," smiled Teri.

Jim and Molly hugged each other while Melissica looked back and forth between the two unfolding transformations. Heavy metal trace elements and helium-4 drawn from the atmosphere and ground areas approached from all directions. Swirls of shiny particles of titanium, aluminum, magnesium, cadmium, iron and beryllium whirled around the two blue plasma spheres.

As beams of white light streamed from their eyes at the ground beyond the dirt road, shiny particles appeared and swirled at that location. Two three-dimensional hologram matrixes rose from the ground. Moments later, Battle Sphere team leaders cautiously exited each Matrix and walked toward the group. They signaled to acknowledge each other before surveying their surroundings.

"Nolia — Nolia Alaur, is that you?" asked Mayla incredulously. At six feet tall with long blond hair, deep blue eyes and ebony skin, it was hard to forget Nolia.

"*Mayla . . . ?*"

"Yes, it's me!"

Mayla ran over and hugged Nolia. "I haven't seen you since we joined the Hologram Protective Force!"

"It's great to see you again Mayla. Wait, you're *human*? *How is that possible*?"

"It's a long story. My Battle Sphere sped up his energy core and the subsequent annihilation event initiated the reverse transformation process."

"You mean the *miracle of life* event? So, it *is* true!"

"*Yes!*"

"But your Battle Sphere, it's such a horrible loss."

"No actually. He's hovering right in front of you."

"Wait. How is *that* even possible?"

"As I said, it's a long story. He has an ability to project protective plasma shields around objects of all sizes. He was able to place one around himself and —"

"Excuse me," said the other hologram, "and I'm very sorry to interrupt your reunion, but *who* are you and *where* the heck are we? My team says that we must be hundreds of light years from home."

Standing six feet seven inches tall, Battle Sphere team leader Lucian Madad had short curly hair, bronze complexion, hazel eyes and a large nose, although his long face and muscular build made it less noticeable.

"And before you answer that, could someone please explain to me how I am supporting Zebulon Park's Battle Sphere? He's *dead*!"

"No, he's hovering right in front of you," smiled Markus.

"And you are?"

"Markus Kilmar."

"*The* Markus Kilmar?"

"Yes," nodded Markus.

"It's truly an honor to meet you Sir," replied Lucian humbly. "I must admit, I'm very confused by all of this. Not to mention the fact that you are presenting yourself in hologram form."

"Ah yes, that. As Mayla said, it's a long story. I'm as surprised as you that Janus was able to transform after all this time."

"Janus?" asked Lucian. "Who's *Janus*?"

"The Thraen immortal Janus Stone, former head of Thrae's GDC. Prior to that, he was Zebulon Park and before that Chancellor Sejus Theron of the World Council.

"*Unbelievable*," whispered Lucian. "And how is it that we're all now here on this planet?"

"It's called Earth. And yes, it's six hundred light years from home. Janus and I came here fifteen years ago with his then infant son Chad to escape the second Mitel invasion of our planet. Chad is the other Battle Sphere you see before you. At the time, we honestly believed that Thrae would be consumed by the rolling energy wave that was inadvertently unleashed during that attack. Thankfully, it turns out that we were wrong."

By now, the Battle Sphere hybrid transformations had completed. Janus and Chad hovered silently side by side, the glass shard mosaic patterns on their short cylinders flashing blue and green hues.

Janus focused his thoughts on opening an encrypted communication link with his Battle Hologram.

"Battle Hologram communications, this is Martin" a male voice responded.

"Hello Martin, this is —"

"Commander Park, it is an honor to serve you," interrupted Martin somewhat nervously. Martin Renner was a typical Thraen: six feet six inches tall with a thin but athletic looking physique. He had a bronze complexion, dirty blond hair and green eyes.

"You can call me Janus. Can you patch in the other Battle Sphere and Matrix?

"Doing it now, Janus."

Suddenly, another voice could be heard above the background chatter of the command cubes.

"This is Darius, how can I be of assistance?" he replied. Darius Ross was *not* a typical Thraen. At almost seven feet tall and very muscular, his father, a former Mitel fighter pilot, had defected during the first Mitel invasion. Darius joined the Hologram Protective Force on his twenty-first birthday, days after receiving the news that his uncorrectable mediocre eyesight disqualified him from becoming a Thraen fighter pilot.

"Hi Darius, Martin here. I think I can see you from my Command Cube. I've patched in both Battle Spheres."

"Hello gentlemen," replied Darius.

"Hi guys," said Chad.

"I'm curious as to what your monitoring systems are showing," said Janus.

"Sir?" asked Darius.

"How do we *look*?" asked Janus.

"Everything looks fully operational on our end."

"Same here," added Martin.

"OK great. How about our propulsion systems and core patterns? Do they also appear normal?" asked Janus cautiously.

"Let me check," replied Darius. He looked around his Command Cube and quickly received positive nods and several thumbs up. "Everything looks normal, Sir."

"Confirmed," added Martin.

"Fantastic," smiled Janus. "Chad, are you thinking what I'm thinking?"

"Yes."

"Prepare to launch," instructed Janus.

"Yes, Sir," replied Martin and Darius in unison.

The Battle Holograms sped up both Chad's and Janus's variable speed flywheels causing their Battle Spheres to spin faster and faster until the surrounding trees swayed. Janus and Chad tracked their rpm surge on their diagnostic mini screen until it leveled off at one hundred twenty thousand.

"Switching to free flight," announced Janus.

"Right behind you, Janus," said Chad.

They flew around the field several times bobbing and weaving. Suddenly, they darted up into the sky.

"A little bit excited, I'd say," smiled Mayla, shaking her head.

At the U.S. Naval Space Surveillance System Command headquarters in Dahlgren, Virginia, General Talbot stood at the rear of the main monitoring room enjoying his afternoon cup of coffee. He had just returned from the NASA Florida complex where he was monitoring the reverse engineering upgrades to the USEP pods.

Sir," said Captain Miller from across the room as he stared intently at his computer screen. General Talbot quickly made his way across the floor, trying not to spill any coffee.

"What is it?" he asked politely.

"Radar has picked up two small objects heading at high speed toward the outer atmosphere."

"From where?"

"Upstate New York Sir."

"Chad appears to be back up and running," smiled General Talbot. "But wait, you said *two* objects?"

"Affirmative, Sir."

General Talbot thought for a moment.

"Captain, reach out to our people at DAAF."

"Sir?"

"I have a hunch Janus Stone just came back on line."

Janus and Chad raced through the upper atmosphere into outer space. For Janus, the experience was exhilarating, like a dream come true.

"How are you doing Janus?" asked Chad.

"It's been a while, but I'm —"

"Race you to the Moon!"

Janus chased after Chad and the two sped toward the Moon. When they arrived, they circled it several times.

"Hey Janus, you want to test out our laser cannons?"

"*Here*?"

"No. The *asteroid belt*."

"Not sure where that is," interjected Martin. "But it sounds good to me. Darius, are you OK with that?"

"No problem here," replied Darius. "We have the precise coordinates from several prior missions. Sending them to you now Martin."

"Received, thank you."

"Computers also confirm we have an active *twelve pack* already established along the travel route," added Darius. "Running systems check on them now."

Darius paused briefly.

"Solar powered signal accelerators are fully operational," he confirmed. "Instantaneous communications and systems monitoring along the mission route has been confirmed. I think we're good to go. Chad, are you ready?

"Yes."

"All set on my end," confirmed Martin. "Janus?"

"I'm ready, thank you."

"Shields are fully operational," verified Darius, "and energy reserves still near maximum."

"Same here," added Martin. "Commanders, we are initiating all out-speed mission launch."

"Launch sequence activated," said Darius. "Initiating all out speed in three, two, and one. *Launch*."

The two Battle Spheres sped away from the moon toward Mars, their S-shaped acceleration profile causing them to gather speed quickly before easing into the highest maximum speed of .95X or ninety-five percent of the speed of light.

"We should reach the inner band of the asteroid belt between Mars and Jupiter in 12 minutes," said Darius.

Under the watchful eye of their Battle Holograms, Chad and Janus slowly rotated their cylindrical cores to study the stars in every direction. At a 180-degree rotation, they watched the Earth become smaller and smaller until it appeared as a bright star.

In a little over eight minutes, their Battle Spheres streaked passed Mars and closed in on the main asteroid belt.

"We're almost there," confirmed Martin. "Initiating deceleration . . ."

"Implementing it on our end also," said Darius.

"Scanners confirm we are approaching our target: a broad, dense, and deep grouping of asteroids up ahead. Initiating target identification."

"Deactivating controlled deceleration and commencing spread formation approach."

"Confirmed."

With that, the two Battle Spheres, now side by side, moved a few miles apart.

"Why are we doing this Janus?" asked Chad.

"It's an attack formation Markus and I used extensively during the first Mitel invasion. It enabled us to deliver maximum damage on a large number of targets."

"Laser cannons energized and ready to go," announced Chad's weapons coordinator.

Chad and Janus scanned their mini screens. Yellow dots with small identification labels appeared on several screens as their Battle Holograms identified, and then tracked, the approaching targets. Within seconds, the yellow dots on his screen multiplied, until they appeared as a swarm.

"Synching target identification," said Martin.

"Synching complete," replied Darius shortly thereafter.

"What are they doing now?" asked Chad.

"They are combining computer systems to eliminate redundant tracking of incoming targets."

Just to be safe, Martin and Darius activated high intensity search lights at the base of each Battle Sphere's cylinders. Seconds later, all four hundred laser cannons opened fire. The light pulses curved away before streaking ahead to intercept the approaching metal, ice and rock. The Battle Spheres effortlessly and systematically obliterated all the approaching asteroids. It was a sight to behold: two bright mini stars sending out thousands upon thousands of high energy plasma bursts that destabilized and disintegrated everything in their path. Such a combination of destructive force had previously occurred only twice before.

Chad and Janus flew through the tiny particle debris. They watched as thousands of bright white flashes caused the next pocket of approaching asteroids to disintegrate.

After fifteen minutes, Darius broke the silence over the communications system.

"Nice work gentlemen. Reserves are down to about thirty percent. Shall we recharge and continue?"

"Sounds good to me!" said Chad.

"Agreed," added Janus.

Martin and Darius quickly charted a course a short distance away from the asteroid belt. The Battle Spheres slowed to a stop. Martin and Darius uncoupled their internal flywheel which caused the Battle Spheres to stop spinning while allowing the flywheel to replenish their energy reserves. As they recharged, Chad remained excited.

"Janus, what do you think?"

"I am very pleased with our performance so far."

"Is it the same as you remember?"

"It is."

"OK gentlemen," said Darius. Are we ready to do it again?"

"You bet!" replied Chad.

They repeated the maneuver twice more. By now, Darius and Martin were confident the two Battle Spheres were operating flawlessly.

"OK, I think we can call it a day," smiled Darius. "Nice work gentlemen."

"Are we ready to head home?" asked Martin.

Yes," replied Chad and Janus in unison.

"Good. Initiating all out speed in three, two, and one. *Launch*."

Under full control of their Battle Holograms, the two Battle Spheres raced past Mars and fifteen minutes later were approaching the Moon.

"Initiating controlled deceleration," confirmed Martin.

"Doing it also," added Darius.

Approaching Earth's outer atmosphere, the Battle Spheres decelerated further to Mach 22. After sliding through it, they raced through the fluffy cirrocumulus clouds toward Earth. Off to their right, the curving view of the blue expanse of the Gulf of Mexico and the Atlantic Ocean was breathtaking. Approaching the east coast, they saw the heavily damaged Manhattan skyline and then the Hudson River. As the Battle Spheres decelerated, they turned north up the Hudson River. They observed the foundations being installed to rebuild downtown Albany, then the racetrack at Saratoga Springs, and finally downtown Coopers Falls partially under construction.

The whirling Battle Spheres slowed to a stop above the old cement pad, hovering briefly before landing next to the two Battle Holograms. Janus watched his mini-screen track the deceleration of his spin surface down to 0 rpm before his translucent blue plasma energy shield dissipated.

Mayla and the rest of the group had returned to the DAAF building complex hours earlier. As soon as their transformations were completed, Chad ran over to Janus.

"Janus, you know what this means don't you?" he asked excitedly.

"No, what?"

"We have to go back and free our people."

"*What?*"

"We have to return to Thrae."

CHAPTER SIX – SOLITARY CONFINEMENT

Ana woke up and stared out her windows at the stone formations. It was early morning and the sun's rays were just reflecting off the stone peaks.

It's time I trained in earnest, she thought. *I need to figure out the limits of my Battle Sphere.*

Ana gulped down a protein drink. Dressed in only a towel, she walked to the middle of the circular opening and carefully laid a change of clothes on the ground before stepping back to concentrate. She moved her legs apart and raised her hands. Standing there, Ana thought about what her Battle Hologram team leader had told her. After that incident she promised herself that she would not be told what to do. Replaying the conversation in her mind, she could feel her anger and resentment growing. Her silver skin mesh quickly spread down her body. Ana let her towel fall to the ground.

Once her hybrid transformation was complete, Ana hovered in place while her Battle Sphere spun slowly. She tried to remember what allowed her to dart up into the sky after her Battle Hologram disappeared. Realizing she had no idea, Ana focused on trying to move to her left which caused her Sphere to move ever so slightly in that direction. She then tried to move higher. Her Battle Sphere lethargically moved a foot higher.

This isn't working, she thought.

Ana tried moving again and again, but the results were the same. She could feel herself getting frustrated.

At this rate, it would take me a million years to get back to Thrae.

She closed her eyes and tried to calm herself. Ana then tried focusing on her mother and two sisters. She could see their faces in her mind's eye. She remembered their smiles. Suddenly Ana felt something click deep inside her. Seconds later, her diagnostic mini-screens tracked her rpm as it rapidly increased before leveling off at 120,000.

Wow, she thought. *Something engages deep inside me.*

Ana instinctively tried to move again to her left. Her Battle Sphere quickly darted across the opening. She then tried to go upwards. Her battle Sphere streaked five thousand feet into the air in a matter of seconds. Down below Ana saw the circular opening surrounded by the expansive Stone Forest and rock formations. Beyond one large stone formation, there was a lush green valley. Ana quickly darted back to the surface.

I'm doing it . . . I'm moving!

Ana darted along the surface toward an opening in the stone formation. She cautiously weaved her way back and forth through the vertical stone shapes that seemed to go on forever. She eventually turned around and carefully made her way back to the opening before repeating the process. After a while, her confidence grew. Ana went further and further into the stone pillars before stopping and turning back. Although she knew she was safe in her hybrid sphere, Ana looked around for the human like creatures Kai had described. Twice she thought she noticed something moving off in the distance. As nightfall approached, she saw something large and very dark crouching on a stone bridge as she passed underneath. Ana turned and darted upwards to the top of the stone outcropping. When she got there, it was gone.

It must be my imagination, she thought. *Who would ever want to live in this desolate environment?*

After Ana returned to the opening, she hovered in its center as her Battle Sphere continued to spin at 120,000 rpm. Her diagnostic mini screens indicated that her power levels had reduced to 65 percent.

What do I do about that? She thought. *I'll run out of power eventually.*

Ana had so many questions for her Battle Hologram team. She wondered where they were and were they watching her. Ana closed her eyes and tried to relax. After a time, she again felt something click inside her, but this time it felt different. Ana opened her eyes and watched her mini screens track her rpm to zero.

Now what? She thought.

Out of the corner of her eye, Ana noticed that her power reserves were increasing to 70 then 75 percent. She watched patiently until the mini-screens flashed that her reserves had reached 100 percent.

OK. So I disengage spinning to recharge my reserves. That's not so complicated.

Like she had done before, Ana focused her thoughts on returning to human form, triggering her hybrid transformation. Once she was standing back on the ground, she quickly put her clothes on and walked toward the series of circular structures. Kai was now standing in the doorway. She moved to one side as Ana entered.

"I see you're making progress," said Kai.

"I guess you could call it that," replied Ana coldly.

"Is there anything I can do to help?"

"Can you free my family for me?"

"Ana I —"

"I didn't think so," said Ana as she closed the door to her quarters.

As time went on, Ana raced faster and faster through the stone maze. With each pass, her confidence grew. To challenge herself, she went further and further into the stone labyrinth. In some stretches, her Battle Sphere barely fit through the maze of stone. In other locations, the maze suddenly opened up to reveal deep and narrow ravines.

Ana occasionally stopped and hovered over the openings. Sometimes, they seemed to go down indefinitely. In others, there were large ledges and stone floors thirty or forty feet below. She noticed water flowing at the bottom of one chasm. Ana eventually realized that an underground river snaked along the bottom of the ravines. The water looked clean and clear.

"Maybe this place isn't quite as desolate as I thought," mused Ana.

In time, Ana went deep into the Stone Forest. By now, she had mapped out several trails for her Battle Sphere to race through. She kept trying to beat her previous best time by racing as close to the stone formations as possible. Every so often, Ana could hear her outer plasma shield scraping against the hard stone.

I've got to be careful, she thought.

The next day, Ana went even further into the Stone Forest. She finally came up against a large stone formation that blocked her path. Ana stared at it for a time before backing up.

Hayden told me I have two hundred plasma laser cannons, she recalled.

Ana focused her thoughts on her laser cannons.

Fire at the rock wall.

Nothing.

She continued to focus.

Still nothing.

Ana then thought about her mother and sisters.

I've got to do this. For them, she thought.

Ana focused even harder.

Nothing.

She strained with all her might as she stared at the rock wall in front of her. Suddenly, a bright flash of light streaked past her into the wall with a loud clap. The plasma burst created a two-foot-deep circular crater, thirty feet in diameter.

I did it!

She focused her thoughts again causing another flash of light to hit the same spot, deepening the crater. She continued to fire at the wall causing a large cloud of dust to rise up into the sky. Ana's mini screens flashed occasionally as her power levels decreased to 60 then 55 then 50 percent. When the levels reached 30 percent, she stopped. The thick dust cloud slowly dissipated to reveal a tunnel about twenty feet deep. Small chunks of rock were everywhere. Ana stared at her handiwork for a time before she turned around and weaved her way back through the stone maze. As she did, Ana couldn't shake the feeling she was being watched.

No, monitored, she thought. *I must've made enough noise to alert everyone and everything that I'm here.*

Reaching the center of the opening, she recharged her reserves, transformed back to human form and put on her clothes. Looking up, she noticed all three Mitel soldiers standing outside, holding their electro laser long weapons. Without saying a word, Ana walked past them toward the living quarters. Kai suddenly appeared in the doorway and stepped outside.

"Are the natives restless?" asked Ana.

"The soldiers are here to protect us," replied Kai. "They take the threat of attack very seriously."

"Well good. So do I."

"It sounds like you have figured out how to fire your laser cannons."

Ana studied Kai for a few seconds before answering.

"Kind of, I guess. Still got a long way to go."

"Understood. I —"

"But at least you have some good news to report to the Mitel Leadership, *right*?"

Kai looked away.

"I mean, that's the real reason why you're here right?"

"Ana, I'm here to help you."

"To do what exactly?"

"To talk if you need to. To offer my perspective —"

"Offer your *perspective*? On what?"

"What you are going through."

"Oh, OK. So, you counsel people who have been forcibly abducted and then torn away from their family? Is that what you do?"

"Listen, Ana —"

"No, you listen! I didn't ask to be a *Battle Sphere*. I didn't ask to be taken from my world. I didn't consent to my body being treated like some kind of *thing*, poked and prodded and forced into a pitch-black enclosure to be forced to transform until I thought I was dead!"

Kai crossed her arms and stood motionless as Ana's eyes turned silver with rage. "You *can't* help me. Not unless you've been through what I've been through!"

After a time, Ana's eyes returned to normal as she calmed herself down. She talked quietly, almost to herself.

"You and all the others: the soldiers, scientists, technicians, pilots, mechanics, and bureaucrats. You are all complicit in the unspeakable suffering and deaths of countless people. Both here *and* on Thrae. Maybe *you* should talk to someone about that."

Kai thought of how to respond but did not answer.

Ana went into her quarters and closed her door. She stared out her window at the stone formations before falling asleep.

Ana got up the next morning eager to continue experimenting with her laser cannons. After transforming, she quickly made her way through the stone formations to the small tunnel she had started. At 98 percent reserves, she focused on her laser cannons. Within seconds, they opened fire. The sheer concentration of firepower cause Ana to move backwards as countless chunks of rock flew in every direction. An enormous dust and debris cloud reduced visibility to only a few feet in every direction. She watched her reserves decrease to 80, then 70 then 60 percent. When her mini screens indicated that her power reserves had reached 40 percent, Ana sensed that the ejecting debris had all but stopped. By thought alone, she ceased firing and waited for the cloud to dissipate. Dust and rock debris were everywhere. The circular tunnel, now forty feet in diameter, extended completely through the rock formation one hundred feet to the other side. Beyond the far opening was the lush green valley Ana had noticed during her initial flight up into the sky.

She darted through the tunnel back into the sun. Ana noticed that her laser cannons had destroyed trees and vegetation beyond the opening. Large burn marks were visible along the grassy fields. Ana then hovered in place to view her surroundings. The view of the lush valley was breathtaking. The underground river exited the rock formation on her right and snaked its way diagonally across the valley before disappearing back under the rock face. To its right, the Stone Forest resumed and continued toward the mountain range Ana had noticed from the opening when they first landed.

It's so beautiful.

Several caves were visible along the sloping stone faces that rose up on either side of the valley. A tree forest stood at the far corner of the valley that received the most sun. Looking around, Ana again had the feeling she was being watched. Now that the blasting noise had stopped, various leaf and grass eating animals reappeared to continue foraging for food.

I'm being paranoid, Ana concluded.

She darted up toward the caves in the rock formation to her left to get a better look. There were no signs of the human-like creatures, although she noticed several well-worn paths leading to the cave entrances.

"Animals probably take shelter there," she said aloud.

Ana eventually headed back through the tunnel and raced through the Stone Forest quickly, pretending that each formation was a military device trying to entrap her. Every so often, she scraped up again the stone, causing her to slow down momentarily.

Be careful Ana.

Exiting the forest into the opening, Ana was excited and proud of her accomplishments. She had taught herself to fly, fire her laser cannons and recharge her reserves. But in the back of her mind, she knew she still had a lot of work to do.

I don't know what I don't know.

She recharged, transformed back to human form, and made her way to the living quarters. When she entered, nobody was around. Ana quickly grabbed a protein drink and went to her quarters to shower. Ana relaxed on her bed, sipping her drink. Fifteen minutes later she was fast asleep.

Ana got up the next morning ready to increase the intensity of her training. After transforming, she raced all the way through the stone formations to the tunnel she had created. She paused briefly to admire her work before darting through it. When she came out the outer side, she immediately turned around and darted back through the Stone Forest all the way to the circular opening.

I've got to go faster.

Ana repeated the *circuit maze* as she called it, three more times, each time faster than the last. To reduce her time, Ana raced closer and closer to the stone formations. On her fifth attempt, her eye caught something, or someone darting across the forest floor. Ana tried to get a better look.

Her Battle Sphere careened off a stone formation causing her to lose control. Ana frantically tried to regain control but it was too late. She plowed directly into a tall stone formation causing it to disintegrate while knocking her unconscious. Her plasma shields flickered then shut down. Ana's Battle Sphere powered down as it bounced once, twice and then a third time along the stone floor before deflecting off the side wall. It rolled slowly to the edge of a ravine before falling in. The Battle Sphere fell another fifty feet before hitting the bottom with a large metallic thud. It rolled slowly before coming to a stop along the underground river. Ana quickly began to transform back to human form. As she laid unconscious, arcs of blue plasma energy raced across her silver skin. An hour later, Ana had transformed back to her human self. Lying motionless beside the river, dusk turned into nighttime.

Tor Aarden and his men made their way along the underground river toward Ana. At eight feet six inches tall and four hundred and fifty pounds, Tor was a giant and the current leader of the Nomas people. The extensive black hair that covered most of his face and entire body made him look more animal than human. The same could be said for the rest of his men.

They had been observing Ana closely and knew the history and capabilities of the Thraen Battle Sphere. The *Nomas*, as they called themselves, knew many things despite their decision to remain in isolation from the outside world. To them, there was no logical reason to do otherwise. The outside world or *Atreus*, was a place of chaos, suffering and destruction.

Their shoulder mounted lights illuminated the chasm as they snaked along the river's edge.

"There she is," pointed one man.

Up ahead, Ana lay on her side unconscious. Two men jumped ahead. As they approached, one of them took off his backpack to access medical devices. He knelt down next to Ana and fumbled through the bag.

"Hurry up," instructed Tor.

"The lighting here isn't the greatest," replied Zeb Maiken, Nomas' senior medical doctor. Zeb was easily recognizable from the graying hair across his entire body. He had trained many doctors and medical assistants over the years, some of whom left for the Atreus to make a difference on Mitel. Although a few eventually returned, most were never heard from again and presumed dead. It was a topic Zeb avoided. He had once left and returned. Tor was another story. He considered those that left as having turned their back on their own people. To him, those who left were no longer Nomas. They were now Mitels. They were now the enemy. Tor was also less trusting of those who returned, regardless of what lengths they may have gone to redeem themselves to him.

Zeb waved his hand-held scanner across the length of Ana's body. He studied the results as they flashed across the screen.

"Well?" asked Tor.

"She's alive," replied Zeb. "She received a concussion and . . ." Zeb paused.

"And what?"

"With such incredibly high levels of titanium, aluminum, beryllium, magnesium and other metals in her bloodstream, it's difficult to fully ascertain her overall condition. She doesn't appear to have any broken bones or major contusions. "

"Is that it? Is that all you can tell me?" asked Tor.

Zeb quickly stood up and faced Tor. He was the same height and size, although his mostly gentle demeanor made him seem smaller and more approachable.

"If you think you can do a better job, you're more than welcome to try."

Tor looked away briefly.

"Sorry old friend," he replied eventually. "Let's get her back safely. The night predators will be out soon. It will be best that we return home without incident."

"OK," nodded Zeb.

He kneeled back down and gently picked up Ana. Zeb carefully placed her on a mobile stretcher on the back of his assistant. As the group made their way back to the valley, Zeb performed updated scans while several armed warriors kept a close watch for any trouble. The Nomas were a peaceful people, but they had their electro laser long weapons ready just in case. Their versions were much more accurate and lethal than those carried by the Mitel military. As they should be since the Nomas invented the technology.

The group walked along the river and through a narrow chasm opening into the valley. They walked up one of the many paths towards the caves. Upon entering one of the larger openings, they strode one hundred yards to its end. Zeb flashed his identification badge towards an optic scanner hidden in the sidewall. A wall in front slid open, revealing HorVert elevators. It had taken the Nomas thousands of years to create their complex underground city that extended miles beneath the surface, and in several directions. A myriad of multicolored lighting systems shined like sunlight throughout the city. Reservoirs of hot springs below the planet surface had been harnessed to produce steam to rotate turbines that activated generators to produce electricity. The hot water was also used to heat their underground city. The Nomas grew large quantities of fruits and vegetables in dozens of natural underground caverns and other manmade enclosures grown by sophisticated artificial lighting systems. Underground high speed electromagnetic rail systems connected the entire city. At the direct center, a complex computer *brain* coordinated the flawless operation of every underground system. It was truly a remarkable and wondrous place. And, aided by invisible highly advanced exterior plasma shields, it was undetectable by the outside world.

Ana was brought to the central medical facility and closely monitored. The next day, she woke up. Seated next to her bed was a female nurse. She was about Ana's height and her face's beautiful pale complexion continued down along her neck and chest. The rest of her body was covered in hair. Ana looked around the room to see it filled with flashing devices.

"Where am I?"

"In our medical facility," smiled the nurse. "You took a pretty hard hit up there."

"*Up there*?"

"Yes. You are now about a mile beneath the surface. You have been unconscious for quite a while."

Just then, Tor and Zeb entered the room.

"Ah, I see you're awake," smiled Zeb. "Good."

Ana stared in awe at them.

"How is she doing?"

"Her vitals are normal. She appears alert although a bit confused."

"Understandable."

"Where am I?"

"I told her —"

"No, I mean what *is* this place?"

"You are in our underground city," replied Tor. "The true extent of our civilization is unknown to the outside world. To them, we are nothing more than sub-humans foraging on the surface."

"But I have been told stories."

"Such as?"

"That you capture and eat people that wander off into the Stone Forest."

"Ah yes, that," smiled Tor. "Let me assure you that we *don't* eat people, although some very formidable creatures on the surface above, if given the chance, most certainly would."

"I see. Is that why you brought me here?"

"That was certainly one consideration."

"Why else?"

"I wanted to meet face to face with a human hybrid Battle Sphere. We have heard the stories of their courage, bravery and firepower. My request to bring you here was met with great apprehension by our elders. I explained to them that Battle Spheres are known for being the most selfless and honorable individuals in the entire universe."

Ana looked away.

"What's the matter?" asked Tor. "Is this not true?"

Ana turned and stared directly at Tor.

"I don't know any other Battle Spheres but me," she replied. "I don't even know how to fight."

"We noticed that," smiled Tor. "But you're learning."

"Not fast enough."

"Not fast enough for *whom*?"

"The Mitel Leadership."

"*The Mitel Leadership?*"

"It's a long story."

"If you don't mind, I'd like to hear it."

Starting from when she was abducted, Ana explained everything. It was like turning on a faucet. It felt good to get everything out. She felt she could trust Tor, Zeb and the rest of the Nomas. They had saved her life and given her medical care, protection and shelter.

"Well that's some story," replied Tor after Ana had finished. "The Mitel commando raid clearly caught everyone on Thrae off guard."

"My family has suffered as a result of Thrae's inability to protect them," replied Ana softly. "For me personally, I felt let down and abandoned."

"Your entire planet has suffered at the hands of the Mitel Leadership Ana. At this point, they have limited resources. I wouldn't be too hard on them if I were you."

Ana didn't respond.

"The Mitel Leadership put you through extensive testing in the underground facility for a reason," he continued. "They must have mapped out your entire systems architecture. I expect they are in the process of reverse engineering your Battle Sphere."

"They want to *clone* me?"

"Not *you*, your Battle Sphere."

"Why? For what purpose?"

"Complete domination over Thrae and whoever else they can reach in the universe. Think about it. With thousands of mechanical Battle Spheres, nothing could oppose them."

"At that point, they wouldn't need me anymore."

Ana knew that also meant her family would be in grave danger.

"No, they wouldn't," replied Tor. "The question is what are you going to do about it?"

"What am *I* going to do?"

"Yes. At the moment, you are the only Battle Sphere on Mitel. You could — "

"I can't put my mother in sisters in danger!"

"They're already in danger Ana. Along with all the innocent men, women and children on Thrae *and* Mitel."

Ana thought for a moment.

"What do you think I should do?" she asked.

"Continue to practice until you are ready to confront the Mitel Leadership."

"I couldn't do it all by myself."

"Yes you could. Ana, you don't fully understand and appreciate the capabilities you possess. You are a *Thraen Battle Sphere*, the most formidable fighting machine in the entire universe."

"*Formidable?* I can't shoot, I can't fly very well, and my Battle Hologram abandoned me."

"You just need to practice. As far as your Hologram Matrix goes, their entire existence was to help you protect your people and planet. When they heard what you planned to do, can you blame them for abandoning you?"

"I guess not. But I have no choice."

"You have choices Ana. You don't fully know and understand everything yet, but as a rare and fearsome Thraen Battle Sphere, your duty is to defend and protect those who can't do it themselves. I think deep down, you know that, and you also know what you have to do."

Ana could feel herself getting angry.

"It's not that easy!" she retorted. "I mean look at you! You and your people decided to cut yourselves off from the rest of your world while the Mitel Leadership killed those who couldn't defend themselves. How is that doing the right thing?"

Tor stiffened as Ana spoke. He then let out a heavy sigh.

"We are among the oldest people to walk this planet. We have been persecuted for thousands of years based in part on our looks alone. We were slaughtered out of fear. Time and time again. We slowly withdrew from the main-stream civilization not out of fear or cowardice, but rather in the interests of self-preservation. A long time ago, we saw the path the Mitel Leadership had decided to follow. Despite everything we had been through, we organized the early resistance movement. We supplied advanced weapons technology, battle planning and manpower. But the majority of the planet was not ready or willing to stand up and face the Mitel Leadership. We pressed on and took the fight to them. We suffered devastating losses. During that time, we became aware of Thraen hybrid technology. We studied it from afar and even came up with a few system architecture *add-ons* as we called them. Along the way, we gained strength and courage from a Thraen Battle Sphere named Zebulon Park who gave his life defending your world from Mitel's first invasion. His courage and selfless devotion to protecting his people gave us renewed energy. We fought on. We eventually started to see the Mitel resistance grow. But it was still not enough. When it became clear that the Leadership was on the verge of locating the existence of this place, we made the decision to withdraw completely. There was nothing more we could do. To do otherwise meant the potential end of our own people. That was something we weren't prepared to consider. Not yet."

Ana sat quietly and listened.

"We now use our appearance to scare away those on the surface who may come looking. *Monsters and man-eaters:* that's how the outside world views us now. That couldn't be further from the truth. At this point, a few of our people still go out into the world to try and make a difference. My younger brother Rad was one of them. He was trained by Zeb and became an exceptional medical doctor. He joined the Mitel military and eventually became the Chief Medical Officer on a Mitel cruiser. Last I heard from him, he was sent off on a deep space mission allegedly in search of another young Battle Sphere. For all I know, he's dead."

Tor looked around the room.

"In some ways he died, at least to me, when he left here and joined the Mitel military."

"What do you mean?"

"What possible good is he doing for our world by joining the Mitel military? How is he helping the innocent men, women and children that need to be protected?"

"I see."

"Ana, I was hoping maybe we could do something together. Something that might give hope to our world. Maybe I am fooling myself."

"How?"

"First, you need to step up your training. Increase your agility and firepower proficiency."

"I know."

"You also need to be ready to defend yourself from the inevitable invasion by the machines."

"How?"

"Watching you train got me thinking. In my opinion, you should fly out to the shared asteroid belt and continue your training there."

"The Mitel Leadership mentioned that too."

"That doesn't surprise me," mused Tor. "Here, take these."

Tor handed Ana two tiny capsules. One was blue and the other green.

"What are they?"

"They're add-ons. The blue one is a detailed three-dimensional display of our shared solar system. The green one manufactures and excretes small solar powered signal accelerators. If you ingest them just prior to your next transformation, they will be absorbed by your Battle

Sphere architecture. The 3-D solar system should pop up as an additional data screen. That will allow you to navigate outer space, at least in our celestial neighborhood."

"Thank you," replied Ana, before placing them in her pocket. "Why are you —"

"Helping you?"

"Yes. I've already told you what I must do."

"You've told me what you've been *asked* to do. The choice to carry out that request is yours and yours alone."

Ana did not answer.

"You need food and rest," Tor continued.

Just then, another nurse walked in with a tray filled with fruits, vegetables and a protein drink. Ana, suddenly realizing how hungry she was eagerly ate. After watching her for a few minutes, Zeb and Tor headed for the doorway.

"Tor," said Ana.

Tor stopped and turned around.

"Thank you for saving my life."

"You are very welcome," smiled Tor.

"I still don't understand why you did it."

"It's quite simple. It was the right thing to do. Now get some rest."

Ana finished eating and quickly drank the protein drink. Minutes later, she felt very drowsy and fell asleep.

The next morning Ana woke up on the soft grass inside the valley. She sat up and noticed she was still wearing the clothes she was given in the medical complex. She reached into her pocket and pulled out the tiny data capsules.

I guess it wasn't a dream.

Ana placed the small capsules back in her pocket as she stood up and looked around. Directly in front of her was the tunnel her Battle Sphere had recently created. It was a beautiful sunny day. There was no sign of Zeb, Tor or the nurses. Ana took her clothes off and, holding the capsules in the palm of her hand tried to transform. Nothing. She tried again. Still nothing.

Don't panic, she thought. *Maybe I just need to get back to my building and take it easy for a while.*

Ana put her clothes back on and carefully placed the capsules back into her pocket. She walked through the tunnel and looked ahead at the Stone Forest. Ana wove her way through the maze of stone formations. By now, she knew the path back to the circular stone opening like the back of her hand.

"It's much more challenging on foot," she grunted.

Working her way back toward the circular stone opening, Ana climbed over, around and between boulders of all shapes and sizes. Every so often she noticed movement above her. Occasionally, Ana noticed something very large, hairy and dark high above her off in the distance. Suddenly, Ana saw a Nomas warrior holding an electro laser long weapon. He was standing on a rock formation high above her.

They're watching over me, she smiled to herself.

After hours of walking and climbing, the path became much easier to navigate. Ana could sense she was nearing the opening. Walking along, Ana again had the feeling she was being watched. Looking up, she saw four individuals dressed in gray pants, brown colored long sleeve, rapid assault shirts, body armor and helmets standing on a large stone outcropping high above her. They were holding electro laser long weapons.

Strange, she thought. *They don't look like Mitel soldiers, and they aren't Nomas.*

Ana glanced up at them twice more while she continued walking. When she looked up a third time they were gone. *Who are they and why are they out in the middle of nowhere.*

A half hour later, Ana entered the large circular stone opening. She was dirty, tired and hungry. As she approached the buildings, Kai raced out to meet her followed by the soldiers.

"Ana! You're OK!" shouted Kai.

Ana flashed a smile before being hugged tightly. She was so dirty, nobody noticed her different clothes.

We were so worried. We thought that maybe —"

"I had been eaten?"

"Yes," whispered Kai, wiping back a tear.

"No. At least not yet anyway . . ."

"What happened to you Ana?"

"My Battle Sphere hit a stone formation knocking me unconscious. When I woke up, I had transformed back to human form. I haven't been able to transform since."

"You're very lucky Ana," replied Kai. "Your body may have suffered some trauma. Come inside so I can run a few tests just to be sure you're OK."

"Sounds good," nodded Ana.

As they walked back to the buildings, Ana glanced over her shoulder for any signs of Tor and the others.

"What are you looking at?" asked Kai.

"Oh, nothing," smiled Ana. "I'm just happy to be out of there."

"I'll bet."

Over the next few days, Ana tried to transform several times without success. After each failed attempt, she carefully placed the tiny capsules back into a small pouch by her feet. She then gathered the rest of her belongings and walked slowly back to her quarters. She was still tired and sore from her crash out in the Stone Forest.

"Give it a little more time," said Kai. "Your body is still healing."

The next morning, Ana woke up refreshed. She could feel that her body was ready. She grabbed a water bottle and headed outside. When she reached the middle of the opening, Ana retrieved the capsules and picked up her water bottle. She then moved her feet apart and concentrated. Her eyes immediately turned silver.

Ana quickly placed the blue and green capsules in her mouth and washed them down with a big sip of water. She dropped the water bottle and allowed her towel to fall to the ground. A minute later, she was hovering above the ground. Ana surveyed the screen displays. Nothing.

I guess Tor was wrong, she thought.

Suddenly, a new three-dimensional display appeared directly below her primary screen. It was slightly larger than the others and contained a distinctive blue boarder. The planets of both solar systems appeared along with the swirling figure eight asteroid belt.

"Where do you want to go?" asked a deep voice that sounded like Tor.

"*Is that you?*" asked Ana incredulously.

"It's not the Mitel Leadership," replied Tor.

"But you're inside me somewhere. It's a bit creepy."

"*Creepy?*"

"I'm sorry. I guess I mean *unexpected.*"

"You have the ability to disable the program at any time."

"How?"

"You just say *deactivate navigation*."

"That's it?"

"That's it. We're just trying to be of assistance. We certainly can't replace your Battle Hologram, but maybe we can keep you company while you're all alone out in deep space."

"Thanks."

"Do you want to try some target practice and agility drills?"

"Definitely."

"OK good. I'm entering coordinates for the divergence region of our solar system's asteroid belt. It should show up as a yellow dot in your 3-D display."

"I see it."

"Good. If you focus your thoughts on that yellow marker, it will activate and help guide you there."

As Ana stared at the marker, it pulsated.

"I'm turning things over to Roe. She will assist you from here."

"Thanks, Tor."

"No, thank you Ana. I've been thinking a lot lately. I guess maybe it's time for our people to stop sitting on the sidelines."

"But I told you, my orders are —"

"Ana."

"What?"

"I know. One day at a time, OK?"

"OK."

"Hi Ana, this is Roe. Are you ready to go?"

"Yes."

"Good. Then let's do it!"

Ana's concentration causing her Battle Sphere to spin faster and faster until she reached full speed. She darted skyward through the upper atmosphere and into outer space. Ana continued to accelerate until her Battle Sphere reached maximum speed. Every few minutes, Ana excreted a small signal accelerator from a mechanical pore that enabled Roe to maintain instantaneous communication with Ana's Battle Sphere. Looking all around, Ana marveled at the size and beauty of outer space.

It's just unbelievable, she thought.

"You will reach the asteroid belt's divergence region in fifteen minutes," said Roe.

"And then what?"

"Whatever you want to do," laughed Roe.

"I'm going to practice firing my laser cannons."

"That's what I'd do if I were you."

Ana's mind wandered while her Battle Sphere sped through the blackness of space. She remained silent for several minutes before speaking again.

"Roe?"

"I'm here Ana."

"What's your family like?"

"*My family?*"

"Yes."

"I have two brothers, both of whom are itching to travel out into the universe. My parents want them to stay here and help our people."

"How about you?"

"Me?"

"Yeah. What do *you* want to do?"

"I want to travel the universe someday too. But first, I want to help my people and my planet."

"Help them how?"

"I want to show Mitel that our people are not some form of prehistoric man-eaters. I want to show the world once and for all that we are creative, highly advanced, trustworthy, and brave. Then I want to help free our world of the Mitel Leadership."

Ana listened quietly.

"Ana, Tor told me what you're going through with your mom and sisters. I'm really sorry about all that. What about your dad?"

"He died during the second Mitel invasion of Thrae. My mom was pregnant with me at the time. She never talked about him. I guess it was just too painful."

"What about your sisters? Did they talk about him?"

"No, but they had a different father. He was a Thraen fighter pilot. He was killed during a mission to eliminate a Mitel terrorist cell. I'm told he was a wonderful person."

"I'm so sorry Ana. My parents were both orphans. They talk a lot about what it was like. The loneliness — "

"What happened?"

"You mean my grandparents? They were all members of the Mitel resistance. One by one, they were killed by Mitel Special Forces."

"Oh . . ."

"But that was their choice, Ana. They died doing what they believed in. Hey, you're entering the asteroid belt."

Ana looked down at her data screens. Yellow dots appeared on several screens. Within seconds, the yellow dots quickly multiplied until they appeared as a moving river.

They are everywhere, Ana panicked.

She instinctively decelerated until her Battle Sphere came to a stop and hovered in place.

"What are you doing?"

"I'm not sure."

"OK. Do you see asteroids?"

"Yes, on my screens."

"Can you see them out in space?"

"Not really."

Roe thought for a moment.

"Don't you have lights? I thought I read somewhere that Battle Spheres are supposed to have search lights on the top and bottom of your core cylinders."

Ana glanced at her mini screens. She noticed nothing that indicated a lighting system. She then concentrated on her cylinders. Nothing. She tried again, activating a thin band of high intensity search lights. A river of ice and rock appeared off in the distance.

"I see them!"

"OK, good. Now follow the asteroids until they start diverging," instructed Roe. "Then circle around and fire at them as they approach you in a diverging pattern. That will be an excellent way to test out your laser cannons."

Located just below its outer spin surface, the Battle Sphere's arsenal consisted of two hundred high energy laser cannons. Positioned in a grid pattern surrounding the sphere, the cannons fired through outwardly permeable openings in the shard mesh skin surface, representing the remnants of porous human skin cells. The sphere's permeable plasma outer defense shield that tightly surrounded its outer spin surface, was permeable from the inside out, allowed the high energy bursts to pass through.

Each laser cannon emitted destructive high energy plasma bursts which on contact, immediately enveloped and destabilized the target's atomic structure, destroying it in seconds. In full battle mode, the sphere appeared as a tiny star emitting streams of bright white mini *stars* in all directions. The energy pulses curved as they exited the spinning orb before quickly straightening out and elongating as they raced toward their target. A Battle Sphere could operate in full battle mode for fifteen minutes at a time before it became necessary to disengage, withdraw and reenergize.

Since Ana no longer had the benefit of her Battle Hologram, she was learning how to fire her laser cannons on her own. She also had to keep track of her energy reserves.

Ana raced beside the asteroid *river* until she reached the cosmic divergence point, where the two solar systems pulled objects towards their respective orbit. She scanned her mini screens to pinpoint the exact location of the split before circling around as Roe had advised her to do. She then cautiously approached the asteroids, focusing her thoughts on her laser cannons. At first nothing happened. She saw a large mass hurtling towards her. Almost instinctively, her sphere fired bright white energy bursts at the asteroid, obliterating it; the tiny remnants of debris harmlessly deflected off of her defense shields.

"I got one!" Ana shouted.

As the asteroids continued to approach, Ana focused her attention on each one individually until her laser cannons opened fire. She then tried looking at two at a time. The results were the same.

"I got two at once!" she said excitedly.

But without the aid of her Battle Hologram, Ana quickly realized that her own abilities were limited. She tried focusing on three, four and then five asteroids at a time but only destroyed two and sometimes three. She circled around and tried again and again but the results were the same. Ana darted back and forth to avoid the approaching chunks of rock, metal, and ice she could not destroy. Noticing that her reserves were getting low, Ana sped away from the asteroid belt to recharge.

"Well? How did you do?" asked Roe.

"I'm getting better at controlling my laser cannons," replied Ana. "But I get the feeling that I might be limited to a few targets at a time."

"That's probably because you don't have your Battle Hologram to assist you."

"What am I going to do?"

"That's easy. You just need to develop engagement techniques that allow you to maximize what you can do."

"I'm not sure I understand."

"For example: if you can only focus on a few targets at a time, teach yourself how to destroy them as quickly as possible and then move on to the next two. Maybe you can line up a series of closely packed targets allowing you to continuously fire at them until they are all destroyed."

That made perfect sense to Ana.

"OK, I'll try it."

Over the next few months, Ana got up each morning and traveled to the asteroid belt. In time, she learned how to focus her entire weapons barrage on up to six discrete targets at a time. It wasn't the most efficient way of doing things, but it was still very lethal. She also became an expert at avoiding concentrated numbers of objects in very difficult conditions. It was as though she had taken her peripheral vision abilities to the next level.

Traveling back and forth, Ana talked to Roe about everything. In time, she felt like she knew Roe's family even better than she knew her own. She also talked to Roe while she recharged her plasma reserves. Occasionally, she just took a break and stared into outer space.

Ana also talked more and more with Kai. While she didn't feel comfortable telling her about Tor, Roe, the Nomas or the valley, she gave daily updates on the progress of her training. Ana also talked about her mom and two sisters. In time, Kai talked about her own family. Her parents were both in the Mitel military. She herself had never married.

"I've just haven't met the right person I guess," Kai explained one night. "Maybe someday . . ."

At the end of the third month, Ana felt she was ready. With Roe's help, she had trained herself as much as she could without the help of her Hologram Matrix. Although she wished her Battle Hologram was with her, she had decided. There was no turning back.

On the way back to Mitel from her latest practice, she decided it was time to end her training. She missed her family and felt she was ready to do what she had to do to secure their freedom.

"Roe? Are you there?"

"Yes Ana, I'm here. *What's wrong?*"

"I think it's time to head home."

"On behalf of the Mitel Leadership?"

"Yes."

Roe didn't respond.

"Roe? Are you there?"

"I'm here Ana. I'm just disappointed, that's all."

"I told you from the beginning that I had no choice. It's the only way I can save my family."

"Ana, I think deep down you know the Mitel Leadership will never let them go. At least not alive."

"That's not true!"

Ana could feel herself getting angry.

"The Nomas know from experience that the Mitel Leadership only cares about themselves," explained Roe.

"By returning to attack Thrae, you are just postponing the inevitable. If you attack the Leadership instead, you probably stand a better chance of saving your family."

"You don't know that!"

"Ana, listen —"

"No! You listen! I *must* do what the Leadership says to save my family. They are all I have left!"

"That's not true. You have us too Ana. We're here for you. You can stay with us. Together, we can help the Mitel resistance defeat the Mitel Leadership once and for all."

"No!" shouted Ana. "*Deactivate navigation.*"

Everything went silent.

Ana flew all the way back to the Stone Forest opening in tears. She felt horrible turning her back on Roe, Tor and the Nomas but felt she had no other option if she wanted to see her family again. When she landed, she rushed into the living quarters, wiping away her tears as she entered.

"Ana, what's wrong?" asked Kai.

Ana did not respond right away.

"Ana?"

"I'm ready to head back," replied Ana. "I've completed my training and am ready to go."

"Ana, that's great news. I —"

"Am I doing the right thing?"

Kai studied Ana intently.

"What do you mean?"

"Am I doing the right thing by trusting the Mitel Leadership to keep their word?"

Kai looked away from Ana.

"Unfortunately, I don't have the answer to that question," she replied.

"What would you do?"

"Ana look I don't think —"

"What would *you* do if you were me?"

Kai thought for a moment before quietly responding. "I would do everything I could to save my family." "Then let's go," replied Ana resolutely.

CHAPTER SEVEN – RETURN TO THRAE – PART II

General Michael Talbot boarded a Gulfstream V and traveled from the U.S. Naval Space Surveillance System Command headquarters in Dahlgren, Virginia to DAAF in Coopers Falls. He wanted to confirm firsthand that Janus was now a functioning Battle Sphere. He also had a hunch what that meant. He was met at the nearby Floyd Smith Memorial Airport in Kingsbury, New York and driven by limousine to DAAF. At the entry gates, the vehicle was delayed momentarily by several dozen picketers who had to be gently herded to one side. Their signs read: ALIENS GO HOME! WE DON'T WANT YOU HERE and MURDERERS! Some containing a stereotypical alien face.

Entering the facility, General Talbot was amazed at all the new construction that had replaced the open fields of the old Davis farm. He smiled to himself as he recalled his first encounter with Janus Stone near the tree grove. He smiled even more as he thought how that meeting and the subsequent events had permanently changed his job. He was no longer working to conceal UFO incidents. Rather, he was busy helping to advance Thraen propulsion technology for bettering all mankind. Major Talbot constantly reminded himself how fortunate the entire faster than light speed technology program has been to have Janus Stone as an invaluable resource for technical information and guidance.

As he stepped out of the limousine, he saw Janus approaching with a big smile. General Talbot noticed that Janus had more energy in his step.

"Hello Michael Talbot, it is a pleasure to see you again," grinned Janus.

The two shook hands.

"Likewise," smiled General Talbot. "I needed to hear everything from the *horse's mouth*."

"Ah yes. Where to begin?"

"For starters, is it *true*?"

"That I've regained my hybrid abilities?"

"Yes."

"It is indeed true," nodded Janus.

"*I knew it!*" laughed General Talbot. "From the moment I heard that two blips were streaking into outer space, I knew. How does it feel?"

"Exhilarating."

"I'll bet. Or at least, I can only imagine."

General Talbot then turned somber.

"I'm guessing this means you will want to return to Thrae to help your people."

"It was originally Chad's idea, but yes, we want to return to our planet."

"Understood. I presume that you will want to take one of the large USEPs."

"We would be deeply indebted to you if that could be arranged. At this point, I believe you are in a position to build as many as you desire."

"Yes, thanks to you."

General Talbot paused briefly.

"Janus, I can't thank you enough for everything you and Chad have done. Not just for me, but for the planet."

"Unfortunately, we also caused the Mitels to come to Earth and do what they did."

"A growing percentage of the world's population is blaming you for what happened, that's for sure."

"And they're right. I had sincerely hoped that after the Mitels discovered our USEP technology, the Leadership would have decided not to come after us; that it was just too far and too risky. I underestimated them. Despite my best efforts, my actions have a way of causing pain and suffering to countless innocents."

"Maybe you're just unlucky."

"Or maybe I don't think things all the way through."

"Janus, you've done so much. Think about it: You may be the only person in human history that has had such a profound impact on two different worlds. In Earth's case, you have single-handedly advanced our propulsion and other technologies by several generations. It's truly remarkable. We are planning several manned missions to Mars. Thanks to you, the time required for our pods to get there will be insignificant compared to the rest of the mission. We will probably colonize the red planet by the end of the next decade. It blows my mind when I sit down and really think about it. Hopefully we will be invited to come visit your planet someday."

"I suspect a visit from your world will happen sooner than we both realize. And thank you for your kind words."

General Talbot and Janus studied the sky for a time.

"Are you still immortal?" he asked eventually.

"I don't know. Time will tell."

"Do you still want to be?"

"That's a good question. In many ways, I would have to answer yes. But a growing part of me has grown weary of that existence. All the decisions I've made and the resulting pain and suffering those decisions have caused, it's a heavy burden to carry around. In time, you forget the names and often the situations, but you never forget the faces of the suffering and the pain in their eyes."

"I can only imagine how those memories can haunt you over such a long life. But I tend to agree with Markus. You are too hard on yourself."

"Maybe."

"Do you think you'll ever come back?"

"I don't know."

"Look me up if you do, OK?"

"I promise."

"And Janus do me one favor?"

"What's that?"

"Don't ever change who you are."

"Don't worry Michael Talbot. After 1,200 years, it's a bit too late for that," smiled Janus.

"Hey, I'm hungry," said General Talbot.

"You sound like Chad. Follow me."

The two men chuckled as they walked towards the DAAF main cafeteria.

Later that day, an informal meeting was scheduled at the DAAF's main cafeteria. Personnel from all over the base attended. General Talbot stood up to get everyone's attention above the talking and laughter.

"OK, quiet! Quiet down everyone," he said loudly.

Everyone in the room turned to look at him.

"Thank you. As you know, Janus Stone is now a fully functioning Battle Sphere. He joins his son in that regard."

Everyone clapped loudly. There were also a few hoots and shouts of encouragement.

"Settle down, settle down," smiled General Talbot. "The really big news is that they plan to return to their planet to help *their* people and we are going to get them there."

"How?" shouted a technician from the crowd.

"We are going to *lend* them one of our large USEP pods," replied General Talbot. He then looked towards Janus. "That means you're supposed to bring it back."

The crowd laughed.

"I've notified our people down at NASA to begin prepping the pod for launch on the Falcon Heavy Launch Vehicle."

General Talbot paused, then looked at Janus.

"Janus, would you like to say a few words?"

As Janus stood up, everyone clapped loudly.

"Thank you, General Talbot," said Janus. "And thank you everyone here in this room for everything you've done and continue to do. I know there is a growing dissent regarding our presence on this planet. I can't say that I blame them, given all the death and destruction associated with the Mitel invasion. But maybe our departure, at least temporarily, will help your world pivot towards the future, one that has great potential."

Personnel in the room clapped loudly.

"I've been thinking a great deal about who should accompany Chad and me. And I agree that it would make sense to bring a seasoned professional from Earth with us.

I have spoken to astronaut Susan Davis, and she indicated that it would be an honor to travel with us."

The crowd cheered.

"I believe that leaves seven more seats," said Janus.

"That's right," replied General Talbot.

"I had thought it would be best to bring Mayla Tallis and Teri Anton to assist our Battle Holograms. Their experience under extreme battle conditions will be invaluable. I must certainly bring Markus Kilmar. His wise counsel will be greatly appreciated during the difficult times to come."

"Are you sure about that?" asked Markus with a grin.

"Yes, old friend, I'm sure," smiled Janus. "I would also like to bring Luna Adair and Denton Millas to provide technical assistance and guidance."

"Whoo hoo!" yelled Luna.

"I thought you would be happy to hear that," smiled Janus. "I think that leaves two spots left."

"Correct," nodded General Talbot.

Janus turned to Jim and Molly Johnson.

"Jim and Molly Johnson, two fledgling astronauts in training, would you be interested in accompanying your son?"

"Yes!" replied Molly quickly.

"I really don't know what to say," added Jim. His mind raced as he processed the magnitude of the offer.

"Just say yes Jim," replied Molly.

"*Yes*," said Jim. "It would be an honor."

"Good," said Janus. "I think that does it."

"Very good," added General Talbot. "I'm very glad you didn't ask me because it would have been a pretty tough decision."

"I thought about it," acknowledged Janus. "But you are needed here. Probably more than you know."

"Let's hope. In the meantime, everyone needs to get ready and say their goodbyes. Launch is in one week."

"*One week?*" asked Jim incredulously.

"Yes, Mr. Johnson, one week. And please don't wander off before then, OK?"

Everyone laughed again, except Jim, who turned bright red with embarrassment.

"It's OK honey," whispered Molly. "I still love you."

The week flew by quickly. Melissica felt as though she was losing Chad all over again. And now she was also losing Molly and Jim. She didn't talk about it with Chad. Melissica realized that Chad would do what he had to do, and that was just how it would be. Instead, she tried to enjoy each minute of her time with him, regardless of what the future had in store. She also spent a lot of time with Molly, whom she now considered a second mother. On the day before the group was scheduled to leave, Melissica and Molly went for a walk up the dirt road to the stream. They sat down next to each other along the rocky embankment and watched the water weave its way over and around the stone filled waterway. Melissica eventually put her head on Molly's shoulder.

"Don't worry honey," said Molly soothingly. "We'll be back. In the meantime, keep an eye on things for us, OK?"

Melissica wiped away the tears as she nodded yes. "I'll miss you all terribly," she whispered. "But I get it. All of this, it's so much bigger than just what *I* want."

"That's pretty brave and selfless of you Melissica. I'm very proud of you." Molly then gave Melissica a long hug.

The day before the launch, the entire group, including Melissica, was flown from the Floyd Smith Memorial Airport to NASA's Kennedy Space Center. As they entered the facility, a large group of protesters blocked the entrance. Some of their signs read GO HOME! YOU'VE DONE ENOUGH DAMAGE, LEAVE OUR PLANET ALONE and DON'T COME BACK!

"Great," said Jim. "They just don't get it, do they?"

"The transition to a cohesive, mutually supportive, and universally tolerant society takes a long time," replied Janus. "The fact that so few are here today is probably a very good sign."

"I guess."

The next morning, they were helped into their launch and entry suits, before being transported to Launch Pad 39A.

"It's truly an honor to be chosen for this mission Janus," said Colonel Susan Davis. "It's a trip of a lifetime."

Susan stood five feet nine inches tall. At 32 years of age, she was athletic looking with short blond hair and hazel eyes. She had been one of the primary test pilots during the USEP reverse engineering project and knew the pod well. A former F18 fighter pilot, Susan had also logged extensive time in outer space as a crewmember on the ISS.

"I'm pleased that you accepted Susan," smiled Janus. "The choice for me was a selfish one."

"How do you mean?"

"You may almost be overqualified for this mission."

"Hardly," laughed Susan. "But thanks."

As they exited the building, Melissica walked up to Chad.

"Hey," she said softly.

"Hey," replied Chad.

"Go save another world, OK?"

"I'll do my best," smiled Chad.

"Please be careful."

"I will."

Melissica lunged forward and gave Chad a long hug. "I love you," she whispered before stepping away.

"Don't worry. I'll come back," said Chad.

"Please do," replied Melissica as she wiped away her tears. "I'll be here waiting."

The group was driven to the Launch Pad in the silver shuttle bus. It was a beautifully sunny day. About five billion people worldwide were expected to follow the launch of the first people from Earth to travel outside the solar system. When they arrived at Pad A, the pad rats were completing their final FOD check.

The crew was escorted to a makeshift launch tower which brought them up to the temporary spacecraft access arm. They strode along the arm's walkway to the large USEP's cabin door. Janus and the nine others climbed into the vertically mounted spacecraft using the series of hand and footholds before strapping themselves into their seats. Before sitting down, Janus and Susan helped Molly and Jim get situated and strapped in.

As Janus scanned the inside of the pod, a voice came over the command and control communications system.

"Welcome everyone," said the voice. "We've completed all preflight checks and are preparing for launch."

"Great," replied Janus as the inner and outer airlock doors automatically closed.

Susan and Janus ran through final flight checks. When she was done, Susan turned to look at Janus.

"Are you ready?" she asked.

"Yes," nodded Janus.

"Mission Control, pod systems fully functional and ready to go," said Susan.

"Affirmative," replied the voice. "The launch tower has been retracted from the pad. Commencing final launch sequence now. Prepare to launch."

"Roger Mission Control."

"T minus 5 minutes to launch . . ."

Janus looked around the pod again. *With all the recent upgrades, I think we are now in excellent shape,* he concluded.

Janus's thoughts then drifted to Thrae.

I hope we can be of some assistance after we arrive.

"T minus 1 minute to launch . . ."

Thirty seconds before launch, the on-board computers assumed control of the launch sequence.

"Ten, nine, eight, seven, six . . ."

The Falcon's main engines ignited, building up to over 90 percent of their maximum thrust. The USEP shook noticeably.

"Five, four three, two, one . . ."

The Falcon Heavy-lift launch vehicle lifted off the pad and streaked towards the sky, its engines now at maximum throttle. Ten minutes later, having separated from the launch vehicle, the USEP entered a low Earth's orbit.

"Deploy and energize the slip ring system," instructed Janus.

"Doing it now," replied Susan.

Satisfied with what she saw, Susan pressed a second button initiating maximum normal speed. The USEP lurched forward as it accelerated. Once Susan confirmed that the energizer gauge had reached *100* percent, she initiated the slip ring which deployed into position. Susan then pushed a third button to activate the departure sequence. Once the ring system was in place and its magnetic field fully activated, the negative vacuum void caused the USEP to accelerate forward above the speed of light and it was gone.

The voyage across deep space was uneventful. Janus was so pleased with the upgraded pod and its performance that things actually seemed boring. Enough food and beverages had been stored on board to feed the group for two full months.

"It's a good thing they did," boomed Denton. "The way Chad eats; we'll probably need all of it."

To pass some time, Chad and Janus taught Molly, Jim and Susan how to speak Thraen. Jim absorbed parts of the language much quicker than the others. He made that fact known to everyone.

"I have a question," asked Susan. "I've heard that you spoke directly with Zan Liss, the former Mitel Emperor. How do you guys understand each other?

"You mean between the Thraen and Mitesh languages?" asked Janus. "Since the two worlds are so close, Thraen and Mitel children have been taught both languages for as long as I can remember. At some point, the Mitel Leadership will probably eliminate that practice, but we have much larger problems to deal with."

"That would be a shame," mused Susan.

"Indeed. Once we arrive, translation devices can be installed inside your inner ears which will allow you to understand spoken Thraen. I brought along a data capsule containing the English language which will facilitate the translation process."

"No thank you," laughed Jim. "I don't want anything installed inside my ears. I'll just keep learning it the old fashioned way."

"You're making progress James, but you still have a long way to go. Unless you receive the translation devices, it's going to take you years to become proficient speaking Thraen."

"That's OK. No implants for me!"

"As you wish," Janus sighed.

Approximately two weeks later, the ten-seat USEP entered Thrae's solar system. Janus disabled the slip speed departure mode, causing the spacecraft transfer to normal power. He then caused the pod to bank toward its final destination. The slip ring unlocked, retracted and rotated the four large, curved sections toward their storage location beneath the pod. As the USEP continued toward Thrae, it sped past the orbits of the four outermost planets in its solar system.

"We're approaching Thrae," confirmed Janus. "I'm reducing speed to minimum normal."

The pod responded immediately and continued to slow down as it quietly passed Thrae's two moons. The group peered out the series of forward-facing windows. Directly in front was the large blue and green planet.

"Wow," said Jim, Molly, and Susan in unison.

Suddenly, the three-dimensional displays detected a large object approaching.

"A Mitel cruiser," said Janus. "And it's bearing down on us fast."

"Invisibility shields would have come in pretty handy right about now," Markus grumbled.

"What are we going to do?" asked Susan.

"We need to outrun it to the upper atmosphere," replied Janus, scanning the console data. "Wait. A much larger object is also approaching right behind it."

"A Mitel Transport vessel," said Mayla.

"They will send Strike fighters to intercept us," added Luna.

"Now what Janus?" asked Chad.

"Before we left, I made sure that the emergency distress beacon was uploaded from our old pod," replied Janus. He activated the signal. "Hopefully somebody is listening."

On the Mitel cruiser's ICC, the scanning specialist detected the small pod. He quickly ran a more detailed scan.

"Commander. My scans show a small Thraen craft headed towards the planet."

"Another one? Where did *this one* come from?" asked the Commander.

"It looks like it came from the same direction in deep space as the other two. The pod's size and configuration is very similar to the two crafts we encountered months ago. Wait, they just sent out a Thraen distress signal."

"Accelerate this vessel to full closing speed. If we can capture it and interrogate the occupants, they might lead us right to the resistance command. "

"Yes, Sir."

"Order the transport vessel to launch a grouping of strike fighters. We *must* block any attempt to rescue it."

"Doing it now, Sir."

In the huge underground Thraen defense base outside Bagan, a hologram technician picked up the new distress beacon.

"Commander, I'm receiving another urgent distress signal from a small craft beyond the outer atmosphere. And just like last time, it's an old indicator signal."

"Contact Liss immediately. Maybe he knows something," replied Arius.

"Doing it now. Tracking antennae also confirm two large Mitel spacecraft are closing in to intercept it."

Zan let out a big sigh as he wiped his hands clean. He had just spent ten hours helping Dru swap out two propulsion units on the first of three gleaming new space cruisers. Zan stood on the rear access platform and gazed around the expansive underground cavity known as Bay Number 1. Workers and equipment were everywhere. He stared with pride at the two identical cruisers parked directly behind him. Zan climbed down from the platform and slowly walked to the cavity entrance. Two huge stone-faced camouflaged doors were slightly ajar. The series of entrance doors, along a mountainous rock face, overlooked Lake Victoria. He stepped outside for some fresh air. A flat granite mesa two hundred feet wide by almost four thousand feet long curved along the near side of the lake. It was formed during Thrae's most recent ice age seventy-five thousand years ago. The far side of the stone mesa dropped fifty feet to the lake. It represented a perfect natural launch and landing pad for both large and small spacecraft for Bays 1 and 2 and was affectionately called the *shelf.*

It's a beautiful view, he thought.

In the underground command center, Arius Court stood over the shoulder of the technician and stared at the computer console. Once again, Arius had a hunch there was something very unusual about the incoming craft.

"Send *twenty* fighters to provide cover fire and safe escort back to the base," he ordered.

"Yes Sir!"

Thraen tactical fighters raced up underground flight ramps, exiting through the heavily concealed access slots and streaked skyward.

Zan watched as two at a time, the silver and black multi-purpose fighters raced skyward. His shoulder mounted communicator then beeped twice.

"Liss here."

"Zan, it Arius. We're receiving another old Thraen distress signal. Any thoughts?"

Zan paused momentarily.

"It might be — "

"Janus Stone?"

"My thoughts exactly. I'm on my way."

Zan sprinted back through the door opening. He powered up a base hover craft and sped along a rectangular tunnel. Bright white ceiling and side lights illuminated the passageway before Zan exited the tunnel into bright sunshine. He banked hard right before disappearing into a second, well-lit tunnel which curved downward. At the repeating series of flashing yellow light strips, Zan slowed the hover craft down as it entered the huge underground cavern. He banked to the right before landing next to several storage units. Zan jumped out and ran toward a cavern door. He flashed his medallion which caused an access door to slide open. Zan sprinted down a hallway toward the command center.

"My monitoring orb just confirmed Mitel fighters are headed our way," said Janus.

"Mine too," said Markus.

"They mean business," replied Denton.

"If there was only a way for us to transform without destroying this pod," said Chad.

"Unfortunately, there isn't," replied Janus.

"The cruiser just initiated a gravity control beam," confirmed Markus.

"Everybody, hold on."

Janus steered the pod to the right, causing the gravity control beam to narrowly miss its target.

"Here comes another one," said Markus as the Mitel cruiser bore down on them.

This time, Janus jerked the pod to the left.

On the Mitel cruiser's ICC, the scanning specialist tracked the progress of the gravity control beams.

"They're successfully evading our gravity beams, Sir," he announced. "And scanners have confirmed that twenty Thraen resistance fighters have passed through the upper atmosphere."

"*Twenty*? They'll be too much for our fighters."

The Commander thought for a moment.

"I have an idea," he said.

"Sir?"

"Order our fighters to withdraw."

"What?"

"Do as I say!"

"Doing it now, Sir."

"Weapons specialist. I want you to launch one of our high-speed stealth drones. Then fall back until we confirm they are all on their way back to the planet's surface."

"Yes, Sir."

"They will lead our drone right to their hidden base."

"Strange," announced Janus, "The Mitel fighters are retreating. And so is the cruiser."

"My orb has identified twenty Thraen fighters headed our way," said Markus. "There's your answer!"

"The beacon worked," concluded Mayla.

"Indeed," nodded Janus.

After realizing that the Mitel forces had retreated, the Thraen fighters escorted the USEP back to their base. Nearing the planet's surface, the fighters again descended directly toward Lake Victoria.

"We're going to crash!" shouted Jim.

"Relax James," smiled Janus.

"But . . ." replied Jim as he watched the lead fighter disappear into an island entrance slot, followed by a second fighter and then a third.

"Our turn," said Janus as he entered the slot. Jim, Molly, and Susan stared at the bright white ceiling and side lights illuminated the passageway. Janus slowed the pod to minimum forward speed and deployed his landing gear as he approached the repeating series of flashing yellow light strips along the bottom and sides of the tunnel. Entering the cavern, the pod was grabbed by a landing-assist gravity control beam. It quickly decelerated, gently landed and rolled to a stop behind the fighters.

"Look at this place!" said Jim. "It's unbelievable."

"Welcome to Thrae," smiled Janus. "Let's get out and stretch our legs."

A minute later, the small stealth drone encased by a rudimentary but effective plasma invisibility shield, landed silently in the corner of the cavern. It immediately transmitted its exact coordinates back into space via an encrypted communications link.

On the Mitel cruiser's ICC, the scanning specialist detected and processed the drone's signal transmission.

"Commander, I've established a lock on the drone's exact coordinates."

"Superb. Weapons specialist," the cruiser commander began, "Launch two high energy cluster pods."

"Doing it now."

Each cluster pod contains several powerful guided missiles. Once the pods pass through a planet's outer atmosphere, they automatically release their missile cluster. Upon release, the missiles activated and separated before streaking toward their pre-programmed targets.

"Cluster pods confirmed launched, Sir."

One pod exited from each of the twin weapons tubes located beneath the cruiser and sped toward the planet.

In the command center, a communications specialist received confirmation that the Thraen pod had entered the underground defense base. Arius immediately headed toward the door. He was eager to determine the identity of the crewmembers in the newest pod.

"Sir! Our long-range scanners have picked up two cluster pods," said the scanning specialist.

Arius abruptly stopped and turned around.

"What? *Are you sure*?"

"Yes, Sir."

"Where are they headed?"

The specialist typed furiously before looking up at Arius.

"Computer modeling say *right here* . . ."

After waiting impatiently for Arius to arrive, Zan and Ard led a contingent of hologram soldiers with both hand-held lasers and electro laser long weapons pointed directly at the USEP pod.

It's very similar to the ones we built, thought Zan.

After the pod doors slid open, Janus and the others slowly climbed down the side of the pod using the hand and footholds.

"Identify yourselves," ordered Zan.

"I'm Janus Stone."

"I had a hunch it was you," grinned Zan "We finally meet face to face. It's an honor."

"You must be Zan Liss," smiled Janus as the two men shook hands. "I see you made good on your word to join the resistance."

"It seemed like the right thing to do. I just hope we can make a difference."

"Agreed."

In the command center, specialists and technicians scrambled to respond to the incoming cluster pods.

"Ground lasers energizing," said a weapons specialist.

"Tracking targets," confirmed a scanning technician.

Having passed through the outer atmosphere, the two pods separated and released their multiple missiles.

"The pods have activated," confirmed the lead scanning specialist tensely.

"How many?" Arius asked calmly.

"Twenty-four sir."

"Re-identifying targets," said the scanning technician. "Tracking confirmed."

In the cavern, Janus introduced the rest of the crew to Zan and Ard. By now the hologram solders had lowered their weapons and listened intently to the conversation.

"I'm glad you made it through OK. And Earth?" asked Zan.

"Chad's plasma shield protected the planet," replied Janus. He motioned over to Chad. "I believe it was your suggestion to place a shield around him that was lifesaving. Thank you."

"I'm happy you all survived. I regret not being able to save more lives. I also regret not being able to walk on that planet. It appeared to me to be exceptionally beautiful."

"Indeed, it is. Markus and I spent 15 years there. Maybe someday you'll return and get the chance to do so."

"Maybe. Any word on Rexx?"

"No."

"Hopefully we've heard the last of him."

"From the little I've heard; word of his demise would be very welcome news."

"It certainly would be. In the meantime, we've been hard at work retrofitting the entire Thraen fleet. The slip ring technology is an incredible success. But I must admit my mechanics are the real architects of the program."

"It's pretty impressive what you've done."

"Thanks. I think we can *actually do it* Janus: end the blockade and rid your planet of the Mitels. It won't be easy. But we also have people on the inside, the Mitel resistance."

"Understood."

"I'm hoping that after we free Thrae, we go on to liberate Mitel and finally realize lasting peace and stability between our worlds."

"The people of Thrae would certainly welcome peace and stability. I believe Chad and I can provide considerable assistance in that regard."

"How so?"

"Thrae now has *two* Battle Spheres at its disposal."

"You're both up and running again aren't you," blurted Ard.

"Yes."

"*Wow*! That's huge. We can *definitely do this* Zan! Are you Zebulon Park now?"

"No, I'm Janus Stone. In many ways, Park died long ago. Chad and I have returned to lend assistance any way we can."

In the underground command center, a sense of urgency filled the room.

"Lasers activated," confirmed the weapons specialist.

"Open fire," ordered Arius.

Eight camouflaged ground laser weapons opened fire at the incoming missiles. The barrage successfully destroyed twenty-one of them. The remaining three continued down toward their destination, cruising just above the planet's surface.

Arius stared at the wall mounted data screens.

"Status report," he requested.

"Two . . . no, three missiles still approaching."

"Are they still headed here?"

"Yes, Sir. They're flying along the surface terrain."

"How long until impact?"

"Two minutes. Can we launch fighters to intercept them?"

"No. We'll risk striking our own population centers."

Arius looked around the command center until he stared at a seldom used weapons cabinet. He suddenly realized what probably happened.

"Alert all base personnel to seek shelter immediately," he instructed.

Arius rushed over to the cabinet, entered the security code, and opened the door. He grabbed a handheld spacial disturbance scanner and ran out the command center and down the long corridor toward the cavern.

"Come with me, *now!*" he ordered a hover craft pilot as he sprinted past her.

Arius entered the cavern, turned on the scanner and, holding it out in front of him, slowly swept it across the opening. The scanner located mass and radiation anomalies. The device flashed yellow.

"There it is," he muttered.

"Sir?" asked the pilot.

Loud beeps sounded over base intercom system followed by an urgent message:

INCOMING CLUSTER MISSLES ARRIVING IN 90 SECONDS. ALL PERSONNEL SEEK SHELTER IMMEDIATELY. THIS IS NOT A DRILL. REPEAT: THIS IS NOT A DRILL!

Zan, Janus and the rest of the group ran towards the nearest shelter opening along the near side of the cavern. Arius and the pilot ran past them in the opposite direction.

"Commander!" yelled a soldier, "Where are you —"

"Stealth drone," motioned Arius as he ran past.

The soldier sprinted after Arius and the pilot. The rest of the group stopped and watched as the trio climbed into a large hover craft, powered it up, and streaked across the opening.

INCOMING CLUSTER MISSLES ARRIVING IN 45 SECONDS. ALL PERSONNEL SEEK SHELTER IMMEDIATELY. THIS IS NOT A DRILL. REPEAT: THIS IS NOT A DRILL!

Standing at the front of the hover craft, Arius kept the scanner positioned towards the invisible drone. He pointed to his left and then gave the thumbs up. The pilot banked the craft sharply in that direction. On cue, the solider reached over and energized a small but powerful magnetic field levitation device located underneath the hover craft. As they flew over the drone's location, the magnetic field surrounded the drone while the levitation feature pulled it up against the craft. Arius and the soldier watched the capture button light up.

"Got it!" shouted Arius. "Let's go!"

Seconds later, the hover craft disappeared up the closest rectangular launch tunnel.

"Quickly!" yelled a soldier, "everyone to the shelter!"

Everyone raced toward the shelter entrance. Everyone except Janus. He stood and stared at the launch tunnel. He knew what Arius knew: a direct hit to the cavern would leave little chance of survival.

The hover craft raced up the opening and into the sunshine.

"Where are they," Arius asked into his headset.

"Fifteen seconds to impact," replied the scanning specialist.

Arius motioned to the pilot to head skyward. At the count of five, he motioned the soldier to release the drone. Arius then signaled the pilot to fly across the lake at full speed. Seconds later, all three warheads, having reached their target, detonated right above the lake. The shock wave quickly overtook the hover craft, causing the pilot to lose control. The craft nosedived into the lake below.

Much further down below, the cavern vibrated briefly, like an earthquake tremor, and then all was quiet. Hazy dust clouds filtered down several launch tunnels. Janus stared silently as the clouds slowly made their way toward him.

Several rescue personnel ran out from the command center hallway, scrambled into three more hover craft, and disappeared up the launch tunnel. After several loud beeps, personnel cautiously made their way back into the cavern from several defense shelters.

"Janus!" shouted Mayla as she ran toward him.

Janus turned to look just before Mayla hugged him tightly.

"I thought I lost you," she whispered.

"Sorry," replied Janus. "I should not have been so thoughtless."

"What happened?"

"The resistance commander and the others redirected the Mitel cluster missiles, saving all of us."

"Are they . . ."

"I don't know."

"That was an incredibly brave thing to do."

"Yes, it was."

On the Mitel cruiser's ICC, the scanning specialist confirmed the detonations. Not noticing the last-minute change in the drone's location, he also noticed that the drone signal transmission had ceased.

"Commander, I've confirmed several detonations on the planet surface at the exact location of the drone."

"Excellent. Send ten fighters to inspect the damage. Hopefully we have taken out a major base of operations."

"Yes sir."

As the fighters neared the surface, they were intercepted and destroyed by four advanced Thraen fighters. On the ICC, the commander was livid.

"What just happened!" he shouted. "We should have destroyed the Thraen resistance base."

He then flopped into his command console in disgust.

"I want a detailed review of the data logs. What good is our technology if it doesn't work properly?"

When the hover craft hit the water, Arius and the others were hurled into the lake. The blunt force of the impact knocked them all unconscious. Sensors on the front and back of their jackets caused their life vests to inflate. An emergency beacon transmitted their exact location. Thanks to the quick response of the rescue hover craft, Arius and the two others were still alive when they were pulled from the lake. They would all survive the incident, but their road to recovery would be long and difficult. Susan was very inspired by the acts of incredible bravery. She approached Janus, who was speaking with Thraen fighter squadron commander Aaron Decker. Aaron was slightly taller than Janus, with light brown skin, charcoal eyes and short curly black hair. As Susan reached the two men, she looked at Janus.

"I can help," she said. "Remember, I was a F18 fighter pilot before becoming an astronaut."

Janus stared at Susan intently. He then shared her offer with Aaron who paused briefly.

"With all due respect Janus, but I don't — "

"You should give her a chance commander. In close proximity combat, Earth's fighter aircraft took out 1 Mitel fighter for every 2 they lost. Not great, but given the technology disparity, it proved that Earth's pilots were extremely capable."

Surprised, Aaron smiled.

"*I stand corrected*," he replied. "We could certainly use more experienced pilots. Tell her to report to our flight simulator next week," he added. "That will give us time to modify the software to accept her language commands."

Janus outlined the offer to Susan.

"Great, thank you," she smiled. "That will also give me time to settle in and get my bearings."

"Sounds good," replied Janus. "In the meantime, I'll arrange for an appointment to have the translation device surgically installed inside your ears. "

Janus then paused.

"That is, assuming you don't share the same reservations as Jim Johnson," he added.

"Not at all," replied Susan quickly. "Just tell me when and where to go."

Realizing her response, Aaron smiled again. He then checked the time.

"If you'll excuse me, I have to get to a briefing," he said. As Susan watched Aaron walk away, Janus turned to her.

"If your training goes well," he said, "I expect that your squadron team will also obtain translation devices in order to be able to understand English."

"That would be fantastic."

A few days later, Janus, Chad, Zan, Ard and Markus boarded a railway module on one of the last functioning sections of the hyper-speed electromagnetic railway. They were headed to meet with members of the Thraen World Council. After a half hour ride, a hover craft brought them to an underground defense fortress near the outskirts of the population center of Retba. Entering the heavily fortified conference center, they were greeted by five men and three women.

"Welcome everyone," smiled Chancellor Jaret Adison, head of the World Council. Janus remembered Jaret from the black patch he wore over his left eye. He found it provincial that someone would wear such a device rather than choose a simple mechanical replacement.

"Thank you all for coming," smiled Jaret.

"Our pleasure," nodded Janus.

"Zebulon Park! On behalf of the entire World Council and the people of Thrae, I want to personally thank you for all you did for us during the first Mitel invasion."

"You are very welcome. Unfortunately, I didn't finish the job. The Mitels attacked Thrae a second time."

"True. But that was not *your* fault. The people of Thrae decided to ignore the threat of further Mitel aggression."

"That's what I've been trying to tell him," Markus replied, "But he refuses to listen."

"Ah, the great Markus Kilmar," smiled Jaret. "Our thanks extend to you as well."

Markus smiled and nodded appreciatively.

"What happened to you Zebulon? After your crash, you just disappeared. Everyone thought you were dead."

"Park did die the day he crash landed in the mountains."

"I don't understand."

"I was lucky to have been found by local villagers and was in a coma for several days. When I awoke, I realized I could no longer transform. That part of my life was over."

"But we have been informed that you can transform once again," replied a second council member. "Is this not *true*?"

"Oh, it's true," smiled Markus.

"Then I don't understand . . ."

"My stubborn mistakes were the reason I could no longer transform. I knew I had to drastically change who I was and how I did things. That's one reason why I went undercover, so to speak. Zebulon Park was not going to be part of my journey going forward."

"In some ways you have changed," said Markus. "In other ways you haven't. I got damaged much worse than you for many of the same reasons. I've told you many times to stop blaming yourself. You did what you thought was best at the time. You can make a difference *now*."

"You're right old friend."

"Markus," said a third council member. "Why do you present yourself as a hologram?"

"It's a long story," replied Markus. "Suffice to say that I wouldn't fit into the USEP pod otherwise."

"You mean for the voyage across our spiral arm to planet 5.1.18.20.9?"

"Earth," said Chad.

"What?"

"The *planet*, it's called Earth."

"Very interesting name," Jaret mused. "And you must be Chad Stone. It is an honor and a pleasure to meet you. It has been a long time since Thrae had two functioning Battle Spheres. I must admit that there is a renewed sense of hope and excitement. I'm told that your bravery and proficiency saved planet *Earth*."

"I couldn't have done it without Janus, Mayla, and my Battle Hologram team. And the people of Earth, they provided the spacecraft to rescue me from outer space."

"You are very modest, young man. And who do we have here? Are you the legendary Zan Liss?"

"Legendary?" laughed Ard. "He set the record for the shortest tenure as Mitel Emperor."

"He's probably right," shrugged Zan.

"And who might *you* be?" asked Jaret.

"Ard was an outstanding Mitel cruiser commander," replied Zan. "Beneath that *humorous* exterior, he is one of the bravest, loyal and dedicated people you will meet."

"I'm not so sure about the brave part," smiled Ard.

"Thank you for joining our cause, Ard," said a fourth council member. "And Zan, we understand you are in the process of retrofitting our new cruisers with the same propulsion technology as the Mitel cruisers."

"Based on what we learned during our trip to Earth, this technology will be even better," nodded Zan respectfully. "But I cannot take credit for that. My expert mechanics are spearheading those efforts. They are the real architects behind the technology upgrades."

"I see," smiled Jaret.

"I would like to think that along with Janus and Chad, we now have an excellent opportunity to end the blockade and free Thrae from the Mitels."

"I concur wholeheartedly," nodded a fifth member.

"We need to formulate a plan of attack that catches the blockade completely off guard," said Zan.

"That won't be easy," replied a sixth member.

"Understood. Janus and Chad do provide us a unique opportunity to do just that. We just need to formulate the most effective surprise attack."

"When you come up with a plan, please let us know. We would be very interested in hearing about it."

"Yes indeed," Jaret concurred. "We will also have to contend with the female Battle Sphere."

"We've been discussing that," said Janus. "Since she does not have the benefit of a Battle Hologram, we believe she won't be properly trained."

"We are considering several tactics to neutralize her," added Zan.

"Such as?" asked the second member.

"Enhanced gravity control beams for one. Chad can vouch for their effectiveness."

"That's for sure," grunted Chad.

"You've brought that technology with you as well?" asked Jaret.

"Yes."

"We'll also try to reason with her," added Chad. "She is just about my age."

"We are also considering some scenarios where we intentionally try to get her to use up her energy reserves, explained Janus. "Without proper energy reserve management, she just might incapacitate herself. However, lethal force will be our last resort."

"It sounds like you have already given this a good deal of thought," replied Jaret. "Please keep us informed."

"We certainly will."

There was a brief silence.

"It's certainly a pity that Commander Court was so badly injured," said Jaret eventually. "He is a great leader who will be sorely missed."

"Yes, he will," replied Zan.

"Would *you* be willing to take his place?"

"Me?" asked Zan incredulously.

"I think that's a great idea," smiled Janus.

"Me too," nodded Markus.

"I don't know what to say," replied Zan humbly.

"Say yes," laughed Ard.

"Yes," nodded Zan.

"Very well then," replied Jaret, "it's decided."

"We think you are destined to do great things," added the second council member.

"Where have I heard that before?" asked Zan.

"Don't let it go to your head," said Ard.

"Don't worry about that," smiled Markus. "We won't let it happen."

"Well, we still have a lot of work to do," said Zan.

"And planning."

"That too."

"Agreed," nodded Janus.

"Excellent," smiled Jaret. "Then please follow me. We have lunch prepared and waiting."

"Great. I'm starving," said Chad.

Walking down the hall, Jaret looked at Janus. "I must say that I am a bit of a history buff," he said.

"Oh really?" replied Janus.

"Yes. I've heard rumors that in a previous immortal identity, you were Chancellor Sejus Theron, head of the World Council. Is that really *true*?"

"It's true."

"Fascinating. What a tumultuous yet exciting time in our history. I don't envy you in the least for trying to navigate through all of that."

"It was a bit challenging."

"If you don't mind, I want to hear all about it."

"I don't mind at all . . ."

CHAPTER EIGHT — LON RETURNS

As Cruiser Number 7 entered the Mitel solar system, Lon Rexx let out a long deep sigh. It had been approximately one year since the Mitel armada had left in search of the young Thraen Battle Sphere. He was not only returning empty handed but was doing so with only two of the original fifty-six vessels. He knew the mission may be remembered as one of the worst military operations in Mitel history. Lon fidgeted as he tried to get comfortable in his command console. At seven feet, one inch tall and three hundred twenty-five pounds of solid muscle, it wasn't easy. Lon was bald, his light complexion, blond eyebrows and small thin nose a stark contrast to his charcoal eyes and large, square jaw.

We lost more assets during the first invasion of Thrae, thought Lon. *But there, at least we neutralized Thrae's two venerable Battle Spheres which set the stage for our successful second invasion fifteen years later. There are no silver linings associated with this mission. At least not yet . . .*

Lon desperately wanted to get off the cruiser and breathe fresh air. He was less eager to face the Mitel Leadership and try to explain what went wrong. Lon had decided to lay the entire blame at the feet of the traitor Zan

Liss. He would also make his case for being appointed Mitel Emperor. Where things went from there remained to be seen.

I must aggressively make my case, he thought. *My survival depends on it.*

As soon as the 1,550-foot-long silver and white wedge shaped cruiser orbited around Mitel, Lon packed his gear into a large duffle bag and headed to the primary launch bay. A well-worn shuttle pod eventually docked with the cruiser and brought him back down to the Hub's space transport facility. Lon was met by six heavily armed members of the elite Mitel Special Forces.

"Commander Rexx?" asked one soldier.

"Yes," nodded Lon.

"The Mitel Leadership wishes to speak with you."

"Well, I —"

"Immediately."

"As you wish," replied Lon quietly.

Lon was brought by hover craft to the Mitel Leadership Complex. After passing the initial checkpoint, Lon was escorted to a second security area for a full body scan.

Once he was cleared, Lon walked slowly across the complex grounds toward the imposing stone and glass Leadership Building. He was careful not to make any sudden or unusual moves. He didn't want to give the snipers any excuses. As he entered the Leadership, several huge security guards surrounded him.

"Commander Rexx?" asked one guard.

"Yes," replied Lon in his deep monotone voice.

"The Mitel Leadership is expecting you."

A second guard pointed a hand-held scanner at Lon. The guard then motioned to him to face the retinal scanner. A green light quickly flashed.

"Follow me, please," said the first guard.

Lon walked up the wide marble staircase followed by three guards, their footsteps echoing loudly. Reaching the second floor, the first guard waved Lon through the set of enormous stone doors into the Mitel Leadership Forum Hall. Across the room, the ten aging Leadership members sat behind the large, curved stone bench looking down on Lon as if he was a prisoner awaiting judgment. As Lon approached them, one of the three guards in front of the bench motioned him to stop. Two of the guards who had accompanied him up the stairs took positions next to him. As he stood motionless, Lon sensed other guards standing behind him.

"Commander Rexx," said the Leadership member directly across from him. "We have many questions for you."

"And for your sake, we hope you have the answers," added a second member.

"Yes, we have many questions," said a third member impatiently.

"I'll do my best to answer them."

"We want to know what happened to our space fleet," asked a fourth member.

Lon quickly glanced around the forum hall. He knew there was no escape.

"Well?" demanded the first member.

"It's complicated," Lon began hesitantly.

"*Complicated*? We lost fifty-six vessels! We've lost *nine thousand strike fighters*! You didn't return with the young immortal Thraen Battle Sphere. *Why not*?"

"Our fleet was in trouble right from the beginning," responded Lon defensively. "The Mitel resistance had infiltrated every aspect of the mission. They systematically started carrying out suicide missions."

"How?"

"They blew up their vessels using small but powerful explosives hidden among the solid fuel canisters, and other locations . . ."

"I see. What did you do to try to stop them?"

"We searched every inch of every vessel. We killed each and every suspected terrorist. I had many of them ejected into outer space while they were still alive to send a message."

"And . . . ?"

"The suicide raids continued, although with much less frequency."

"What about Emperor Liss?"

"You mean the *traitor*?" Lon bristled.

"What do you mean?" snorted the second member.

"Once we reached our destination —"

"Planet 5.1.18.20.9?"

"Yes. After we arrived, we demanded return of the young Thraen. Liss subsequently used his own cruiser to attack the rest of the fleet."

"We don't believe you," replied the third member.

"It's true! Ask the crew."

"He's telling the truth," said the fourth member. "Many crew members have independently said the same thing."

"Why would he do such a thing?" asked the first member.

"He was corrupted by the resistance, that's why. Per this Leadership's orders, we launched a large cluster pod strike on the planet's largest and most densely populated areas. The goal was to force the young Battle Sphere out of hiding. Liss called it genocide and terrorism. He vowed to stop us. He destroyed several of our cluster pods."

"Where's Liss now?"

"I don't know. The coward, Ard Lindar and several Mitel resistance fighters escaped in two small pods hidden in his cruiser. He had clearly planned his escape well in advance."

"Interesting," said a fifth member, "Several months ago one of our cruisers in the Thraen blockade identified two small pods approaching from deep space. The tracking data confirmed they came from the general direction of planet 5.1.18.20.9."

"*That must have been them,*" Lon replied. "They didn't have the courage to return to Mitel."

"And what about Leadership member Gen Zandt?"

"He was assassinated by the resistance."

"A pity. But you brought back his body, correct?"

"Our cruiser was badly damaged and had to be abandoned. In all the confusion, his body was left behind. The vessel was eventually destroyed by the annihilation."

"The *annihilation?*" asked a sixth member incredulously.

"Yes."

"Please explain," requested the first member.

"During the conflict, we partially disabled the young Battle Sphere. Instead of being captured, he sped up his energy core which produced a significant amount of antimatter. The subsequent annihilation event wiped out all but two vessels. Despite the resistance *and* the traitor, we still almost captured him."

"What did you do to disable the Battle Sphere?"

"It was my idea actually," Lon began. "Once our strike fighters lured him into outer space, we surprised him with a swarm of about one thousand fighters. During that engagement, I instructed our vessels to form a perimeter around the Battle Sphere. We used our enhanced gravity control beams to initially immobilize him. The crushing weight of the beams would render him unconscious causing his transformation back to human form. At that point, he would have been ours. Unfortunately, the traitor disrupted our efforts just long enough to allow the young Battle Sphere to reverse his core and initiate the annihilation event."

"That was very unfortunate. But how would he even know how to do such a thing?"

"I don't know. Ian Micron, my second in command and a self-proclaimed Thraen historian, had theorized that Zebulon Park had accompanied the young Battle Sphere across deep space and trained him."

"*Zebulon Park*? He perished during our first invasion of the Thraen planet," said the second member.

"Micron said that his death was never confirmed."

"Where is Micron now?"

"He perished in the annihilation event."

"I see. Ultimately, the mission was a complete failure. We lost a sizeable portion of our space fleet with absolutely nothing to show for it!"

"I respectfully disagree," replied Lon.

"And why is that?"

"We proved that we could overpower and immobilize a Thraen Battle Sphere."

"There are no Battle Spheres left to *immobilize*!"

"That's not *technically* true," said the third member.

Lon noticed the first member give a quick look to the third member.

"Wait," said Lon. "*What's not true*?"

"I don't recall asking you a question," replied the first member tersely.

"My apologies. With all due respect, I did everything in my power to carry out your express orders. I mobilized the other cruiser commanders. I organized and initiated the cluster pod strike. I authorized the swarm which allowed my gravity control beam containment plan to be implemented."

"I see. What is it that you *want* Commander Rexx?"

"I want the chance to finish the job."

"And that *is*?"

"Eliminate Zan Liss *once and for all!*"

"We don't have time for your petty vendettas!"

"That's not what I mean. If the Leadership is correct in their assessment that Zan Liss fled to Thrae, *an assessment I happen to agree with*, then he may present an even greater danger to Mitel than before."

"And why is that?"

"He oversaw the reverse engineering program for our entire fleet, correct?'

"True."

"And the enhanced gravity control beam project."

"Also, true."

"Liss will probably now upgrade the Thraen fleet."

"But Thrae does not have a viable space fleet!"

"Maybe not yet but given time they will."

There was a brief silence.

"I ask you again. Rexx . . . what do you want?"

Lon paused before answering.

"I want to be named Mitel Emperor."

"*Is that all?*" the first member smirked as the rest of the Leadership laughed at the request. The first member quickly motioned everyone to be quiet. He then stared intently at Lon.

"We will consider your request Commander Rexx. Your loyalty has not gone unnoticed. But it takes more than that to be Mitel Emperor. *Much more*."

"I understand," nodded Lon. "But if this Leadership decides to appoint me Emperor, I will crush both resistance movements once and for all."

"We are not impressed by words Commander Rexx."

"I always let my actions speak for me."

There was a brief silence. Suddenly, the large stone doors slowly swung open. Two security guards entered the chamber followed by Ana.

"Falon Ross. Your visit is quite unexpected," said the first member.

Walking toward the bench Ana stared briefly at Lon. He could tell she was sizing him up. Lon also sensed there was something very different about her.

"I'm ready," announced Ana.

"Oh?" replied the first member as he looked around the chamber. "Today seems to be the day for requests and pronouncements."

He then glared down towards her.

"We alone will decide when you are ready! *Do you understand?*"

Ana knew she had to control her emotions. She took a deep breath before responding. "Yes, Sir," she replied.

"Good," smiled the first member. "Explain to us why you think you're ready?"

"My Battle Hologram team abandoned me as soon as they found out I was going to use my abilities to attack the Thraen resistance. First, I taught myself how to fly. Next, I taught myself how to fire my plasma cannons and dodge stationary targets in the Stone Forest. After that, I went to the diverging asteroid belt. I practiced dodging moving targets and then shoot at them. Finally, I taught myself how to destroy multiple targets."

"That's what we've heard. But can you operate all two hundred of your plasma laser cannons?"

"Wait," said Lon, "she's a *Battle Sphere*?"

"That's correct."

"Why did we just travel six hundred light years in search of another one?"

"Because we ordered you to!"

Lon cringed slightly as the words echoed around the chamber hall. Ana bit her lip to keep from laughing out loud.

"As I'm sure you are aware Commander Rexx," the first member continued, "Thraen Battle Spheres are *very* rare. We owed it to Mitel's safety and security to attempt to capture the young boy before he decided to attack us. And as you said yourself, you almost did."

Lon nodded silently.

"Now, answer my question Falon Ross," instructed the first member.

"I can't fire all of them yet," replied Ana. "But I'm able to continuously fire several cannons at specific targets. The concentrated barrage allows me to disrupt and destroy them quickly."

"That could be very useful," said the fourth member.

"Is she Thraen?" asked Lon.

"Falon Ross?" the first member sighed. "Yes."

"Then how is she here?"

"We ask the questions!"

Lon's face turned bright red.

"Falon Ross, we're told you had an incident in the Stone Forest early in your training. Tell us about that."

"I was practicing my dodging skills. I kept going faster and faster until I lost control of my Battle Sphere and crashed into one of the stone formations."

"We're also told you were missing for more than a day. Is that true?"

"Well, yes but —"

"The Stone Forest is known to be a very dangerous place at night. Large human-like creatures and man-eaters are thought to roam there. Some historians believe that an advanced civilization, who call themselves the Nomas, also live somewhere deep within the Stone Forest. These people are thought to be responsible for inventing many of Mitel's most advanced technology and weaponry. The whole idea seems absurd to me, but then again, there have been many mysterious disappearances in there over the centuries. Workers and soldiers alike have simply disappeared without a trace. It makes you wonder if the stories are true. You didn't happen to meet them by chance?"

"No," replied Ana as she tried to downplay the incident. "I was unconscious the entire night. When I awoke the next morning, I had transformed back to my human form. I walked back to the large opening since I knew the way from my training."

"I have heard of those woods," said Lon. "Some of our best Special Forces soldiers have been killed out there. I've heard stories that a few of the Nomas people joined the Mitel military. As a matter of fact, the Chief Medical Officer assigned to the traitor's cruiser was thought to be from there. He was enormous. They say he looked more animal than man. Regardless, I don't see how an unarmed, not to mention unconscious *girl* could survive out there an entire night on her own."

"This *girl*, Commander Rexx, is also a Battle Sphere."

"Understood, but —"

"She is the same type of human hybrid that fifty-six of our spacecrafts went in search of, returning empty-handed with only two!" admonished the second member.

"And *you* want us to appoint you to be the next Mitel Emperor?" asked the third Member.

"What?" said Ana impulsively. "*Him*? You've *got* to be kidding me."

In a fit of rage, Lon stepped angrily towards Ana.

"I'll show you!" he growled.

Ana turned to face Lon. Her eyes turned bright white. The guards immediately stepped away from Lon.

"Her eyes," said one guard nervously. "*Watch out.*"

Lon stopped in his tracks. He realized that one more move in Ana's direction meant that his life was over. Lon slowly stepped back, forced a smile, and waved at her.

"Just kidding," he said.

Ana stared at Lon intently.

"You *must* control yourself Falon Ross," scolded the first member. "Your family's safety depends on it!"

Ana shifted her gaze toward the Mitel Leadership causing several members to move about uncomfortably in their seats.

"I'm ready," she announced firmly. "I want to complete the mission to Thrae so I can see my mother and sisters again."

"And so, you shall," replied the first member stoically. "Report to the Arman Matrix immediately and await your orders."

Ana nodded, her eyes returning to normal. She glared at Lon before being escorted out of the chamber by three security guards. Everyone listened silently to the echo of their footsteps as they walked down the stairs.

"Your life almost came to an end Commander Rexx," said the first member eventually.

"Understood," replied Lon quietly.

"She can be of great use to us, do you understand?"

"How were you able to force her to do your bidding?"

"We are holding her family hostage. Mitel Special Forces captured all of them as part of a surprise raid before she even knew she was a Battle Sphere. She has agreed to attack the Thraen resistance in return for their safe release."

"That's excellent news!"

"Indeed."

"I want to be a part of it."

The first member stared at Lon before responding.

"I will discuss your request with the Leadership. I will recommend that you be placed in charge of an operation to eradicate the Thraen resistance movement once and for all. If you are successful, we will then consider your other request."

"To be named Emperor?"

"Yes."

"Thank you. I will not disappoint you."

"Let us hope not. Please report to the Arman Matrix and await your assignment."

"As you command," nodded Lon.

"And Commander Rexx, you must protect and defend the young Battle Sphere at all costs. Do you understand?"

"I do."

"Good."

Lon nodded once more before exiting the chamber followed by the rest of the security guards. The large stone doors closing behind them like they were sealing off the entrance to a huge vault.

There was a long silence.

"What do you think?" asked the second member eventually.

"About the girl or Rexx?" the first member asked.

"Both."

"As long as we hold her family hostage, Falon will do exactly as she is told."

"I tend to agree," nodded the third member. "As for Rexx, he is loyal and brave. But he's still a liar and a cheat."

"I thought we all decided that we *liked* those traits," said the fifth member, "I mean to a point . . ."

"His temper concerns me," added the sixth member.

"It should," replied the first member. "It will cause him to make mistakes. For all we know, it was his temper that doomed the recent mission in search of the young immortal Thraen Battle Sphere. But no matter, he will still be useful to us. If Rexx believes that eliminating the Thraen resistance will allow him to become Mitel's next Emperor, so be it."

"But what if he's successful?" asked a seventh member. "What will we do then?"

"We will have him eradicate the Mitel resistance."

"And then . . . ?"

"We will instruct our Special Forces to eliminate him."

"Based on what?"

"For being a traitor to the Mitel people of course," smiled the first member. "Isn't that *always* the reason we use?"

"And what about the girl?" asked the second member.

"As I've said before, when she has done what we've asked, we will eliminate both her and her family."

"I *know* you've said that before, but how do you propose eliminating her? She's a Thraen Battle Sphere."

"Not when she's in her human form."

"True. But going forward, I suspect she will be very careful who she shows herself to in human form."

"You may be right. But she is also not a fully functioning Battle Sphere. She said so herself."

"But a Battle Sphere nonetheless," grunted the third member.

"Don't forget, our mechanical Battle Sphere prototypes have passed their agility and weapons tests with flying colors. They will not be as fast and maneuverable and only shoot fifty plasma cannons, but with one thousand under production they will easily overwhelm her. And as I've also said before, we won't have to worry about their loyalty. They will simply carry out their preprogrammed orders."

"I hope you're right," said the second member.

"I know I'm right. And even if they can only keep her at bay, the final design of our second-generation Battle Sphere has been completed. Once they come into service, *nothing* will be able to stop them, not even the venerable Thraen Battle Sphere."

CHAPTER NINE – THE ENCOUNTER

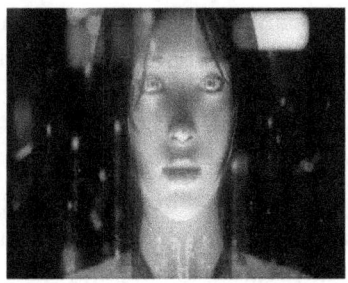

Janus leisurely strolled into the base's underground cafeteria and sat down next to Chad, Luna, Jim, Molly and Susan.

"Good morning, everyone," smiled Janus.

"Where's Mayla?" asked Jim.

"Sleeping. She's still adapting to daily life as a human after being a living hologram for so long. But when she gets up, we would like to show you around a little bit. There are so many beautiful things to see, despite the Mitel attacks and ongoing blockade."

"We would like that," grinned Molly.

"Having spent long periods of time on the ISS," said Susan, "I can relate to the struggles acclimating from one environment to another, although it's a far cry from being a hologram."

"That's for sure," added Jim. "And I'd love to see as much of Thrae as possible."

"OK great," replied Janus. "Let's plan on meeting in the base's underground cavern in an hour. Right now, I'm going to get some food. I'm starving!"

"I hope Chad left you some," smiled Jim.

Two hours later, the group climbed into a large base hover craft accompanied by two of the base's hologram soldiers. Twenty-four transparent retractable overlapping curved roof sections closed tight just before the craft took off. With a hologram soldier at the controls, the hover craft sped up one of the many rectangular tunnels, illuminated by the bright white ceiling and side lights. The craft exited the tunnel into the bright sunshine. It was a beautiful warm and sunny day and side and floor vents allowed the outside air into the craft. The air was cleaner and fresher than anything Molly, Jim and Susan had ever experienced before and the visibility due to the air quality was incredible. The craft banked slightly to its left over Lake Victoria. Some twenty miles off in the distance was the large population cluster of Tryden. It contained 80 gleaming glass covered sky structures. Circular at their base, the structures curved up into the sky to form a group of tightly bundled cylinders of different heights. The structures were positioned in a descending pattern from the cluster's center with air traffic grids weaving their way between them. From a distance, the grids appeared as glistening rivers suspended high in the air. However, after the second Mitel invasion, many grids had been shut down.

Everyone's eyes suddenly caught a gleaming reflection from the region's most famous landmark, the Assal sky structure. At two thousand feet high and located at the exact midpoint of Tryden, it was the tallest vertical sky structure on the planet. Even though it had suffered some damage during the rolling energy wave, it was still an impressive sight. Much further beyond that was the majestic Micron mountain range, their peaks covered in glistening white snow.

As the hover craft flew toward the population center, Jim, Molly, Chad, and Susan stared in awe at the foliage below. Several types of trees covered the surface. Some looked like mushrooms, their densely packed branches forming a circle at their top. Others looked like fat gray carrots, partially exposed above the ground with irregularly shaped branches reaching toward the sky. Still others looked like pine trees, only much thicker and wider. The hover craft crossed a wide and shallow river filled with circular sand dunes as far as the eye could see. On the opposite side of the river, the fields were lush and light green, followed by more trees. Clusters of circular dome-like structures and Thraen underground shelter entrances dotted the landscape. As the craft approached the population center, the dome-like structures became more concentrated. People were walking about in all directions. By now, other types, sizes and shapes of hover craft and transport vessels flew above and below their craft in various preprogrammed directions.

The hologram soldier banked the craft gently to the left as they entered the large population center. The craft had been scanned, identified and allowed admittance. The hover craft flew into a large rectangular slot at the midpoint of one of the peripheral sky structures which served as landing ports. The pilot followed the yellow flashing arrows imbedded in the floor directing him to his landing spot. The group climbed out of the hover craft and took the closest HorVert elevator to the main level, located five full levels above the true ground area. Janus led the group onto a wide blue acrylic walkway with clear acrylic railings. Up ahead, the walkway split in several directions that led to other sky structures.

"Wow," whispered Jim. "This is incredible."

Molly and Chad walked to the railing and looked below. Another level of interconnecting walkways traveled in different directions. Below that were two levels of air transportation grids with the lower level used for commercial transportation. At the bottom was the hyperspeed electromagnetic railway system. Due to the infrastructure damage from the rolling energy wave, rows and rows of railway cars sat silently in the shadows.

"This is amazing!" shouted Jim.

"I'll say," smiled Susan.

"It's even better that I imagined," said Chad.

"Just wow," added Molly as she looked up at the Assal sky structure.

Chad and Luna walked up ahead together. Every so often she would elbow him and laugh.

"Luna has been good for Chad," Jim grinned.

"She has," replied Molly.

"Do you think they could become more than just friends?"

"No. I mean, she is quite a bit older . . ."

"What? 18? *Maybe 19?*"

"She was a hologram Jim, *remember*? She's probably more like 500 years old."

"I guess that would give a whole new meaning to dating an *older woman*. But you can't count the hologram years . . ."

"Why not?"

"You just can't. That was all business."

Molly gave Jim an incredulous glance.

"You know who I feel bad for?" she asked.

"Who?"

"Melissica. I wonder how she's doing."

"Me too. One day at a time, right?"

Jim looked up at the air traffic grid.

"Listen," he said eventually, "Let's take day trips to as many population centers as possible, OK?"

"OK," smiled Molly. "That's one of the reasons we came, right? To see and experience all of *this*."

"Let me show you around," said Janus from behind. As everyone turned around, he motioned toward an approaching hover-tran. The covered silver and black transportation device were long and narrow and contained 2 rows of twenty seats. The group climbed in and headed to the center of Tryden. When they arrived, they walked along the open walkways and stared at everything. Thraens were walking in every direction. Others rode the tram which passed by occasionally. Still others rode small hover craft with baskets in the front and back. Most people were dressed in tight-fitting jumpsuits or what appeared to be more formal versions of sweat pants and shirts. Occasionally, the group received curious stares as people passed by.

"Everyone is so tall," whispered Jim.

"And thin," mused Susan.

"I bet everyone stays very active and watches what they eat," added Molly. "Jim? Do you hear me?"

"That reminds me," smiled Jim. "I'm hungry."

Janus took everyone to a popular marketplace where they all got something to eat. Molly and Susan got a protein salad with blue, red and yellow vegetables. Chad and Ard ordered traditional Thraen squash burgers with purple fries. Jim got a steak-like dish.

"This is delicious," said Jim. "What is it?"

"It's called a bug steak," smiled Janus.

"I'm sorry I asked. Oh well, I'm hungry."

After lunch, Janus took the group to the Thraen Historical Science Museum which chronicled the development of nuclear fusion, weather control technology, living holograms, space exploration and propulsion technology. There was no mention of immortality or human hybrid technology.

"Why is that Janus?" asked Chad.

"It's such a painful part of our past," he replied pensively. "Everything associated with those discoveries was expunged from Thraen history long ago."

"But that's not right. I mean, how can you keep from repeating past mistakes if you don't have those reminders to help guide you?"

"Good question. In expunging the technology, in one sense they did. But you raise a good point. Maybe someday soon, Thrae will confront that part of its history."

"I think hologram technology was the most impressive thing of all," mused Jim.

"I would tend to agree with you James," nodded Janus. "Speaking of holograms, I'd like to introduce Chad to a very special one, if you are up to it."

"I don't understand," replied Chad.

"Well, not too far from here, there is a vault. On Earth, you call them cemeteries."

"It's a hologram of his mother, isn't it," said Molly quietly.

"Yes," nodded Janus.

"Are you serious?" asked Chad.

"Very. You *don't* want to go?"

"I don't know . . ."

"Chad," said Molly, "of course you need to go see her. I mean, wouldn't you go see me?"

"Of course, I would. You know that. But it's a topic I really don't want to get too deeply into. At least not yet."

"I don't think anyone is asking you to. Would it help if we all went there with you? Janus? Is that, OK?"

"Fine with me. Chad? Are you up to it?"

"I guess," he responded nervously.

With the hologram soldier at the controls, the group flew fifteen miles to the vault complex. They again stared at the wondrous landscape and structures along the way.

When they arrived, the group walked a short distance through a large and beautiful garden. It was filled with bushes and small trees and brightly colored flowers. Small birdlike creatures hovered around them.

"It's so peaceful," whispered Molly.

"And beautiful," added Susan.

Up ahead, a white, one-hundred-foot-tall circular building appeared from behind the foliage. The walls were made of marble. The top of the structure spiraled to a point, like a vine reaching for the sky.

"Wow," whispered Jim.

Near the entrance was a circular meditation pond. The middle of the pond contained a fountain that mirrored the top of the building. In the water, millions of silver stones shined brightly. Marble benches lined the perimeter of the pond.

"The stones are in memory of all the innocents killed during the Mitel invasions," explained Janus, "They also represent the countless people who perished during our four world wars."

"*War*," grunted Jim. "Such a waste . . ."

"That's for sure," replied Janus, "but it also forced Thrae's population to confront how they were doing things. They voted to eliminate regional boundaries in favor of a global society governed by a World Council. Thraens also voted to institute an equitable or *inclusive* capitalistic system that intentionally distributed the profits to the stakeholders *who directly contributed to a business's financial success*. A worldwide vote was necessary since those who stood to lose the most with such a new system were the ones who held the most power; Thraens who stood to gain the most from such a modified system had none of the power.

It took a long time to institute such a system since there was no *one size fits all business model*. Equitable capitalism was designed and implemented with the idea of *empowerment*. Profits were to be distributed in ways that offered equitable rewards to those people or stakeholders who directly contributed to a company's success; people now being fairly rewarded for their efforts. And this new system required constant monitoring to ensure accountability and integrity of the newly applied approach."

"That's fascinating," replied Jim.

"Indeed," acknowledged Janus. "OK everyone, why don't you sit out here while I take Chad inside," he added.

"Sounds good," replied Molly. "Chad honey, are you OK?"

Chad nodded and followed Janus inside the building. It was brightly lit due to a spiral ceiling constructed with a translucent material that let light pass through it.

"This way," motioned Janus. They walked down a hall to a black door near the center of the structure.

"OK Chad. Walk through that door," pointed Janus. "In the center of the room is a retinal scanner. All you have to do is look at it."

"But how —"

"I added you to the database soon after you were born. I assumed one day you would visit this place."

"Oh . . ."

Chad walked into the circular hologram viewing room while Janus waited outside. Unlike the rest of the building, the room was dimly lit, almost dark. Chad slowly approached the scanner in the direct center of the room and looked into it. Seconds later, it activated the pre-programmed hologram image. A beautiful young woman surrounded by a light blue hue appeared before him. She was tall, with shoulder-length black hair and pale blue eyes. Her complexion appeared light, despite the blue hologram hue.

"Hello Chad," smiled Liana.

"Hello," he replied tentatively.

"My scans tell me that you are approximately 16 years old. By now you must look a lot like your father, tall, handsome and I'm sure very smart."

Chad grinned nervously.

"Can you see me?" he asked.

The hologram did not respond.

"I mean, are you like Markus? Can you understand what I am saying?"

"There are limitations to my programming. But I am very happy that you are here today to see me."

"Me too."

Liana again did not respond.

"I just wanted to tell you how sorry I am. It's my fault that you died."

Liana once again did not respond.

"Can you hear me?"

"I can hear you, Chad. Unfortunately, I am unable to respond to those specific questions other to say that I love you."

"You can't *respond*? How many questions can you answer? Twenty? Fifty? Is that your limit?"

There was no answer.

Chad's nervousness was quickly replaced by feelings of anger and disappointment. This was not how he wanted to meet and see his mother. Chad was about to turn and leave when suddenly, Liana's hologram image glowed until it became blinding bright white. Chad reached up to cover his eyes. When the brightness subsided, he looked at her. Liana's hologram looked different somehow. It also sparkled brightly.

"Hello Chad."

"You said that already."

"No, *I* didn't. Look at you, my beautiful baby, you're all grown up now."

"What? I mean —"

"I'm so happy that you survived your core detonation and reverse transformation process. That was such a wonderful, brave and unselfish thing you did to risk your life like that. You have so much of your father in you. I love you so much, more than I can ever put into words."

"I don't understand. How do you know all that?"

The hologram stepped forward and hugged Chad tightly. The room filled with an incredible brightness. Chad felt his mother's spirit flowing through every inch of his body. It was so wonderful and peaceful. After what seemed like an eternity, Liana stepped back and gazed at Chad intently.

"I'm so sorry Mom. I'm so sorry that I caused your death," whispered Chad as tears streamed down his cheeks.

"Oh honey," replied Liana soothingly. "You did no such thing. What happened to me was the result of the many curses of immortality. I was just one of countless many."

Liana then smiled broadly.

"And you know what?" she said.

"What?"

"I'd do it all over again, without hesitation."

Chad wiped away his tears.

"I have so many questions," he said. "I don't know where to begin."

"I bet you do," smiled Liana. She then looked intently at Chad. "But I don't have much time. I want you to listen to me. OK?"

Chad nodded.

"Stay true to who you are, my beautiful Chad. Always know that I'm with you and love you with all my heart. And *please* don't blame yourself for my death."

"But you just got here."

"There isn't time to explain other than to say that I can't maintain my presence in this device very long. As it is, I think I've corrupted it."

"Oh."

"I want you to tell Janus that I'm so very happy that he found true happiness once again with Mayla."

"Mom I —"

"And please tell him to always remember me and his daughters. Promise me that you will do this?"

"Yes, I promise."

"Good. I love you so much Chad."

"I love you too Mom . . ."

Liana hugged Chad tightly once more before stepping back to look at him. She then smiled and waved to him before her hologram sparkled brightly, forcing Chad to close his eyes once again. When he opened them, the room was dark and empty. Chad tried to reactivate Liana's hologram program several times without success. By now he could feel she was gone. Chad slowly walked back into the hallway; his eyes once again filled with tears. Janus could tell right away something was wrong.

"Chad, what is it? What's wrong?"

Suddenly, Chad smiled broadly as he wiped away his tears.

"Janus, Mom told me to tell you that she loves you."

"I know that," smiled Janus weakly.

"And she told me to make sure I tell you not to forget about her and my sisters."

"I never will . . ."

"She also said how proud she is of me."

"She is —"

"For helping save Earth from the Mitels and surviving the reverse transformation process. She said what I did was so brave and unselfish and that I am so much like you."

"*What?*"

"And she said how happy she is that you met Mayla."

Janus stared dumbstruck at Chad.

"Chad I . . ."

"*Dad*. Mom was in there. She hugged me tightly. *I felt her*. It was so wonderful. She was so warm and loving and beautiful. And she told me not to blame myself for what happened to her. She said she couldn't maintain her appearance very long. I think she's gone now. The hologram doesn't work anymore either."

Janus stepped forward and hugged Chad tightly.

"I believe you," whispered Janus. "And I love you too my son. Always."

CHAPTER TEN – REACHING OUT

Exhausted, Rad Aarden flopped on his bed and let out a deep sigh after yet another long day. He was helping coordinate the staffing and final hardware configuration of the medical facilities on every new cruiser. Although significant progress was being made, there was still a lot of work to do. After a while, he stared at the computer on the far side of his quarters. He eventually got up and sat down in front of it. He typed an encrypted message to an old, but reliable destination.

Hello Tor. It's Rad.

He hit the transmission key and then stared blankly at the computer. Nothing. Just as Rad was about to get back up, a response came through.

Hello brother. It's nice to finally hear from you.

Rad grunted and smiled. He then typed more.

Sorry for being silent for so long. I'm sure you can understand. You'll be happy to know I am no longer in the

Mitel military. I'm now on Thrae, as a member of their resistance, providing medical assistance and guidance.

There was a long silence, followed by a short response.

Please explain.

Rad rubbed his beard for a moment before typing.

Where to begin. I was one of the few who escaped the failed mission in search of the immortal hybrid. The six-month journey to the planet was very challenging. The Mitel resistance destroyed several crafts by detonating suicide bombs. The resistance has successfully infiltrated every level of the Mitel military. They are selfless, brave and committed to their cause and stronger than ever. The young Thraen Battle Sphere was well trained and selfless. He not only reversed his energy core to wipe out the remaining fleet, but as we later discovered, he survived intact. I traveled to Thrae with former Emperor, Zan Liss, who is now Thrae's resistance commander. We are making great strides upgrading their modest fleet. Thraens are truly remarkable people. The resistance reminds me of our own people as they are operating mostly underground to avoid detection.

Nice, my brother, I am proud of you. Liss may have been your Emperor, but he wasn't mine. Can you trust him?

With my life, Tor. When we attacked the planet and kill large numbers of innocent men, women, and children, Liss finally realized his destiny: to follow in his parent's footsteps. They were both Mitel resistance commanders, killed in front of him by Mitel Special Forces when he was a child. As soon as the Mitel armada launched cluster pods targeting defenseless population centers, he attacked his own fleet, destroying several cruisers and transport vessels. He is brave, resourceful, smart, and determined. He is the only reason I am still alive today. We were recently joined by the young Thraen Battle Sphere.

The boy followed you back?

Yes, along with his famous father.

Who?

Zebulon Park. He trained his son knowing full well that we would come one day, which explains the boy's incredible proficiency is battle. After the annihilation event, Park himself is once again a functioning Battle Sphere. Thrae now has two Battle Spheres at one time. They will be a formidable team.

Are you serious? This is incredible news.

Yes. Helped by the Battle Spheres, Liss intends to free Thrae from the Mitel blockade and secure its independence. He then hopes to persuade Thrae to help us free our planet from its repression. It would be in Thrae's best interests to do so. We may finally have a legitimate opportunity to not only be free, but to also achieve long lasting peace and prosperity. I know it won't be easy. The big questions in my mind are: are the Mitel people willing to join the effort? Is the Mitel resistance willing to throw their full support behind Liss and Thrae? Are our own people, the Nomas, willing to once again assist in these efforts? Are portions of the Special Forces willing to defect? These questions need to be answered. Tor, there is a sense of determination and excitement here. Hopefully we can all work together to achieve these goals.

I will get the word out. If a coalition is to be formed, we will need to meet Liss face to face at some point. I will be in touch my brother. And again, I'm so proud of you.

Rad smiled to himself. *Maybe there is hope,* he thought.

The next day, Tor Aarden called an emergency meeting of the Nomas elders. They met in the grand chamber, once part of a natural underground cavern. Tor stood up front and looked out at the ascending semicircular shaped seating area. There wasn't an empty seat in sight.

"Thank you all for coming on such short notice," he said.

"What is the meaning of this?" asked one elder.

"I received an unexpected series of communications from my brother Rad —"

"The *Mitel military doctor*?" interrupted a second elder.

"He is still a doctor, but he is no longer with the Mitel military. He is now a member of the Thraen resistance."

"*The Thraen resistance*?" asked a third elder skeptically.

"Yes. There have been some major developments which I want you all to be aware of. The young Battle Sphere, the one the Mitel armada went searching for has returned to Thrae. *Zebulon Park* has also resurfaced, and he is once again a fully functioning Battle Sphere."

The chamber suddenly burst into loud commotion.

"Quiet down please," shouted Tor respectfully. When order was restored, he continued. "Former Emperor Zan Liss is also there —"

"Traitor to his own people," shouted a fourth elder.

"No. He is now a Thraen resistance commander."

The Chamber erupted a second time.

"Quiet *please*," shouted Tor.

Once the chamber settled down, the oldest and most respected elder stood up. Everyone turned to look at her. Given the size of most Nomas men, Nya Wellas, at five feet two inches tall and short white hair, was difficult to see even when standing.

"Why are you telling us this now?" she asked.

"Once Liss helps free Thrae from the blockade and secure its independence, he intends to come back to Mitel and help free our world from the repressive Mitel Leadership."

"That will be a tall task, very tall indeed."

"I don't think he intends to do it alone. He expects to earn the trust and respect of the Thraen people and their military —"

"They are not the formidable power they once were."

"Not at the moment. But with Zan's help, that may quickly change. They will also have the two Battle Spheres at their disposal."

"The Mitel Leadership has secured the loyalty of the young female Battle Sphere."

"For now, perhaps since she is being blackmailed."

"The Mitel Leadership is also developing mechanical Battle Spheres, isn't that right?"

"Correct. Although my hunch is that they will be a significant downgrade from Thraen Battle Spheres."

"If they are able to mass produce them, it won't really matter, will it?"

"I don't disagree. That's why they need our help."

For a third time, the chamber erupted into a loud and heated discussion between the elders.

"Please," Tor shouted. "Quiet down."

When it grew quieter, the oldest elder spoke again.

"When the time comes, you want us to enter into the conflict, don't you?" she asked.

"At this point, I am only requesting that I be allowed to meet with leaders of the Mitel resistance."

"We've tried influencing Atreus events before. Those efforts did not end well for us."

"I realize that, but things are different now."

"With all due respect Tor, that has *always* been the rationale for us getting involved."

"I hear you Nya. But *this time*, the Mitel resistance is stronger than ever. They have infiltrated every level of the Mitel military. Rad said the resistance played a key role in facilitating the recent defeat of the armada sent in search of the young Thraen immortal. That fleet was essentially wiped out, leaving their military vulnerable right now."

"That is welcome news."

"Yes, it is. So, if those discussions result in an alliance, I would then seek the backing of the Thraen military and the two experienced Battle Spheres before we decide to go any further."

Nya looked around the chamber.

"I tend to agree with Tor that things really are different this time," she began. "This may represent our best *and last* chance to rid ourselves of the brutally repressive Mitel Leadership. I fear that if they are allowed to deploy their mechanical Battle Spheres, our window of opportunity for lasting peace may close indefinitely."

With that, Nya sat back down. The chamber was somberly quiet.

"If we get involved, there's no turning back," replied the first elder eventually.

"I concur," nodded the second elder.

"It could result in our total destruction," added the third elder.

"What other options do we have?" asked Tor. "If we sit and wait until the Leadership creates an unbeatable fleet of mechanical Battle Spheres, we as a people are doomed anyway. The stakes couldn't be any higher."

There was silence.

Nya raised her right hand.

"I vote yes, for our people and for the future of our planet," she announced.

After a brief pause, one by one hands rose until everyone in the chamber had their right arm up in the air.

"Ok then, it's settled," said Tor. "I will report back to all of you as soon as I have more information." As he walked out of the chamber, the elders again talked loudly amongst themselves.

Tor got word to his most trusted contact within the Mitel resistance he wanted to meet with its senior leadership to discuss something of great importance and urgency. Upon receiving the request, Zi Liss knew it *must* be important. The Nomas people were so reclusive and secretive; any form of preemptive correspondence was most unusual.

"Let's meet them right away," instructed Zi. "And I know just the place."

Zi selected an old, abandoned storage facility tucked away in the rolling Montes Mountains to the east.

"It's not easy to get to and only a handful of people still know of its existence," he concluded. "We'll meet at midnight to minimize detection."

Tor climbed into a sleek multipurpose Nomas HorVert war craft accompanied by three heavily armed Nomas warriors. The wedge-shaped craft carried eight small high energy cluster pods and an array of plasma laser weaponry. The pods exited twin weapons tubes located beneath the craft. Tor liked the craft for two reasons. Its twin ultra-high output engines were dampened to be both quiet and dissipate heat; and once the high-speed invisibility shields are activated, it is impossible to detect.

Tor flopped into the pilot seat and ran through the pre-flight checklist. He put on his fiber optic headset.

"Everything looks good here," he said.

"We just completed a sweep of the surface," replied a deep voice. "Preparing to open door number 2."

"Engines activated," replied Tor.

As he looked ahead, a large cavern door slowly slid open. Made of graphene on the inside and faced with surface rock on the outside, it blended in seamlessly with the outside cliff surface. Once the door was wide open, Tor looked around the immense cavern. The outside light reflected off hundreds of advanced fighters and HorVert war craft parked tightly in several rows nose to tail.

"Activating invisibility shield," said Tor.

"Confirmed active," replied the voice. "You are clear to launch."

Tor's war craft streaked out the entrance into the sky, the door closing behind him. He flew for three hours before landing vertically in an open field surrounded by dense woods, the location about an hour on foot from the storage facility. As they walked away from the craft, Tor pushed a button on his belt, activating a static invisibility shield. The war craft immediately disappeared.

When they finally arrived, Tor stood at the edge of the forest and surveyed the area. Beyond the opening was a single story structure once the primary research facility.

Checking the time, Tor confirmed they were about a half-hour early. It was eerily quiet, except for the constant chatter of the small tree reptiles. They all wore super sleek high resolution night vision glasses and *chameleon* uniforms, body armor, helmets, boots and gloves, all Nomas inventions.

"It looks all clear," mused Tor.

"Yes," nodded a Nomas warrior.

The four huge men emerged from the shadows and cautiously proceeded to the entrance, their hand-held ball laser weapons ready and activated. As they opened the door, the warriors activated small high intensity lights on each side of their graphene-mesh helmets. They proceeded down the main hallway, stopping to inspect each room to make sure they were alone. After checking the last room next to the rear entrance, Tor let out a sigh.

Now we wait," he said. They took up positions inside the largest room at the center of the building and turned off their lights.

About thirty minutes later, twenty-five heavily armed Mitel resistance fighters emerged from the forest. Zi and Jun Rexx headed to the entrance while the rest of the contingent took up defensive positions around the perimeter of the building.

As they entered, Zi signaled Tor.

"There're here," said Tor jumping to his feet.

As the two men entered the center room, the Nomas warriors reactivated their helmet lights. It was the first time Tor had laid eyes on Zi Liss.

"Whoa, could you turn those things down?" asked Zi.

Tor motioned to his warriors who quickly dialed down the lighting intensity.

"Thanks. You must be Tor," smiled Zi. "I was told to look for the biggest guy in the room."

"It's an honor to finally meet you," smiled Tor as the two men shook hands. "Who is this?" he asked pointing toward Jun, dressed all in black including a full-face mask, the lights reflecting off his high-definition night glasses.

"This is Jun Rexx. He is my second in command." Jun was an impressive sight. At seven feet two inches tall, 320 pounds of solid muscle, Jun exuded quiet confidence. Tor couldn't get over the number of knives and weaponry strapped to Jun's body.

"I see you like to travel light," said Tor as he shook Jun's hand. Jun shook his hand and nodded slightly.

"I see you are also a man of few words," added Tor. Jun nodded respectfully a second time.

"Jun lets his actions do the talking," replied Zi. "Isn't that right Jun?"

"As best as I know how," replied Jun in a deep voice.

Over the next hour, Tor explained everything to Zi. In return, Zi frankly assessed who could be counted on to help overthrow the Mitel Leadership.

"The Mitel resistance has never been stronger," said Zi. "At the end of the day, if the coalition holds together, I think we have a very legitimate chance at success," he concluded. "But I think you should also confirm things with Zan Liss."

"I will," replied Tor as the two men shook hands firmly. Suddenly, the sound of muffled laser fire could be heard outside.

"Mitel Special Forces," said Zi. "They hunt us relentlessly. Despite our best efforts, they must have found out about our meeting."

Zi spoke into his helmet mounted communicator. "What's going on out there?" he asked.

"We are under attack from all sides," the voice responded above the noise. "They're — "

Zi then only heard ball laser weaponry.

"Anton? Can you hear me?" he asked.

Nothing.

"OK," said Zi. "We've got to get out of here. *Now*."

Outside the structure, Mitel Special Forces quickly overwhelmed the resistance fighters. About a dozen remaining fighters reluctantly retreated into the dense woods to regroup. Seconds later, eight Special Forces personnel simultaneously entered both the front and rear entrances. Jun quietly disappeared into the shadows.

As the Special Forces converged on the center room from either side, the team leader barks instructions.

"Drop your weapons, *NOW*!"

Zi, Tor and the warriors did what they were told. The dual mounted helmet lights on each Special Forces personnel brightly illuminated the center of the room. After a brief delay, the team leader stepped into the light.

"*Well, well, well*. Zi Liss. Captured at long last," he said. "I'm sure you know the Mitel Leadership would love to *talk* to you."

"Don't you mean *torture*?" asked Zi.

"Call it what you'd like."

Zi glanced around for a way out.

"I wouldn't do anything stupid if I were you," said the team leader.

At the back of the room, beyond the glare of the lights, Jun reappeared like large and silent predator, unnoticed by anyone else. Jun quietly stepped forward, and with his huge left hand covered the mouth of a Special Forces soldier standing at the back of the room. With his right hand, he slit the soldier's throat. Jun quietly lowered the dying man to the floor without a sound and stepped forward.

"We've been trying to capture you for a very long time," the team leader continued. "It would be a shame for you to go and ruin it."

Jun grabbed the neck of the next soldier standing with his back to him, twisted it forcefully with a loud cracking sound, severing his spine. Before anyone could react, Jun stepped forward and slit the throat of an adjacent Special Forces soldier. He pulled the dying man up against him knowing full well that all Special Forces soldiers are outfitted with graphene body armor. What protects them will also protect him.

The three closest soldiers raised their weapons at Jun. He calmly raised his right arm exposing the dwarf ball laser weapon strapped to it. He methodically shot all three soldiers in the face in rapid succession. Without hesitating, Jun reached for his favorite weapon, also invented by the Nomas, a hand-held spray fire ball laser weapon with graphene piercing charge.

"*Drop,*" he ordered.

Zi instinctively shoved Tor to the ground while the warriors also dove down.

The Special Forces Personnel across the room opened fire at Jun, their laser blasts harmlessly bouncing off the dead soldier's graphene body armor. Jun returned fire, unleashing a brilliant spray of ball laser, killing everyone else standing in the room. He then let go of the dead soldier and sprinted across the room.

"Wait here for me," he instructed before disappearing into the darkness down the hall.

As Tor, Zi and the warriors lie on the ground, they heard shouts, followed by the unique sound of a second barrage of spray ball weapons fire. Then silence.

Jun then reappeared.

"Let's go," he ordered.

The men jumped to their feet and followed Jun down the hallway toward the front entrance. They maneuvered around several dead Special Forces personnel lying in various positions by the front entrance; their helmet lights still on, smoke rising from their ball laser wounds. Exiting the building, the group immediately came under intense ball laser fire. Zi, Tor and the warriors returned fire.

In the middle of the firefight, Jun stepped forward, having drawn a second, energized spray ball laser weapon.

"Run" he shouted before opening fire, dropping several soldiers in their tracks. Tor, Zi and the three Nomas warriors sprinted toward the woods. Jun continued his barrage, pinning down the rest of the Mitel unit. He then turned and ran. Two dozen Special Forces personnel jumped up to give chase. As they did, the Mitel resistance fighters opened fire from the woods, wounding several soldiers and forcing the rest of the unit to retreat.

"OK, let's get back to the hover crafts before they regroup and come after us," instructed Zi. He then turned toward Jun.

"Nice work my friend. You saved me once again."

"I owe you my life," replied Jun. "It's the least I could do. And besides," he added pointing to one of his Nomas produced spray laser weapons. "We all might be dead if it wasn't for these."

"I won't even ask how you got those," said Tor.

"I know a guy who knows *a lot* of weapons people."

"I guess Zi wasn't kidding about you."

Jun pulled the black mask from his head revealing his rugged looking face and short blond hair. Except for the large scar across his left cheek, he was a dead ringer for his brother Lon. Tor did a double take.

"You look just like Lon Rexx."

"*My twin brother*? That's what I've been told. The only difference is I'm not a sociopathic coward."

"I don't think he can fight like you either."

"Have you ever met him?"

"No. But I've studied a fair amount of surveillance footage."

"Well, if you ever do, do me a favor."

"What's that?"

"Kill him."

"*Let's go!*" barked Zi.

The group hurried through the woods to an open field to a waiting hover craft. They all scrambled in before the craft took off. As they raced above the trees, loud explosions erupted behind them. Tor looked back towards the storage facility. Over the trees, he could see several bright yellow fireballs rising into the night sky.

"I left them some presents," said Jun. "Murderous butchers."

"I'm sure glad you're on our side," replied Tor.

Before heading home, Zi dropped Tor and his men off at the open field.

"Are you sure you want to be dropped off *here*?" asked Zi.

"Yes, I'm sure. We'll talk soon," waved Tor just before the resistance hover craft took off and disappeared over the trees.

Upon his return, Tor immediately called a meeting of the elders. Like before, the meeting chamber was full.

"Thank you all for coming," announced Tor.

"Well?" asked the first elder. "What was the outcome of your meeting?"

"It went very well," replied Tor. He did not want to mention the surprise attack. To do so would only make it harder to convince the elders to commit to helping the resistance. "The resistance is organized, brave, and has some exceptionally ferocious fighters," he added.

"It will take more than *that* to defeat the Mitel Leadership," quipped a second elder.

"I understand," nodded Tor. "The good news is that the resistance has infiltrated the military even further than we thought. We can count on their full support. I have been told that as much as twenty percent of the Special Forces units are willing to defect if they perceive that we have a fighting chance of success. Those men are tired of what they have seen and done. They are willing to put their lives on the line if real change is plausible."

"That sounds promising," said a third elder. "What about the young female Battle Sphere?"

"She remains an unknown. I personally feel she can be won over, but we must assume for now that she is loyal to the Leadership."

"She will learn that loyalty is *not* a two-way street when it comes to the Mitel Leadership."

"I don't think she's under any illusions, but she is holding out hope for the safe return of her family."

"What comes next?" asked a fourth elder.

"And when do you plan to meet with Zan Liss?" asked a fifth elder. "We need to make sure both he and the Thraen military will be part of the coalition.

"Don't forget about the Thraen Battle Spheres," added the first elder.

"OK. OK. I will reach out to my brother Rad to try to arrange an in-person meeting as soon as possible. Given that the Mitel Leadership now considers him a traitor, it will have to be meticulously planned. It might even be too risky at this point."

"Risky?" asked the second elder incredulously. "You said last time that if we wait until the Leadership creates an unbeatable fleet of mechanical Battle Spheres, we as a people are doomed. The stakes couldn't be any higher."

"The stakes are very high, and *yes*, the future of Mitel will be decided on how strong a coalition we are able to pull together," replied Tor. "*All I'm saying* is that we don't want to take unnecessary risks. For example, we could also arrange an encrypted video meeting."

"I want you to look into his eyes," replied the second elder.

"I understand," grinned Tor. "But at the end of the day, all you have is his word. Which I might add, appears to have the full support and trust of my brother and the people of Thrae."

There was a somber silence in the chamber.

"I call a vote on whether to allow Tor to speak with Zan Liss on behalf of the Nomas people to form a military alliance to oppose the Mitel Leadership," announced the third elder. "All in favor raise your hand."

"What if we fail?" asked the first elder.

"Failure is not an option," quipped Tor. "Now can I have a show of hands?"

One by one, the elders slowly raised their hands until it was unanimous.

"Good. I will reach out to Rad to continue to move our plan forward. Thank you all for coming."

As Tor exited the chamber, the elders talked loudly amongst themselves.

"Failure is *not* an option," he muttered to himself determinedly.

CHAPTER ELEVEN – FLIGHT TRAINING

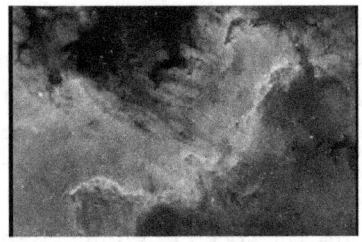

Susan underwent intensive training in the Thraen tactical fighter flight simulator for several days before her initial test flight. She attended daily squadron meetings, and in the evening studied flight and technical manuals translated into English on her computer. Susan also learned to fly base hover craft, which was mandatory training for all pilots. It also provided her with a much-needed break from both the simulator and her studies.

In the simulator, Susan quickly became proficient with the voice controls and computer pad inputs. Using the Thraen equivalent of a throttle and stick, she acquired the feel and responsiveness of the fighter's four inline high output plasma thrust engines, thrust vectoring and gyroscopic directional systems. Susan also learned to interpret the fighter's three three-dimensional hologram displays: ground terrain, the region within relatively close vicinity of her fighter, and tracking and prioritization of approaching targets. She was assigned a hologram technician to assist her in target tracking and prioritization, both hostile and friendly. In addition, Susan practiced several simulated dogfights, firing all six superheated high energy hydrogen plasma burst laser cannons.

The cockpit itself was intuitive and user friendly. Flight controls switched automatically when the craft flew back and forth between Thrae's atmosphere and outer space. While it took getting used to, Susan enjoyed using the voice controls, although she could override them at any time with the push of a button. The entire cockpit was constructed and powered as a single sealed unit which made the enclosure quiet. If the craft became badly damaged or inoperable, the unit could be safely ejected into any environment. The cockpit lighting adapted automatically to the constantly changing conditions.

On the morning of her first flight, Susan had butterflies in her stomach as she sat in her cockpit. She entered her keypad code activating her computer voice command system and verbally ran through her preflight checklist. She then listened to the chatter over the squadron's communication system as two other fighters took off, disappearing into the underground flight ramps.

"Fighter number 13 cleared for takeoff," said a voice over the communication system. "Exit ramp 2-0."

"OK Susan, it's your turn," instructed Aaron. "Do it just like you practiced."

Aaron, as squadron commander, was intensely protective of all his pilots. Before Susan's first flight, he already had the translation devices installed inside his inner ears just in case.

"Commence takeoff," said Susan, "slot twenty."

Her fighter engines automatically sped up and aided by a gravity control beam, the craft raced up the underground flight ramp and exited through the heavily concealed access slot on the lake's largest island. As her tactical fighter raced skyward, she gave more commands.

"Level off at thirty thousand feet, power level 4, climb rate 3."

Susan quickly caught up to the other two fighters. Her three-dimensional hologram quickly displayed, tagged, and tracked their locations.

"OK Susan," said Aaron closing in from behind, "let's start slow and practice some basic maneuvers. I want you to switch over to manual and follow the lead fighters. Just replicate what they do."

"Will do," replied Susan, pushing a keypad button.

The fighters ran through several maneuvers of increasing complexity. Every time, Susan performed the task flawlessly.

She's a natural, thought Aaron.

After several high altitude turns, Aaron spoke over the squadron communication system.

"Nice job Susan. Let's take it into outer space, OK?"

"Sounds good," replied Susan, trying not to show she was nervous.

The fighters streaked through the upper atmosphere into outer space. The view was spectacular. Stars shined brightly in all directions.

Wow, thought Susan.

The fighters again ran through maneuvers, this time using the outer space controls and propulsion system.

"Nice job everyone," said Aaron. "Let's head back to base."

Susan's fighter vibrated slightly as she passed back through the upper atmosphere. Her plasma heat shields, having automatically deployed, absorbed, and attenuated the intense heat generated by the re-entry. As she headed toward the surface, she listened for her instructions.

"Fighter number 13 cleared for landing," said the voice over the communication system, "Entry ramp 1-2."

Susan input the data into her computer keypad and switched to autopilot as she had been trained. A few minutes later, her fighter entered the rectangular tunnel and headed downward. She stared at the white ceiling and side lights illuminating the passageway. Seconds later, she reached the repeating series of flashing yellow light strips along the bottom and sides of the tunnel. Her craft automatically slowed down to minimum forward speed and deployed its landing gear. Entering the underground base, Susan's fighter was grabbed by a landing-assist gravity control beam which quickly decelerated and gently landed the craft. As her engines powered down, she ran through her post flight checklist. By the time her canopy released and swung open, a portable stairway was positioned next to the cockpit. She released her harness and climbed out. Looking down the stairs, she saw Aaron standing at the bottom holding his helmet, smiling broadly.

"You did great Susan," he shouted.

"That was the most incredible ride I have ever been on. Just unbelievable," she replied.

"It should be. It's the best fighter Thrae's ever built."

Aaron then motioned her to follow him.

"We don't want to be late to the debriefing. Given how well you did today, we will probably begin target practice at the *junkyard* tomorrow."

"Where's that?"

"About five hundred miles above Thrae. It's filled with targets, decommissioned spacecraft mostly. You'll start to get a feel for your laser cannons there."

"What about the blockade?"

"Since our fighters have superior firepower *and* maneuverability, they leave us alone out there, at least for now . . . "

"Are you saying we're not worth their while?"

"Too much trouble at this point in time is a better way to put it. The Mitel blockade is currently focused on much bigger ambitions, but hopefully we will soon disrupt all their plans."

"Hopefully . . . "

Over the next two days, Susan continued to train under Aaron's watchful eye. She excelled at target practice and her confidence grew. Debriefing, Aaron informed Susan that since she was doing so well, it was time to begin air to air combat maneuvering.

"Bright and early tomorrow morning," he said. "Get a good night's sleep."

That night, Susan tossed and turned.

What if I do poorly, she thought. *Thraen pilots are incredible. I will make a complete fool of myself.*

The next morning, Susan woke up exhausted. She meditated for almost an hour. Realizing she had lost track of time, she put on her flight suit and rushed to the underground base. When she arrived, she was greeting by Aaron.

"You're late," he said.

"Sorry," replied Susan.

"Let's go."

Four fighters took off and raced skyward. On the way up, Aaron notified Susan she was assigned to protect one fighter while he flew with another. When they reached forty thousand feet, the two sets of craft flew in opposite directions for several miles before turning around to confront each other. Instead of firing their plasma weapons, the craft used their high-resolution laser systems. A laser lock set off an alarm in the cockpit. After four consecutive seconds, it meant that a fighter had been fired upon and destroyed. It was sobering to know that in real combat, the same alarm would also sound.

As the fighters approached, Susan tracked them on her three-dimensional display.

"Targets approaching," confirmed her hologram technician. "Almost within range. Preparing target locks."

Seconds later, and without notice, Susan's partner suddenly veered skyward. Surprised, she raced after him and was quickly chased by Aaron.

This was a setup, she thought angrily. *And I stupidly fell for it.*

As he bore down on her, she dodged back and forth to avoid his laser lock. As his laser locked on for a second, her cockpit alarm sounded.

Susan veered left and then raced ahead at full speed. Looking at her display, Aaron was almost right behind her. A few seconds later, her alarm sounded again. She decelerated and veered to her right. As she straightened out, Aaron moved in behind her. Seconds later, her cockpit alarm sounded for a third time.

OK, she thought *let's see if you're ready for this.*

Susan jerked her controls causing her fighter to perform a three-hundred-and-sixty-degree roll. Even before settling in behind Aaron's fighter, she initiated her laser lock. As the alarm sounded in Aaron's cockpit he glanced down at his three-dimensional display.

What the . . . he thought.

A few seconds later, his alarm sounded again, indicating that four seconds had passed.

"You did it. *You got him,*" shouted her hologram technician. "Whoo-hoo!"

"She tagged you!" said one pilot.

"Nice job," added the other.

Inside her flight helmet, Susan was beaming.

"That's what I get for trying to surprise you," said Aaron eventually. "Nice work, Susan."

The four fighters continued practicing for almost an hour. Susan performed well, only being *tagged* twice while also tagging the second fighter once.

The next day, Aaron ran into Janus in a base hallway.

"I want to thank you," he said.

"For what?"

"Recommending Susan to be a fighter pilot. Her training is coming along extremely well. She is an exceptional pilot and a pleasure to be around. We would be very grateful if you could get us more just like her."

"I wish I could. Unfortunately, they are six hundred light years away."

"Wow," replied Aaron.

"But I'll see what I can do," grinned Janus.

"Thank you," Aaron said with a smile.

CHAPTER TWELVE — THE REBELLION BEGINS

Zan and Ard relaxed in the underground base cafeteria slowly sipping a protein drink. Rad's large frame suddenly appeared in the doorway. Seeing the two, he walked over and sat down.

"I heard from my brother," announced Rad. "He met with Zi Liss. Based on that conversation, the Nomas elders want to meet with you to discuss forming a coalition to take back Mitel from the Leadership."

"*The Nomas*?" asked Zan.

"They are my people. Are you saying that you haven't heard of us?"

"Zan doesn't get out much," said Ard.

"Are they all as big as you?" asked Zan, sipping his protein drink.

"Just the men," replied Rad.

"My condolences to the Nomas women," said Ard.

Rad grunted.

"Anyway, about the coalition meeting," he began, "I think it is imperative that it happens very soon for a number of reasons."

"Aren't we getting a little ahead of ourselves?" asked Zan.

"Who's Zi Liss?" inquired Ard.

"My father's younger brother. Before we left for Earth, he tried to persuade me to join the resistance."

"Which one?"

"Does it really matter?"

"Yes."

"Why? Both organizations are fighting repression."

"Yes of course. But on Mitel it's more personal."

"Well, I'm *here* Ard. And besides, we can only focus on one conflict at a time."

"I disagree. We can — "

"*Anyway*," interrupted Rad, "about the meeting . . ."

"An in-person meeting is too risky right now," replied Zan, shaking his head, "regardless of the reasons for it."

"How about using an encrypted video conference?" asked Ard.

"That's what Tor suggested as a backup," replied Rad.

"*That* we can do," nodded Zan. "But again, regardless of the outcome of that meeting, everything depends on us successfully breaking the blockade."

"The cruisers are almost ready," smiled Ard.

"Just in time too. We have a follow-up meeting with the World Council three days from now to discuss next steps. Rad, you could bring up the subject of a coalition then."

"That would be great," nodded Rad. "I'm sure they've heard of the Nomas people. They will also understand the importance and significance of our willingness to enter into such an alliance."

"We'll find out and take it from there, agreed?"

"That sounds fine."

Three days later, a delegation from the base headed to the underground defense fortress near Retba. Zan, Ard,

Mayla and Janus traveled in one hover craft accompanied by two heavily armed hologram soldiers while Rad, Chad, Teri, Lia and Markus followed closely behind in another. When they arrived, the contingent was escorted to the conference center where they were once again greeted by Chancellor Jaret Adison.

"Welcome everyone," he smiled, "please come in." Inside the chamber, the seven other council members sat silently.

"It's very good to see you again," nodded Janus. "I've brought a few more people I'd like you to meet. To my right is Mayla Tallis. She was Chad's Battle Hologram Commander prior to his miracle of life event. Standing next to her is Teri Anton. He was Chad's scanning and logistics specialist."

"It is an honor to meet both of you," smiled Jaret. "Our Hologram Protective Force has had a long and storied history. And I must say, it's not very often that one meets members who have changed *back* to human form."

"Indeed," replied Janus. "For a long time, I believed the whole concept of the reverse transformation process to be Thraen folklore. I was proved wrong by my own son."

"Our children have a way of doing that," acknowledged Jaret.

"Yes. Now standing next to Teri is Lia Saar who was working undercover as a Mitel cruiser communications specialist. Lia is a member of the Mitel Resistance who possesses many valuable skills."

"A pleasure," nodded Jaret. "Thank you for assisting in our cause."

"Last but not least, Rad Aarden, former cruiser Chief Medical Officer and member of the Nomas people."

"I am most pleased to meet you," said Jaret almost in a whisper. "Your people are an inspiration to us all."

"As are the Thraen people to us," replied Rad.

"Thank you. You are the first Nomas I have ever met in person. I must say you are even larger than I had visualized."

"I can't speak to that," Rad grinned slightly. "But our people are committed to forming a coalition with both the Mitel and Thraen resistances. Working together, we believe the Mitel Leadership can finally be defeated."

"This Council has been discussing the possibility of forming a coalition," replied Jaret. "The Nomas people would be a most welcome and valuable addition."

"Why would the Nomas people be so important to our cause?" asked Janus.

"We were the earliest humans to inhabit Mitel."

"OK, but —"

"Although we chose to essentially remain isolated from the outside world, the Nomas underground population center hidden deep within the Stone Forest rivals anything found here on Thrae. The same goes for our medical technology. We have also designed and developed certain weapons technologies that are more advanced than anything currently in use here or on Mitel. The biggest difference between my people and you are that we never became so preoccupied with our physical selves to pursue human hybrid technology or immortality. I personally consider that choice to be a good thing although my people have great respect for both the Hologram Protective Force and Thraen Battle Spheres."

"I'm very surprised you have not heard of the Nomas people before now," said Jaret.

"I have," replied Janus. "It's just that I was under the impression that they were . . ."

Janus paused as he tried to select his words carefully.

"Primitive man eaters?" asked Rad.

"Well . . . Yes."

"You need to get out more Janus," said Ard.

Rad grunted then smiled. "*For once* I agree with him," he said.

"We would welcome the help of the Nomas people with open arms," added Lia. "The Mitel resistance will fight to the death to defeat the Leadership. In our opinion it is now or never. They have been committing genocide against the Mitel people ever since they seized power. They must be stopped."

"I don't disagree," nodded Janus respectfully.

"Good," smiled Jaret. "We are all in agreement. Now please, all of you, this way. We have much to discuss."

As everyone sat down around a large clear acrylic table, Jaret continued to speak.

"We have been told that the new space cruisers are ready to launch. Zan, is this true?"

"Yes, including the last-minute upgrades. For their size, I believe they are the most technically advanced war craft in the universe, except of course the Thraen Battle Sphere."

"That's great to hear."

"There's one problem."

"And that is?"

"How to launch them without getting shot out of the sky by the blockade before they reach outer space."

"Since we now have two Battle Spheres, can't they engage the Mitel cruisers until our cruisers are launched?"

"Coverage is an issue since there are four Mitel cruisers circling the planet and we have only two Battle Spheres. But that's not my real concern."

"What is?"

As soon as the cruisers detect the Battle Spheres, they will unleash a cluster pod attack targeting our population centers."

"How can you be so sure?"

"Battle Sphere engagement countermeasures are now a required course at the Mitel Military Academy." replied Zan. "Cruiser commanders and ICC personnel are trained to immediately deploy cluster pods at predetermined population centers to force the Battle Sphere to break off its attack in order to destroy the incoming pods. That will allow the cruisers to escape or regroup."

"I see," Jaret mused. "Then what do you suggest we do?"

Mayla placed a thin square computer pad on the table. She pushed a button activating a three-dimensional image of planet Thrae. Circling the image in four equally spaced orbits were Mitel cruisers, each followed by a transport vessel.

"Over the past several months, we've closely tracked the Mitel blockade's movements," she explained. "As you know, it consists of four cruisers, each followed closely by a large transport vessel. What stands out is that their highly coordinated patrol patterns have not changed. The craft orbit Thrae approximately 250 miles above the planet surface, circling it every hour and a half."

"Sixteen times a day," added Teri, "and they orbit the planet at four distinct inclination angles: zero degrees, or around the equator and three geosynchronous rotation angles of 45, 90, and 135 degrees. Their orbits are staggered about twenty-two minutes apart to avoid collision since their paths intersect twice, on opposite sides of the planet at the equator. As you can see from the 3-D display, it also helps reduce surveillance gaps."

"It's a very effective deterrent for any craft attempting to travel to and from outer space," said Ard. "Our USEP pods wouldn't have made it through without the last minute intervention of the Thraen fighters."

"And we can't keep doing that for fear of provoking a cluster pod strike on our population centers," Jaret grumbled.

"You're absolutely right," replied Zan. "We, therefore, needed to come up with a creative, yet plausible plan to attack the blockade."

"Which is?" asked the first council member.

"Lia? Could you please elaborate?"

"Certainly," she replied. "As I've said before, our resistance fighters have painstakingly, and with great personal sacrifice, infiltrated the entire Mitel space fleet. For example, we have a dozen embedded resistance fighters on Cruiser Number 4, circling at an inclination angle of 135 degrees." Lia then paused.

On the three-dimensional image, Cruiser Number 4 and its transport vessel both flashed.

"With all due respect Lia," replied Jaret. "They are twelve against two hundred. They cannot possibly seize control of the cruiser."

"Not by themselves," acknowledged Lia. "But they do have the ability to release a powerful airborne opioid that will incapacitate the rest of the crew."

"You mean *kill*," added Ard.

"Call it what you want. They don't deserve any better than what they've done to their own people."

"Very interesting," Jaret considered.

"Then what?" asked a second Council member.

"We'll launch a space pod small enough to fit into the cruiser's primary launch bay," replied Lia. "We plan to rendezvous with it just before the equator."

A bright dot curved up from the three-dimensional planet to the rear of Cruiser Number 4.

"Once we reach the ICC, we'll launch two cluster pods which will curve back around us and destroy TV4," explained Zan. "We'll immediately change course and accelerate toward Cruiser Number 3 at full closing speed."

Everyone watched the cruiser change direction toward the inclination angle of 90 degrees on the 3-D representation once the transport vessel disappeared.

"But how will you get up there without being detected?" asked a third Council member.

"We are going to place an invisibility shield around our small space pod *and* its launch pod," replied Janus.

"The space pod is barely large enough to squeeze in a full ICC crew of myself, Ard, Lia, Mat and Dax," added Zan. "And before the rest of the blockade registers the destruction of TV4, we'll be within firing range of Cruiser Number 3 and TV3 circling at 90 degrees."

"Won't that attack alert the remaining two cruisers?" asked a fourth Council member.

Everyone stared at the 3-D image while the attack continued to unfold.

"Cruiser Number 2 at the inclination angle of 45 degrees will be headed in our direction only fifteen-hundred miles away. Still traveling at full closing speed, we'll head straight for it and launch a series of cluster pods. Before the cruiser or the transport vessel registers any activity, the pods will be bearing down on them. By then, it'll be too late for both craft to perform evasive maneuvers."

"What about the remaining cruiser?"

"Cruiser number 1 will be at the equator, but on the opposite side of the planet."

"This is where things start to get a little tricky," said Ard.

"*Starts* to get tricky?" asked a fourth Council member.

"Yes. We will have lost the element of surprise by that point. Cruiser Number 1 will have been alerted by this point. This is when Janus and Chad enter the fight to help finish off the remaining cruiser and transport vessel *and* intercept any cluster pods launched in response to our attack."

"Do you think there is a chance the remaining Mitel vessels will flee?" asked a fifth Council member.

"Doubtful. It's just not in their DNA."

"It all sounds very risky," Jaret pondered.

"With all due respect," said Zan. "Going forward, everything we do is going to be risky."

"Have we taken *everything* into consideration?"

"We think so," replied Janus. "Chad and I will spring into action earlier if the plan begins to unravel. Between the two of us, we should be able to destroy every cluster pod before they reach the surface."

"And if you don't?"

There was a long silence.

"I think we all know the answer to that question," replied Zan softly.

"Zebulon," Jaret began. "You, better than anyone in this room, know how much our people have suffered at the hands of the Mitels. It is very difficult for this Council to authorize a mission that risks endangering the lives of countless more Thraens."

"The Mitels have gotten to where they are by taking huge risks. The Council *must* adopt a similar approach if Thrae is going to have any real chance of freeing itself. We have a solid plan and the ability to implement it. We now have two Battle Spheres ready to assist in these efforts. Now is the time to act."

Jaret looked at the other World Council members soberly. "Now is also the time to voice any concerns."

"I agree with Janus," replied the second member.

"We must discretely instruct the general population to seek underground shelter before the mission is launched," added the third member.

"That would be difficult," mused the fourth member. "The blockade will register all the activity and switch to a heightened alert. If they do, we may sabotage our own surprise attack."

"I concur. At the very least, we must alert the general population at the first hint of trouble."

"Alerting our people at that late stage won't provide enough time to get everyone to a shelter," interjected Jaret. "If we're going to proceed, it's a risk we'll have to take." He then sighed deeply. "Our people are *very* weary of conflict. But they are equally weary of the blockade and its debilitating effects on their quality of daily life, not to mention the constant threat of attack."

"I agree wholeheartedly," nodded the second member.

"Then it is decided. When is the mission scheduled to start?"

"Fourteen hours," replied Janus.

"*That soon?*"

"Yes," nodded Zan. "We must strike while we have the element of surprise."

Jaret rubbed his chin.

"So be it," he replied soberly. "Once you engage their cruisers, we will alert emergency response teams around the planet. Good luck everyone and thank you."

Fourteen hours later, Zan, Ard, Lia, Mat, and Dax were transported down a short tunnel to the waiting launch pod. Entering the circular launch area, the group peered up at the vertically mounted space pod positioned in the direct center of the one-hundred-foot-high launch cylinder. Glancing above that, Zan noticed the roof retracting. The bright white electromagnetic glow at the base of the launch pod signaling that launch was imminent.

The crew was taken by hover lift to the small craft's cabin door. Zan and the others climbed into their seats using hand and footholds before strapping themselves into their seats.

"Commander Liss," said a voice over the communications system. "We've completed all preflight checks and are prepared for launch."

"Good," replied Zan, "we're all secure." The inner and outer airlock doors quickly closed.

"Invisibility shields activated and fully operational; preparing to launch in five, four three, two, one . . ."

The launch vehicle lifted off the pad, streaked out of the tube up into the sky. Minutes later, having separated from the launch vehicle, the small space pod entered Thrae's outer atmosphere.

Zan instructed the pod's computer to scan for Cruiser Number 4. Nothing showed up.

He pushed the second of three propulsion buttons causing the spacecraft to shudder and lurch forward under the power of its twin high output plasma thrust engines. Seconds later, the pod was cruising two hundred and fifty miles above the Planet surface. Zan directed the computer to perform a second scan. Two small objects appeared on the three-dimensional display.

"There they are," confirmed Zan. He pushed the third button initiating maximum normal speed. The pod lurched once again as it accelerated towards the cruiser and transport vessel. As the small undetectable spacecraft passed the enormous transport vessel, Zan activated reverse thrusters which decelerated the pod while it quickly closed in on Cruiser Number 4. Zan skillfully used the pod's thrust vectoring system to guide the small pod parallel to the primary launch bay at the bottom rear of the large space cruiser.

Zan transmitted the pod's coordinates just before a corkscrew gravity control beam locked onto the craft and guided it safely into its rear bay from outer space. As the silver bay doors slowly slid closed, countless stars shined brightly against the blackness of deep space. Zan waited impatiently while he and the rest of the crew listened to the familiar hiss of the bay pressurization system. After what seemed like an eternity, the 'all safe' light flashed yellow releasing the clear acrylic sliding doors. Several resistance members hastily entered the bay and opened to pod's access door. As Zan stepped out, he was greeted by several determined faces.

"*Zan Liss?*" asked Vin Arnn, a 20-year-old resistance commander.

"Yes," he replied.

"It's a pleasure to finally meet you sir. We've heard a lot about you."

"Hopefully not all bad."

"It would be if it came from the Mitel Leadership," said Ard from behind. He stepped past Zan into the launch bay. Standing behind Vin were eleven more resistance fighters.

"Nice to meet you guys," smiled Ard. "I see you've cleaned the place up already. Nice job."

"We jettisoned most of the dead into outer space as you requested," Vin replied, "a few at a time to avoid detection."

"Good," replied Zan. "Timing for this mission is very critical so let's get moving. And remember to use these." Lia passed around several small handheld communications devices.

"What are these for?" asked Vin.

"We don't want to use the cruiser's communications system going forward. We don't want to leave a trail."

Accompanied by Vin, the group hurried to the HorVert Elevator located outside the launch bay. The elevator whirled toward the front of the cruiser before heading up to the highest level. As the doors opened at the rear of the ICC, everyone rushed to their stations. Ard scrambled over the railing to the weapons console. Vin stood at the rear of the ICC to observe.

Ard sat down and typed furiously. He paused, typed again and then frowned. The cluster pod's launch mechanism had been deactivated.

"Uh, we have a problem," he announced.

"*What?*" groaned Zan.

"We have been locked out of the weapons system."

"How?"

"The weapons specialist must have realized what was happening. I'm guessing they're starting to catch on to the resistance's opioid purge."

"Can you unlock it?"

"I tried."

"Lia?" asked Zan, do you think you can hack into the weapons system?"

Lia rushed over to the weapons console and inserted a program module into the computer. It commenced high-speed searches for encrypted programming signals.

Streams of data quickly appeared. Lia refined her search focusing her attention on the most recent weapons activity.

"I think I've found something," she announced. Lia instructed her module to search for the signal 'back door'. A few seconds later, she heard a long beep.

"I'm in."

Lia typed more instructions before pausing. She typed again and stared at the console.

"I'm able to unlock the lead cluster pod in each tube. But for some reason, that's all I can do. The laser weapons are also operational."

"That's better than nothing," Zan mused.

"Remind me again after we've used those pods up," grunted Ard. "The lasers might help us fend off a few dozen strike fighters, or a cruiser just *happens* to be sitting next to us."

"I understand that Ard, it's still — "

"*Better than nothing.*"

"Sir," said Mat. "Scanners have located Cruiser and Transport Vessel Number 3."

"Let's go," instructed Zan.

"What about TV4?" Ard asked.

"It'll have to wait for now. We must continue with the surprise attack plan."

"But it's no longer a surprise," cautioned Ard. Everyone in the ICC turned and stared at Zan.

"Maybe, maybe not Ard. But there's only one way to find out. *I said let's go.*"

Dax entered instructions causing the cruiser to turn and accelerate toward Cruiser Number 3. Lia, now back at her communications console, received an urgent transmission.

"Transport Vessel Number 4 is trying to contact us," she confirmed.

"Scanners show the two other cruisers have changed course," announced Dax. "They're headed this way."

"Do you think they were alerted?" asked Zan.

"Yes," replied Ard.

"OK, change of plans. Activate the slip ring. We'll close quickly, launch the pods at cruiser number 3 and TV3 and then veer off. Hopefully we'll take them by surprise so that they won't have time to launch a return strike."

"The slip ring isn't fully energized," replied Ard, "and I know I've said this before, but we're pushing our luck with this maneuver. Launching the pods at high-speed risks a spontaneous pod detonation in the launch tubes."

"I don't think we have a choice. *Activate the slip ring.*"

"Doing it now Sir," replied Dax.

The large spaceship accelerated at lightning speed. Everyone stared intently at the large rectangular monitors that curved across the front of the ICC.

"Cruiser Number 3 is directly ahead," confirmed Mat. "And Transport Vessel 3 is veering to our right."

"Both targets locked," confirmed Ard.

"*Fire!*" ordered Zan.

Ard launched both cluster pods in rapid succession.

"Disengage the slingshot, hard left!" Zan directed.

Cruiser Number 4 decelerated and vibrated noticeably as it scraped along the edge of Thrae's outer atmosphere. Shortly thereafter, the vibrations were replaced by the normal hum of the propulsion units.

"We are back to maximum normal speed," said Dax.

"Scanners confirm both spacecraft were destroyed," added Mat, "but not before the cruiser launched four pods at us."

"Where are they?"

"About 40 degrees to our left and closing . . ."

"How long until impact?"

"Approximately five minutes."

On Cruiser Number 2's ICC the scanning specialist registered the destruction.

"Commander!" he shouted. "Scanners have confirmed that both Cruiser Number 3 and Transport Vessel Number 3 have been destroyed!"

"*What*?" barked the commander, jumping up from his console seat, "*How*?"

"Cluster pods from the Cruiser Number 4."

The commander spun around to face his communications specialist. "You said their pod launch tubes had been disabled!" he growled.

"Yes Sir. The last transmission we received from the cruiser's ICC was unambiguous —"

"ARGH! They must have got them working again!"

Zan continued to stare at the ICC monitors.

"Ard, initiate the departure mechanism recharge," he ordered."

"Already done. It's going to take more than five minutes for the system to fully recharge."

"I know. Do you think we can take out the pods with our rear mounted lasers?"

"Maybe. Trying to identify targets now."

"Wait," said Mat, "the clusters pods just separated."

"There goes that idea," groaned Ard.

Zan closed his eyes and concentrated. After a brief time, he jumped up from the command console.

"I've got another idea," he said. "Lia, notify the base that we are unable to launch our pods. And tell Janus and Chad to get up here."

"Will do," replied Lia. She opened an encrypted communication link from her portable communications device in her backpack."

On the ground, Lia's message was relayed to Janus and Chad. They had been meditating on the shelf outside the huge stone-faced doors. The two quickly stood up and concentrated. Janus's eyes turned bright white just before he levitated fifteen feet up into the air. Seconds later, Chad was levitating next to Janus. Heavy metal trace elements and helium-4 approached them from all directions. Swirls of shiny particles of titanium, aluminum, magnesium, cadmium, iron, and beryllium whirled around the two blue plasma spheres.

"Commander," said Cruiser Number 2's scanning specialist. "We successfully unencrypted a transmission from the renegade cruiser."

"What did it say?"

"They can no longer launch their cluster pods."

"Do you think it's a decoy?"

"No. They've requested assistance."

"From whom?"

"It's unclear Sir."

On Cruiser Number 4's ICC, Zan looked over Mat's shoulder.

"Where's Transport Vessel 4?" he asked.

"Five hundred miles to our left," replied Mat. Zan then turned toward Dax.

"Head right for it, maximum speed."

"Yes Sir," replied Dax.

"You're going to use TV4 as a shield like we did back at Earth," said Ard. "There may be too many warheads for the transport vessel to absorb before disintegrating. The rest of them will continue on through."

"We'll find out," replied Zan firmly. "What's our departure energizing level?"

"40 percent and climbing . . ."

"Impact in three minutes," confirmed Mat.

Vin, who had been standing silently at the back of the ICC, quickly stepped forward.

"You're saying *we'll find out*?" he asked. "Are you sure that's our best course of action here?"

"Welcome to my world," Ard muttered to himself.

On the platform outside the huge stone-faced doors, two three-dimensional battle hologram cubes appeared. By now, the Battle Sphere hybrid transformations had completed. Janus and Chad, their hybrid transformations now complete, hovered silently side by side.

"Janus, Martin here," said Martin over the encrypted communication link. "I'm patching in Chad's Battle Hologram now."

"I'm here," confirmed Darius.

"We don't have much time," replied Janus. "Zan successfully commandeered one of four Mitel cruisers forming the blockage above the planet. But it's now under attack. As soon as we take off, the remaining cruisers are going to launch cluster pods at our population centers."

"We've got to shoot them down *and* save the cruiser," replied Nolia.

"Yes," replied Janus.

"Then let's get going."

"Battle Sphere systems confirmed fully operational," said Darius.

"Same here," added Martin.

"Prepare to launch," instructed Nolia.

Each variable speed flywheel engaged causing the Battle Spheres to spin faster and faster until they leveled off at one hundred twenty thousand revolutions per minute.

"Launching in three, two and one," said Martin, "launch."

Janus and Chad raced towards the upper atmosphere at all out speed.

On Cruiser Number 2's ICC the scanning specialist did a double take.

"Commander!" he shouted. "Scanners have detected *two* Battle Spheres entering Thrae's outer atmosphere!"

"*What*? Are you *sure*?"

"Positive! Their identification profiles match with a 99.98 percent certainty."

"This is outrageous! *Where did they possibly come from*?" growled the commander. He then paused. "Notify Cruiser Number 1 and initiate Battle Sphere defense protocols. *Do it now*!"

"Yes, Sir!"

Seconds later, both cruisers launched eleven cluster pods on two dozen population centers at the planet surface below.

"Pods are launched," confirmed the weapons specialist.

"Good," replied the Commander. "Make sure the departure mechanism is fully charged. Before we activate the slingshot and escape, I want to destroy the defecting cruiser before it falls into rebel hands!"

"Understood, Sir."

"Commanders," announced Nolia, "Mitel cruisers have launched cluster pods toward the planet's surface."

"Right on cue," grunted Lucian.

"Identifying targets," confirmed Darius.

"Synching databases now," added Martin.

"Synching confirmed."

"Prioritizing and distributing targets between Battle Spheres."

"Intercept trajectories confirmed. Modifying current route in three, two and one . . ."

Chad and Janus darted in opposite directions.

"We just passed the Transport vessel," said Mat. "The approaching cruisers launched a series of cluster pods at the planet surface."

"Battle Sphere engagement countermeasures directed at the population centers," replied Zan.

"The Battle Spheres have changed course to intercept them."

"There goes our help," moaned Ard.

"Impact in one minute," confirmed Mat. "Transport Vessel 4 is firing laser weapons at us," said Mat.

"Decrease to minimum speed and pull in well behind the spacecraft," instructed Zan.

"Doing it now," confirmed Dax.

"What? *You want to slow down*?" asked Ard.

"Dozens of strike fighters are exiting the transport vessel from all three levels," exclaimed Mat. "They're headed right for us."

Janus and Chad raced to intercept the cluster pods descending rapidly through the upper atmosphere.

"We are within firing range," announced Martin. "Targets identified and . . . wait. The pods just separated. Re-identifying targets."

Right after Cruiser number 4 disappeared from sight far behind the huge transport vessel, the TV was hit broadside by cluster warheads. The vessel quickly disintegrated in bright flashes, throwing debris in all directions. The remaining warheads raced through the wreckage toward Zan's cruiser.

"Incoming warheads!" said Mat. His screen suddenly flashed more bad news. "Incoming laser fire from the approaching fighters."

Above the planet surface, both Battle Spheres were continuously firing their 200 laser cannons at the descending cluster warheads.

"Four warheads are about to reach their targets," said Darius.

"We're not going to catch them in time," added Janus.

Chad focused his thoughts on the four population centers. *I'll try to place plasma shields over each.*

A semicircular shield appeared over the first population center, then the second and third just before impact. The cluster warheads detonated harmlessly against the outer surface of each shield. As Chad focused on Amer, the fourth population center, the warhead struck its target. At ground zero, the destruction was absolute.

"NOOOO!" yelled Chad.

"Impact in twenty seconds!" shouted Mat.

"Activate the departure mechanism!" ordered Zan. The cylindrical ring rapidly sped up until it was spinning at lightning speed.

"Ten seconds!"

The outer space directly behind Cruiser Number 4 distorted like an invisible tsunami. The lethal strike fighter laser bursts exploded harmlessly against its approaching wake, followed instantaneously by dozens of exploding cluster warheads. The approaching Mitel fighters began evasive maneuvers, but it was too late. They were all hit by the approaching distortion and instantly obliterated.

Mat grimaced for impact while keeping one eye on his computer screen. Seconds later, the approaching yellow dots along with their identifiers were gone.

"Hey! It looks like everything has been destroyed!" he shouted.

A loud cheer erupted throughout the ICC.

"Of course!" shouted Ard. "The distortion wave! That was your back up plan."

"Yes," signed Zan. He slumped into his console seat. "Luckily for us it worked."

"For the record," Ard grinned, "I never doubted you."

"You always doubt me Ard, and for good reason."

"Nice work Commander," said Vin. "I thought we were goners."

"I was starting to have my doubts," replied Zan.

"Sir," interrupted Mat. "The two remaining cruisers are closing in at maximum normal speed."

"The celebration is officially over," replied Ard.

"Where are the Battle Spheres?" asked Zan.

"Down at the planet surface," replied Mat.

"Tell them to get up here."

Seconds later, Lia sent an encrypted message.

"Commanders," said Nolia, "Our cruiser is under attack by two approaching Mitel cruisers."

Above the smoldering population center of Amer, Janus stared at the ruins in anger.

"Nolia, Lucien. Get us up there," he ordered tersely.

An instant later, both Battle Spheres were racing toward the upper atmosphere at all out speed.

On the ICC of Cruiser Number 2, the scanning specialist again registered the two small objects.

"Commander," he said nervously, "The Battle Spheres are headed this way again."

"Notify Cruiser Number 1 and initiate Level Two defensive protocols. Launch six more pods at population centers much farther away. We need to buy ourselves as much time as possible to finish off the renegade cruiser and escape. In the meantime, order our two remaining transport vessels to slingshot into deep space and return to Mitel."

"Yes Sir."

A short time later, six more cluster pods from each cruiser exited the launch tubes in opposite directions along the edge of outer space.

"What is the energizing status?"

"65 percent and climbing rapidly. Cruiser Number 1 reports the same."

Darius stared intently at his console screen.

"Commanders," he announced. "The Mitel cruisers just launched another round of cluster pods. Tracking suggests they are targeting the far side of the planet."

"Trying to buy more time," replied Lucien.

"The two groups of pods are diverging rapidly."

"We must redirect our Battle Spheres."

Seconds Later, Janus and Chad raced at all out speed toward each group of pods.

On the ICC of Cruiser Number 4, Mat's scanners detected the cluster pods. "The two cruisers have fired another round of cluster pods. Only this time, modeling trajectories confirm the targets are much further away."

"The Battle Spheres have no choice but to chase them all down," Ard grumbled.

Zan rubbed his chin. He then jerked his console seat towards Lia.

"Try to activate our cluster pods again," he ordered.

"OK," nodded Lia. She hurried over to the weapons console and reinserted her program module. Lia stared at the streams of data. She typed, paused, and typed again. After a long beep, she typed more instructions.

"I unlocked one more cluster pod in the left tube but that's it."

"Excellent," replied Zan. He jumped to his feet.

"Zan," said Ard. "We may have one more pod, but there are two cruisers headed our way."

"I understand Ard. Dax, prepare the slingshot aimed at the closest grouping of cluster pods."

"What?" Ard asked. "A pod grouping? *Why*?"

"If we can destroy them before they separate, we can free up the intercepting Battle Sphere to go after the cruisers and catch them off guard."

"We should notify the Battle Holograms," replied Lia.

"No."

"*What*?" Ard asked.

"By now the cruisers have breached our encrypted communications network. We can't risk tipping them off."

"But the slingshot will deplete our remaining energizing reserves. We won't be able to escape the cruisers."

"We don't have enough reserves to escape as it stands now. Do you have a better idea?"

"No."

"OK then. *Execute the slingshot*."

"Sir," said the Scanning Specialist on Cruiser Number 2, "the renegade cruiser appears to be trying to escape!"

"What are our energizing levels?"

"95 percent."

"Good. They won't be able to out run us," scoffed the Commander. "Instruct the other cruiser to prepare to slingshot into deep space. We'll overtake the renegade cruiser with our own slingshot, destroy it and escape from there."

"Doing it now, Sir," replied the Communications Specialist.

Darius continued to stare at his console screen.

"Commanders," he announced. "Our cruiser just executed another slingshot."

"*What are they doing?*" asked Nolia.

"They're headed directly toward one of the groupings of cluster pods. I think they're trying to destroy them before they separate."

"Agreed," nodded Martin. "Which Battle Sphere is chasing down those pods?"

"Janus."

"If Zan's cruiser takes out the pods, we can divert his Battle Sphere to take out the cruisers."

"We could," Nolia replied, "but what if we're wrong."

"Zan didn't give us the heads up for a reason. He must believe the encryption channel has been breached."

"Let's do it," replied Darius.

"I tend to agree," nodded Nolia. "But we mustn't tip our hand."

"Understood," replied Martin. "Let me try, OK?"

"Go ahead."

"Janus, this is Martin."

"Yes Martin."

"Change of plans."

"*What?* What do you mean?"

"Just what I said."

"We are within firing range," confirmed Ard.

"Can you lock onto all the targets?" asked Zan.

"Already done. The tricky part will be to get the pod to release its warheads almost immediately."

"And how do you plan on doing that?"

"It's a trick I learned at the Academy from a fanatical instructor in a course called Advanced Munitions."

"What's the trick?"

"You hit the launch button and manual detonation button at the same time."

"That doesn't sound right, or safe."

"It worked every time."

"And if it doesn't this time?"

"We'll never know."

On the ICC of Cruiser Number 2, the Scanning Specialist stared intently at his monitoring Screen. A yellow light flashed in the top right-hand corner.

"We're within firing range," he announced.

"Prepare to fire Ard," ordered Zan. "And just for the record, I think I'm starting to rub off on you."

"That's a scary thought," Ard grinned wryly. "Well here goes."

He grimaced slightly as he pushed both buttons simultaneously. The pod launched and immediately separated.

"Missiles are on their way," confirmed Mat with a sigh of relief.

"Janus, we need you to eliminate two big problems," said Martin.

"But —"

Out of the corner of his eye, Janus detected the second set of missiles on his diagnostic mini screens. They were quickly closing in on his targeted pods.

"I understand now," he replied.

"Initiating course correction in three, two and one."

Janus's Battle Sphere changed direction and closed in on the two Mitel cruisers at all out speed.

"Fire two cluster pods," ordered the Commander.

"Yes, Sir," replied the weapons specialist.

"Commander," said the Scanning Specialist. "The renegade cruiser just launched a cluster pod. It immediately separated its missiles somehow."

"*What*? I thought they were unable to launch. Where are the missiles headed?"

"They're bearing down on our pods and wait, the Battle Sphere!"

"What about it?"

"*It's headed straight at us!*"

"*What*? It's a trap! Launch the slingshot, do it now!"

"What about the renegade cruiser?"

"Launch the pods and get us out of here! *NOW!*"

As Janus's Battle Sphere approached firing range, the weapons specialists eagerly rotated through their targets.

"I haven't seen targets this big and fat since the first Mitel invasion," said one specialist.

"You got that right," added another.

"Let's get to work," added a third.

"We are within range," confirmed Lucien.

All two hundred of Janus's laser cannons fired in full battle mode. Janus's Battle Sphere appeared as a tiny star emitting streams of bright white mini *stars* in all directions. The energy pulses curved as they exited the spinning orb before quickly straightening out and elongating as they raced toward the cruisers.

"Executing the slingshot now!" confirmed the navigation specialist. The other cruiser is —"

The two cruisers lit up brightly as hundreds of plasma energy pulses struck repeatedly along the full length of each vessel. Cruiser Number 2 destabilized and disintegrated in a matter of seconds, followed by Cruiser Number 1. All that remained were two expansive debris fields which Janus flew through before streaking toward the two pods closing in on Zan's cruiser.

"Incoming cluster pods," said Mat nervously.

"How many?" asked Zan.

"Two."

"How long until they arrive?"

"Twenty seconds."

Zan glanced over at Ard as he tried to figure out what to do next.

Janus switched to free flight and accelerated toward the speeding pods at all out speed.

Identifying targets," said Martin, "and locked."

Two weapons specialists immediately fired a series of plasma bursts.

"Ten seconds," said Mat nervously.

"Turn hard left," ordered Zan. "*Now!*"

"There isn't time," replied Ard.

The two pods destabilized and disintegrated after being struck by plasma pulses. Janus raced past Zan's cruiser before circling down toward the planet surface.

"*The Battle Sphere,*" said Mat excitedly, "it took out the pods!"

"*That's a relief*," Zan sighed. He then flopped back into his console chair. "Dax, shut down all power," he ordered.

"*Sir?*"

"Just do as I ask. The auxiliary power will kick in."

"Yes, Sir."

"Lia, terminate all communications channels."

"For what purpose?" Lia asked.

"I'm trying to fake the destruction of this cruiser for our spacecraft logs."

"Ohhh," replied Ard. "That's a great idea."

"We'll find out. Lia, can you also terminate our mission logs?"

"Doing it now," she replied, typing quickly. Lia then paused and typed again. "Done and . . . done."

The cruiser went dark for a few seconds before the auxiliary power came on-line.

"Those few seconds *always* makes me uncomfortable," Ard complained.

One Thousand miles away, Chad bore down on the other group of pods as they streaked along the outer atmosphere.

"Let's destroy them before they separate," said Nolia.

"Scanners confirm we are within range. Identifying targets, and locked," confirmed Darius.

"Open fire," ordered Nolia.

Chad's weapons specialists cycled through their targets unleashing a lethal barrage which destroyed one pod after another until Darius confirmed they were gone.

"Cease fire, cease fire," ordered Nolia. "You're simply wasting plasma energy at this point."

"Lucien confirms that the two remaining cruisers have been destroyed," said Darius.

"We did it," smiled Nolia. "Thrae is finally free of the Mitel blockade. Let's get Chad back to the base."

"Doing it now," replied Darius.

Powered by its electromagnetically charged super-conductor disc antigravity propulsion system, Cruiser Number 4 descended from the upper atmosphere and slowly landed on the shelf next to Bay Number 1. Zan and Ard walked down bulkhead number 3's retractable stair-case beneath the cruiser and headed straight to the under-ground conference room for debriefing. When they entered, Janus, Chad and Markus were already standing before the seven-member World Council.

"Please come in," motioned Jaret. "We were about to discuss the results of the mission. We thank all of you for your courage and heroism. Although the mission was successful, it came at a cost."

Zan thought about how to respond.

"The population center of Amer was devastated," added a second council member. "We estimate that thirty-five thousand men, women and children were killed."

"Innocent civilians," added a third member.

"You said that the plan would work," added a fourth.

"And it did," responded Zan quickly.

"The destruction and loss of life was not Zan's fault," said Janus. "It was mine. As an experienced Battle Sphere, I should have done a much better job of evaluating the situation including identifying and prioritizing the incoming warheads. If I had done that, we would have destroyed all of them."

"Bah," said Markus. "You're being too hard on yourself as usual. If the Mitels would simply leave us alone, none of this would have happened."

There was an awkward silence.

"If I may speak," Zan began. "We will all carry the guilt of the loss of innocent life for the rest of our lives. Unfortunately, we can't undo what just happened. But the loss of life would have been far greater if our plan had failed, or through inaction, we simply waited for the Mitels to attack us again. But we didn't. We now control the skies for the first time in over fifteen years. The next order of business is to get our cruisers into space and establish a viable defense perimeter. In the meantime, I hope that the World Council will accept my resignation as commander of the Thraen resistance."

"*Let's not be hasty*," replied Jaret. "Markus is right. The responsibility for the loss of life rests at the feet of the Mitel Leadership. They are the ones who must be held accountable for the death of countless innocent Thraens. It is my hope that they will be brought to justice during my lifetime. As head of the World Council, I will *not* agree to accept your resignation Zan Liss. We must move forward. We must be prepared for whatever response the Mitels put forth."

"Very well," nodded Zan. "The Mitels *will* return to Thrae that much is certain. If we are not prepared, the loss of life will be much worse when they do."

"What about the remaining transport vessels?" the second member asked.

"They escaped into deep space," replied Janus. "Presumably back to Mitel."

"Mitel also knows that Thrae has two Battle Spheres," added Markus.

"But won't that make them more cautious?" the third member asked.

"It might. But they will respond eventually. They always do."

"And we will need to be ready when they do," replied Zan. "We have six new cruisers under construction, and the modules for another six ready to be rolled in once the first six are completed and launched. We have Transport vessels in another underground base to refurbish and new fighters to build. We must also establish a working outer space defense perimeter using high energy lasers and cluster pods."

"Agreed," nodded Janus.

"Look," said Ard, "The Leadership was going to find out about the Battle Spheres eventually."

"Yes," replied Jaret, "but the World Council and people of Thrae wanted it to be on our terms."

"True, but unfortunately, we didn't. So, let's make the best of it."

"We have no choice," acknowledged Jaret.

There was a brief silence.

"Not to change the subject," said Zan, "but I'd like you to meet twelve people waiting outside who were instrumental in the success of our mission."

"By all means," motioned Jaret.

Zan opened the conference room door and waved for the Mitel resistance members to come into the room."

"These are the members of the Mitel Resistance that helped us secure the Mitel cruiser."

"But they are all so young," said the forth council member.

"Yes, they are. These young men and women are the future of Mitel. They have hopes and dreams for a better life for all their people back on Mitel, not to mention the people here on Thrae. We must not forget them."

"I'm sorry if we come across as being unappreciative or unnecessarily critical," Jaret conceded. "This has been a very difficult period for our people. But I can speak for the entire World Council when I say that I fully understand and sincerely sympathize with the seemingly endless pain and suffering that the Mitel people have endured. We, as a world civilization, should have done more to help you when we were better positioned to do so. Instead, we watched from a distance and did absolutely nothing. We are now paying a steep price for that inaction. From the bottom of my heart, thank you all for your bravery and assistance. In time, hopefully, Thrae will be in a position to return the favor."

"Thank you," Vin replied. "We will protect the people of Thrae with our lives. Just tell us what we can do to be of assistance."

"Thank you," smiled Jaret. "I'm sure Commander Liss can put all of you to good use."

"Yes," replied Zan. "We've got a lot — "

"Of work to do," interrupted Ard.

"Yes."

"Then let's get started," said Janus.

"Oh, by the way," Zan remembered. "Dru has several modifications he would like to incorporate into our newest *acquisition*. I think they could come in very handy under the right circumstances."

"What do you mean?" asked Ard.

Zan looked at him but didn't respond.

"I get it. *You'll tell me about it later.*"

"You're finally starting to understand how I operate."

"Just don't wait until the last minute this time, OK?"

"Deal . . . I mean, I'll certainly do my best."

"Why don't I believe you?"

After the meeting, Chad made his way back to his living quarters. By now, he was exhausted. As he walked past the sliding entry doors, he was greeted by Mayla and Teri. They had grim expressions on their faces.

"What are you doing here?"

"Chad, your Mom and Dad . . ." replied Mayla somberly. Her eyes began to well up with tears.

"What's wrong?"

"They were in Amer when the Mitel pod hit," replied Teri.

"We are trying to contact them," added Mayla.

Chad stared at the two in stunned disbelief. Mayla walked over and hugged him tightly.

CHAPTER THIRTEEN — CHAOS

Men, women, and children began cautiously emerging from Amer's underground defense shelters. The subterranean labyrinth had dozens of entrance points to maximize access when time was short. It also provided alternative escape routes in areas where falling debris sealed off the access stairway. At ground zero, almost every entrance point was partially blocked. In some cases, entrances were completely sealed off. This slowed movement through the passageways down to a trickle. In one sense, the blockages were fortuitous. Men, women, and children were forced to exit far away from severely damaged and unstable structures.

Molly followed the long line of people down the crowded passageway. She was worried sick about Jim ever since they had been separated in all the confusion to find shelter.

The day before, Jim desperately tried to locate Molly as everyone hurried back and forth. He walked up and down the raised walkways trying to glimpse her. He eventually realized that he was the only one still outside.

Jim reluctantly gave up his search and ran toward a shelter entrance point identified by a red and white diamond shaped sign. He ran down the stairs and pulled on the heavily reinforced door. It wouldn't budge. He then pounded on it as hard as he could, his identification badge falling to the ground.

It's been sealed off, he thought.

Jim rushed back up the stairs. At the top step, he looked around in all directions for Molly one last time. By now, the population center was deserted. Jim ran along an elevated walkway until he saw a second diamond shaped sign. Looking down the stairs he saw it too had been sealed shut. Jim panicked.

Stay calm and think.

Jim walked along curving structures trying to decide what to do. He then heard a loud screeching noise. Looking up at the sky, he saw what appeared to be a shooting star streaking down toward the population center.

The missile.

Jim stared at it transfixed. He could feel his life racing in front of his eyes. Suddenly, a large hand grabbed him firmly by the shoulder. Jim was pulled into a narrow passageway. He spun around to see a tall man wearing a backpack staring down at him. His eyes flashed metallic green, and his skin texture was almost flawless. To Jim, it appeared as though he wasn't human.

Without saying a word, the man pulled Jim down the passageway to a long set of stairs. The man then pointed down the stairs. Jim instinctively followed him to the bottom. Turning the corner, he saw a second set of stairs going further down. Jim hesitated just as the missile hit. Everything went black.

Chad stayed up all night watching the reports as they came in. At ground zero, the population center had been leveled. Nobody outside the underground shelters was expected to have survived the blast. Chad's heart sank. He felt helpless and vulnerable. He now understood what Thraens have been living with for generations.

The intercom buzzed. Chad lunged at it hoping to hear his parents' voice.

"Hello?" he asked anxiously.

"It's Markus, let me in."

Chad entered a four digit code into the wall keypad causing the door to side open. Markus entered, followed by his monitoring orb. Markus reached out and gave Chad a big hug. The room sparkled brightly. "I'm so sorry to hear what happened," he whispered.

Markus then stepped back.

"You look exhausted," he said.

"I've been up watching the reports. I was hoping to hear some good news."

"I can tell you from experience a large contingent of first responders are at the scene. The authorities are also starting to run through their activation lists."

"*Activation lists?*"

"A miniature heartbeat monitor and tracking device is in the waistband and collar of most civilian clothing. The system is not perfect, but it has shown itself to be very reliable. The database can only be accessed during a global emergency. Unfortunately, it's the reality of the times we live in. If the device fails to detect an individual, that means the device did not register a heartbeat. It helps the first responders quickly locate injured civilians and provides swift closure to loved ones who otherwise might agonize for years wondering what happened. We hope to locate Jim and Molly safe and sound this way. Odds are they made it safely to a shelter before the missile strike."

"I hope so . . ."

"Listen Chad, you need to get some sleep. I'll wake you if we hear something."

"Promise?"

"I promise," replied Markus softly.

"OK."

Chad lied down on a long couch and covered himself with a blanket. In less than a minute he was fast asleep. Markus watched him for some time before letting himself out.

Jim woke up on the floor of a dark passageway. He was completely covered in dust and his forehead ached. He slowly sat up on the foam cot stretched out beneath him. Jim reached up and touched his forehead. It was covered by a large patch.

Ouch, he thought.

Jim felt something wet between his fingers. He looked at his hand but could only make out a dark blotch. He then put his fingers to his nose. It smelled like blood. Jim looked around the darkened corridor. To his right, there was a large, blackened door about thirty yards away. A few smaller doors were located almost directly across from him. To his left, the hallway seemed to go on indefinitely. Long thin ceiling lights were along the top of the walls every few hundred yards. Bundles and bundles of different sized wires and conduits covered the ceiling. Between the lights, the hallway was dark.

Where am I?

Jim struggled to stand up. His arms and legs ached, and his back was stiff. He looked up and down the hallway again. It was quiet. Jim limped over to the large, blackened door. He pushed and pulled on it repeatedly to no avail. It wouldn't budge. Jim let out a long deep sigh. He turned around and leaned on the door for support as he stared down the long hallway. Then it dawned on him.

Who am I?

Suddenly, a tall man appeared through the wall down the corridor. He was surrounded in a light blue hue. Jim rubbed his eyes and looked again. The man noticed Jim standing against the door and floated toward him. Jim pushed on the door as hard as he could. It still wouldn't budge. The man kept approaching.

Chad woke up to the sound of the intercom buzzer. He jumped up and pushed the button.

"Hello?"

"It's Markus."

Chad punched in the code. The door slid open.

"Well?" asked Chad anxiously, rubbing his eyes.

"Nothing yet. Last I heard, the authorities were having some problems accessing the activation lists."

"Isn't there anything else we can do?"

Markus thought for a moment.

"You and I could go over there by hover craft. I could instruct my monitoring orb to search for them while we look around. It's worth a try."

"Let's go."

"Who are you and what do you want?" shouted Jim anxiously.

The man surrounded by the light blue hue didn't respond as he kept floating closer.

Jim looked around for something to defend himself with. He saw what looked like a piece of pipe on the floor. Jim picked it up and prepared to throw it.

"Stop!" he shouted.

The man drew closer.

Jim threw the pipe as hard as he could. It went right through the man, clanging along the floor down the hallway. The person stopped.

"I'm not going to hurt you," said the man softly. He then appeared to fade out for a few seconds before returning.

"Who or *what* are you?" asked Jim.

"I'm a hologram," he replied.

"A what?"

"*A living hologram.* I was human a long time ago. Then I volunteered to be transformed into a hologram. I'm one of the first ones, actually."

He then flickered once again.

"Why do you do that?" asked Jim.

"Do what?"

The hologram flickered again.

"That."

"Unfortunately, I'm so old that I'm starting to run out of power. Early hologram versions weren't designed and created with the type of energy reserves that today's holograms have."

"How old are you?"

"1,350 years."

"What happens when your energy reserves run out?"

"I cease to exist."

"Oh, I'm sorry. What's your name?"

"Atlas Root. What's yours?"

Jim rubbed his head again.

"I don't know."

"You aren't from here that's for sure."

"I don't even know what city I live in."

"No. I mean you aren't from this *planet*."

"What? How do you even know *that*?"

Atlas frowned. "Isak ran a scan on you. Your internal organs are configured differently. And besides . . ."

Atlas then raised his hand.

"You don't have four fingers."

Jim looked at his own hands.

"You mean I'm some kind of *freak*?" he asked.

"I'm not saying that at all," Atlas chuckled. "You're just different. Since you speak fluent Thraen, you must have lived here for a long time."

Jim thought for a moment.

"I don't know," he muttered. "I can't remember anything . . ."

"You were hit in the head by large chunks of falling debris," explained Atlas. "Scans of your brain showed signs of medically significant trauma. For a while we thought you weren't going to make it. I applied a curing patch which should speed up the healing process."

"Thank you. What *is* this place?"

Atlas faded slightly then returned. Jim studied his features. He had a kind and caring face; big expressive charcoal eyes, short black hair and an unusually large nose for his long and thin face.

"You are below the population center of Amer," replied Atlas, "on planet Thrae."

"Why are we down here?"

"Amer was attacked by a Mitel cluster pod. The buildings and infrastructure above us were destroyed. Isak found you wandering above just before the missile struck. He grabbed you and brought you down here."

Suddenly the large, blackened door flung opened. Isak stepped into the hallway carrying a large sack over his shoulder. Seeing him for the first time, Jim was taken aback by his sheer size. As Isak walked toward the two, his eyes flashed metallic green.

"Did anyone see you?" asked Atlas.

Isak shook his head no.

"Good."

Accompanied by three hologram soldiers, Chad and Markus traveled via base hover craft to the outskirts of Amer. Upon landing, the twenty-four curved clear retractable overlapping roof sections immediately opened. They all climbed out of the craft and headed toward Amer on foot. Markus directed his orb to race ahead to scout things out while digitally mapping the entire population center. A constant stream of men, women and children trudged along in the opposite direction toward temporary shelters. The looks on their faces were all the same: helpless, exhausted, and sad.

"When will this senseless violence ever end?" Markus muttered.

As they approached ground zero, everything was in total ruins. Chad's heart sank as he thought about Jim and Molly.

"How could they have survived that?" he asked.

Markus motioned to the long stream of people walking past them.

"They survived," he said. "We need to stay optimistic."

"Isak, you know I don't like you going out there," said Atlas. "You might get captured by Thraen soldiers."

Isak shrugged and waved his arm dismissively.

"I hope someday I won't have to say *I told you so*," added Atlas. "Anyway, show me what you found."

Isak flung the large sack off his shoulder down to the floor and opened it. Atlas reached into the bag setting off his focused energy. He rummaged around and pulled out a shirt and pants. He held them up against Jim. "Too small," he mumbled. He reached back in and pulled out another set and held them up again. "These should do it."

"What are you doing?" asked Jim.

"Isak found you some clean clothes to wear. You can take a shower over there." Atlas pointed to one of the side doors. "It's rudimentary, but it works."

"But — "

"Listen, you're filthy dirty and need to get clean. And don't worry, the patch won't come off. It eventually gets assimilated by your body. Besides, the clothes you're wearing have an imbedded tracking device. The ones we gave you don't."

"*A tracking device*? Why?"

"They say it's to help find you. We believe it's to track everyone's whereabouts."

Atlas handed Jim the clothes.

"Now hurry, take these with you. We need to get moving before the Scavengers find us."

Jim went through the doorway. As he entered, a light came on. In the corner of a long, narrow room was a makeshift re-circulating shower system which continuously purified and re-circulated the water. Next to it was a self-sustained nano membrane toilet. Towels were hanging on pipes along the wall. Jim took off his shoes and clothes, turned on the water and stepped into a square clear acrylic pan. The hot water felt good against his body. He felt a sharp radiating pain on his forehead as he drenched himself. After a few minutes, the pain faded. Jim stood motionless under the pulsating water for a while.

Who am I? he wondered. *And who are the people who Atlas says are tracking my location? I need to be very cautious until I figure out what's going on.*

Jim reluctantly turned the water off and stepped out of the shower. He stared for a time at his face it a make-shift mirror.

Who are you? he thought. *What was your life like before the explosion? Why can't I remember anything?*

Jim got anxious. To push back those feelings, he dried himself off and put on the clothes Atlas had given him.

They fit ok.

Jim put his shoes back on and quickly used the toilet. As he washed his hands, he noticed a synthetic yellow flower sitting on a small shelf in the corner. He picked it up and studied it for a time.

It's beautiful, but it seems kind of strange for it to be down here, he concluded.

Jim carefully placed it in his pocket. He then grabbed his dirty clothes and walked out. Atlas and Isak were standing in the hallway. They were both wearing huge backpacks.

"Those look heavy," said Jim.

"They are," smiled Atlas. "Give me your old clothes."

Jim handed the dirty clothes to Atlas who promptly threw them on the floor. Isak, now carrying a long solid rod, tamped down on the waistband and collar with the butt end of the rod.

"What's he doing?" asked Jim.

"He's destroying the tracking devices," replied Atlas.

Isak eventually stopped and looked up. He mouthed a few words to Atlas.

"OK good, let's go," instructed Atlas.

Isak and Atlas walked down the long corridor. Jim stood silently and watched them. Atlas eventually stopped and turned around.

"Aren't you coming?" he asked.

Jim could feel the anxiety growing inside himself. To control it he quickly walked to catch up, before the three slowly disappeared into the darkness.

As they made their way toward the worst of the destruction, Markus's orb received a transmission.

"The activation database is up and running," he announced. "Hopefully we'll receive good news soon."

Chad didn't respond. He was simply too anxious and worried. As they kept walking, Markus's monitoring orb reappeared. Markus closed his eyes to review the data. He then looked at Chad.

"There is a primary access point six hundred yards to our left," he said, "and another one four hundred yards beyond that. Many people are exiting from the underground shelters. It appears that a few people are simply waiting there. Let's check it out, shall we?"

Chad's eyes lit up.

"Let's go."

Atlas, Isak and Jim walked along for about twenty minutes. Up ahead was another large, darkened door. Jim noticed that it was slightly propped open at the bottom by a piece of debris. After they passed through, Isak kicked the chunk out of the way and closed the door tightly.

"Makes it harder to follow us," smiled Atlas.

They walked up a short hallway that turned ninety degrees. Directly ahead was another long dark hallway with bundles of different sized wires and conduits along the ceiling. At the end of the hallway was another door.

"Our next stop," pointed Atlas.

The three walked along until they reached the large, blackened door. Before Atlas could reach through it, Isak used the thin flat wedge on the other end of his pole to pop the door open at its midpoint. Beyond the door was a large brightly lit circular enclosure. Plants and trees filled the cavity. High above was a gray acrylic dome.

"What *is* this place?" Jim asked.

"It's a conduit hub below the center of a recreational area. The dome is normally clear, but the explosion wave must have covered it with a layer of dust. The loss of innocent life is unimaginable, but ever since Thrae turned their backs on us, we really haven't felt much of a connection to the surface dwellers."

Looking around, Jim noticed a small shallow stream running through the middle of the cavity.

"This opening as originally constructed was exposed to the elements," Atlas continued. "The hub provided ventilation to the several corridors that branch off from it. In order to protect the infrastructure from the elements and also for safety and security, it was ultimately covered with a transparent dome. Over time, cracks developed in the circular walls and foundation, resulting in the stream over there. The groundwater allowed dormant foliage seeds to take root and grow. Isak says the water is drinkable."

Atlas walked closer to the center of the opening before turning around.

"Many population centers have very similar underground corridor systems for ease of access to utilities," he explained. "I've been through most of them so many times that I know the layouts by heart. Across this opening is a small room that contains a basic shower and toilet. They are also located along the hallways. They were originally installed by maintenance workers long ago. Eventually they fell into disrepair once the need to come down here vanished due to advancements in energy and utility delivery technologies. Over time, some have been repaired by drifters like us."

Isak motioned and mouthed several words to Atlas.

"OK, we'll wait here."

Isak lowered his backpack to the ground and walked off. Jim watched Isak disappear into the foliage as Atlas took his off his backpack.

"Where's he going?" asked Jim.

"To look around and make sure nobody else is here. Small groups of Scavengers make the rounds down here. Because the underground systems are so extensive, we rarely cross paths. But they can be very dangerous."

"Where did they come from?"

"They were once surface dwellers. A long time ago, they rejected Thrae's advanced technology and the direction it was going. As a people, they went into seclusion. Surface dwellers poked fun at them, referring to them as the *Recluses*, but they didn't care. They grew their own food, made their own clothes, and lived in modest structures far away from the population centers. They were very proud, hardworking, and surprisingly neat and clean in their appearance."

Atlas gathered his thoughts.

"The Mitel invasions changed everything. Especially the second one, since it caused significant swaths of land to be badly scorched. Growing crops became difficult, so the Recluses started venturing out in search of food which brought them back to the population centers. Since they still didn't want anything to do with modern civilization, they started using the tunnel systems to get around, only coming out late at night. That's when they came to be known as *Atseleters* or Scavengers. You can recognize them easily by their loose-fitting homemade clothes, mostly grays, browns and black. No color whatsoever. I think it helps them blend into the shadows and darkness. They also wear large black and gray homemade backpacks."

"What do they want?"

"Food mostly. Occasionally, they're bored and just looking for trouble. For a long time, we had an understanding with them. They left us alone and we'd leave them alone. But that changed after the last Mitel invasion. Their quality of life steadily deteriorated, which has made some of them much more aggressive. The ones we run into nowadays appear unkempt and dirty. We've heard rumors that they have broken apart into competing factions, some in worse shape than others."

"Why doesn't anyone help them?"

"Many have tried, but the Scavengers no longer trust the surface dwellers."

"I see," nodded Jim. "Can I ask another question?"

"Sure."

"Who or *what* is Isak?"

"Isak Sone is his full name," replied Atlas. He then thought for a moment. "Where to begin," he said aloud. "Suffice to say that Isak is a very unique person. He was also the first recorded Thraen Battle Sphere."

"A *what*?" Jim asked.

"Isak is, or I should say *was*, a human hybrid also known as a *Battle Sphere*. He had the ability to transform into a twenty-foot diameter device that is still considered for its size to be the most formidable war machine in the entire universe. He could fire up to two hundred plasma laser cannons at one time. He could also fly at speeds approaching the speed of light. He was, really, truly remarkable."

"How do you know all this?"

"I was his Battle Hologram commander. I directed a highly trained team of human holograms that monitored his speed, energy reserves, propulsion and other internal systems. At first, he didn't have us. We were invented, or should I say *created*, about a hundred years later. Before us, Isak did everything on his own. When we were assigned to him, we helped maximize his performance and destructive powers."

"Were you *evil*?"

"No," Atlas laughed. "Our job was to protect innocent men, women and children of Thrae."

"Well, that's a relief. But you said *was*. What happened?"

"It's a long story, but about fifty years later, a second Battle Sphere was discovered named Val Rand. He was young, self-confident, and flashy. Many viewed him as an arrogant risk taker. After a while, even his Battle Hologram team didn't like him. But for one of the few times in Thraen history, it had *two* Battle Spheres at one time. And they would need them both."

"Why?"

"Because twelve hundred and ninety-five years ago, an advanced civilization called the Saturs, discovered Thrae and began to threaten it. At first, the Thraen World Council simply ignored them because they were located so far away. I mean, they were located on our galaxy's *adjacent spiral arm*. But as the threats increased, the Council issued a condemnation transmission. What the Council didn't know was that the Saturs possessed incredibly advanced propulsion technology. They proceeded to launch a vast armada toward Thrae which our long-range scanners detected. Instead of waiting for them to arrive, the World Council sent Val and Isak to confront them."

"Wow," replied Jim softly. "What happened?"

"Val did what Val does. He was reckless and quickly got into trouble. Isak fought bravely to try to rescue him. His reserves ran out, but Isak refused to give up. He was so badly damaged his Battle Hologram was essentially destroyed. I was the only hologram survivor. Isak was left for dead, adrift in deep space. Val, realizing he was out of options, reversed his energy core. In doing so, he caused his Battle Sphere to internally produce significant quantities of antimatter. He was somehow able to contain it at least temporarily with his outer plasma defense shield. A Saturs war pod eventually pierced the shield exposing the antimatter to outer space. The instantaneous annihilation event was on a cosmic scale and wiped out the entire armada. Isak, floating along at the outermost periphery of the blast, survived.

Through sheer determination, he was able to generate just enough propulsion power to return to Thrae while also projecting the last remnants of his Battle Hologram. The trip took five long and lonely years. We kept each other company along the way. Isak was eventually rescued when he stumbled across an interplanetary trade route. Upon his return, he allowed himself to transform back to human form. But he was a hideous mess. His skin was mostly burned away, and he had lost his arms and legs along with his chest and shoulder muscles. His facial bones were fractured, and his jaw was crushed. He was also blind."

"Oh my God," whispered Jim.

"In the hopes of restoring his Battle Sphere abilities, surgeons reconstructed his face, replaced his arms, legs, shoulder and chest muscles with robotics and robotic muscle mesh made entirely of graphene. The replacement parts were all imbedded with high concentrations of titanium, aluminum, magnesium, cadmium, iron and beryllium; elements that facilitate his hybrid transformation. He also received robotic eyes and synthetic skin across most of his body. But no matter how hard he tried, Isak could no longer transform. I personally think he was traumatized beyond his ability to focus on transforming. He also lost some of his memory due to the annihilation event. To this day, he still can't speak. He occasionally grunts and thrashes about when he has a bad dream. He gets those often. I think he's tormented by his past."

"So sad."

"It gets worse. Val's supporters blamed Isak for his death. They relentlessly stoked public opinion until finally, Isak was put on trial before the World Council. With his memory of the Saturs confrontation unreliable, Isak couldn't defend himself at trial. Had he been able to transform, his Battle Sphere computer logs, history and streaming data videos would have exonerated him. At trial, I argued on his behalf only to be disparaged and dismissed."

"Why?"

"Because I was the first and only Battle Hologram commander to ever lose its entire hologram support team. To the world, I was considered an incompetent failure. But I wasn't. We fought hard and bravely. If Val had not been so reckless and selfish, none of that would've ever happened. But in the end, he gave his life for all of us so I had to forgive him. Before the mockery of a trial was over, I helped Isak escape. We have been in hiding ever since."

"I see . . ."

"But I'm now very worried about Isak."

"Why is that?"

"I'm his caretaker. I'm the one who usually finds food and clothing and searches for new places for us to live temporarily until we feel it's time to move on for fear of being discovered. Since I'm nearing the end of my life, I worry about what will happen to him after I'm gone. As it is, my memory is starting to fail due to the lack of an adequate electric charge. I'm starting to forget important details about the past. Details that could help exonerate Isak's name."

"How is it that Isak is also still alive after all this time?"

"That's *my* fault."

"What? *Why?*"

"After immortality was discovered on Thrae, thirteen hundred years ago, I was able to obtain a few doses of the serum. I tricked him into trying it. Isak got violently ill. I thought I had killed him. He forgave me eventually. In the end, the serum interacted with his new mechanical self to cause him to become a *natural* immortal. He didn't need the serum going forward. It was the strangest thing. After immortality and human hybrid technology was expunged from Thrae due to the spiraling adverse effects, essentially, history forgot about Isak."

"Then why do you still hide?"

"Out of fear, and shame, I guess. We also came to view ourselves as misfits."

"But why not explain things to the Thraen leaders? Surely, they will understand."

"I tried. Long ago, I reached out for help from Chancellor Sejus Theron, head of the World Council. To me, he was a sensitive deep thinker who cared greatly about all his people, unlike most bureaucrats. If anyone was going to help us, it was him. When he dismissed my story as a hoax and folklore, I decided to give up. I felt that Thrae had turned its collective backs on us. We were deemed to be expendable. So here we are . . ."

Atlas faded again, this time longer than usual. It looked to Jim like he would fall over. He reached over and grabbed Atlas, his arm and shoulder sparkling brightly.

"Are you OK?" asked Jim. By now Atlas had reappeared.

"Yes."

"Why is it that you sparkle when you touch things?"

"For us to operate in the physical world, scientists created *focused energy*. By thought alone, we can direct discrete electrical particles to become concentrated in specific areas such as the hands, arms, feet and legs. This allows us to perform physical activities. Otherwise, we can float through anything without fear of injury."

"That's pretty cool."

"It has its advantages."

Isak suddenly appeared through the trees. He gave the thumbs up.

"OK," smiled Atlas. "This is going to be our *new* temporary home. It's one we've used before. I'm the one who found it originally," he added proudly. "It's warm during the daytime and not too cold at night. Come, let me show you around."

"Sounds good," grinned Jim.

Markus, Chad, and the soldiers reached the first underground access point. First responders dressed in orange were assisting people as they exited up the underground stairs.

"Wait here," said Markus.

Chad surveyed the area for Molly and Jim as Markus walked up to a group of first responders. They talked briefly. When Markus came back, he appeared excited.

"They said an alien woman is being helped at the next access point. They also confirmed that she's in very good health. Let's go!"

Markus sent his monitoring orb on ahead as the group hurried toward the next underground access point. As they made their way around a large pile of debris, Chad noticed Markus's orb hovering above a large group of people. Sitting directly below it was Molly.

"Mom!" yelled Chad. He sprinted toward her. Molly jumped up and did the same. They embraced as if they had been separated for years.

"I was so worried about you," whispered Chad. He eventually stepped back and looked around. "Where's Dad?"

"I don't know," replied Molly, wiping away tears. She then looked at Markus.

"Thank you, Markus," she said.

"You're welcome," he nodded. "Although I must say, I really didn't do much of anything."

Suddenly, Markus closed his eyes and concentrated. When he reopened his eyes, they were filled with tears.

"Markus, what's wrong?" asked Molly.

"I just received an updated transmission from the activation database. Jim's imbedded clothing device failed to register a signal."

"What does that mean?"

"They were unable to detect a human heartbeat."

"So?" asked Chad, his heart racing.

Markus initially looked away. He then stared directly at Chad.

"Chad . . . I'm sorry — "

"It doesn't mean *anything*," interrupted Chad defiantly. "The devices aren't foolproof. You said so yourself."

Molly walked over to Chad and hugged him tightly as tears streamed down her cheeks.

CHAPTER FOURTEEN — THE PLOT THICKENS

In his darkened quarters, Lon stared blankly at the colored lights emanating from his computer hardware. He had just received news that two transport vessels on their way back to Mitel were all that's left of the Thraen blockade. Like everyone else, he was stunned and surprised to hear that the fleet had identified two Thraen Battle Spheres. And despite initiating defensive protocols, the cruisers were still destroyed.

That's how Liss did it, he thought. *He had the help of not one, but two Battle Spheres. But where did they come from and why didn't we know about them before now? The Battle Sphere defense protocols were obviously ineffective. My swarm maneuver and gravity control beam perimeter is the only proven method to incapacitate a Thraen sphere.*

Lon let out a long sigh.

Two spheres will represent a significantly more difficult task. Hopefully Falon Ross can neutralize one while I focus on the other.

Lon stood up and paced impatiently around his darkened quarters.

If it wasn't for Liss, I'd be Emperor right now. That traitor will pay with his life for what he's done. I will not rest until he's dead.

Lon's intercom beeped.

"Rexx here," he said, lunging for the button.

"The Mitel Leadership has instructed you to appear before them at day break tomorrow," said the voice.

"Did they say why?"

"No."

"OK, thank you." Lon let out another deep sigh after the intercom beeped a second time. He paced around his quarters with even more pent-up energy.

What do they want now? Crazy old fools. They probably want to discuss the failed blockade and the appearance of the two Battle Spheres. They have no idea what they are up against and how to defeat them. Only I do.

Lon eventually turned on his perimeter wall lighting and packed his duffle bag before flopping onto his bed for a restless night's sleep. As he drifted off, the lighting slowly dimmed and then turned itself off.

Early the next morning, Lon boarded a base hover craft which flew him straight to the Leadership complex. When he arrived, Lon was escorted up the wide marble staircase by two huge security guards. He followed them through the massive stone doors. As usual, the ten elderly Leadership members sat stoically behind the large, curved stone bench above the forum floor. As Lon approached, he was motioned to stop by the middle guard standing in front of the bench. The two guards that had accompanied him up the stairs took positions diagonally behind him.

"Commander Rexx," said the Leadership member seated directly across from him. "Thank you for coming."

"I am honored to be here," Lon replied. *I hope that at least sounded sincere,* he thought. *Frail, useless old men . . .*

"We have confirmed that another small pod arrived at Thrae quite recently. Were you aware of that?"

"No, I wasn't."

"The pod's distress beacon was very similar to that of the earlier pods."

"Zebulon Park must have returned to Thrae," replied Lon calmly. "He must have trained the new Battle Spheres to defeat our blockade."

"That is one possibility."

"What else could it be? Those Battle Spheres obviously were very proficient in taking out four of our best cruisers."

"It appears they had additional help. During the engagement, the commanders repeatedly referred to a renegade cruiser."

"The Mitel resistance . . ."

"That part appears certain."

"What happened to the renegade cruiser?"

"The commander of Cruiser number 2 launched two pods at it just before they themselves were destroyed, presumably by a Battle Sphere reported to be in the vicinity. Flight logs confirm that the renegade cruiser ceased all communications seconds later, followed by a complete loss of power. As the auxiliary power came on-line, the cruiser's logs abruptly terminated. Our forensic team has concluded the renegade cruiser was destroyed by either the pods or the Battle Sphere or both."

"What a waste. But it's better that it was destroyed rather than falling into enemy hands."

"You're right . . ."

"Now what?"

"We must retaliate before the Thraen forces regroup."

"How?"

"We are putting you in command of a fleet of eight cruisers accompanied by six transport vessels and a full accompaniment of supply and weapons craft."

"What about the Battle Spheres? They will surely confront us once we arrive."

"We understand. That is why we are sending *our* Battle Sphere ahead of you. She will draw them off long enough for you to begin a cluster barrage targeting their largest population centers. That will further distract the Thraen Battle Spheres. Hopefully, you can employ your gravity beam measures to capture one or both."

"Well, I . . ."

"*What* Commander Rexx? Last we spoke, you were quite confident that your method would incapacitate a Battle Sphere. *Are you less confident now?*"

Lon paused several seconds before answering.

"I am not less confident. But you are sending a young, untested Battle Sphere up against two experienced Thraen Spheres that just wiped out our blockade, *in the hopes of distracting them?*"

"Yes. She will buy you the time you need. We feel that your combined forces will be quite formidable. We want you to closely coordinate your attack plan with Falon Ross."

"But we will also face an unknown Thraen force."

"We have no reason to believe that the Thraens will mount a significant defense. Our plan is as follows: Falon Ross will arrive first. She will be instructed *not* to engage any Thraen vessels, at least initially."

"*Why not?*"

"We want her to head directly to the planet surface and draw the two Thraen Battle Spheres out into the open to confront her. Falon will use her concentrated fire power to catch them off guard. Since she is a Thraen Battle Sphere herself, they will be conflicted as to how to deal with her. Your force will arrive immediately thereafter and unleash a barrage of cluster pods at their population centers. If all goes well, Falon will inflict significant damage on one or both Thraen Battle Spheres. From there, you and Falon shall coordinate your efforts to crush the rebellion once and for all. Before returning, you will employ your enhanced gravity control beam system to incapacitate and capture one or both Thraen Battle Spheres."

"And if it doesn't work?"

"*It must work*!" a second member berated.

"Quiet please," motioned the first member. "We have a backup plan which we will reveal in due time Commander Rexx. In our opinion, this mission represents an opportunity for you to redeem yourself. Wouldn't you agree?"

"Yes," replied Lon hesitantly.

"*Good.* The mission will commence in three weeks' time."

"*Three weeks?*"

"That's correct. It is significantly much more time than the armada was given before leaving in search of the young Thraen immortal. It will allow you to plan and coordinate your strategy with Falon Ross. It will also allow you and your fellow cruiser commanders time to identify and target suspected Thraen resistance bases and related infrastructure. We must not allow the Thraen resistance any time to prepare a cohesive defense strategy."

"Understood."

"Do you have any questions, Commander Rexx?"

"No, not at the moment."

"Very well. You are free to go."

As Lon was escorted down the stairs, he mulled over the attack plan.

The mission plan is much too optimistic, he thought. *There are too many unknowns. The Thraens must have established at least some rudimentary form of deep space surveillance by now. If so, there goes the element of surprise. And even if they haven't, everything must come together in perfect sequence for the mission to succeed. That's never a good sign. I don't understand why Leadership would sacrifice so many vessels for that stupid planet. I will also have to work with that lunatic Battle Sphere. Good luck with that. And what is the 'backup' plan. They seem to have a lot of confidence in it, enough to throw away more of our spacecraft. I must contact my sources to discover what they might know. If I am to lead a rebellion, I must build a coalition while I still can . . .*

After the large stone doors closed, the first member looked around the room.

"Well?" he asked the rest of the members.

"I don't believe Rexx thinks much of our plan," replied a second member.

"Or of us," added a third member. "I don't trust him. I never have."

"I agree that we need to watch him very closely," replied the first member. "But it doesn't matter *what* he thinks about our mission or whether he agrees with it as long as he carries out his orders. Best case scenario, he returns triumphantly with one or more Thraen Battle Spheres in his possession."

"And the worst-case scenario?" asked a fourth member.

"Rexx is defeated and killed. It will represent one less problem for us to deal with. But the mission also buys us more time to bring the mechanical spheres on-line."

"Yes," replied a fifth and sixth member in unison while the remaining members nodded affirmatively.

"And while they're gone, it will provide us an opportunity to try the immortality serum our scientists have recently engineered," explained the first member.

"What if the serum doesn't work?" asked the second member.

"What have we got to lose?"

"Our lives . . ."

"We are already old men," scoffed the first member. "There isn't that much life left to lose. Does anyone disagree?"

The forum hall was quiet.

"Good. I will make the final arrangements."

Later that evening, Lon again sat silently in his darkened officer's quarters. This time he was seated in front of his computer and large split-screen monitor. Suddenly, the faces of several Cruiser commanders appeared across the monitor.

"Fellow commanders, thank you for joining me," said Lon. "None of us are satisfied with the actions being taken by the Mitel Leadership. These frail old men, who have never seen even a *minute* of military engagement, continue to send us out to slaughter. The time has come for us to decide whether we will accept our fate or begin preparations to take charge of our own future."

Nobody spoke for several seconds.

"Rexx," said one commander eventually. "You are talking about a rebellion. That is a *very* dangerous game. In fact, we are all risking our lives just participating in this meeting."

A few of the other commanders nodded in agreement.

"Relax," Lon sneered. "This communications channel employs the most advanced encryption software on the planet."

"We had all better hope so."

"Getting back to the *rebellion* as you so fittingly called it, what other options do we have?"

"I'm not saying that we have any at the moment."

"*At the moment*?" replied Lon impatiently. "If we don't do something, and do it soon, we will all find ourselves floating around the universe in very small pieces."

"Enough with the dramatics Rexx," said a second commander. "We all understand our current predicament. That's why we're here. The question is: how do we pull off a successful coup?"

"I have been thinking about this for a long time. I had almost a full year to do so as we traveled in search of the young Thraen immortal and then all the way back home."

"And?"

"We need to form a coalition."

"Between whom?"

"It must be broad in scope. We will need to secure the allegiance of as many Special Forces units as possible. We will also need the Leadership complex guards to join us. A cousin of mine is married to one of them. I have become friendly with him. Just think: the guards have the ability to eliminate, or at the very least, allow us to kill the entire Leadership in their own chambers."

"What motivation would they have for doing so?" grunted a third commander. "They are very well compensated for their loyalty not to mention the threat of harm to their families in the event they do not comply."

"That's a very good question," replied Lon. "In my opinion, we need to show them three things."

"*Which are*?"

"That our plan has a very high probability of success; that we will financially compensate them beyond their wildest dreams for their change of loyalty; and that our coalition is sufficiently broad enough to insure that there is not a second rebellion in response to our takeover."

"They can't *all* be bought Rexx," hissed the first commander.

"And that goes double for Special Forces commanders," added the second commander.

"Then we will have to convince them that it will be for the greater good of the Mitel people and the safety of their families. Either that, or we target them for elimination during our takeover."

There was another silence.

"We will also need to secure the loyalty of the young female Battle Sphere," Lon continued.

"But she is Thraen," said a fourth commander. "She can never be trusted."

"I'm not so sure," Lon mused. "And besides, I've been told that her family is being held hostage in a secret location. I will find out where. If we seize them, that will insure her loyalty. At least for as long as we require it."

"And then?"

"We kill her," smiled Lon.

"I think Rexx is on to something," said a fifth commander. "If we can put together a broad-based coalition, the plan should work. And as Lon said, if we do nothing, we will all eventually die defending the Mitel Leadership. I lost two brothers on that wild goose chase across the universe. Only two of our spacecrafts made it back."

"That's all true," Lon replied. "By sheer luck, I was one of the fortunate survivors. Look. This is going to take some time and delicate planning. But the sooner we start the better. I am scheduled to meet in secret with a few

Special Forces commanders that I know are sympathetic to our cause. Then I must head to Thrae with some of you to crush the Thraen rebellion once and for all. Hopefully we will all return safely and go from there."

"*Another mission to Thrae?*" asked the first commander.

"Yes," scoffed Lon. "The Leadership is obsessed with that planet and their secrets of immortality. I've been told that the secret or *blueprint* no longer exists. I for one have neither the time nor the patience to sit around and wait for them to die off and see what happens. I also don't want to wait around for them to send me off to my death. In any event, if the secret meetings go as planned, I will approach my cousin's husband. My sense is that he will join us. He can then help convince the rest of the Leadership guards to join our cause. This newly formed coalition will win over a majority of the regular Mitel forces. But first, I need to know that all of you *and* your crews are with me."

"My crew will do what I tell them," said the first commander.

"So will mine," added the second commander.

"Mine too," added the third.

"Good," nodded Lon. "Are you all with me?"

"Yes," replied the commanders in unison.

"You will need to meet with Adrian Sidd," said the first commander.

"*Who's he?*"

"He is a retired Special Forces Senior Commander and one of the wealthiest people on the planet. Spanning several generations, his family amassed a fortune in weapons development, procurement, and sales. That's before the Leadership seized all their manufacturing facilities."

"Strange that I've never heard of him before . . ."

"Well, without his involvement, the coalition will go nowhere."

"Can you arrange a meeting?"

"Yes."

"Excellent," smiled Lon, "set one up as soon as possible."

"I'll see what I can do. He's a very busy guy."

"Let me know and thank you all."

With that his monitor went black.

CHAPTER FIFTEEN – ON THE MOVE

When Jim awoke the next morning, he stared at the many long, thin tree leaves up above him. His forehead still ached, but not as bad as the day before. He rolled over on his foam cot to see Isak sitting against his backpack reading a hologram book. Isak's big hands almost covered the small book which amused Jim.

"Good morning," said Jim.

Isak looked up from his book and waved.

He's a giant, thought Jim.

Just then Atlas appeared through the foliage carrying his backpack. It seemed fuller than normal.

"I found food and clothes," he announced. "The good news is there is a *lot* of food available right now. The bad news is that it's going to spoil very quickly. And once it's gone, it's gone. More bad news: all my usual sources of food have been destroyed."

"If you don't mind my asking," Jim began, "where do you go to find *food*?"

"I've made friends over the years with older holograms like myself who now work in food shops and food incinerators. Some of the food is quite good. You just have to pick through it. I *never* steal food."

Atlas put down his backpack.

"I noticed emergency crews have begun removing debris from underground shelter access points," he said.

"Can you get into the shelters from here?" asked Jim.

"Not typically. The underground shelters are located beneath our corridor network. Since the corridors were not constructed to the same high standards, they are considered a liability to connect to. There are a few special access bulkheads."

"Have you ever used them?"

"Not yet."

Atlas then turned to Isak.

"I saw more signs of them," he said.

Isak put down his book and quickly stood up. He mouthed several words to Atlas.

"I think we are OK for now, but that could change."

"What's wrong?" asked Jim. "Did you see evidence of the Scavengers?"

"I'm afraid so."

Isak mouthed several more words to Atlas.

"I think that is a great idea."

"What is?" asked Jim.

"Isak wants to teach you self-defense."

"What *me*?"

"Yes, you. In case we are attacked, you need to help fend them off rather than becoming a liability to us."

"Makes sense, I guess."

"How about we start after breakfast?"

"That sounds good. Right now, I'm hungry."

After breakfast, Isak stood in front of Jim. The big man was surprisingly communicative with his body and hand motions. Although Jim was tall and physically fit, Isak was over a foot taller and weighed well over one hundred pounds more than Jim. As he watched the two, Atlas immediately sensed Jim's trepidation.

"It's not always how big you are, but how well you fight," offered Atlas.

"You're reading my mind," replied Jim somewhat apprehensively.

Isak flashed an amused expression as he gently patted Jim's shoulder. He then showed Jim how to stand as though he had a pole running through the top of his head down through his body. The objective was to pivot with the shoulders, using minimum motion in close combat situations. Isak tried to impress upon Jim that while size and weight matter during a fight, the important thing was to maintain balance, use key defensive moves and always be ready to counterattack. Always.

Defensively, Isak had Jim practice positioning his head downward to minimize direct blows to more fragile areas such as his nose and jaw. He taught Jim how to contain an attacker's arm that grabbed him by restricting its movement at the elbow. Atlas also showed Jim how to turn side to side to avoid blows and to raise his hands and arms close to his own body to deflect punches.

"Minimum movement," said Atlas occasionally.

Offensively, Isak instructed Jim how to punch the throat when given a clear shot. Isak showed Jim how to strike effectively and repeatedly with an open palm, and how to use his elbow to chop down on an opponent and even gouge eyes if necessary. They practiced until Jim was exhausted.

"I think you have some potential!" exclaimed Atlas.

To Jim, Isak was physically intimidating. He could almost feel the mechanical parts of his arms, legs and shoulders. He knew deep down that Isak could probably kill him with little effort. Near the end of the practice session, Jim unexpectedly shoved Isak off balance.

"Whoo hoo!" shouted Atlas. "Nice move!"

For the first time, Jim saw Isak smile as he reached over and patted Jim on the back.

"OK," said Atlas. "That's enough for today. It's time for the two of you to get something to eat."

As they ate, Jim noticed that Atlas had not faded away the entire day. When he mentioned it, Atlas responded "I have good days and bad days I guess."

Afterward, they sat around and listened to Atlas tell many stories of when he was Isak's Battle Hologram commander. Jim listened intently while Isak occasionally clapped his big hands together and grunted in delight.

As it grew dark, a perimeter light came on near the dome. It reminded Jim of moonlight. By now, he was very tired from all the training. Jim stretched out on his cot and fell into a deep sleep.

Over the next few days, Jim and Isak trained right after breakfast. Isak enjoyed the exercise and Jim could feel his confidence growing. He realized how his low center of gravity helped contain a much bigger opponent. Isak continually challenged Jim to counter attack whenever possible.

"You must always counterattack," urged Atlas.

Isak also showed Jim how to use a long pole, which was the weapon of choice for most Scavengers. He taught Jim how to use it to his advantage during a fight; how to avoid and deflect the pole's blows; and techniques to quickly wrestle the object away from an attacker's hands in close combat situations.

In time, Jim's favorite move became a shoulder and head twist to avoid a punch followed immediately by open palm counter punches. As time went on, Isak held back less and less. Jim learned how to take a hit and still relentlessly counterattack.

"OK, OK, enough for today," smiled Atlas.

By now, both Jim and Isak were exhausted.

As he lay on his cot later, Jim tried to remember details from his past.

Why can't I remember anything? he wondered. *Who am I? Are people looking for me? Do they want to help me or capture me?*

Getting anxious, Jim rolled over and tried to go to sleep. He tossed and turned for over an hour before eventually falling into a restless sleep. Jim then dreamt that he was suspended in water. He couldn't breathe or get to the surface. Looking up above, he saw a shimmering orb with a monitoring screen on it. Jim reached desperately toward it for help before the orb suddenly disappeared. He panicked as he knew he was about to drown.

Jim sat up in his cot, his heart pounding.

"It was all a dream," he told himself. Looking around the opening Jim saw Isak sleeping nearby. Atlas was gone.

Probably out looking for food.

As he sat there, Jim was again haunted by his loss of memory.

Who am I? Where am I from? What is my past and what did that dream mean?

Jim was now sweating profusely.

I need fresh air.

He quietly got up and put on his backpack. He glanced at Isak as he silently made his way across the opening to a corridor door. As Jim exited, he propped the door open with a small stick. He made mental notes as he walked down one corridor to the next. Jim eventually came to a blackened door that led to two flights of stairs going up. He reached down, grabbed a chunk of debris lying on the ground next to the door, and placed it in the doorjamb to keep the door ajar. He then glanced up the stairwell.

They must lead to the surface, he thought.

Reaching the top of the double flight of stairs, Jim stared down a long, darkened corridor. Off in the distance was a well-lit opening. After his eyes adjusted to the darkness, Jim cautiously made his way toward the light. Reaching the entrance, he slowly stepped out onto a deserted elevated walkway. Looking up, he saw two full moons shining down at him. Small puffy clouds, illuminated by the moonlight, moved silently across the night sky.

Jim took a long deep breath of fresh air before cautiously walking along the walkway. Once again, he made mental notes as to the location of the passageway leading to the stairs. As he walked along, badly damaged and collapsed structures were everywhere.

Jim eventually stopped in front of another passageway. Sensing a large opening, Jim slowly walked toward it. Down the passageway to his left was a large room with no roof, the bright moonlight illuminating the entire opening. Inside the room were several piles of debris. It was eerily quiet. As Jim surveyed the destruction, something in a pile of rubble off in the corner caught his eye. As he cautiously approached it, he realized a person was lying in the debris. As he slowly approached, Jim realized that it was a young girl buried up to her chest in twisted metal and stone. Her upper body, face and hair were completely covered in a thick layer of dust.

Jim slowly knelt next to the young girl, the light of the moon illuminating her upper body. Although he knew she was dead, she looked like a sleeping statue. He then noticed that she was wearing a loose-fitting top that appeared handmade.

I bet she was a Scavenger. Maybe she was out looking for food after the pod strike when the roof collapsed.

He stared at her for a long time, the passing clouds occasionally causing the moonlight to fade in and out.

She's kind of like me, he thought. *No identity and now lost forever.*

Staring at her, Jim was suddenly overcome with emotion. He cried, his shoulders heaving violently. After a while, he pulled himself together, wiping the tears from his face. Jim took off his backpack and pulled out a small blanket. He carefully placed it over the young girl's face and torso. He then rummaged through his backpack a second time until he found the synthetic yellow flower he had taken from the corridor bathroom. He gently placed the flower on top of the blanket. Jim sat next to the young girl for several minutes, occasionally staring up through the opening at the moons and clouds.

I've got to figure out who I am, and then try to help end the Scavenger crisis, he thought. *Nobody should die alone like this, especially a young defenseless girl.*

Jim gently touched the blanket one more time before forcing himself back up. He then put on his backpack and slowly made his way out of the room, glancing back one last time at the blanket and flower before heading down the long dark passageway to the walkway. He stopped and quickly glanced both ways. It was still deserted.

I should get back, he thought.

Jim retraced his steps to the first passageway, down the two sets of stairs to the blackened door he had left slightly ajar. He kicked the debris toward the stairs and closed the door tightly behind him. He then hurried down the corridors to the second door. It was also still ajar. Jim quietly walked into the opening. He noticed that Isak was still sleeping, and Atlas had not yet returned.

Jim slowly took off his backpack and silently lay back down on his cot.

I probably shouldn't tell Isak and Atlas I ventured out to-night, he concluded. *Leaving the doors open was probably not the smartest thing to do. Scavengers could have snuck in here and taken our supplies . . . or worse . . .*

As he lay there, Jim could not get rid of the image of the young girl lying in the rubble, the moons illuminating her dust covered body. Tears streamed down his cheeks as he stared across the opening for a time. He eventually drifted back off to sleep.

As Jim slept, Molly sat alone in her quarters looking up at the moons. She wondered if Jim was somewhere safe, or even still alive, tears running down her cheeks.

The next morning, in the underground base cafeteria, Chad stared dejectedly at his protein drink. Luna, Susan and Molly sat silently across from him. Chad was realizing how much he missed Melissica. Molly was lost in thought, worrying about Jim, and thinking about their shared life.

She would hug me and tell me everything will be OK, thought Chad. *I wish she was here.*

So many memories, Molly thought. She wiped the tears from her face.

Just then, Janus and Markus appeared in the doorway accompanied by Markus's hovering monitoring orb. They walked over and sat down on either side of Chad.

"How is the lad doing today?" asked Markus.

"Not good," replied Molly. "None of us are."

"I'm truly sorry," said Janus. "I wish I could have done more to prevent what happened."

"I'm the one who told him to go," said Molly, "first to Thrae and then to Amer that day."

"It's not your fault Molly," replied Markus. "Jim was so excited to visit our population centers. He talked about it constantly."

Chad cleared his throat.

"I'm not going to give up looking for him. Not until they find a body," he said resolutely.

"I'm sorry lad," responded Markus, "but after a cluster pod detonation, there really isn't much left to find. That's why they use tracking devices. It helps the survivors get closure."

Chad's face turned red with frustration and anger.

Markus suddenly froze and closed his eyes. He raised his finger for everyone to be quiet. When he opened his eyes, he looked directly at Molly.

"They found Jim's identification badge in the rubble outside an underground entrance door."

"He was trying to get in," replied Molly sadly.

Tears welled up in her eyes.

"That's what I was thinking," nodded Markus.

"But they didn't find a body?" asked Chad.

"No . . . "

"Then I'm *not* giving up. I'm going to keep looking for him. Markus, can you bring me to where they found the badge?"

"Yes, but —"

"Like *right now*?"

"OK. Let's go."

Chad and Markus traveled by hover craft back to the underground access stairway. Hover cranes, loaders and hover transport craft were busy removing debris from ground zero. Chad stood at the top steps and surveyed the scene. He then looked toward the sky.

What would I have done? he thought.

Chad walked briskly toward the next access point followed by Markus. A man dressed in orange raised his hands as they approached.

"You can't go any farther," he said. "The demolition crews are everywhere."

Chad reached into his pocket and showed the man his Thraen base identification.

"We're looking for a missing resistance fighter," Chad explained.

The man stared at the badge for a moment.

"OK," he replied. "But be careful."

As they kept walking, Markus looked at Chad.

"Looking for a resistance fighter?"

"Hey, it worked, didn't it?"

At the next underground access point, Chad stopped and looked around again.

"What are you doing?" asked Markus.

"I'm deciding what to do?"

"What?"

"If I was looking for shelter knowing a missile was about to hit, I'm trying to decide where I would go."

Chad walked further. Out of the corner of his eye, he saw something. It was a passageway covered mostly by debris.

"Markus, could you look in there?"

"Sure thing," he replied. Markus's hologram disappeared through the rubble to a set of stairs filled with chunks of debris. He made his way down one, and then a second flight of stairs to a blackened door. Pieces of debris were everywhere. He noticed a few dents in the door. There also wasn't a handle on the outside.

The debris must have caused the dents, he thought.

Markus looked back up the stairs before sticking his head through the door. To his surprise he saw a long hallway with ceiling lights every few hundred yards. Bundles of different sized wires and conduits covered the ceiling. Between the lights, the hallway was dark.

Markus passed through the door and floated several yards down the hallway. Along the way, he saw dirty clothes lying on the ground. He then poked his head through a side door. He then reached his left arm through the door and temporarily enabled focused energy in his left hand to illuminate the room. Markus noticed a simple shower and toilet.

Odd, he thought.

He looked down the long corridor again before heading back to Chad.

"Well?" asked Chad as Markus reappeared through the pile of debris.

"There is a stairway leading to a long subterranean passageway. It must be accessed *at least* occasionally as I saw some dirty clothes lying on the ground outside a makeshift bathroom."

"Do you think Dad could have gone in there?"

"The door doesn't open from the outside."

"Maybe he had help."

"Chad, I —"

"*Maybe he had help,*" repeated Chad stubbornly.

"Maybe he did."

"We've got to keep looking for him."

"In order to have survived, Jim would need to have found adequate shelter near the location of his badge."

"Why don't we check out the passageway?"

"It was pretty desolate down there Chad. Besides, if he was there, don't you think he would have come back out by now?"

"Maybe he doesn't know that it's safe to come out."

"He's going to need food and water."

"I know . . ."

"From what I understand, the corridor network runs underneath the entire population center. If he's down there, maybe Jim will exit somewhere else. In the meantime, let's continue searching the area close to where they found his badge, OK?"

"OK . . ."

Chad and Markus spent the next four hours looking for any sign of Jim. They searched the two underground access points in every direction in an expanding grid pattern. Along the way, they located more entrances to the underground corridor network. Each time they did, Chad had Markus float through the debris down to the blackened entry door. Markus poked his head through the door, called out Jim's name and listened for a response. Each time he returned to the surface; Chad's hopeful expression turned to disappointment.

When they returned to the base, Chad was greeted by Molly and Janus. From the sad look on Chad's face, Molly knew they had found nothing.

"There must be more we can do," urged Chad. "How about putting out a missing person's report?"

"That feature is available as a menu option on the holographic news feed," contemplated Markus.

"Really?" asked Chad.

"Chad, I don't mean to come across as callous," replied Janus. "There are literally thousands of missing persons. We can't expect any kind of special treatment in this case, nor do we deserve it. Countless families are suffering the same way we are."

Chad thought for a moment.

"But he's an alien, right? Isn't that *special* news? A missing alien caught up in the Mitel cluster pod attack?"

"It's worth a try," urged Molly. "Isn't it?"

"OK, OK," replied Janus. "I'll see what I can do."

To his surprise, the news service took interest in the story and agreed to stream a missing person narrative and posting a prominent picture of Jim on their separate missing person sub feed.

"If nothing else," said one staff member, "It will bring more awareness to the plight of all the missing, not to mention the shared suffering."

"Hopefully it will help us unite and heal as a people," added another.

"I can't thank you enough," said Janus to the staff.

That night, Atlas went back to a badly damaged clothing store. The structure was unsafe and might collapse.

As long as it doesn't shift or fall down when I'm using my focused energy, I have nothing to fear, thought Atlas. *I can float right through the debris.*

He floated up to the second level. Dust and debris were everywhere. Sifting through all the clothes and other supplies, Atlas felt a twinge of guilt.

It's all going to be thrown away anyway, he rationalized. *Either that or it will be ruined by the elements eventually.*

Atlas found a large backpack for Jim. He then filled it with the clothes he had picked out for both Jim and Isak.

OK, now the tricky part, he thought.

Atlas pulled the backpack through the crevices in the badly damaged structure. He was now using his focused energy in his arms, putting himself at risk. A few times along the way he thought he heard the building creak and settle. Once outside, he looked up and down the walkway. It was quiet. A strong breeze blew across the now deserted population center. A minute later, it rained.

As Atlas made his way back toward an underground entrance, he suddenly had the feeling he was being watched. He put down his backpack and quickly looked around the perimeter. He noticed silhouettes moving near piles of debris.

Scavengers, he thought.

Atlas knew they would not attack a human hologram. But he feared they would follow him back to Isak and Jim. Atlas picked up the backpack and floated as quickly as he could to another corridor entrance much farther away. He rushed down the steps, reached through the large, blackened door, and using his focused energy, turned the L-shaped handle. Opening it, Atlas entered the hallway and quickly closed the door tight behind him. He used the same technique to open an adjacent makeshift shower room door. He then closed that door behind him and listened silently until he heard noises outside the large, blackened door. The door was being pried open. He then heard the Scavengers enter the hallway. They paused briefly outside his door before making their way down the long corridor.

After a while, Atlas slowly poked his head through the door and peered down the hallway. There was no sign of the Scavengers. He grabbed his backpack and headed out the large, blackened door and up the stairs. At the top, Atlas looked around. He saw no one nor did he have the same feeling of being watched as before. He quickly set out toward his original entrance point. As he entered the circular area, he could hear the rain pelting against the acrylic dome. Since Isak seemed happier than he had been in a long time, Atlas decided not to tell him about the Scavengers.

I'll just keep a lookout, that's all, he thought. *I technically don't need sleep anyway. It's just a way to conserve my electric charge.*

The next morning, sunshine streaked through the now clear acrylic dome. Jim and Isak practiced again, Isak practicing defensive techniques and counterattacks. He mouthed something to Jim. For the first time, he actually understood what Isak said.

Be decisive. Every second counts.

Jim nodded, smiled, and redoubled his efforts. At the end of their session, Isak smiled and nodded his approval.

That night, after Jim and Isak had fallen asleep, Atlas floated up one of the long corridors looking for any signs of the Scavengers.

Nothing.

Every now and then, Atlas faded in and out.

Not a good day today, he thought.

Atlas floated down another hallway, poking his head through side doors.

Still nothing.

He eventually went up an entrance stairway to look around.

I need to find out if they're still searching for us.

He floated through the large, blackened entry door, then up two long flights of stairs to the narrow passageway. When he reached the walkway, he saw several Scavengers walking toward him. It was too late to hide. Instead of fleeing back down the passageway, Atlas glided onto the walkway. The Scavenger closest to him pulled out his knife and pointed it toward Atlas. As others yelled loudly, he then sprinted directly at Atlas who did not move. The Scavenger thrust his knife repeatedly at Atlas to no avail. It was like trying to kill a ghost. When the Scavenger stopped, Atlas activated his focused energy in his arms and feet. He grabbed the Scavenger by the neck and tossed him across the walkway into a pile of debris like a rag doll. It was a painful lesson for the novice ruffian. Living Holograms possess exceptional, almost lethal strength. A second more experienced Scavenger rushed Atlas with a metal pole. He knew that living holograms were only vulnerable when their focused energy is activated. As he reached Atlas, he swung the pole with all his might. Atlas reached out and grabbed onto the pole, abruptly stopping it in mid swing. He jerked the pole out of the Scavenger's hand. He then bent it in half before tossing it to the ground with a loud clang. Before the Scavenger could run, Atlas grabbed him by the arm and tossed him through the air into the same pile of rubble. The man landed with a thud.

Atlas then looked at the others who stood frozen in fear.

"Leave us alone!" shouted Atlas. "Now *go!*"

He floated toward the group of Scavengers. They quickly ran off into the night. Atlas turned and stared at the two men lying limp on the pile of rubble. For all he knew, they were dead.

That is the price they pay for threatening me, he thought. *If they try to hurt my friends, I'll do the same without hesitation.*

Atlas looked down the walkway one last time before making his way back down the stairway to the corridor.

Atlas didn't know that a small group of Scavengers had noticed Jim, Atlas and Isak when they peered down through the acrylic dome earlier that evening. When they got word of the human hologram encounter, they notified the larger Scavenger group what they had seen. The group's leaders were eager to exact their revenge.

When Atlas returned to the circular enclosure, Jim and Isak were sleeping on their cots.

They're vulnerable, he thought.

Atlas floated over to several tall bushes and silently kept a lookout for any trouble. As time passed, he had mixed feelings about his confrontation with the Scavengers.

It was unnecessary, he thought. *It only puts Isak and the alien in more danger. I should have stayed down in the corridors.*

He then looked around the circular enclosure.

We still would have crossed paths eventually, he rationalized.

Atlas kept the encounter with the Scavengers to himself. The next morning, before Isak and Jim trained, Atlas suggested that it was time to move on to the next location.

Why? I like it here, mouthed Isak.

"It's important that we keep moving," replied Atlas. "And besides, the food is starting to run out."

Isak waved his arm dismissively.

That night, after Jim and Isak had fallen asleep, Atlas floated up and down the long corridors looking for any signs of the Scavengers.

I know they are close, he thought. *I can feel it.* He headed back to the circular enclosure. At that instant, Jim was having another bad dream. In it, he was lying in a tight rectangular box with long silver nails pointing down at him. One nail was up close against his neck. He didn't know how to move or what to do. Jim awoke to see a Scavenger crouched over him, holding a long knife against his throat.

Just as he was taught, Jim swung his left hand up along his body and swatted the knife away. With his right hand, he hit the Scavenger in the face with open palm blows. The Scavenger groaned and fell to one side, his nose bleeding profusely. Looking up, Jim saw several more Scavengers standing nearby.

"Isak, Atlas!" he shouted, scrambling to his feet. Several Scavengers rushed toward him. Out of the corner of his eye, Jim saw Isak race out of the darkness. His eyes flashing metallic green, Isak used a brutal elbow chop to down one rushing attacker while punching another in the face repeatedly. Both men crumpled lifeless to the ground.

Before he could react, Jim was grabbed tightly by the shirt. Using his right arm to contain the attacker's arm, Jim lowered his head just before being punched in the forehead and ear. The pain was intense, but Jim kept his focus and deflected the next punch with his left arm. The Scavenger then tried to shove Jim off balance, but he held firm. Jim deflected one punch, then another. Seeing an opening, he punched the Scavenger squarely in the throat, dropping him to the ground.

A wild punch from another Scavenger hit Jim squarely in the side of the head. He staggered but kept his center of gravity. Two Scavengers grabbed him before one was pulled off and pummeled by Isak. When the second Scavenger took his eye off Jim for an instant, he hit him in the face repeatedly with his open palm, dropping him. Jim saw another Scavenger lunging toward him with a right hook punch. He automatically turned his shoulder to avoid the punch altogether. As the Scavenger's momentum caused him to continue forward, Jim hit him in the neck with an elbow chop. He heard a cracking noise as the Scavenger fell limp to the ground. Jim, now tired, looked ahead toward the next attacker.

Suddenly, Atlas appeared through an entrance door with a blood curdling scream. The remaining Scavengers turned and ran as fast as they could out the same door they entered, disappearing down the corridor. Just like that, the fight was over. Atlas, Jim and Isak surveyed the scene. Several Scavengers lay unconscious on the ground. A few others quietly moaned but didn't move.

"Isak, are you OK?" asked Atlas. "I'm so sorry I left. I was out scouting."

Isak waved to Atlas he was OK. He then looked at Jim and grinned.

Nice job, he mouthed.

Jim could feel his heart racing. His head and ear hurt badly as Atlas floated over to check on him.

"Your ear and forehead, you're bleeding pretty good," he said. "Let me get you something."

Atlas glided over to his backpack and returned with a hand-held device. He activated it, causing one end to glow bright blue. Atlas administered absorption pain relievers around each wound.

"Give it a minute," he said.

Isak reached over and touched Atlas's shoulder. As he turned around, Isak mouthed instructions.

"OK," replied Atlas. "Let's pack up quickly and get moving. The other Scavengers will return soon and this time with electro laser weapons."

The trio hastily packed up their belongings and quickly headed toward the perimeter wall.

"That door," Atlas pointed.

With his long pole ready, Isak opened the door and peered down the long corridor. It was empty. He motioned to Atlas and Jim to follow. On his way out, Jim glanced back through the foliage at the motionless Scavengers lying on the ground. He adjusted his backpack then closed the door behind him. As they silently made their way down the hallway, Jim looked at Atlas.

"Where are we going?" he asked.

"This corridor, or should I say *series of corridors*, will take us to a hyper-speed electromagnetic railway tunnel. We'll follow the tunnel to the surface."

"Isn't that *dangerous*?"

"No. That section of the hyper loop hasn't been used since the last Mitel invasion. When we exit the tunnel, the terrain is pretty much unpopulated. We'll then follow the surface loop to Pisco. We'll either camp there or continue to Timad. Both population centers have underground networks very similar to Amer."

Twenty minutes later, they exited the corridor into the more dimly lit hyper speed tunnel. Below them, two hyper loop channels were sandwiched between eight-foot-tall rectangular structures. On one side, the structure provided a positive conducting current. The opposite side supplied a negative conducting charge. When operational, the currents created opposing magnetic fields that pushed the high-speed trains along the hyper loop channel. Jim and Isak swung themselves down onto the left channel. Atlas simply floated down.

"This way," he pointed.

The tunnel slowly curved around before straightening out. A few miles off in the distance, daylight was visible. As he walked along, Jim replayed the previous night's fight in his mind. He was proud of how he held his own against the Scavengers. But he also had a nagging feeling he was part of something else.

I'm an alien after all, he thought.

Isak, with his longer stride, slowly moved ahead of Jim. Atlas kept glancing back to make sure Jim was OK. Eventually he drifted back next to him.

"Are you OK?" he asked.

Although Jim's head and ear still hurt, he replied yes.

"Good," replied Atlas "I've been thinking . . ."

"About *what*?"

Atlas paused before answering.

"How you could look after Isak. *I mean,* after I'm gone."

"It looks to me like Isak can take care of himself."

"You don't know him like I do."

"Did you ask him? Maybe Isak doesn't want anyone looking after him."

"There are things he can do and things he can't."

"I think that pretty much describes every living creature, doesn't it?"

Atlas laughed. "You are correct, it does."

CHAPTER SIXTEEN – A CLUE

After another grueling day of flight training, Susan was given a much-needed day off. Entering the cafeteria that morning, she noticed Molly sitting alone staring at her breakfast. Susan walked over to her.

"Hi," she said. "OK if I join you?"

Molly looked up.

"Sure," she replied.

Sitting down, Susan noticed that Molly looked exhausted and sad.

"How is your flight training going?" asked Molly.

"It's going very well, thank you. But forget about that. Is there any update on Jim?"

"No," replied Molly glumly. "It's so frustrating. I feel utterly useless at this point."

"It must be an awful feeling. I wish there was something I could do to help."

Susan then got an idea.

"Hey," she said. "Today's my day off. I've already been cleared to fly hover crafts on my own. How about we go back to Amer and look around for Jim?"

Molly face brightened.

"That would be great," she replied.

"OK great. I'll grab something quick to eat. We can get ready to leave right after that."

Less than an hour later, the two climbed into a medium sized military hover craft. They were accompanied by a heavily armed hologram soldier who had volunteered to have the English translation software imbedded into his hologram architecture. Susan looked at Molly.

"I was instructed to bring him along just in case," she explained. She then turned to the soldier. "Thank you."

"My pleasure, and *thank you*," smiled the soldier. "I hear you have impressed Squadron Commander Decker. That's not an easy thing to do."

Susan entered the coordinates for Amer into the flight computer and powered up the hover craft. Sixteen curved clear retractable overlapping roof sections closed tightly above them as the craft took off. They exited through an auxiliary tunnel into the bright sunshine. Susan banked to her left, flying directly over Lake Victoria and headed south. Off in the distance, they caught the gleaming reflection of the Assal sky structure. Molly then turned her attention to the majestic Micron mountain range off in the distance, their peaks still covered in glistening white snow.

As the hover craft flew along, Molly and Susan studied the foliage below. Occasionally, Susan checked her controls and readouts to make sure everything looked normal. Molly again stared at the mushroom and carrot shaped trees, with their unusually shaped branches up on top. As they flew over it, Molly remembered the wide and shallow river filled with circular sand dunes as far as the eye could see. On the opposite side of the river, Susan banked right and headed toward Amer.

As they approached the population center, the familiar clusters of circular dome-like structures and underground shelter entrances dotted the landscape. Looking off in the distance, Molly noticed the crater like area at the direct center of Amer. The rising dust cloud had since disappeared. As they got closer, other types, sizes and shapes of hover craft and transport vessels flew above and below their craft in various preprogrammed directions.

Entering the population center, Susan banked the craft gently to the left. The craft was scanned, identified and allowed admittance.

"Maybe his tracking devices are working again," said Susan. "I think we should scan the entire area just in case."

"Sounds good," nodded Molly.

Susan made several passes over the impact zone, repeatedly scanning the surface for any signs of Jim. Nothing. As Molly surveyed the wreckage, tears welled up in her eyes.

How could he have possibly survived that? she thought.

Molly wiped away the tears and pushed the negative thoughts from her mind. As Susan flew over a large acrylic dome, Molly pointed down at it.

"What's that?" she asked.

"It's an old underground maintenance hub," explained the soldier. "Pretty much abandoned at this point. It connects to a bunch of underground hallways once used to service older technology cables and conduits."

"Maybe he sought refuge there."

"It's possible."

"Let's go down and look around," suggested Susan.

"OK," replied Molly.

Susan headed to a makeshift landing area designated for military craft. As she approached, a hologram soldier on the ground directed Susan where to land.

After powering down the craft, the clear retractable overlapping roof sections opened and the trio exited a sliding side door. The hologram soldier quickly looked at Susan.

"Let's be careful," he said. "Everything here is still a bit unstable."

"Do you mean the buildings, or are you referring to everyone's personal safety?"

"Both."

The soldier drew his electro laser long weapon. With one hand on the trigger, he carried it in front of him as a precaution.

"Understood," replied Susan.

They walked silently toward ground zero. Reaching the entry checkpoint, Susan and the soldier flashed their IDs.

"She's with us," said the soldier, motioning toward Molly.

They made their way to the same elevated walkway Jim was on just before the blast. They walked along until they reached the now bent diamond shaped sign next to the stairway where Jim's identification badge was found. At the bottom, the entry door was sealed shut. The trio surveyed the area for a brief time. A few Thraens could be seen walking off in the distance. The continuous sound of hover cranes, loaders and hover transport craft removing piles of debris could be heard in the distance. Otherwise, it was eerily desolate.

"Let's go this way," pointed Molly.

They walked until they saw a second diamond shaped sign. The stairs led down to the same sealed entry door.

Molly kept walking. Out of the corner of her eye, she saw a narrow passageway between two badly damaged structures. She stopped and studied it closely. Although the passageway was littered with debris, it was passable. She looked up and down the walkway before entering the passageway.

"Where are you going?" asked Susan.

"Jim had to find shelter somewhere. Maybe it was here."

When she reached a long set of stairs, she stopped and examined them.

"It leads to the old underground hallway system I was talking about," said the soldier.

"Let's go," she instructed.

Molly headed down the stairs followed by the others. Reaching the bottom, she turned and descended the second flight of stairs. At the bottom was the dented blackened door without a handle. Pieces of debris were everywhere.

"Allow me," offered the soldier.

He stuck his head through the door. The long hallway was deserted. He then reached through the door and opened it from the inside. Stepping inside, Molly and Susan looked down the hallway.

"Wow," said Susan. "It seems to go on forever."

Molly crossed her arms in front of her as she walked several yards down the hallway.

"We could spend days looking around down here," said the soldier. "That's how complex this old hallway system is."

Molly stopped and turned around. Looking down she saw dirty clothes lying on the ground. She bent down to look at them.

They look oddly familiar, she thought. *Could it be?*

She picked up the clothes and studied them. The top was covered in blood.

"What are you doing?" asked Susan.

"I found something," replied Molly. "You might think I'm crazy, but these look like the clothes Jim was wearing that day."

"Let's bring them back for testing," suggested the soldier. He then quickly removed a plastic pouch from his backpack.

"Give them to me," he instructed. "We need to minimize DNA contamination."

He placed the items in the pouch and secured it in his backpack. After walking down the corridor for a time, they returned to the elevated platform and searched the area a few more hours for any signs of Jim before heading back to the base.

Later that evening, Molly and Susan met at the cafeteria for diner. Molly barely touched her food.

"Thinking about Jim?" asked Susan.

"Yes," nodded Molly quietly. "And all the damage, I don't see how he could have survived that blast on the outside."

"They found his ID badge by the doorway. So he was trying to get in right? A body wasn't found there or by another nearby entrance for that matter. He must have gotten in somehow."

"Then why hasn't he contacted us?"

"I don't know. But Jim knows from the Mitel attacks back on Earth that you need to seek *real* shelter."

"Maybe he just stood there and watched the missile hit knowing that it was the end . . ."

As Molly cried, Susan quickly moved over and hugged her.

"I'm sorry Molly," she said quietly. "Please don't give up hope. I'm told the tracking devices aren't fool proof. Maybe he got hurt and can't reach out to us."

"We checked all the medical facilities in the population center."

"Maybe he was taken in by someone else."

"Maybe," sniffed Molly.

"Let's —"

"Excuse me," said a Hologram technician. "Are you Molly Johnson?"

"Yes, why?"

"I've been asked to bring you to the medical facility."

Molly's heart raced as she and Susan followed the technician. When they entered the medical area, they were greeted by Rad, Janus, Chad, and Markus.

"What?" Molly asked nervously. "What's going on?"

"The test results," replied Rad. "The blood found on the clothes is not Thraen blood. We then compared the DNA profile to Susan's which had recently been added to our military database. It's clear that —"

"It's Jim's, isn't it?" interrupted Molly.

"Yes."

"He survived the blast!"

"It appears so," smiled Janus.

"Based on the amount of blood on the shirt," Rad began, "It appears that Jim walked away from the blast."

Molly was so happy she cried.

"But how do you explain destroying the tracking chips?" Markus asked.

"That's a good question," replied Janus.

"We need to perform a thorough search down there," said Chad.

"I'll organize one for first thing tomorrow," stated Markus.

"Thank you everyone," replied Molly.

Over the next few days, a contingent of Hologram soldiers searched the entire underground hallway system. Jim was nowhere to be found. However, some samples of dried blood in the circular enclosure matched the blood found on the bloody clothes. Some of the dried blood was also Thraen.

"Strange," mused Janus.

"He's out there somewhere," replied Chad optimistically. "We just need to keep looking."

Chad's thoughts turned to Melissica.

I wish I could tell her all about what's going on, he thought. *I miss her so much.*

CHAPTER SEVENTEEN – THE SERUM TEST

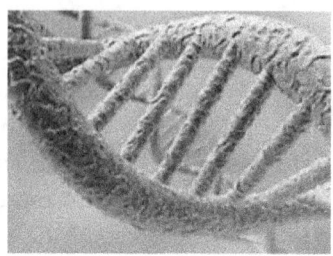

Lon awoke in his quarters after a restless night's sleep. The night before, he stayed up late studying the official mission orders, flight plans, spacecraft maintenance updates and digital maps of Thrae's suspected military installations. Before breakfast, he was to meet Ana to discuss her role in the attack. He was not looking forward to it.

It's her eyes, he thought. *She can kill me where I stand, by mere thought alone.*

Lon jumped out of bed and quickly got dressed.

I must win her over somehow, he concluded. *You can do it Lon. Use your charm and humor!*

Lon walked briskly to the large cafeteria at the direct center of the Hub. He grabbed a super-sized protein drink before looking across the cafeteria for Ana. He noticed her seated at the far end of the room, studying her tablet.

Lon zigzagged past the larger tables filled with military personnel. He sensed their stares as he passed by. Reaching Ana's table, he cleared his throat, causing Ana to look up.

"Hi Falon," smiled Lon awkwardly. "Is it OK if I join you?"

"Sure, go ahead," she replied. "And please call me Ana. Falon Ross is just some name the Mitel Leadership gave me."

"That figures," Lon mused, rolling his eyes.

"What can I do for you?"

"We need to discuss the upcoming mission."

"OK. What about it?"

"You have reviewed your mission orders, correct?"

"Yes."

"What do you think?"

"The mission is challenging. I'll do my best —"

"Do your best?"

Ana frowned.

"I mean," smiled Lon clumsily, "I *know* you'll do your best, but are you confident you can handle two Thraen Battle Spheres at once?"

"I don't think I'll need to take them both on at the same time."

"Why not?"

"Because *you* and the rest of the fleet are going to arrive right after me and launch the cluster pods, remember? That will distract at least one of them, maybe both."

"True, but aren't you at least a little bit worried?"

"Of course, I am."

"Two experienced Battle Spheres! Ana, it's a formidable challenge and we don't have any room for error."

"What other choice do we have?"

"Maybe none."

Lon then hesitated. He was reluctant to raise the topic of the rebellion so instead changed the subject altogether. "Hey, you trained quite a bit in the Stone Forest. How was that?"

"It was pretty desolate. But it helped me teach myself to control and develop my abilities."

"Folklore says that an advanced civilization lives out there somewhere."

Ana looked away.

"The creatures out there," Lon continued, "are said to be *gigantic* and look more animal than man. With all the flying around you did, you *must* have seen something, no?"

"No."

"I'm told they also eat humans."

"*They don't eat* . . . Lon, *who* told you that creatures out in the Stone Forest actually eat humans?"

"Mitel soldiers. And I've heard many rumors."

"You're telling me you've heard firsthand accounts from people who actually witnessed it happen?"

"*No*, but over the years, I've heard that many soldiers have disappeared out there searching for the Nomas creatures and their population center."

"Did anyone have any luck finding the population center?"

"No."

"Well, neither did I. Lon, did it ever occur to you that the soldiers simply got lost and ran out of supplies? I can tell you from experience that it's a desolate and unforgiving place out there."

Lon could sense Ana was getting agitated. He glanced quickly at her eyes. They were still normal. *I know she knows more than she is telling me. I'm certain of it.*

"Look Falon, *I mean Ana*," Lon winced, "I don't want to argue with you. As far as the mission goes, we need to trust each other and work together, OK?"

Ana studied Lon's face.

"OK," she replied.

"Good," Lon sighed. "We're *both* in a difficult situation."

"What do you mean *both*?"

Lon glanced around the cafeteria before responding.

"Look Ana, I know you're being forced to do the Leadership's bidding. I get that, OK? But I'm also being forced to lead an operation which I fear could be a suicide mission."

"How are *you* being forced?"

"*Are you kidding*? If I don't carry out their orders, I'll be killed. That is how the Leadership works."

Lon again looked around the cafeteria.

"But it doesn't have to be that way," he whispered.

"What do you *mean*?"

"We can stand together and oppose our oppressors."

"Who, *us*?"

"Not just us. I'm talking cruiser commanders and their crew, Special Forces commanders and their units, Leadership complex guards and untold numbers of regular Mitel forces."

"They're all ready to rise up against the *Mitel Leadership*?"

"Not yet. But I'm trying to put that together."

Ana rolled her eyes, sighed and fell back against her chair.

"I'm *serious* Ana. Look, I know you don't think very much of me, and maybe you're right to feel that way. But if we don't do something, and do it soon, we'll all die anyway. And so will your family. Is that what you want?"

Ana sat back up.

"My *family*?"

"Do you think for one minute that the Leadership can be trusted to keep them alive?"

"I don't know . . . I mean —"

"The answer is you can't."

"What do you *want*?"

"If I put together a coalition, I want you to join us. If we can defeat the Leadership, and those loyal to them, your family will be freed, and you will be released from your servitude."

"They'll be killed at the first hint of trouble."

"I'll make sure they don't."

"*How*?"

"Before we start the rebellion, we'll use our contacts to locate and rescue them."

Ana was silent for a moment. She didn't want to tell him what she knew about the mechanical battle spheres. At least not yet.

"*Well*?" asked Lon. "Are you with us?"

"I'll have to think about it."

Lon stared at Ana.

"If we proceed, we'll need to act quickly and decisively," he explained. Lon then checked the time before continuing. "A word of advice: If you value your own safety and that of your family, I would *not* repeat any of this to anyone."

"Is that a *threat*?"

"*No* Ana. It's just the realty of the Mitel civilization. You must be very careful who you trust. Rule of thumb: trust nobody, at least initially."

"Including you?"

"That's your choice to make. I'm offering you a path to freedom for both you and your family."

Ana stared at Lon intently.

"Before we depart," Lon added, "we still need to go over the mission plans in more detail. We *must* be on the same page if we are to succeed."

Ana nodded in agreement.

"You will depart first —"

"I know that, Lon."

"OK. What you may not know is our propulsion system limitations will force you to travel slow enough to insure that we're not far behind you once you arrive."

"What limitations?"

"Although we can now travel through deep space at mind boggling speeds, it's impractical to attempt to do it over relatively short distances, in cosmic terms that is."

"How fast can *you* go?"

"In *deep* space when the slip rings are engaged? We can travel light years in a matter of seconds."

"That's pretty fast."

"It sure is. My understanding of the phenomenon is that when the spacecraft reaches approximately twelve times the speed of light, its gravitational field causes the craft to resonate at the exact same frequency as deep space. Once that happens, the craft instantaneously darts forward, like electricity running through a wire. It's called *slip speed*. Unfortunately, the slip triggers the cylindrical ring to slow down causing the craft to decelerate to less than the speed of light. Once the ring comes back up to speed, the process repeats."

"I see."

"The problem is that we can't control the length of the slip. Once fully initiated, we would likely overshoot Thrae by twice the distance it takes to get there. In order to deal with that, our *scientists* have come up with a crude solution. They dialed down the slip ring so that it will allow us to get to Thrae in about 3 days while still maintaining control of the spacecraft. It's better than the two weeks it used to take us, but still much slower than the speed of light, which would get us there in half a day."

"Then I'll just have to go slower so you can keep up."

"But it will take us three days."

"I heard you the first time Lon."

"So . . . how will you eat and . . ."

"*Poop*?" laughed Ana.

"Well, *yes*," Lon blushed.

"When I'm in mechanical form, I don't eat *or* poop Lon. I simply stop for a short time and recharge myself."

"Interesting," Lon mused. "We'll have to factor your recharging stops into our flight plan."

He then checked the time and stood up.

"Listen, I must be going. I'll be in touch soon, *OK*?"

Ana nodded.

Lon smiled, turned, and walked away. Ana watched him stride across the room, ignoring several stares along the way, and then disappear through the cafeteria doors.

That evening, Rad Aarden flopped on his bed. He let out an exhausted sigh after another long day. Everyone's hard work was paying off as the new cruisers were almost ready to launch. Rad heard a beep from his computer. He groaned as he got up and shuffled across his quarters. He sat down in front of his computer and opened an encrypted message.

Hello Rad. It's Tor.

He quickly typed and hit the transmission key.

Hello brother. It's good to hear from you again.

Indeed. Listen. We've received word from Zi that the Mitel military is close to launching a surprise attack on Thrae. The size and scope have not been verified. However, sources believe it will consist of four to eight high speed cruisers and several upgraded transport and supply craft. Smaller than previous attacks, but with the upgraded propulsion systems, still very formidable.

Rad rubbed his jaw and stared at the screen as he contemplated yet another military confrontation. He wanted to tell his brother all about Thrae's technological advancements. Worrying that the transmission could be intercepted and unencrypted by the wrong people, he decided not to.

Thank you for the head's up, Tor. I will pass this information along immediately. Tell Zi we thank him also.

Will do. Be safe my brother.

You as well.

A few days later, Lon requested three days leave to visit with his family before leaving on the mission. His request was granted. During the middle of the night, Lon piloted a small base hover craft to an old abandoned military base located deep in the Black mountains. He had scheduled a secret meeting with several Special Forces Commanders to discuss his plan. When he arrived, Lon landed his vehicle next to three large silver and black hover crafts glistening in the moonlight.

Good, he thought. *Everyone's here early. That's a good sign.*

Lon grabbed his backpack and jumped out of the hover craft. As he approached the command center's rear entrance, he was confronted by several soldiers holding electro laser long weapons.

"Don't move," ordered a soldier.

Lon stopped and squinted at their helmet mounted lights. A soldier stepped forward and scanned Lon's uniform which contained an imbedded identification.

"Sorry Commander, we're just doing our job."

"That's a good thing," smiled Lon.

"Please, this way," motioned the soldier, "they've been expecting you."

Lon followed the soldiers through the rear entrance and down a dark hallway to a conference room. Lon was warmly greeted by several commanders. He proceeded to explain his plan and the recent conversation with the young female Battle Sphere.

"I like it," said one commander. "There's someone else you will need to present this to."

"*Who*?" Lon asked.

"A retired Special Forces Senior Commander. His name is Adrian Sidd. You'll need his blessing."

"Another commander recently told me the same thing. Why is Sidd so important to the rebellion?"

"You'll understand when you meet him. Other than the Mitel Leadership, he's probably the richest man in the world. His family made their money building advanced weapons systems over several generations. Rumor has it that the Sidd family hid their wealth before the Leadership seized the family's manufacturing facilities. They've since re-established a secret manufacturing network."

"Why doesn't the Leadership just attack him?"

"They currently have their hands full with the Mitel resistance, not to mention their obsession with planet Thrae and the search for its secrets of immortality. Rumor also has it that he has enough weapons, strike fighters and ground-based cluster missiles to mount a serious defense. And the Leadership probably knows it. Sidd also employs a significant number of former Special Forces technicians, commanders, soldiers and Leadership guards. At a time where the Leadership is trying to maintain loyalty and support, killing large numbers of former military won't help their cause."

"That all makes sense."

"And although Sidd owns a lot of property, he spends most of his time at a sprawling heavily fortified compound, making it hard for the Leadership to attempt to eliminate him."

"Wow . . ."

"In my opinion, the Leadership has decided to leave him alone until they have either defeated the Mitel resistance or develop a weapon capable of eliminating both threats at the same time. I'm guessing Sidd doesn't want to wait until that happens which is why he is interested in your *plan*."

"Understood. I'm eager to meet him."

"I'll set up a meeting at his compound in two days' time. I understand he wants to talk to you before you leave for Thrae."

"Excellent."

In the dense woods, a large contingent of heavily armed resistance fighters led by Jun Rexx quietly closed in on the abandoned base. Their state-of-the-art night vision glasses allowed them to navigate the rugged terrain. The Mitel resistance had been tipped off that a secret but undesignated military planning meeting was scheduled to take place there at midnight. Better yet, it was rumored that Jun's twin brother would be in attendance. That alone was incentive enough for Jun to lead the mission. Their goal: ambush the meeting and kill everyone there.

As the contingent crept within fifty yards of the tree line opening, an operations specialist's hand held scanner flashed red multiple times. He waved toward Jun, but it was too late. A resistance fighter on the periphery set off the first of many temporary infrared motion sensors placed on trees around the perimeter. Realizing what happened, the operations specialist broke the silence via his helmet communications system.

"We've been located," he announced.

"Let me guess," grunted Jun, "tripped a motion?"

"Affirmative."

"Let's go," Jun ordered. "I didn't come all this way for nothing."

Jun darted ahead followed by the rest of the resistance fighters. As he approached the tree line, Jun pulled out a spray ball laser weapon.

Here we go, he thought.

Just as Lon finished answering questions, the sound of ball laser fire could be heard outside.

"We're under attack," concluded one commander.

"This was *supposed* to be a secret meeting Rexx," growled a second commander.

Just then, a Special Forces soldier entered the room.

"*The resistance*," he blurted.

"How many are there?" asked a third commander.

"Based on the motion sensors? Fifty, probably more."

Lon reached into his backpack and pulled out a small black device attached to a harness.

"Here," he said. "Give this to your commander. He'll know what to do with it."

The soldier grabbed the device and disappeared back up the hall.

"What did you give him?" asked the first commander.

"It's a small but very powerful bomb," Lon explained. "Launching it at the leading edge of the resistance force should slow them down. In the meantime, let's head out the back to the hover crafts."

In front of the command center, the intense firefight was cut short thanks to Jun's spray ball laser weapon. Several Mitel soldiers regrouped at the command center entrance while others retreated along the exterior sides of the structure. Jun motioned his resistance fighters toward the front entrance. At that instant, the soldier carrying the black device and harness emerged through the front entrance. Lightly tapping the side of his night vision glasses, Jun zoomed in on the small device. He recognized it immediately.

"Get down!" he yelled.

As he neared the rear entrance, Lon reached for his belt and pushed a remote controlled detonation button. The thunderous explosion caused the entire front of the building to collapse, killing the soldiers positioned there. Smoke, dust and debris swirled up the hallway toward the retreating commanders.

"*What was that, Rexx?*" asked the first commander.

"The resistance must have inadvertently hit the device with their laser fire," replied Lon. "Let's keep moving!"

In the dust and debris, Jun instinctively jumped back up. "Follow me!" he ordered.

Running along the left side of the building, Jun fired his spray laser weapon at the retreating soldiers. In the open field behind the building, the three large hover crafts took off. Reaching the open field, Jun and the rest of the resistance fighters came under heavy laser fire from Special Forces soldiers in the retreating craft. Disregarding his own safety, Jun knelt down and returned fire at the closest hover craft. After receiving a sustained barrage, it lurched out of control, nosedived into the woods and exploded.

Jun methodically turned his attention toward the next closest hover craft. He unleashed a spray ball laser barrage, killing three soldiers as they returned fire. One of the dead soldiers slumped against Lon who was crouching against the side wall. He pushed the dead man to the deck.

The craft quickly accelerated skyward. Now out of range, it banked to the left. Lon cautiously peered over the edge. He lightly tapped his night vision glasses to zoom in on the rear opening. Standing in the field was a large muscular figure staring back at him. Studying the physique, Lon realized that he was looking at himself.

It's Jun, he thought. A slight chill quickly ran down his spine. *I've got to kill him before he kills me.*

Lon sighed heavily before lowering himself back down to the deck. He watched silently as soldiers tended to the wounded.

That was too close, he thought. *Putting together a reliable and trustworthy coalition will be more challenging than I thought.*

On the ground, Jun watched stoically as the two remaining hover craft disappeared over the treetops off in the distance. Using his night vision glasses zoom feature, he had seen Lon's face peering over the side of the second hover craft.

"We'll meet again, my brother," he muttered, "and when we do, you will *not* be so fortunate. *That I promise you.*"

On the way back to the Hub, Lon was dropped off in an open field so he could detour to his private dwelling near the Black Mountains.

"Sorry about your hover craft," said a commander. "There wasn't enough time to get it."

"No worries. When I get back to the base, I'll say it was stolen by the resistance," smiled Lon.

Lon waved and headed toward his dwelling as the large hover craft flew off. He planned to stay there for the remainder of his three-day leave, other than his day trip to meet with Adrian Sidd. After he arrived, Lon expected to be visited by the Leadership security forces. On the first night, Lon sat in the dark with two charged dwarf laser weapons next to him. But to his surprise, nobody came.

The next morning, Lon plugged the location coordinates of Adrian's compound into the computer of his single seat transport craft and headed east. Although he tried to relax, he kept replaying the ambush in his mind. He also thought about all the obstacles that lie ahead.

Ten miles from the compound, Lon received an incoming communication signal on his center console. He reached over and turned it on.

"Identify yourself immediately. You are in restricted airspace. Repeat: Identify yourself immediately," said the voice.

"I am Lon Rexx," he responded. "I am here to meet with Adrian Sidd."

"Please provide your password phrase."

"New beginnings," grunted Lon. *Not sure who came up with that one,* he thought.

"Thank you, Mr. Rexx. Our antigravity landing system will guide you in from here."

Lon could feel the antigravity beam grab onto his small transport craft. It steered his vehicle for about five miles before being handed off to the next beam.

Off in the distance, Lon noticed the sprawling compound built on the top of a sweeping mountaintop. Several structures of various sizes, shapes and colors were surrounded by tall, thick stone walls.

It's huge, he thought.

A multiuse landing area was visible off to the left. Lon noticed several military style hover crafts parked nearby. Immediately adjacent to the craft was a large strike fighter storage building. He counted approximately two dozen silver strike fighters parked in rows beyond the structure.

When he touched down, Lon was greeted by a man and a woman in a small hover vehicle. They flew him up to Adrian's living quarters located high above the rest of the facility. It was a huge multi-level glass and stone structure. After the hover craft landed, Lon followed the escorts up stone steps and through a tall set of sliding front doors. Immediately inside he was greeted by three enormous former Leadership guards.

"Are you Lon Rexx?" asked one guard.

"Yes," replied the female escort. "He is here to see Director Sidd."

A second guard pointed a hand held scanner at Lon. It beeped several times. Lon slowly removed the two dwarf laser weapons from under his jacket and handed them to the guards. He was then scanned a second time.

"We'll return these to you on your way out Mr. Rexx," said the first guard.

"Follow me, please," instructed the female escort.

Lon followed the escort up a set of stairs and down a long hallway. As he walked along, Lon studied the several paintings and sculptures on either side.

They're probably priceless, he thought.

At the end of the hallway, two more tall sliding doors opened, revealing a three-story high room. The entire far wall was made of glass. More paintings and sculptures were situated throughout the room. The back of Adrian's head was visible above his silver and black chair behind a clear polymer desk. Adrian was staring out the windows at his massive compound below.

"Lon Rexx to see you Sir," said the female escort.

"Thank you. Commander Rexx, please have a seat."

Lon sat down in one of several chairs in front of Adrian's desk.

As the doors slid closed behind the female escort, Adrian turned his chair around. He was a very large man, with unusually broad shoulders. He had steely looking eyes, a light complexion, short black hair and a matching black anchor style goatee mustache.

Fifteen years ago, on a secret Special Forces mission, Adrian stumbled across a small but powerful explosive. His motion triggered the device which would have killed him if he hadn't been wearing his custom-made body armor. The force of the blast blinded him and eventually required his arms and legs to be amputated. After multiple surgeries, Adrian was fitted with robotic eyes, arms, legs and pectoral muscles. In some ways he was now more machine than man, also possessing incredible strength. In time, Adrian used his wealth to customize his robotic arms; adding thought activated laser weapons.

Adrian eventually went back to the bomb site and recovered several small pieces of shrapnel. Although tests were inconclusive, he was convinced that the advanced device was made and distributed by the Nomas.

Only they could have created such a device, he had concluded.

To Adrian, the Nomas were always a direct threat to his business interests and power. There was also some family history. While he had heard rumors that his grandfather had defected to the Nomas, he refused to believe them. After the blast, things suddenly became much more personal. They had almost killed him.

"Thank you for coming, Lon Rexx."

"My pleasure. I see that you hire many ex-military."

"I compensate them quite well for their services. I'd like to think that I receive their fierce loyalty in return."

"One would hope."

"Indeed. I've heard a lot about you and your *plan*. I must profess that I am very intrigued by it. Did you come up with it yourself?"

"Yes."

"And despite the dangers, you reached out to others to begin to form a coalition. I must say, I admire that kind of courage."

"What kind is that?"

"The fearless kind . . ."

"Thank you. But I'm also a firm believer in advance planning, preparation, mission risk assessment and execution. I also assign a high value to loyalty."

"Good! We think alike in that regard."

Lon nodded.

"I'll get to the point," Adrian began. "My sources tell me that the Mitel leadership is close to launching a fleet of mechanical Battle Spheres, maybe a thousand or more. From what I can determine, they will not be as fast, mobile or possess anywhere near the same level of firepower as a Thraen Battle Sphere. However, their sheer numbers should prove to be more than a match against any opponent."

"This is the first I've heard of *mechanical battle spheres*," replied Lon.

"That's why your takeover plan is so intriguing. If we can implement it *before* the launch, we can take control of the Battle Spheres."

"And if we don't?"

"Then I fear we might all be doomed. You see Lon, my family has been involved in the weapons procurement for many generations."

"That's what I've been told."

"When the Leadership seized power, they not only murdered my great-grandfather, but his brothers, sisters and many of their families. Because of our longstanding ties and allegiances with the Mitel military, the Leadership realized that their purge of my family risked alienating many top commanders. They ultimately, and *reluctantly*, decided not to kill us all. The Leadership left my immediate family alone and *instead*, seized all of our production facilities. We were lucky in the sense that my great-grandfather realized what was coming and went to great lengths to hide the family's vast wealth."

Adrian stood up and walked toward the windows.

"What you see out there would not have been possible otherwise. By expanding our military strength, we have been able to keep the Leadership at bay *until now*."

"With all due respect," said Lon. "Your compound, while very impressive, would not last long against the Mitel military."

Adrian turned around quickly to face Lon.

"On the contrary, we have about two thousand strike fighters hidden in several underground bases around the planet. Getting to that point was painstakingly difficult. More importantly, we have several land-based cluster pods ready to launch when I give the word. The Leadership is aware *to an extent* of our overall resources. In my opinion, that is the real reason why they have left us alone. Not to mention they have had their hands full with the Mitel resistance and continue to be distracted by their obsession with planet Thrae.

In any event, we eventually resumed weapons procurement and sales to the resistance in secret. That has enabled us to fund most of our own military expansion."

"I had no idea," said Lon.

"We will need to deploy all of our resources when the time comes to seize power from the Mitel Leadership and those loyal to them."

"I'm ready to go."

"Good. As soon as you return from your mission to Thrae, we must finalize plans and put them in motion."

"Sounds good to me . . ."

"And our second order of business will be to locate the Nomas underground city —"

"The *Nomas*? Everyone says they don't exist, that they are just legend."

"On the contrary Lon, they do exist. Do you know how I know?"

"How?"

"My grandfather would tell us stories of how he would leave partially constructed weaponry at the base of the Stone Forest. He did it time and time again. And each time my grandfather's curiosity grew. He eventually started sending men into the forest looking for the Nomas. In some cases, they never returned.

"I've heard similar stories."

"Eventually, the orders stopped altogether. My grandfather concluded that the Nomas became so afraid of being discovered that they started doing everything themselves. And to this day, we occasionally come across stories of incredibly advanced weapons being used in military skirmishes. In my opinion, the Nomas have advanced the art of weapons design and production to the point where they are second to none. That makes them a *threat*. That is why we must find them and eliminate them."

"I see."

Adrian turned back toward the window.

"As for my grandfather, he went searching for them one day and was never heard from again. I'm *convinced* that they killed him. That is another reason why I want to eliminate them."

"To extract revenge . . ."

"Correct."

Adrian turned back around and walked to his desk. "Are you on board with that part of *our* plan?"

"I don't see why not," replied Lon. "Once we're in charge, we can do whatever we want."

"True enough. And oh, before I forget, have you spoken about this with the female Battle Sphere Falon Ross?"

"Yes. Unfortunately, she has yet to commit to our cause. She did say she wanted to see how our mission goes before she decides."

"She's smart. Why commit to a significant challenge unless you have confidence in those around you. Listen, I wish you the best of luck with your mission to Thrae. I hope it is very successful and you both return unharmed."

"So do I."

"We'll speak about the implementation details of the plan right after your return, agreed?"

"Sounds good," nodded Lon.

Adrian then extended his hand across his table.

"Thank you," replied Lon standing up. The two shook hands firmly. Lon could feel an unnatural, almost vice like grip in Adrian's hand.

Very odd, he thought to himself.

Adrian pressed a button on his desk. Seconds later, the large doors slid open as the female escort reappeared.

"My assistant will see you out."

"Please follow me Mr. Rexx," she motioned.

Lon followed the escort out the tall doors which slid closed behind them. Adrian walked back to the windows and watched Lon return to his hover vehicle.

When he returned to the Hub, Lon tried his best to act nonchalantly. Except for some stares and an occasional whisper, it was business as usual.

I've got to relax, he thought. *Being paranoid will not help me pull together a coalition.*

The Thraen mission was quickly approaching. It was time to meet with Ana once more to discuss specifics of their invasion strategy. Lon messaged Ana and she agreed to meet him at the cafeteria the next morning.

After a restless night's sleep, Lon pulled himself out of bed and made his way across the Hub. Upon entering the cafeteria, he grabbed a super-sized protein drink and again looked across the room for Ana. She was seated at the same table as last time, studying her tablet. Lon zigzagged past the larger tables filled with military personnel and strolled up to Ana's table.

"Hi Falon," smiled Lon before wincing. "Sorry. *I mean Ana.*"

Ana motioned Lon to sit down.

"I've been thinking," Lon began.

"About the mission?"

"What else?" he grunted. "Well, you know *what else*, but we can talk about *that* later."

"OK," sighed Ana.

"Anyway, since you are one of their own, my feeling is that the Thraen Battle Spheres will be reluctant to engage you, at least initially. I also believe they will hold back and not use their full complement of laser cannons when they face you in the beginning. So I think it's crucial that you take full advantage of their hesitancy before they decide to change their approach."

"Don't worry, I will."

"Good. After you arrive, you are to head directly to the planet surface."

"I know —"

"I'm just walking both of us through the attack sequence."

Ana nodded.

"Make sure you fly high enough to allow the ground forces to quickly detect you. That will draw out the Battle Spheres. And since our forces won't be far behind, it is critical that you preoccupy them until we've launched our cluster pods and establish our perimeter."

Ana looked away. Lon could tell she was upset.

"*What's wrong?*" asked Lon.

"Why does the mission have to include killing innocent civilians?"

"It's either them or us Ana. If it turns out you cannot contain them, the cluster pods will keep the Battle Spheres preoccupied as they chase them down and destroy them. That will give you a second opportunity to attack them."

"I just don't see how killing countless innocents will help our cause. Won't it just strengthen their resolve not to mention the fact that its morally wrong in the first place?"

"War is terrible Ana," replied Lon, "there's no getting around that. And strengthening their resolve is always a possibility. But we have little choice. If engaged head-to-head, without our defense protocols as a distraction, an experienced Battle Sphere can wipe out a larger force than the one we are sending there. And if we can inflict enough pain and suffering on the general population, it may force the Thraen resistance to abandon their cause, for the sake of their own people."

"I don't think they'll ever give up Lon."

"We shall see. In the meantime, by following our orders, we will also insure our own survival, not to mention the safety of your family. Agreed?"

Ana nodded.

"OK. With your concentrated firepower, I want you to focus on distracting and degrading the Battle Spheres shields. If you are lucky —"

"*Lucky*?"

"Yes, *lucky*. There's a great deal of luck involved in these encounters. The difference between victory and defeat often turns on split second decisions in the heat of battle."

Ana sighed.

"Anyway, if you are *fortunate*, your concentrated laser cannon fire will damage one or both spheres. Degrading their capabilities will put us in a position to capture them.

It's also very important that you engage them within the planet's atmosphere. That will allow us time to establish our outer space perimeter."

"And that's when I lure them into outer space for you to capture them using your enhanced gravity control beams."

"Hopefully, yes."

"What do you mean *hopefully*?"

"Ana, no disrespect whatsoever, but we are talking about two experienced Battle Spheres here. It's not going to be easy. I've said that from the start. And even if we incapacitate them, they have the ability to choose to self destruct rather than allowing themselves to be captured."

"*What?*"

"Unfortunately, yes," nodded Lon, "another possible complication. I don't know how, but they have the ability to modify their propulsion system to produce significant quantities of antimatter."

"*Really?*"

"Yes. The resulting annihilation event is on a cosmic scale. My hope is that being so close to the planet, they will not go that route. Even though . . ."

"Even though what?"

"The Battle Sphere that our Armada went in search of self-destructed not far above Earth. Before it did, it projected a plasma defense shield around the planet."

"Did it work? Did it protect the planet?"

"We didn't stick around to find out. We've also never heard of another Battle Sphere possessing that ability. It was probably an anomaly. It's gone now, so I guess it doesn't really matter, does it? Hey, maybe you can figure out how they do it. But don't blow yourself up or Mitel in the process, OK?"

Ana grunted.

"Sorry. I'm trying to interject some levity. My point is this: you must use everything at your disposal to achieve your goals. There are so many variables that can work against you in life, not to mention warfare. You can't take anything for granted and you must never, ever, let your guard down or allow the feelings of others get in your way."

"I won't."

"Good. That philosophy has kept me alive so far. Take it for what it's worth. Do you feel ready for the mission? Do you feel confident?"

"Yes."

"Very good Ana. I can't stress it enough. You *must* distract the Battle Spheres until our fleet not only arrives, but also initiates defensive battle protocols. That should occupy them long enough for us to set up the outer space perimeter. Hopefully you can damage one or both of them at that time. We will contact you over the encrypted communication system as soon as we arrive. From there, we'll coordinate our maneuvers to lure them into outer space. Timing is critical. We must make sure we synchronize our arrival sequence consistent with the mission plan to stay on track. I think that's it. Any questions?"

"Not at the moment. I promise you I will do my best, Lon."

Lon looked around the cafeteria.

"Excellent. Now about the other matter . . ."

Ana slumped back into her chair and let out a deep sigh.

"*What?*" Lon asked, his impatience showing. "This is important!"

"It is to *you*."

"And you as well."

"*Why?*"

"As I said before, your family's safety depends on it."

"I don't know if I believe that, but assuming you're right, what have you done since the last time we talked?"

"For starters, I had a secret meeting with several Special Forces commanders."

"How did *that* go?"

"Other than the ambush intended to kill all of us, it went very well."

Ana sat up quickly. "*Ambush?*" she asked.

Lon looked around the cafeteria before responding.

"I don't know by whom, but the Mitel resistance was tipped off about our meeting. I had a hunch that word would get out, so I brought a small high energy explosive that helped save our lives. That's what I mean when I say don't trust anyone. Anyway, a few days later I met with an incredibly wealthy ex-Special Forces Senior Commander who is very well connected. He is all in with the plan."

"Are you *sure* you can trust all of these people?"

"You can never be completely sure Ana."

Why don't you join the resistance?"

Lon hesitated. *I can't tell her my true ambitions; or that my twin brother is a resistance fighter,* he thought.

"Because they're terrorists," he replied eventually.

"How is your rebellion any different?"

"We are trying to help the Mitel people."

"And they're not?"

Lon struggled to control his growing impatience.

"I don't know what they stand for quite frankly."

"Wouldn't it be worth finding out before you move forward?"

"Maybe."

"*Maybe?*" grunted Ana. "I don't know Lon. It seems *way* too complicated."

"You're not kidding," Lon sighed. "And everything is becoming so urgent. I just found out that the Leadership is about to launch a fleet of mechanical Battle Spheres. They might not be as fast or maneuverable or possess nearly the same amount of firepower, but they will shift the balance of power heavily in their favor."

"How did you . . . ?"

"How did I what?"

"Find out about the mechanical Battle Spheres?"

"From Adrian Sidd, the incredibly rich ex-Special Forces Senior Commander. Why? Did you know about them too?"

I can't let Lon know how I found out, she thought.

"No not really. I mean, I've heard rumors . . ."

"That's why we must do this now. At some point, resistance will be futile and they will have no incentive to keep your family alive."

"OK. OK. I get that. What are the next steps?"

"I plan to speak with a member of the Leadership guard before we depart. It will give us more options if they join our cause."

"And if they *don't*?"

"We'll still move forward."

Ana looked around the cafeteria for a moment.

"Let's see how both your meeting and the mission go first before I make my decision, OK?" she replied finally.

"Fair enough," Lon nodded. "If we don't survive the mission, I guess it won't make a difference anyway."

Lon stood up.

"I'll see you the morning of the mission departure."

"Yes," smiled Ana weakly.

"Let me know when your encrypted communications link is up and running. When is the synching scheduled for?"

"Tomorrow . . ."

"Good. Please review the mission plans and course trajectories one more time. We've corrected our arrival to allow you two recharging stops. Please contact me with any questions."

"I'll be sure to do that," nodded Ana.

Lon smiled awkwardly before making his way back across the cafeteria. As he exited the dining hall, Lon couldn't believe how truly naïve Ana is.

Unless she joins our cause, she will never see her family alive again, he thought. *And if we take power, we'll continue to use them as leverage to force her to do our bidding.*

The following evening, Lon slipped away from the base in a small multipurpose hover craft and traveled to his cousin's dwelling unit. During the approximate one hour trip, he repeatedly went over his plan in his mind.

This could go very well or very bad, he thought.

Just in case, Lon had brought two dwarf electro lasers under his shirt. *If they turn out to be loyalists, I will have little choice but to eliminate the entire family. It will be blamed on the resistance,* he concluded.

As he landed, Lon quickly surveyed the area using his night vision glasses.

All quiet, he thought. *Well here goes.*

Lon climbed out of the hover craft and walked briskly to the dwelling entrance. He pushed the intercom button. It beeped twice.

"Yes?" asked a female voice.

"It's Lon."

His cousin opened the door and motioned him inside. Seated in the middle of the room was her husband, a Leadership complex guard. Lon stepped inside and spoke.

"Hi, thank you for —"

A second guard stepped out from behind the entrance door and placed a hand-held electro laser against the back of Lon's head.

"Don't move," said the guard sternly.

The first guard sprung up from his seat. He was perhaps a foot taller than Lon, maybe more. He stepped forward and frisked Lon for weapons. He grabbed the two dwarf lasers from under his shirt and tossed them across the room.

"You came prepared I see," he growled.

"I didn't know what to expect."

"So expect the worst?"

"Wouldn't you?"

Without warning, the Guard punched Lon in the jaw causing him to stagger to one knee.

"What the . . ." Lon mumbled.

"That's for coming here and putting my wife and children in danger!"

"We are all in danger already." Lon grimaced as he slowly stood up.

The second guard again placed the electro laser at the back of his head. The first guard stared at Lon intently before motioning to the second guard to stand down.

"I've done a lot of research on you Lon Rexx," he said. "I don't like all the things I've learned. You are described as a self-centered opportunist. But you are also cunning, brave and a strong leader."

He then smiled.

"And it appears you can take a punch. In my opinion, you possess the traits necessary to stand up to the Leadership and those loyal to them. But that's still not enough. We cannot unseat the Leadership by ourselves."

"Understood, that's why I am pulling together a coalition."

"Oh?"

Lon explained his recent meetings with Ana, Adrian Sidd and the Special Forces commanders. "Can I count on you and the other guards?" he asked eventually.

"I must present all of this to the guards sympathetic to our cause. And there are many."

He then paused.

"If any of this gets out, we'll deny it. We will also kill you; do you understand?

"Yes," nodded Lon.

"We also know that Leadership scientists are close to launching a new weapon they believe will make the Leadership unstoppable."

"Adrian Sidd said they are developing a mechanical Battle Sphere."

"That makes sense. We know they performed many tests on the young female hybrid after she was captured."

"They probably mapped out her system architecture and reverse engineered it. When do you think the mechanical spheres will be operational?"

"We don't know. It's being done in total secrecy. I'm sure the Leadership threatened to eliminate each scientist's entire family if they leak any information."

"The Leadership is aggressively moving to consolidate power to the point where it will be futile to oppose them. We will need to act and do it quickly."

"That's why I decided to meet with you."

"I am commanding a mission to Thrae in a few days. Hopefully we will crush the resistance forces there once and for all and do it quickly."

"The Thrae resistance has proven to be very stubborn and resourceful."

"Indeed. Leadership wants us to decimate the planet's remaining infrastructure. In doing so they believe it will turn the population against the resistance."

"Do you think that's realistic?"

"I'm beginning to have my doubts. The Leadership is also trying to send a message: they don't want anyone here to get any big ideas."

"It's already too late for that," the guard grunted.

"I agree," Lon smirked. "So, while I'm gone, I need you to recruit as many guards as possible."

"I will."

"Upon my return, we must meet again to finalize and coordinate our plans going forward."

"That sounds good. Oh, and here," said the guard. He retrieved Lon's dwarf lasers from across the room. "No hard feelings?"

"None whatsoever," nodded Lon, tucking the devices back under his shirt.

They shook hands before Lon departed. Stepping outside, he surveyed the perimeter. Lon rubbed his jaw as he walked to his hover craft underneath the night shy.

That went better than expected, he thought. *The mechanical Battle Sphere has them on edge, and for good reason. I wonder if Ana has known about this. That might be the reason she's resisting joining us.*

Powered by its refurbished antigravity propulsion system, the captured Mitel cruiser took off from the shelf and headed into outer space for routine flight testing. Shortly thereafter, six Thraen space cruisers took off one by one into outer space for more exhaustive testing. After that, they were scheduled to establish overlapping crossing defensive orbits. Following their launch, partially constructed sections of six more cruisers were transported along underground tunnels to underground bays 1 and 2 for final assembly.

The next day, twenty newly constructed outer defense globes were successfully launched and located five hundred miles beyond Thrae's atmosphere. This newest generation spherical defense matrix both destroyed approaching asteroids and defended the planet against large and hostile attack forces. Each globe was twice the size of its predecessor and armed with twenty laser guided high energy missiles. In addition, each satellite had fifty pulsating laser cannons to identify, track and destroy cluster pods both before and after they separate. To maximize the element of surprise, their outer defense shields absorbed and attenuated scans of their weapons bays. Given the opportunity, they could be a formidable challenge for an unprepared cruiser commander.

"It took a lot of testing, but we finally got it right," mused Arius in his exoskeleton body wrap. Now that Zan was Thraen resistance commander, Arius had assumed command of the Global Defense Center or GDC. His rehabilitation was progressing slower than expected, but he was both stubborn and tenacious. "The Mitels are in for a big surprise when they show up."

"Agreed," replied Teri. "They just can't seem to leave Thrae alone. Jealously perhaps?"

"I think that's part of it, but also because we are the closest planet to Mitel and a threat to the Leadership's authority. Whatever the reason, the Mitel Leadership appears determined to exterminate us."

"I'm just glad we launched the new cruisers and got our air defense system established *before* they arrived," acknowledged Mayla.

"That's for sure," replied Arius. "Hopefully, next time, things will be much different."

"They should now that we have two Battle Spheres to back us up."

"I am cautiously optimistic Mayla. Unfortunately, the Mitels are not only relentless and ruthless, they are also resourceful."

"True enough."

Ana sat in the base cafeteria sipping a fruit drink as a young Mitel officer walked up to her. He was about six feet five inches tall, thin, with blond hair, gray eyes and cleft chin.

"Excuse me. Are you Falon Ross?"

"My real name is Ana."

"Do you mind if I sit down?"

"No. Go right ahead."

"Forgive me if I'm a bit nervous, but I have never met a real live Thraen Battle Sphere before. I mean, I saw plenty of digital footage and photos at the Mitel Academy, but that was different —"

"What's your name?" asked Ana.

"Xavier Sidd. I've recently been assigned to the Hub. I am a cruiser navigator at the moment, but one day hope to be a commander."

He's so young, she thought. *What a waste of life if he serves on a doomed cruiser.*

"I'm sure you will someday," Ana replied.

"Thanks for the vote of confidence."

Xavier then glanced around the cafeteria nervously.

"Listen," he said. "My uncle, Adrian Sidd, is really eager to talk to you."

"*Who* is Adrian Sidd?"

"He just happens to be one of the richest people in the world who also used to be a Special Forces Commander."

"Is that how he got so rich?"

"No," laughed Xavier. "Our family made their money in weapons procurement."

"Oh, I see."

"Yup, for better or for worse, I guess, depending on how you look at it. Anyway, like I said, he really wants to talk to you."

"Why?"

Xavier paused before answering.

"He said it had something to do with your recent conversations with Lon Rexx and that you would know what he meant."

Ana nodded. Xavier then pushed a small computer chip across the table.

"These are the directions to a secret location three population centers to the east. You can get there by taking the local high speed transportation system. Adrian was hoping to meet you tomorrow."

"*Tomorrow?*"

"Yes. He wants to meet before you head out on your mission. Can I tell him you'll be coming?"

"I guess so . . ."

"Great. Thanks Ana. It was a pleasure meeting you and I hope we meet again."

Ana watched Xavier as he walked out of the cafeteria.

That night, Ana loaded the chip into her computer. Three-dimensional displays appeared above her bed showing the route and location. It also confirmed that a private hover vehicle would pick her up at the public transportation port near the base and bring her to the high speed transportation link, all expenses paid.

At least he's making it easy, she thought.

The next morning as Ana stood outside the port, a sleek black hover vehicle landed next to her. The door slid open. A male and a female escort sat inside.

"Welcome Ana," said the female escort. "Director Sidd wanted me to thank you for agreeing to meet with him on such short notice. Climb in."

"No problem," replied Ana. She stepped into the craft.

The doors slid closed, and the vehicle whisked her to the transportation link.

"You depart in three minutes," said the female escort. "You'd better hurry. Accelerator Track 4."

"Thanks," replied Ana as she jumped out.

"Look for the same model hover vehicle once you arrive," said the escort as the door automatically closed.

It will be hard to miss, thought Ana.

When she arrived, the second vehicle sped her toward the population center before turning and heading up over a rolling hill to a large, secluded living structure. Ana stared out the window as they landed.

It's beautiful, she thought.

A female escort brought her inside to a large room with ceiling to floor windows. The Black Mountains, covered in a blue haze, could be seen off in the distance.

"Please be seated," said the escort. "Director Sidd will be with you momentarily. Ana stared out the windows for a time before a second set of doors slid open.

"Sorry to keep you waiting Ana. I'm Adrian Sidd."

Ana nodded and smiled.

"I'm glad that you were able to wander out of the Stone Forest unharmed. It can be a very dangerous place."

"*What*? How did you know about *that*?"

"I know about a lot of things Ana," chuckled Adrian. "Intelligence gathering is a hobby of mine."

"But —"

"No buts. Remember the four men you saw high above you dressed in gray and brown when you were making your way out on foot?"

"Yes . . ."

"They work for me."

"What were they doing there?"

"Trying to find the Nomas people."

"The *Nomas*?" Ana's heart was now beating rapidly.

"Correct. Their population center is hidden in there somewhere. I'm certain of it. The question I have for you is what were *you* doing walking around in there?"

"Is that *why* you asked me here?"

"No, but I *am* curious."

"I had a training accident and temporarily lost the ability to transform into Battle Sphere mode. So I had to walk out."

"I see." Adrian studied Ana's face. "I understand you did a lot of training in there. I expect it made a great obstacle course."

"It did, actually."

"And during all that training, you never saw the Nomas people or their hidden city?"

"No."

"OK. Full disclosure. The Nomas and my family had a business relationship that spanned several generations. Many years ago my grandfather disappeared in the Stone Forest searching for them and was never heard from again. I've been trying to find out what happened to him."

"Like you said, it can be a very dangerous place."

"Indeed. And not just because of the fierce predators that hunt out there during the night."

"What do you mean?"

"The Nomas people are not what the outside world perceives them as. They are a uniquely advanced civilization. Probably the most advanced on Mitel and in my opinion, very dangerous."

"Why do you say that?"

"Our family business consisted primarily of advanced weapons procurement. And to a large degree it still is. We used to supply materials and weapons components to the Nomas, leaving them at the entrance to the Stone Forest. They would use those items to build weapons the likes of which Mitel had never seen before. One day they stopped using us. We concluded they started doing everything on their own. That's when my grandfather went looking for them."

"I see . . ."

"They are very dangerous, Ana. Almost as dangerous as the Mitel Leadership —"

"Then why haven't the Leadership mentioned them to me before?"

"The Leadership is very selective in what it discusses and when. Have they mentioned *me* before?"

"No. Are you dangerous *too*?"

Adrian smiled.

"I can be," he replied, "if I believe strongly enough about something."

"And you believe in Lon's rebellion plan?"

"In general, yes. He will certainly need my help."

"Which you are willing to provide?"

"I'm like you Ana. I'm trying to decide."

"Lon told you that?"

"Yes. But I understand where you're coming from. First and foremost, you are worried about how the uprising would impact the safety of your family. Second, you have doubts about Lon Rexx. I have my doubts, too. He is prone to letting his anger dictate what he does and while he may be fearless and a good military tactician, he does not possess the strongest intellect. But none of us are perfect, are we," grinned Adrian.

"No. I told Lon —"

"That you want to decide after the Thraen mission."

"Yes."

"Understood. Please know that I would highly value your commitment to our *team*. You are a formidable asset and clearly smart and determined. Please understand that I would fully commit my substantial resources to rescuing your family *before* defeating the Mitel Leadership. And based on my extensive military contacts as a former Special Forces Senior Commander, I am quite confident we can count on the majority of elite elements of the Mitel military to support us."

"How would you rescue my family?"

"I would launch a covert rescue operation to free them. You would make sure Mitel strike fighters do not interfere with that mission."

Ana nodded.

"And one more thing," said Adrian. "If the mission to Thrae goes poorly, don't despair. It may be a sign that the Mitel military is not as big an impediment to defeating the Leadership as some might think."

"I'll keep that in mind."

"Please do. Thank you for coming and good luck with the mission."

The doors slid open as a female escort entered the room.

"My assistant will show you out," motioned Adrian.

After the doors slid closed, he stared out the window and watched Ana climb into the hover vehicle. It took off seconds later.

She knows more about the Nomas than she's telling me, he thought. *I can feel it. If she joins us, I will gain her trust and coax that information out of her. If that doesn't work, I'll use her family as leverage.*

Atlas, Jim and Isak eventually settled into the circular enclosure at the center of the underground hallway network. Although the enclosure was very similar, it didn't have a stream running through it. It did however contain a few damp areas and as a result, the ground foliage was not as well developed as in Amer.

Late that night, Atlas went out looking for food. It had been awhile since he had stayed in Pisco so he wasn't sure if any of his contacts were still around. The elevated walkway was quiet as Atlas floated along. Off in the distance, he saw the changing screens of the news feeds shown on four sides of an eight-foot-high rectangular free standing structure. The news feed stations were located at various intervals throughout Pisco and somewhat bored, Atlas approached the screens to scan the news for a time. He read the detailed updates about the recent cluster pod attack on Amer. Suddenly, on a smaller adjacent screen, he saw a familiar face.

That's him, he thought. *That's our travel companion.*

Below the picture listed the name *James Johnson,* and a description stating he and his family were recent arrivals from planet Earth. It further described how he went missing during the attack.

"Where's *Earth*?" muttered Atlas. "I've never heard of it."

Atlas continued to stare at Jim's picture.

"*Recently arrived*? If that's the case, how come he's able to speak fluent Thraen?" he muttered.

Atlas then remembered Jim's head injury.

I wonder if that had something to do with it . . . maybe he's suffering from a language syndrome.

Impulsively, Atlas glanced up and down the elevated walkway before lowering his backpack to the ground. He rummaged around the bottom of his bag until he found a small black hand-held device. Atlas quickly activated it and pointing the device directly at the adjacent screen inside the clear Plexiglass case. He scanned the smaller screen device until he heard a beeping noise, confirming he had copied the content of the streaming video. He deactivated the device and carefully placed it back inside his backpack. As he floated away, Atlas was conflicted about what to do next.

I want to show this to James to see if it helps him remember who he is, but I also want him to take care of Isak after I'm gone.

Suddenly, Atlas felt dizzy. He lowered his backpack to the ground before fading in and out a few times. He stood motionless for a time before things returned to normal. He then picked up his backpack and continued on his way.

Crouching in a small, darkened passageway, a Scavenger watched Atlas float down the walkway. He had heard how two Scavengers had been critically injured in Amer by the former Hologram Matrix commander.

I wasn't there the night of the fight, he thought. *But I know the Scavenger group is keen on exacting revenge. And by the look of things, Atlas may be vulnerable now.*

He watched as Atlas disappeared into the night. The Scavenger emerged from his hiding spot and hurried back to tell the rest of his group who he had just seen.

At the Hub, the time had come to launch the Mitel mission to Thrae. Lon reported to the space transport facility at dawn. After a bumpy ride into space aboard a well-worn shuttle pod, the craft docked with the 1,550-foot-long silver and white wedge-shaped cruiser. The sleek and slightly bulbous craft had two sets of small triangular wings up front that transitioned into two long narrow wings in the stern. Two vertical tails were positioned along the rear of the craft. After crossing through the airlock, Lon handed off his duffle bag to a young specialist and headed for the ICC.

"Good morning, Commander," said the Communications Specialist. "And welcome aboard. Are you eager to get the mission started?"

"Thank you and yes," nodded Lon, "but there is still a lot to do before we depart."

"Understood Sir."

Lon went through the pre-departure inspection checklist and over the next few hours scoured the vessel checking the operational readiness of major systems, propulsion and weaponry.

Despite all the recent upgrades, these craft are still aging rapidly, he thought. His mind then wandered to thoughts of Zan Liss, who as Mitel Director had overseen the propulsion refurbishment program for the entire fleet.

The traitor knew what he was doing. But how? It would be poetic justice if all his upgrades helped me track him down and kill him once and for all. He then smiled to himself. *Yes, it would.*

Lon took the HorVert elevator back to the ICC. As the doors opened, the crew members all turned to look at him.

"Everything is operational and ready for launch," announced Lon. "What is the status of the Battle Sphere?"

"Synchronized tracking confirms she is about to depart," replied the Navigator.

"Good. And what about the rest of the fleet?"

"They await your word," replied the Communications Specialist.

Lon flopped into the command console.

"The Battle Sphere has launched," announced the Scanning Specialist.

"Excellent," nodded Lon. "Instruct the fleet to commence slip ring energizing and begin to line up along the launch perimeter."

"Doing it now, Sir," replied the Communications Specialist.

Lon stared at the several monitors along the front of the ICC. He watched impatiently as the energizing levels climbed to 40 then 60 then 80 percent.

It's ironic, Lon thought. *We are too close to Thrae in cosmic terms to initiate normal slip speed. If we did, we'd overshoot the planet and end up on the far side of their universe. The make shift solution? Dial back the slip ring speed to one-third the speed of light allowing the fleet to travel five times faster than previous propulsion technology but still slow enough to maintain complete control over where we're going. A crude fix, but effective, I guess. It's also a huge waste of time and resources given how fast we can now travel in deep space.*

Lon sighed.

Scientists should be working on solving that problem rather than spending all their time inventing mechanical Battle Spheres. I mean how effective can they be against the real thing anyway? No matter. At least we'll arrive in three days time rather than the two weeks it used to take us.

A few minutes later, slip ring indicator flashed that the system was charged. One by one, all the other vessels confirmed that they too were charged and in position. Once the Coordinated Launch Center received confirmation from the last craft, the ready for mission launch notice was transmitted across the entire fleet. The Communications Specialist turned toward Lon.

"Sir, the entire fleet is ready to go," he said.

"Let's do it," signaled Lon.

The Propulsion Specialist pressed the launch button, causing the cruiser to lurch forward. The Specialist studied the system readouts and controls. Satisfied with what he saw, he pushed a second button initiating maximum normal speed. The cruiser lurched again and accelerated. Confirming that the slip ring was deployed and in position, the third button was pushed, and the cruiser streaked away from Mitel. In rapid succession, the rest of the fleet launched and raced after Lon's cruiser.

The Mitel Leadership slowly made their way to the underground transport shuttle system located directly beneath their building. From there, they were transported to the medical facility at the far end of the complex. The time had come to administer the long-awaited immortality serum scientists had painstakingly developed. It consisted of oral fluids followed by transfusions administered through the arms, back, abdomen and thighs. The oral fluids relaxed the body and temporarily neutralized its immune system to ward of possible rejection of the highly invasive chemical mixture. As they traveled across the compound, members looked at each other silently. Their emotions ranged from muted excitement, to apprehension, ambivalence and even fear. During the development process, the serum was administered to dozens of captured resistance fighters and their families. The early results were nothing less than tragic, as each and every patient died a horrific and painful death. As time went on, the recipients survived for longer and longer periods of time until the serum, based on the monitored results, appeared to work. Ironically, the Leadership ordered the newly created immortals killed. Although the scientists cautioned that the process was not perfected, the Leadership decided that they were out of time. It was now or never.

The members were brought to the serum transfusion quarters. The state-of-the-art facility was exceeded only by the Nomas underground medical complex hidden deep beneath the Stone Forest.

"We are giving ourselves the best possible chance of success," said the first member when the decision was made.

"Yes, but that may not be enough," replied the second member. "More testing is still needed."

"By the time the process is finally perfected," scolded the third member, "we will all be dead!"

"So instead, you choose to die now?"

"I choose no such thing. There are risks in everything we do. This is no different."

"I disagree."

"Why?"

"We are doing this out of fear. Fear of death, fear of the unknown, and fear of losing control. Our judgment is clouded. Nothing good is going to come of this. Mark my words."

"Let's hope you're wrong," replied the first member.

The aging old men were escorted one by one to medical platforms in a row along a wall of the serum transfusion room. Each platform was surrounded by computers and diagnostic and monitoring equipment of all shapes and sizes. The men were strapped into position once serum delivery tubes were inserted at various points along their bodies. They were then handed a small tray of oral fluids.

The first member held up his glass as he looked toward the rest of the members.

"To immortality!" he announced loudly.

"Yes," replied one member enthusiastically, "to immortality."

"Indeed," replied another apprehensively.

"Let's hope," mumbled a third.

In a matter of minutes, the fluids took effect as the members lay silently, their eyes closed. A team of four dozen scientists, physicians and medical technicians, were closely monitoring their vital signs and several other indicators for each member. Everything appeared normal and the signal was given to deliver the serum.

At first nothing happened. The leadership members appeared relaxed and pain-free. But within a matter of minutes, pain radiated throughout their bodies.

"Ahhhh!" screamed one member in horrific pain.

"Something is wrong," moaned another, "I cannot feel my body."

The pain became unbearable. One by one, members groaned and twitched. A few became very agitated and tried to free themselves from their platforms. The medical staff looked on with alarm as every member showed signs of extreme physical duress.

"I don't understand," muttered the lead scientist.

"Maybe they are simply too old and frail," whispered a physician. "They are the oldest recipients we have ever administered the serum to."

Suddenly, alarm warnings sounded from one, then a second, and a third medical platform, signaling those members had slipped into cardiac arrest. Seconds later, two more members succumbed to the same thing. As the medical team scrambled to respond, the remaining members were placed in a medically induced coma. Two of the five cardiac victims were revived and quickly placed in a coma. The other three, including the ambivalent third member, died.

The remaining seven members remained in a coma for five days. When they awoke, each member was visibly more energetic, stronger and active. By all indications, the serum had succeeded. Unfortunately, the Leadership members were also noticeably more impatient and easily agitated; to where both scientists and physicians had become alarmed. Their fears were soon realized. The following week, the membership ordered killing the lead scientists, physicians, and their families.

"This shall serve as a warning to everyone," lectured the first member. "Going forward, we rule Mitel indefinitely. Opposition and incompetence will be dealt with swiftly and forcefully. There will be no leniency."

A new and even more brutal era on Mitel had begun.

CHAPTER EIGHTEEN – THE INVASION

Once the Thraen deep space surveillance system detected the approaching Mitel fleet, the six new Thraen cruisers were sent beyond the far side of Thrae's larger moon to minimize detection. Since that moon rotated around its own axis once every twenty-nine days, the cruisers had little trouble adjusting their relative location to stay hidden.

"The Mitels don't have the Centural magnetic storm to cloak them this time," mused Arius.

He watched the rows of hologram technicians track the approaching fleet from the GDC's elevated command platform. He stepped forward in his exo-skeleton body wrap to better view the screen monitors along the front wall. "They must have concluded we still lack a deep space surveillance system," he added. "They have become arrogant or careless *or both*. We shall make them pay dearly. Their continued aggression *must* be brought to an end."

"I completely agree," nodded Markus. "But as I've said before, the only way to end it once and for all is to bring the fight to them."

"You're right. But first things first. If this encounter goes as planned *and* we continue to aggressively restore our cruiser fleet, someday we'll be in a much better position to do that, but not before."

Beyond Thrae's atmosphere, the retrofitted renegade Mitel cruiser orbited the planet. Before it joined the other six Thraen cruisers, Zan piloted a USEP pod into outer space accompanied by Ard, Rad and three of his medical staff. As the pod bore down on the rear of the large craft, Zan initiated the craft's thrust vectors which caused the pod to decelerate and turn around 180 degrees. After the doors to the cruiser's left launch tube opened, a gravity control beam locked onto the USEP and guided it flawlessly into the launch tube. While the pod was robotically secured, the bay's rear doors closed. The bay was then quickly pressurized and once the all-clear signal was given, a large reinforced acrylic door opened. Dru and his assistants made their way toward the bright silver USEP. As the airlock doors slid open. Dru poked his head in.

"Welcome aboard," he said. "How was the trip?"

"Short and sweet," smiled Zan. "How is —"

"The cruiser? It's even better than expected."

"That's good news," smiled Zan. He stepped out of the pod and patted Dru on the back. "Nice work. Tell me, did you enjoy being cruiser commander?"

"Very much so. Lia, Dax and Mat are exceptional to work with. But my heart will always be down here in the propulsion area."

"I knew you would say that," chuckled Zan. He then turned toward Ard. "Let's get to the ICC. We must join the rest of the fleet."

"What about us?" asked Rad.

"The medical facility is waiting and ready to go," replied Dru. "You'll see that we made a few more equipment upgrades. I hope you will approve."

"Thank you," nodded Rad. "And as long as Zan lets us know what's going on *before* it happens, we should be fine."

"I'll do my best. Let's go," motioned Zan. He walked toward the HorVert elevator.

Entering the ICC, Dax, Mat and Lia smiled and nodded.

"The team is back together," clapped Ard, quickly making his way to the weapons computer station. Zan flopped into the command console.

"Let's join the rest of the fleet," he instructed. "Lia, is our encrypted tracking device up and running?"

"Yes Commander," she replied. "We register as just another Thraen cruiser to the rest of our own fleet."

"Good. This engagement is going to be tough enough without risking friendly fire."

Seconds later the refurbished renegade cruiser turned and headed toward the dark side of Thrae's larger moon. As it passed behind the large natural satellite, the six sleek new cruisers lined up in a row came into view.

Ana grew nervous and apprehensive as she entered the Thraen solar system. She constantly glanced at her mini screens to make sure she was not too far in front of the Mitel fleet. When Thrae appeared as a small marble up ahead, she became even more conflicted.

It's so beautiful, she thought. Memories of her childhood all came flooding back to her. Her thoughts then drifted to her family still being held captive.

I must do this to free my family. There's no other way.

Decelerating rapidly, her scanners detected the ring of Thraen defense globes.

Not my problem, she thought. *I'm here to engage the two Battle Spheres, nothing more.*

In the GDC, the hologram first officer rushed to the command platform.

"Sir, the Mitel Battle Sphere has arrived and is just beyond our outer atmosphere approximately twelve hundred miles southwest."

"Has it engaged our defense globes?"

"No, Sir. At least not *yet*."

Arius's instincts told him that the Battle Sphere was searching for only two objects: Janus and Chad.

"Instruct the globes to stand down unless attacked first," instructed Arius. "Initiate full tracking protocols."

"Yes, sir," replied the first officer before rushing back to the main floor.

Arius quickly punched in the three-digit code on his console communication device. It beeped twice.

"Janus Stone."

"The Battle Sphere has arrived. We are sending the tracking link to your Battle Holograms."

"OK, thanks. Chad *let's go!*" shouted Janus.

The device again beeped twice.

Markus turned to face Arius. "If you'll excuse me, I'm going to return to the underground base to see if I can be of any assistance."

"Very good my friend," nodded Arius, "good luck."

"You too," replied Markus. Once outside the GDC, he returned to his monitoring orb and sped off.

Ana hovered beyond the planet's atmosphere and studied the beauty of its curving surface. She was again filled with conflicting emotions.

I need to free my family, she kept reminding herself.

At that moment, Ana felt so alone. She checked her mini screens to confirm that the armada was on schedule.

OK, she thought. *It's time.* She darted down toward the planet surface.

Janus and Chad ran outside Bay Number 1 onto the shelf and took up positions fifty feet apart. Janus glanced toward Lake Victoria before closing his eyes to concentrate. Chad looked up at the sky and wondered where Jim might be at this exact moment before closing his eyes. He had Molly promise she would remain safely in the underground base after the approaching Mitel fleet had been detected.

Janus was the first to transform as the silver metallic mesh pattern resembling shards of glass quickly spread from his eyes to cover the rest of his body. Janus's eyes turned bright white before he levitated fifteen feet up into the air. Seconds later, Chad was also covered in the same silver mesh. Shortly thereafter, they were levitating side by side as heavy metal trace elements and helium-4 approached from the atmosphere and ground areas. Swirls of shiny particles of titanium, aluminum, magnesium, cadmium, iron and beryllium whirled around the two blue plasma spheres.

Beams of white light streamed from their eyes toward the ground across the Mesa. The same shiny particles appeared from all directions and swirled there too. Two Battle Holograms formed from the ground up while Hologram personnel moved back and forth inside each holo-gram structure.

"OK Commanders let's get this mission started," said Nolia.

"Agreed," added Lucian.

Janus and Chad listened to the background chatter while they scanned their computer mini screens.

"Propulsion systems on-line . . ."

"Core patterns normal . . ."

"Laser cannons fully operational . . ."

"Energy levels normal . . ."

Then a familiar voice was heard above the chatter.

"Hi Darius. Martin here. I can see you again from my Command Cube."

"Hello Martin," waved Darius. "We've completed preflight diagnostics. Everything is a go."

"Same here," confirmed Martin. "Ready to synch target identification?"

"Affirmative."

"OK great. Synching commenced."

There was a slight pause.

"ID confirmed," replied Darius, "and . . . databases synched."

"We are ready to launch when you are, Command-ers," instructed Nolia.

"Let's go," replied Chad.

The Battle Hologram teams sped up Chad's and Ja-nus's variable speed flywheels causing their Battle Spheres to spin faster and faster until they leveled off at one hundred twenty thousand revolutions per minute.

"Launching in three, two and one," said Martin.

Both Battle Spheres raced skyward and headed south. A short time later, Ana's Battle Sphere appeared on their diagnostic mini screens.

"There she is," said Chad. He then realized Ana had stopped and was hovering in place. "What's she doing?"

"Waiting for us," replied Janus. "Let's approach her very slowly."

"OK," replied Chad. The two spheres slowed to a stop three-hundred yards from Ana's spinning sphere. "We need to try to reason with her," he added.

"Opening up a communications channel now," said Martin.

"Hello, my name is Chad —"

"I know who you are," interrupted Ana abruptly.

"*You do?*"

"You are part of the Thraen military. The same people who failed to protect my family from the Mitels."

"*What?* That's not true."

"Chad is right," added Janus. "The two of us came back to Thrae only recently. Regardless, who are you?"

Ana did not respond.

"I said, who —"

"My name is Ana."

"Ana *who?*"

"What does it matter at this point?"

"A great deal, actually since you are Thraen."

"I may be Thraen, but I'm *not* one of you."

"Of course, you are, Ana."

"NO! I am not. Thrae turned its back on me *and* my family."

"Ana, you were abducted in a surprise raid. That's not Thrae's fault. As a matter of fact, you were being *guarded* by our military. They were killed defending your family during that raid."

"OK then, why didn't anyone come to rescue us? We waited and waited. I was eventually taken from my family and repeatedly tortured and forced to partially transform like an experimental animal. I was held prisoner in a spherical chamber in complete darkness. I was triggered to partially transform over and over until I became violently ill. I was poked and prodded, strapped into painful harnesses and given countless injections until I passed out. I wanted so badly to be with my family and be hugged by my mother and told that everything was going to be OK. I cried and cried and I begged for help, but nobody ever came."

"It must have been horrible. Ana we're sorry for all of that."

"If I refuse to do what the Mitel Leadership wants me to do, my mother and sisters will be killed."

"We're here to help you."

"*Help me*? I was deserted by my own people and left for dead. Even my Battle Hologram refused to help me!"

Ana grew silent for a moment.

"But none of that matters anymore," she added.

"Ana, listen —"

"No, you listen. I taught myself how to fly and how to use my laser cannons on my own. And now, I have come here under orders to confront the two of you."

"Ana, we're very sorry for what happened to you. Like I said, Chad and I weren't here at the time. And besides, Thrae was so badly damaged after Mitel's second invasion they really didn't have the ability to rescue you."

Ana didn't respond.

"Listen Ana," said Janus gently, "things are changing. We can help you now. You can choose not to obey them."

"I have no choice at this point. I must do what I've been ordered to do. *My family's life depends on it!*"

"Ana —"

Ana opened fire at Janus with a continuous stream of plasma laser pulses from twenty laser cannons.

"Janus, watch out!" blurted Chad.

The force of the concentrated attack pushed Janus's Battle Sphere backwards fifty yards. His outer defense shields quickly weakened. In Janus's Command Cube, the hologram personnel were taken aback by the magnitude of the energy barrage.

"His plasma shield is weakening," said Martin.

"She can't maintain that barrage very long," replied Nolia. "She'll have to retreat and recharge."

"She's one angry kid," mused Darius, "and she's venting that anger through her laser cannons. I don't know how she's doing it, but I'm going to bet she can keep this up for a *while*."

Chad stared dumbfounded at the unfolding attack. He didn't know what to do.

"Chad, we need to open fire," said Darius.

"But what if we destroy her?"

"If we don't, she'll destroy Janus."

"Commence fire," instructed Nolia. "Medium energy bursts. Do it now!"

One hundred of Chad's cannons fired, the light pulses curved away from Chad's spinning surface before streaking ahead toward Ana. The onslaught forced Ana to retreat.

"Let's go after her Chad," ordered Janus.

From his command console in Cruiser Number 1's ICC, Lon gazed at the screen monitors. Thrae appeared as a large marble in the center monitor, its two moons visible almost directly behind it.

"Ana preoccupying the Battle Spheres was our first critical step," he said. "There's cause for optimism."

Lon glanced at his communications specialist.

I want to move in closer," he said. "Order three transport vessels to follow us."

"Yes, Sir," replied the communications specialist. "What should I tell the rest of the fleet?

"Instruct the cruisers to fan out as we approach the planet. Have the remaining transport vessels and supply craft stay back for now."

"Sir, I've detected a network of spherical satellites around the planet," confirmed the scanning specialist.

"How many?"

"Twenty. Scans suggest they are military defense satellites but they don't match anything in our database."

"Perform a more detailed scan."

"I did. Those scans confirm the presence of laser weapon systems and possibly laser cannons."

"We've encountered those satellites before. Our fighters should have little trouble eliminating them."

In the GDC, Arius monitored the continuous updates flashing across the large wall mounted monitors.

"Commander," said the First Officer, "the eight Mitel cruisers are fanning out. I'm guessing they're preparing to launch their cluster pods. Shall we send in our cruisers?"

Arius stood up and approached the elevated railing.

"Order the two closest outer defense globes to launch cluster pods as soon as their cruisers are within range," he said firmly. "With a little luck we'll catch them off guard. If so, we'll instruct our cruisers to move in for the attack."

Janice and Chad closed in on Ana's Battle Sphere. Tracking their approach, she darted toward the ground.

At the last second Ana turned and sped along the surface, hugging the terrain.

"What's she doing?" asked Chad.

"She's trying to keep us pre-occupied," replied Janus.

"I agree," added Lucian.

"The Mitel cruisers have fanned out," said Darius.

"You know what that means," replied Martin.

"Cluster pods, "confirmed Nolia.

"We've got to try to stop them," said Janus. "Chad: I'll follow Ana while you go after the Mitel cruisers. Hurry and be careful!"

"On my way," replied Chad, immediately streaking skyward.

Registering that Chad was headed toward outer space, Ana stopped to face Janus. As he slowed down, she opened fire with an even more intense barrage of plasma laser fire.

In the ICC of Cruiser Number 1, the scanning specialist detected the approaching Battle Sphere.

"Commander, a Thraen Battle Sphere is entering the outer atmosphere."

"ARRGH!" growled Lon. "I knew it! She cannot handle both at once. This mission could unravel in a hurry if we don't neutralize those Battle Spheres."

"Incoming cluster pods."

"*What*? From where?"

"The Thraen defense globes, Sir."

"Why didn't we pick that up in our detailed scans?"

A few seconds later, incoming pods plowed into the cruisers on either end of the Mitel cruiser row. The vessels destabilized and broke apart in bright flashes of white light.

"We just lost two cruisers," announced the scanning specialist nervously.

Lon angrily pounded his fist on the arm of his console seat.

Receiving their instructions, the six Thraen cruisers raced forward.

"Aren't we going to join them?" asked Ard, somewhat confused.

"Not immediately," replied Zan. "We don't want to give up our stealth advantage. Let's wait until things get just a little more hectic. At that point, we should be able to join the fight undetected."

The scanning specialist in Cruiser Number 1 stared at his scanners in disbelief.

"Sir, scanners confirm six Thraen cruisers headed our way!"

"*What*! Thraen cruisers? From *where*?"

"They appeared from behind the far side of their largest moon, Sir. Their configuration doesn't match anything in our database. They are significantly larger and faster!"

"How did our blockade fail to detect those cruisers being fabricated?" Lon asked tersely. "I told Leadership that the Thraens must have re-established their deep space surveillance capabilities by now. But did they listen? *No*! Pompous old fools! Thrae knew we were coming and we walked right into their trap!"

Then it suddenly dawned on Lon.

"*The traitor*! He must have overseen their propulsion upgrades! Commence defensive protocols. *Do it now*!" he barked.

All six Mitel cruisers launched a barrage of cluster pods toward predetermined population centers. As Chad entered outer space, his mini-screens registered dozens of pods streaking toward the planet. He immediately thought of Jim and the devastation of Amer.

I must stop every single pod, he thought.

"Identifying targets," said Darius calmly.

Battle Sphere weapons specialists stared impatiently at their individual weapons screens as the incoming pods propagated as alpha-numerically identified white dots. As the pods released their clusters, the number of target increased dramatically.

"Targets locked," confirmed Lucien, "one thousand four hundred and fifty-two to be exact."

Now within range, weapons specialists opened fire at the pods, each cycling through their assigned cluster of five laser cannons. Chad's Battle Sphere appeared in space as a bright white mini star, emitting thousands of high energy plasma bursts that curved away from his spinning sphere before streaking ahead to intercept, destabilize and disintegrate the cluster warheads on impact. The closest outer space globes also targeted and fired plasma bursts at the incoming projectiles. One by one they were all destroyed.

"Order the transport vessels to launch their strike fighters," directed Lon from his console seat. "We must eliminate those outer space defense globes before they wipe out our entire fleet!"

At four thousand feet long, the Mitel transport vessels contained three stacked flight decks which accommodated 100 Mitel strike fighters per deck. The fighters entered and exited through a large slot at the rear of the vessel which used a permeable plasma shield to buffer the decks from the effects of outer space. From a distance, the vessel appeared as an enormous, partially squashed cigar with a tapered profile that widened from front to back. The vessel contained two large wings and matching winglets on either side of the back end and three equally spaced vertical tails up above. The 900 strike fighters streamed out the rear slots of the three huge transport vessels and quickly destroyed the nearest outer space globes.

In the GDC, the second officer approached the raised command area. "Commander, Mitel strike fighters have joined the conflict. They are systematically eliminating our outer space defense globes."

"Notify every underground base to launch as many tactical fighters as possible." Arius ordered.

In less than a minute, Thraen tactical fighters raced up dozens of underground flight ramps, exiting through heavily concealed access slots. The fighters streaked skyward; their four inline high output plasma thrust engines at max power. Within four minutes, four hundred and thirty-two fighters had entered outer space and joined the fray, their six superheated high energy hydrogen plasma burst laser cannons firing continuously.

Susan was performing her first combat mission as a Thraen fighter pilot. She singlehandedly eliminated thirteen Mitel Strike Fighters before returning to base.

In the renegade cruiser's ICC, the crew monitored the developing battle. They also listened to the back and forth between Ana, Janus and Chad.

"It looks like our forces are off to a great start," said Ard, "although it appears to be turning into a free for all."

"That's what I was hoping for," Zan mused.

"*Why*?" asked Lia.

"Thrae possesses superior technology and firepower and will excel in a freewheeling engagement. In my experience, Mitel battle plans have always been somewhat rigid. They tend to unfold in stages to be successful."

"I tend to agree," replied Ard. "By the way, what's up with that Battle Sphere anyway? She seems pretty angry."

"Ana?" asked Lia. "Maybe *you* should pay more attention Ard. She has been mistreated and taken advantage of almost her entire life. Wouldn't *you* be angry?"

"I guess so. But she could also channel that pent up anger in positive ways."

Lia rolled her eyes. "*Such as*?"

"Helping her own people defeat her oppressors."

"At this point, I don't think she trusts anyone. And for good reason."

"You're right and I'm truly sorry. We have to find a way to earn her trust."

"I think that's what Janus is trying to do, although he may not know it yet."

"I hope he figures it out before she beats him into the ground."

"Me too Ard," added Zan. "It's also time for us to join the fray. Navigator: full power."

"Yes, Sir," replied Dax.

The renegade cruiser streaked forward out from behind the moon, banked right and raced toward Thrae.

On the planet surface, Ana relentlessly fired concentrated plasma streams at Janus forcing him to retreat for short distances at a time. He was feeling sluggish and drained, but stubbornly refused to allow his battle Hologram to return fire. Although he wasn't sure why, his intuition told him he shouldn't, at least not yet.

"Energy reserves are down to 15 percent," announced the Battle Hologram energy specialist.

"Commander," said Lucian, "you must withdraw and recharge *now*."

"Understood," replied Janus wearily.

He turned and raced away at all out speed. Ana chased after him but simply could not match his explosive acceleration. Janus eventually ducked underneath a grove of dense foliage and came to a stop. Janus's flywheel was quickly disengaged causing his sphere to cease spinning. He tried to relax while his Battle Sphere started to reenergize. Janus then heard a familiar noise as Ana streaked by up above him.

She's searching for me, he thought. *Hopefully I can recharge before she finds me.*

"You OK Janus?" asked Martin.

"I think so."

"I'm surprised by your restraint."

"For whatever reason, she is reluctant to engage our outer space defense forces. If that's the case, then it makes sense for me to keep her occupied down here, rather than risk her destroying some of those forces."

"I think so too."

"How are we doing up there?"

"Chad is doing great and our defenses have clearly caught the Mitels fleet off guard. So far so good."

Janus switched to a secondary communications channel. "Please turn off our outgoing communications link with Chad," he instructed.

"What? *Why?*"

"I don't want to distract him."

"But . . ."

"Do as I ask."

"Yes Sir."

Janus sat silently and listened to the chatter between Chad, his Battle Hologram and the rest of the Thraen defense forces.

On the ICC of Cruiser Number 1, Lon studied the screen monitors as Mitel and Thraen fighters clashed in outer space. It quickly became clear to him that the Thraen fighters were superior to their Mitel counterparts. After Chad arrived, the conflict turned into a rout, leaving the remaining six Mitel cruisers defenseless. Growing visibly frustrated, he turned toward the Communications Specialist.

"Order the three remaining transport vessels, supply and weapons craft to withdraw! We can't risk losing the entire fleet."

"Doing it now," replied the communications specialist. "What about our cruisers?"

"Instruct them all to launch a second round of cluster pods. That should draw the Battle Sphere away and allow us to regroup. In the meantime, Navigator: position this cruiser in between the two nearest transport vessels. Do it now!"

"Yes, Sir."

That should shield our cruiser for now, he thought.

Seconds later, the five other Mitel cruisers launched a second round of cluster pods before turning and racing forward to confront the approaching Thraen cruisers.

Janus checked his power level.

It's only 28 percent, he realized. *Something's wrong.*

"Nolia, why am I recharging so slowly?" He asked.

We don't know," she replied. "We are running several diagnostic scans. Ana's constant plasma cannon barrage may have temporarily affected your core energy signature. The other possibility is that your renewed ability to transform came with a slower ability to recharge."

"Wouldn't it have been flagged during initial diagnostics, not to mention early weapons testing in the shared asteroid belt?" asked Darius.

"It should have, yes."

Explosions erupted all around Janus turning his concealed foliage enclosure into a flaming inferno. He reengaged his flywheel and darted skyward only to come under yet another fierce barrage from Ana's laser cannons. Janus's energy reserves quickly dwindled.

"This is *not* good," muttered Darius shaking his head.

The Thraen cruisers moved within firing range of the five Mitel cruisers and launched several high ordinance missiles. The two leading Mitel cruisers took numerous direct hits before disintegrating in bright white flashes. Two other Mitel cruisers took evasive action; one turning hard right toward Thrae while the other banked hard left away from it. The fifth cruiser raced head on toward the approaching Thraen vessels, releasing a barrage of lethal cluster pods.

Chad's Battle Sphere, having abandoned the outer space fray, bore down on the second round of cluster pods as they entered Thrae's upper atmosphere.

I've got to get them, he thought.

"Identifying targets," said Darius.

The Battle Sphere weapons specialists stared impatiently at their individual weapons monitors as the pods appeared on their screens. As the pods released their clusters, the number of targets proliferated.

"Chad," warned Lucian, "a grouping of Mitel strike fighters are bearing down on you from two different directions."

"I see them," replied Chad.

"Identifying new targets now," confirmed Darius.

The Mitel fighters opened fire at Chad, the force of their high energy ordinance against his plasma shields caused Chad's Battle Sphere to jerk back and forth. Chad glanced down at his energy reserves. They were now down to 34 percent. Seconds later, the weapons specialists opened fire at the cluster missiles, cycling through their assigned cluster of five laser cannons. Chad's erratic motion made their job much harder as his plasma laser pulses repeatedly missed their mark.

"I can't get them!" barked a weapons specialist.

"Stay focused," encouraged Nolia. "We can't let them reach the surface."

Beyond Thrae's atmosphere, the cluster pods from the lead Mitel cruiser found their mark. Thraen Cruiser Number 2 buckled before disintegrating into countless shards. Only seconds later, high energy ordinance from another

Thraen cruiser plowed into the lead Mitel cruiser, obliterating it.

"Commander," said Mat, "wide range scanners show a Mitel cruiser is positioned between two transport vessels off to our right."

"Are you thinking what I'm thinking?" asked Ard.

"Lon Rexx is commanding that cruiser," grunted Zan.

"Yes! That's his trademark move. Let's go after him."

"Several stray cluster pods approaching," announced Mat.

"Navigator: veer hard left toward the planet," instructed Zan. "We *must* avoid that ordinance."

"Yes Sir!" replied Dax.

"Commander," said Mat, "two of our cruisers are in pursuit of a Mitel cruiser that is headed toward the far side of the planet."

"This is what I was hoping for," replied Zan, jumping up from his command console.

"What do you mean?" asked Ard.

"I'll explain later. Navigator: set a course around the near side of the planet. I want to intercept that cruiser."

Near the planet surface, Ana continued her laser barrage at Janus causing him to briefly plummet toward the planet surface. He finally recovered about fifty feet above the ground before swerving and racing along the planet's surface contour.

"Janus! Watch out!" shouted Nolia.

But it was too late. Janus struck the corner of a large moss covered stone outcropping, exploding the ledge into millions of little pieces. The force of the impact knocked him unconscious. Janus's Battle Sphere stopped spinning as it arched through the air before descending toward the surface. It plowed through a heavily wooded region known as the Stygian Forest before coming to a stop, partially buried in a small crater. It became eerily quiet as a haze settled over the region.

"Janus, can you hear me?" Nolia asked urgently.

There was no response.

The Command Cube scrambled to run diagnostic checks.

"I need an update *now*," snapped Nolia impatiently.

"It appears his weakened shields held up through the crash landing," said Darius. "That's all we know so far."

"We must get to him right away," replied Nolia, "before Ana inflicts more damage."

"Sending twenty Thraen fighters to that location now," confirmed Arius, "along with several medical and military hover crafts."

Ana followed the half-mile long path of destruction through the fog covered forest in search of Janus' Battle Sphere. Tree limbs and wood splinters of various shapes and sizes were everywhere. Reaching the crater, the light blue hue of Janus's plasma defense shield was now gone, signaling the initial phase of his reverse transformation process. Ana stared at it in disbelief.

I caused that, she thought incredulously. *But he didn't fight back. I just don't understand. After all I've heard about Thraen Battle Spheres. Even Lon Rexx fears them . . .*

In the sky three hundred miles to the south, Chad's weapons specialists cycled through their plasma laser cannons, firing at the Mitel fighters and cluster missiles. One by one, the fighters and several missiles were eliminated. Once all the fighters were destroyed, Chad focused on the remaining cluster missiles.

"There isn't much time," he said. "We need to hurry."

Ana hovered above Janus's Battle Sphere for a time. Her diagnostic mini screens registered the approaching Thraen fighters and support craft heading in her direction. Ana tracked their approach for several seconds before darting toward the sky in search of Chad.

Beyond Thrae's atmosphere, Zan's cruiser circled around the planet. Cruiser Number 5's scanning specialist registered its approach.

"Sir," he said, "One of our cruisers is approaching."

"We're in luck. Which one is it?"

"I'm not sure. It's not registering . . ."

"Request their assistance immediately."

On the ICC of Zan's renegade cruiser, Mat's scan detected Cruiser Number 5.

"Sir," said Mat, "the Mitel cruiser is approaching around the horizon."

"They're trying to contact us," confirmed Lia.

"Patch them in," instructed Zan.

"Repeat, Cruiser Number 5 here. We are being pursued by two Thraen cruisers. We require your immediate assistance."

"On our way," replied Zan. He then turned toward Lia.

"Can you hack into their database?"

"I'll try." She inserted a program module into her computer launching high-speed searches of encrypted communications signals. Almost immediately, streams of data appeared. Lia refined her search before instructing her module to search for the highly classified systems *back door*. A few seconds later, she heard a long beep.

"I'm in."

"OK," replied Zan, "I want you to download everything about the cruiser: crew, mission logs and plans, specifications, identification, *everything*."

"Doing it now."

"Hurry, before they lock you out."

"Don't worry," smiled Lia. "I've already locked them out."

"What are you doing?" asked Ard.

"Stealing its identity," replied Zan.

On Cruiser Number 5's ICC, the communications specialist noticing something strange. "Commander. It appears someone has breached our classified database."

"What?" the Commander hissed. "*Who*?"

"I don't know."

"Lock them out!"

"I'm trying Sir. Wait . . . *We've been locked out!*"

On the ICC of Zan's renegade cruiser, he stared at the screen monitors.

"Lia, shut down their communications and monitoring systems," he instructed. "We mustn't allow them to transmit any logs of this encounter back home."

Lia typed furiously. "Doing it now," she announced. "And . . . data download complete.

"Excellent work." Zan then pivoted toward Ard.

"Fire cluster pods now!" he ordered.

At the weapons console, Chad typed quickly. He then looked at Zan. "On their way."

On the ICC of Cruiser Number 5, the scanning specialist confirmed that the approaching Mitel cruiser had fired several cluster pods.

"Commander, the cruiser has launched several pods," he announced.

"Hopefully they will shake the Thraen cruisers off our tail," replied the commander.

"Wait!" blurted the scanning specialist.

"*What now?*" the Commander asked.

The shaken scanning specialist turned toward the Commander.

"The pods are aimed at *us!*" he blurted.

"*What?*" the Commander shouted. "Navigator, hard right!"

"Yes Sir!"

As Cruiser Number 5 executed its evasive maneuver, several cluster pods detonated along its front and side. An instant later, the large craft disintegrated in bright white flashes.

Above the planet surface, Chad closed in on the remaining cluster warheads at all out speed.

"Identifying targets," said Darius. "Wait. The Battle Sphere is closing in on you from the North."

"I see her," replied Chad.

"Targets locked."

Ana and Chad's weapons specialists opened fire almost simultaneously. Chad's Battle Sphere vibrated under the force of Ana's assault causing several of the plasma bursts to miss their mark. Undeterred, the Battle Sphere weapons specialists continued to cycle through their plasma laser cannons. They destroyed all the incoming cluster warheads but one. It detonated directly above the population center of Altar. The force of the detonation vaporized everything within a half mile diameter sending shock waves in all directions. The destruction was absolute. At ground zero, there would be no survivors.

"*Nooooo!*" shouted Chad, "all those *innocent* men, women and Children!"

Ana listened to Chad's grief-stricken response over the communications channel, her anger replaced by sadness, shame and remorse. She turned and darted toward outer space.

Chad was furious. He immediately chased after Ana at all out speed. As he closed in on her, Lucian spoke.

"Chad, your father crash landed. Crews are trying to get to him."

"What's his status?"

"We don't know much yet. He ceased communications so as to not distract you."

First Jim and now Janus? he thought.

Chad was now within firing range.

"*It's all her fault.* Lock in on her," he ordered.

"Chad, I don't think he would have wanted you to destroy her."

"What? *Why not?*"

"He refused to return fire once she showed no interest in attacking our outer space defense forces."

"But she caused me to miss eliminating the last cluster missile!"

"Janus would probably tell you that the Mitel cruisers fired those missiles, not Ana."

Chad did not respond.

364

"Listen Chad, what she did was misguided, but she's obviously very angry and confused."

"Where's Janus?"

"The Stygian Forest. Rescue and recovery crews are arriving now."

Chad stared at his mini-screens one last time. Ana was now well within firing range. With a sustained high energy barrage, he would quickly wear down her shields and destroy her. Chad paused, reversed direction, and darted back toward the planet surface.

In outer space, two Thraen cruisers closed in on the three huge, but now empty, Mitel transport vessels. They failed to register Lon's cruiser sandwiched between two. Lon's Scanning Specialist detected their approach.

"Sir," he said. "Thraen cruisers headed this way."

"Energize our slip ring," replied Lon.

"Yes Sir," replied the Propulsion Specialist.

"What about the transport vessels?" the Communications Specialist asked.

Lon did not immediately answer.

On Zan's cruiser, Lia monitored the Thraen defense communications.

"Zan," she said. "Our cruisers are closing in on the three transport vessels.

"Did they register Lon's cruiser?" asked Ard.

"Not yet. Wait, they just detected an energy spike."

"Lon's preparing to escape," concluded Zan. "Instruct our cruisers to open fire."

"Slip ring fully charged," confirmed Cruiser Number 1's Propulsion Specialist.

"Excellent," replied Lon. "Now order the remaining transport vessels to withdraw."

"Incoming missiles!" shouted the Scanning Specialist.

"Full speed ahead!" ordered Lon.

Mitel Cruiser Number 1 emerged from between the two enormous transport vessels, turned and accelerated away from the planet. A third transport vessel sped after it. Seconds later, high energy ordinance detonated along the side of the first transport vessel. It destabilized and disintegrated. Several alarms sounded throughout the neighboring transport vessel indicating that shrapnel from the adjacent blast had penetrated portions of its outer hull. Before anyone could react, high energy ordinance exploded along its length, instantaneously destroying the vessel.

Lon's cruiser, followed by the remaining cruiser and third transport vessel, sped off into deep space. Ana, realizing that the mission was being abandoned, reluctantly raced off after them.

In the conflict, Thraen military forces lost one new cruiser, thirty-eight fighters and seven outer space globes. More important, fifty-five thousand civilians perished in the cluster missile strike.

"Such a tragedy," reflected Chancellor Jaret Adison sadly, "and so soon after the destruction of Amer. So many more innocent lives lost."

He stopped to wipe his eyes.

"What's the saying *we always use*? Oh yes. *But it could have been so much worse.*"

Jaret sighed.

"Maybe someday there will finally be lasting peace on Thrae. One can hope, and struggle to move forward."

Mitel forces lost six cruisers, three transport vessels and nine hundred strike fighters. It marked the second straight engagement where Mitel came out on the losing end against Thraen forces.

Lon let out a deep sigh as he flopped into his bed. He was not looking forward to his return to Mitel. Lon knew full well that he would face the wrath of the Mitel Leadership.

CHAPTER NINETEEN – THE PLAN

Chad followed the half-mile long path of destruction through the fog covered forest until he reached the recovery crews. His mind raced as he thought about Jim and Janus. He landed nearby, transformed back to his human form, and ran to the crater. Janus, still covered in his silver shard mesh, was being carefully lifted into a medical hover craft.

"How is he?" asked Chad.

"He's unconscious, but we think he's going to be OK," replied the medical officer. "With any luck, he'll escape with only a concussion and some contusions. We are considering placing him in a medically induced coma just to be safe."

Out in space, Zan and the rest of the ICC crew poured through the newly acquired data.

"The commander and crew appear to have been relatively green," said Zan. "That should be a plus for us."

"How so?" asked Ard.

"It should allow us to return to Mitel."

"Return to Mitel? *Are you crazy?*"

"We need to rescue Ana's family. Once we do that, she will return to Thrae. I'm certain of that."

"You're probably right. But a rescue attempt sounds like a pretty tall task."

"You think it's more challenging than heading six hundred light years across the universe in search of Chad Stone?"

"No. But it's probably just as dangerous."

Zan entered a code into his console intercom. It beeped once.

"Dru here."

"Can you activate the *crew*?"

"Right away." The intercom beeped again.

"What's that all about?" asked Ard.

"Dru worked with Thraen scientists to create a small device that when scanned from a distance, mimics a human life form. They can also be programmed to travel up and down hallways. An exterior scan will reveal a standard crew on board."

"That's a neat trick."

Zan then contacted Arius who appeared on one monitor in front of the ICC. He explained his plan.

"You'll need to locate the family first," said Arius.

"True," replied Zan, "I'll reach out to my uncle Zi, a senior commander with the Mitel resistance. I'm confident they will be motivated to help release Ana from her involuntary servitude."

"I agree, but are you *sure* you want to do this?" asked Arius. "It's going to be very risky."

Zan looked around the ICC. Everyone nodded their heads in support. "Yes," he replied, "I'm positive."

"Then I wish you a safe journey Zan Liss," responded Arius. "In the meantime, whom do you want to assume your role as Thraen resistance commander?"

"Since Janus is currently unavailable, Mayla Tallis and Teri Anton should make a very capable team."

"Good choices. I'll let them know. Before you depart, I want to have a Mission Departure Teleconference to walk us through the specifics of your mission plan."

"We don't have much time. We need to catch up to the returning fleet."

"Understood, but I need to make sure that this rescue mission is not just a one-way suicide voyage."

The screen monitor went black.

"I get the impression that Arius isn't too keen on the rescue mission," Ard mused.

"You're right," Zan sighed. "There's not going to be much room for error."

Minutes later, Rad sat down in front of his computer station in Cruiser Number 5's medical facility. He typed an encrypted message and hit the transmission key.

Hi Tor. It's Rad.

He stared at his screen for a time.

Hello brother. It's good to hear from you again.

Same here Tor. And thanks to your timely warning, we successfully repelled the Mitel attack force. Suffice to say that Thrae has been tenaciously upgrading their defense fleet and it paid off. Zan Liss has been invaluable. He and his mechanics helped upgrade the propulsion systems on several new cruisers, which proved crucial to our success.

That is very good news.

Indeed. We are now planning a return to Mitel.

What?

Given the immediacy of the mission, Zan had given Rad authorization to reveal details of the rescue. Rad quickly typed a brief explanation and hit the transmission key.

That wasn't a mistype. Thanks to several imbedded Mitel resistance fighters, we seized a Mitel cruiser during the previous conflict to end the blockade. Helped by another resistance member, we hacked the database and assumed the outward identity of Cruiser Number 5 just before we destroyed it. We are preparing to return in disguise to free the family of the young Thraen Battle Sphere. In doing so, Zan believes she will abandon her forced allegiance to the Mitel Leadership.

Tor responded quickly.

I am very impressed and Zan is probably correct in his assessment. When are you due to depart?

Soon.

OK. I will contact Zi Liss immediately. He will ascertain the whereabouts of the captives and pull together the resources on his end. I will report back to you.

Thank you, brother.

On the ICC of the renegade cruiser, Lia, Zan and Ard poured through the captured data logs.

"The Commander's name was Del Alline," Lia read aloud. "He graduated from the Mitel Military Academy just last year. He was only twenty-one . . ."

"The Mitel military is assigning young, untested officers to lead their cruisers in battle," Zan sighed.

"Maybe nobody wants the job," replied Ard.

"Maybe. Dax, you are now Commander Alline."

"Why *me*?" asked the 21-year-old incredulously.

"Once we make contact with the returning fleet, Lon will be suspicious. Despite our outward appearance, he will want to see and talk to you. We need someone very young and poised to convince him that we are the missing cruiser."

"But I won't know what to say."

"Don't worry. We'll prep you beforehand."

"But what if he asks a question that only a Mitel Academy graduate would know?"

"Relax. We'll set up a teleprompter for you to read from. Ard will act as the Propulsion Specialist and feed you the answers if necessary. *Commander Alline,* go to the cruiser supply area and find some clothes that fit you."

"Groan," replied Dax, rolling his eyes.

Two hours later, Zan's console seat intercom beeped. He stepped away from reviewing the computer flight logs and pushed the button. "Liss," he replied.

"It's Rad," said the voice. "Your Uncle Zi wants to speak to you."

"Great. Now would be a good time for the MDT. Lia: can you patch everybody in?"

"Doing it now," she replied.

One by one Arius, Mayla, Teri, Chad, Markus and then Zi appeared on each of the several monitors located along the curved front wall of the ICC.

"Hello nephew," nodded Zi. "It is good to see you again."

"Likewise," replied Zan.

"It is even better to know you are no longer affiliated with the Mitel military. Your parents would be extremely proud of you."

Zan nodded respectfully but didn't respond.

"Unfortunately," Zi continued, "I cannot talk long. Special Forces are in the area. Jun tells me we must keep moving."

"This is GDC Commander Arius Court. Do you know the whereabouts of the young Battle Sphere's family?"

"Yes," nodded Zi. "They are being held in a heavily fortified complex at the base of the Black Mountains. It was once the summer palace of the ruling family before the Mitel Leadership came to power. It's located above a relatively small population center. Access on foot from there without being discovered will be difficult. The Black mountains rise sharply on the other three sides. We originally believed that Mitel Leadership families were being protected there. Instead, we received confirmation from an imbedded resistance member that the young female Battle Sphere's mother and her two sisters were being held captive there."

"Can the imbedded resistance member be of any assistance to us?"

"No. They've since been eliminated."

"That's a pity."

"Zi," said Zan. "I know that fortress. Isn't it relatively close to our old development complex?"

"It's within the range of our hover craft, yes."

"Is the complex —"

"Still abandoned? Yes."

"How about the landing strip? Is it serviceable?"

"We probably need to clear away some debris, but we can get our people up there right away to secure the facility and get the landing-assist system up and running."

"OK great. We could land the USEP at night and travel by hover craft to the complex."

"Don't forget how tough it is to land there," said Dru from the back of the ICC.

"Understood."

"How would you get to the planet surface undetected in the first place?" asked Zi.

"We would exit the cruiser as we pass that region's outer space commerce entry point. We could shadow a large cargo vessel as it transitions through the upper atmosphere. From there, we would quickly veer off onto the high altitude flight lane before abruptly descending to the old development facility."

"You'll be detected as soon as you exit the flight lane."

"*For further evaluation*, yes. But we'll be labeled as an illegal commerce vehicle and given low priority. Mitel fighters won't arrive for at least two hours to sweep the area."

"OK. Assuming you're correct, we still have the bigger problem. The rescue itself will be a challenge."

"It will obviously need to be a surprise attack," Zan acknowledged. "I'll give you my thoughts and people can let me know if they agree, OK?"

Everyone nodded.

"After we land, Markus will fly over there in his monitoring orb to scan the complex. He'll map out the best access point; the location of Ana's mother and her two sisters; and the most direct pathway between the two. Chad will transform and swoop in to create a diversion by firing a barrage of low energy plasma pulses all around the complex."

"I like the idea of a controlled diversion," replied Zi. "It would distract attention away from our approaching hover craft."

"We used a similar diversion back on Earth," added Mayla. "It was very successful."

"OK good," replied Zan. "Chad can provide cover fire on the way back to the development complex."

"He can do the same as you depart in the USEP and then the cruiser," said Teri.

There was a brief silence.

"Is there anything anyone wants to add? Concerns?" asked Arius, "Now's the time."

"It's going to be tricky, that's for sure," replied Zi.

"And we'll need to adjust on the fly," added Mayla.

"You have our full support no matter how it unfolds."

"Thank you," nodded Zan. "I'll be down in the USEP to get Chad and Markus within the hour. We'll leave immediately thereafter, OK?"

"Sounds good," replied Chad.

"I must go now," said Zi. His monitor turned black.

"Thanks everyone and good luck," said Arius.

Once Zan returned to the renegade cruiser with Chad and Markus, it sped off to catch up with the rest of the returning Mitel fleet. Markus showed Chad around the cruiser since it was his first time aboard one.

Soon thereafter, Zan stepped out of the HorVert into the ICC and made his way to the command console. Ard, still reviewing the log reports, stood up to stretch before approaching Zan.

"Zan, what are we going to tell them?" he asked.

"Tell who?"

"Lon Rexx and the rest of the returning Mitel fleet."

"Why we were missing in action?"

"Yes."

Zan thought for a moment.

"We'll tell them what the cruiser commander *should* have done. We were forced to flee into deep space from the opposite side of the planet to escape three Thraen cruisers."

"Do you think they'll believe us?"

"We'll find out."

Tor called another emergency meeting of the Nomas elders in the grand chamber to discuss the Thraen rescue plan. He looked out at the ascending semicircular shaped seating area. Once again, there wasn't an empty seat.

"Thank you all for coming on such short notice," said Tor.

"What is the emergency *this time*?" an elder asked.

"Zi Liss notified me that Zan Liss is coming back here to rescue Ana's family."

"Why does that concern us?" a second elder asked.

"If the family is successfully rescued, Ana will no longer be forced to serve the Leadership. I want to help."

"Are you *sure* about that?"

"I'm sure enough that I think we should help."

"And if the mission fails? What then?"

"*Then it fails*," replied Tor. "But at least we'll have done something to influence events in ways that benefit our people." Tor then explained the rescue plan. When he finished, the hall remained silent for a time.

"*It's too risky*," said a fourth elder eventually.

"Yes, it is," added a fifth.

"Why?" grunted Tor.

"*Why*? What if our warriors are captured during the raid?" asked the first elder. "They will most certainly be tortured for information. What if one of them relents and reveals the location of this underground city? What then?"

"We both know that a Nomas warrior would *never*, under any circumstance, reveal the location of this place."

"One can never be certain of anything that happens in the Atreus."

"I agree," nodded the second elder.

The chamber erupted in discussion. Once it settled down, Nya, the oldest and most respected elder stood up. Everyone turned and strained to look at her.

"Why do you believe this one particular mission is so critically important that we get involved?" she asked.

"The Thraen resistance is working side by side with the Mitel resistance," replied Tor. "That's huge. Together they have identified a strategic mission that benefits all of us. If Ana's family is successfully freed, she will most certainly defect back to the Thraens. There would be no reason for her to do otherwise. In return, the Mitel resistance will have taken a formidable asset away from the Mitel Leadership. But as I said, the two organizations working together and trusting each other is an enormous step forward. We owe it to ourselves to insure that this mission is successful. We also owe it to the entire populations of both Thrae and Mitel."

"I see. What if the mission is unsuccessful and the family is *killed* in the process? Thanks to you, Ana now knows we exist. She also knows our approximate location. Wouldn't she find a way to extract revenge?"

Tor thought for a moment.

"In my opinion, we can't think in terms of failure," he replied. "If we choose to act based solely on that, we have *already* failed."

There was a brief silence.

"Tor is right," acknowledged Nya. "However, I also believe that the mission is very risky and prone to failure. And if it does fail, I fear Ana will not only come back here to destroy us all, but she will also bring the Mitel military along with her. I'm sorry Tor, but I must vote against participating in this mission." She then slowly sat back down.

"I agree with Nya," said the first elder.

"It could result in our total destruction," added the second elder.

"In my opinion the mission is very sound," replied Tor, growing frustrated.

I say we put it to a vote," said a third elder.

"All in favor of *not* participating in the rescue mission raise their hand."

One by one hands rose until three-quarters of the elders in the Chamber held their right arm up in the air.

"Very well, this Chamber has spoken," said Tor. "While I disagree with its decision, I will abide by it. Thank you all for coming."

As Tor walked briskly out of the Chamber, the elders talked loudly amongst themselves.

I will officially abide by the elders' decision, Tor thought. *What I do unofficially is a different matter altogether.*

CHAPTER TWENTY – THE DECEPTION

With the upgraded propulsion units operating at maximum normal speed, Zan's renegade cruiser caught up to the rest of the returning Mitel fleet. Along the route one of Dru's mechanics jettisoned solar powered signal accelerators from the rear of the cruiser at predetermined intervals.

In the ICC, Dru and the rest of his mechanics were putting the finishing touches on a makeshift intercom system.

"The teleprompter is all set up," announced Dru. He had placed it directly in front of the command console to allow Dax to stand and face the monitors as he spoke. Dru then glanced over at Ard seated at the weapons console.

"Type something," he instructed.

Ard complied.

I sure hope this works.

There was a small beep in Dax's ear indicating that he had just received a tele-message.

"Dax, can you read the message OK?" asked Dru.

"I can read it fine."

"OK. But can you read it *without* staring directly at it?"

Dax, wearing a Mitel cruiser commander's uniform, looked at the ICC screen monitors before quickly peeking back at the teleprompter.

"Umm, yeah. No problem."

"OK. Let's try it again. *Ard?*

Lon Rexx is a murderous psychopath . . .

Dax glanced again quickly at the teleprompter. "Yes," he grinned.

"Good," replied Dru. "Now Ard: talk into your fiber optic communicator."

Ard reached up to touch the almost invisible clear optic line that curved from his ear to his mouth.

"Hello boss, can you hear me?"

Janus, seated at his computer in his commander's quarters, stared at his view of the ICC.

"I hear you loud and clear Ard," he replied.

Ard gave Dru the thumbs up without looking back.

"OK," said Dru. "I think we're good to go."

On the ICC of Cruiser Number 1, the scanning specialist noticed a signal from out in deep space.

"Sir," he announced. "Scanners have detected something approaching us from behind."

"What is it?" asked Lon.

"It's too far away to perform a detailed scan. But whatever it is, it's slowly gaining on us."

"Could it be a Battle Sphere?"

"No Sir. It's much bigger."

"Strange . . . keep a close eye on it."

Zan's intercom beeped from across his quarters. He walked over and pushed the button.

"Liss here."

"Hi it's Lia," said the voice. "Mat said we were just scanned."

"Was it —"

"Preliminary? Yes."

"That means a detailed scan is not far off."

"Correct."

"Notify everyone to get ready."

"OK." The intercom beeped again.

Zan then punched in the code for Markus's mobile communicator.

"This is Markus," said the voice.

"It's Zan. Can you and Chad meet me in my quarters as soon as possible?

"We're on our way."

On Cruiser Number 1, the scanning specialist continued to track the approaching object. Once in range, he performed a detailed scan.

Seconds later, the communications specialist received an incoming signal. The specialist turned toward Lon.

"Sir," he said, "I just received an incoming beacon signal from Cruiser Number 5."

"*What*?" asked Lon.

"Detailed scans confirm that the approaching craft is in fact Cruiser Number 5," added the scanning specialist. "It shows a full and active crew."

"I thought that cruiser was *destroyed*," replied Lon incredulously.

"We never actually confirmed that, Sir."

"Contact them immediately," instructed Lon. "I want visual verification."

On the ICC of Cruiser Number 5, Lia received a transmission request.

"They are asking for a visual conference," she said.

"Here we go," muttered Ard. "You ready Dax?"

"Yes," he replied. He quickly positioned himself next to the teleprompter.

"Zan, are you there?" asked Ard.

"I'm here," he replied. Seconds later, the door slid open as Markus and Chad entered his quarters.

"Lon Rexx is contacting us now," explained Zan. "This is our first big hurdle."

Suddenly, Lon's stoic face appeared on the ICC's center wall monitor.

"So this is the famous Lon Rexx," said Markus.

"*Infamous is more like it,*" whispered Ard. "The guy *never* smiles."

"Would you if you were him?" asked Zan.

"*Uh, no,*" whispered Ard. Lon spoke.

"This is Lon Rexx, commander of the Mitel forces. Whom am I speaking with?"

"Cruiser commander Del Alline," replied Dax.

"Our detailed scans have confirmed your electronic ID, computer logs and physical configuration as Cruiser Number 5."

"That's correct, Sir."

"Where have you been, commander?"

"During the confrontation, we found ourselves being pursued around the planet by three Thraen cruisers. I gave the order to retreat into deep space to escape them."

"Why didn't you turn to confront them?"

"We were badly outnumbered, Sir. To do so would have been suicide. I thought the best course of action was to escape the three cruisers and then circle back to assist the rest of the fleet."

"I see . . ."

"Once we determined that we were no longer being pursued, I immediately ordered our cruiser to return to the planet. When we realized the rest of the fleet had withdrawn, we raced to catch up."

"Understood. I noticed you are a recent graduate of the Academy."

"Yes I am," replied Dax. "Are you inferring that my inexperience affected my judgment?"

"*Good one,*" whispered Ard.

"Well, no," replied Lon defensively. "I've just never heard of a cruiser catching up so late on a return voyage without giving prior notice. Why didn't you send out a distress signal?"

"We didn't have time."

"There's *always* time for distress signal."

"Lon is clearly suspicious," said Zan. "We need to change the subject, and do it quickly."

Ard typed.

Dax's fiber optic communicator beeped. He quickly glanced at the Teleprompter.

"Well, I didn't and I'm sorry. I was thinking about the safety of my crew."

Lon didn't immediately respond. He looked around his ICC. Everyone was staring at him. They all knew he had positioned his cruiser between the two transport vessels to avoid being destroyed.

"A noble gesture certainly," he answered eventually. "But given how the Mitel resistance has infiltrated every aspect of our military, I must make absolutely sure you are not one of them."

Ard continued to type.

"Commander Rexx. I'm sorry I didn't follow proper protocol. And I must admit, I'm a bit nervous since you are such a legend at the Academy."

"*Ard what are you doing?*" hissed Zan.

"*Don't worry,*" whispered Ard.

"What do you mean?" replied Lon awkwardly.

"Everyone there knows about your accomplishments in CCCF," explained Dax.

"*They do?*"

"Yes," replied Dax. "You won more CCCF matches than any other combatant. From what I've been told, you were undefeated other than the one competition against an outsider. Rumor has it that he cheated and then pinned the blame on you."

Well, I —"

"What was his name again? The *cheater*?"

"*Zan Liss,*" replied Lon disdainfully.

Zan grunted in disgust.

"Easy my friend," said Marcus, "in due time, we'll make him pay for all that he has done."

"He went on to become Mitel Emperor," Lon continued, "and soon after that, a traitor to us all. He sabotaged our mission to planet Earth. I have a feeling that he had a hand in the ambush we narrowly escaped."

"*You don't know the half of it big guy,*" whispered Ard as he continued typing.

"I hope that one day I can help you catch him," said Dax. "It would truly be an honor."

Lon stared at the screen momentarily. He felt confident that the young commander was telling the truth and could be trusted.

"With the help of loyal commanders such as you, one day we shall," he replied eventually. "Commander: please position your cruiser alongside the transport vessels for their additional protection while we complete the voyage to Mitel."

"Yes, Sir."

"And Commander . . ."

"*Sir*?"

"It's good to have you back."

"Thank you, Sir."

The screen monitors suddenly went blank. Everyone was silent initially. Zan let out a deep breath.

"I wasn't sure where you were going with that at first, Ard," said Zan finally.

"Neither was I," added Dax.

"The guy is an egomaniac, plain and simple," explained Ard. "I'm just glad we were able to turn the focus back to him before things got out of hand."

"Agreed," replied Zan. "Nice job gentlemen. But our job only gets harder from here on out."

A day and a half later, the remaining fleet entered Mitel's outer orbit. Chad and Markus stood at the rear of the ICC and stared at the planet. It was the first time either of them had been to Mitel.

"It's not Earth or Thrae," Chad mused. "But it's still beautiful."

"So is a venomous spider," replied Markus.

"OK," said Zan. "Our next step is to carry out a night landing at the old development complex. Ard: can you figure out the upcoming times we'll be passing by that region's outer space commerce entry point?"

"I'll get right on it," Ard replied.

Zan then entered a code into his console intercom. It beeped once.

"Dru here."

"Is the USEP ready to go?"

"We're finishing up pre-flight checks now. Should be ready to go within the hour."

"Great. Thanks."

The intercom beeped. Zan then looked over at Lia.

"Any word from Zi?"

"Yes. The development facility has been secured and the landing strip is clear. He says everything is quiet, at least for now. They have four military grade hover crafts on site, ready to go."

"Good, thank you."

Zan turned his attention back to Ard.

"Any luck?" he asked.

"OK," replied Ard. "Objects rotate around Mitel once every hour and thirty-six minutes. The regional commerce entry point is as of this moment . . ."

Ard Glanced at his multi-view computer screen.

". . . twenty-one minutes ahead of us. It will be dark in a little less than six hours. That means our earliest night-time departure would be approximately six hours fifty-seven minutes from now."

"And every hour and thirty-six minutes from there," replied Zan.

"Correct. But at this time of the year, there is only seven hours of actual darkness at the old development facility."

"Your recommendation would be . . . to depart at the first available night cross-over to in order to maximize our time under the cover of darkness."

"Yes."

"OK. Let's start the departure clock and begin final preparations."

"Clock started . . ."

Relaxing in his quarters on Cruiser Number 1, Lon received an urgent transmission requesting that he return to the Hub immediately. From there, he was to head straight to the Mitel Leadership building.

I am not looking forward to this, thought Lon. *Those grumpy old men will be in a foul mood. I just hope I can talk my way out of this mess one more time. After that, I'll set my plan in motion. If all goes well, I'll no longer have to care what any of them think.*

CHAPTER TWENTY-ONE – A NEW HOME

In the circular enclosure, Atlas organized his back-pack as he prepared to head out in search of food. Hearing Atlas moving about, Jim sprung up from his cot.

"Can I go with you?" he asked.

"It's really not very exciting," replied Atlas.

"I don't care. I just want to get out for a little while. You know, smell the fresh air."

"OK, sure. Just stick close to me. Scavengers come out at night."

"OK," nodded Jim.

The two headed down a long tunnel toward a large, blackened door. Jim noticed that Atlas was fading in and out more than usual tonight. He wanted to ask how he was doing but decided against it. When they reached the door, Atlas used his focused energy to turn the inside handle and push the slab open. They climbed the two sets of stairs to a small passageway in silence. At the top, Atlas turned to Jim.

"Wait here," he instructed.

Atlas floated to the passageway opening. He stopped and looked both ways for a short while. After adjusting his backpack, Atlas motioning Jim to follow.

"All quiet," said Atlas as Jim approached.

Jim stepped out onto the elevated walkway and took a deep breath. The fresh air smelled great. He could feel a slight breeze against his face.

"This way," instructed Atlas.

Atlas brought Jim to another passageway several hundred yards down the elevated walkway.

"Follow me," he said.

At the end of the passageway was a HorVert elevator. The tube itself was clear acrylic. Atlas stood in front of the sliding doors, activated his focused energy in his legs and waited.

"Don't you have to push a button?" asked Jim.

"No," chuckled Atlas. "The elevator senses people's feet in front of the door."

Seconds later, the silver and clear acrylic car came sliding down the tube.

"You really aren't from around here are you?" joked Atlas.

As the doors slid open, Atlas walked in followed by Jim. As the doors slid closed, Atlas said "Level four, fifth stop please."

Above the door, Jim noticed two lights go on, labeled L4 and S5. A second later the HorVert rose up into the air past one elevated walkway, then a second, then a third. Jim stared out at the population center. It was breathtakingly beautiful at night. The sixty glass covered sky structures, circular at their base which curved up to form a group of tightly bundled cylinders of different heights, were all lit up.

"Wow," whispered Jim.

At the fourth elevated walkway, the HorVert changed direction and headed horizontally past four exit ports. At the fifth port, the HorVert stopped, and the doors slid open.

"Let's go," instructed Atlas.

Jim followed Atlas three hundred yards to a narrow passageway. As Atlas entered, he motioned to Jim to follow. The dimly lit passageway took them behind a popular food establishment. Atlas knocked three times on the rear door. Several seconds later, the door opened and a beautiful female hologram emerged.

"I thought you said you weren't coming," she said. "Hey, and who's your friend?"

"He's our new traveling companion," replied Atlas.

Finch studied Jim momentarily. She sensed there was something different about him. She could tell he was a kind and gentle soul.

"You have pretty eyes," she smiled. "What's your name?"

"I don't —"

"He's having some memory issues," said Atlas.

"Oh, were you in the military?"

"Maybe," replied Jim.

"OK, well my name is Glade. People call me Finch. Nice to meet you. I was in the HPF for a long time, and I witnessed a lot of people suffer with memory loss. Anyway, come on in and have a look. It was a busy night so there isn't much left to pick through."

Jim followed Atlas and Finch down a short hallway to the prep room. On a counter were several baskets. Atlas rummaged through each one. As he did, Finch watched Jim intently.

"How's Isak?" She asked eventually.

"He's doing well," replied Atlas. "He's been training quite a bit with our friend here."

"Really! You must be a pretty good fighter then," she grinned.

"I'm not so sure about that," replied Jim shyly.

"Well, you've got a big bump on your head, not to mention a few nicks here and there. Do they hurt?" She reached over and with her focused energy, touched Jim's patch gently. The feeling of her hand against his skin felt good, almost tingly.

"Scavengers," replied Atlas as he put down his backpack. "A large group of them tried to ambush us back in Amer. Isak and our friend here took care of them."

"See, I told you. You *are* a good fighter."

"You said that already," Atlas smirked. He inspected several small bags of food from each basket before placing a few into his backpack.

"Where are you staying?" asked Finch.

"The usual," replied Atlas.

"Down there?" frowned Finch. "It's so dirty."

"It's pretty clean actually."

Finch then looked Jim directly in the eye. Her eyes were a beautiful pale blue.

"If you need a place to stay for a while, let me know."

"Finch, what's gotten into you today?" asked Atlas.

"*What*? I have extra sleeping quarters."

"I'll keep that in mind," replied Jim meekly.

"Good," smiled Finch. "You know, you look familiar somehow. It's like I've seen you somewhere before."

"I don't think so . . ."

Atlas quickly picked up his backpack.

"OK, it's time to go," he said. "We need to make a few more stops before everything closes."

Finch followed Atlas and Jim to the back door. As they exited, Atlas turned to Finch. "Thanks for the food.

It's greatly appreciated. I hope I can make it up to you someday."

"You keep saying that," she smiled. "I tell you what. Bring your friend back with you next time and we'll call it even, OK?"

"Sounds good."

Finch waved goodbye to Jim as she slowly closed the door. They walked to the elevated walkway in silence.

"This way," said Atlas.

As they walked along, Atlas looked at Jim.

"I've known Finch for a long time," he said. "She was a dedicated and reliable member of the HPF."

"HPF?" asked Jim.

"Hologram Protective Force. Long ago, we were just like you. Flesh and blood. But we volunteered to become members of the HPF."

"How?"

"Our bodies were infused with a gamma ray energy burst which instantaneously transformed it into an almost infinite number of discrete electrical signals that activated our living hologram. It included our electrical DNA, our brain's discrete memory, feelings, preferences and physiological traits. I mean, we were still us, but in a different physical form. Instead of blood and tissue, we used modest amounts of electricity and plasma energy to maintain our physical structure and appearance."

"That's incredible."

"It's probably Thrae's greatest scientific achievement. A hologram's initial transformation charge was supposed to last thousands of years due to the minor resistance or impedance of the hologram representation. Unfortunately, early versions like me don't seem to have been perfected. My charge appears to be running out much sooner."

"So that's why you are fading in and out."

"Yes."

"Can't you just get another charge?"

"I don't know. But since Isak and I are now outcasts, I don't think that's a realistic possibility."

"You won't know unless you try."

"True."

The two walked along in silence for a time.

"She seems to like you."

"You mean Finch?"

"Yes. She's not normally like that."

"But I'm human and she's a hologram."

"So what?"

"I mean how . . . you know?"

"Focused energy. If you close your eyes you can't tell the difference."

"I see. Well anyway, tell me more about her."

"Finch? She was under my command in Isak's Battle Hologram. Like many, she grew increasingly concerned about Val Rand's reckless behavior. After one particularly dangerous incident, she lodged a formal complaint with the World Council. After a brief investigation, Val was completely exonerated. It was a mockery. And instead of being listened to, Finch was punished."

"What happened?"

"She was released from the HPF."

"How did she handle that?"

"She was understandably angry and bitter at first. Imagine allowing your body to be forever changed to serve a cause you strongly believed in, only to be betrayed for doing the right thing and speaking up."

"That's sad."

"Indeed. Val was so flashy and popular and such a formidable fighting machine, that nobody dared to speak out against him. At least not back then. But time has a way of healing deep emotional wounds. Maybe *healing* is not the right term. Over time you simply learn to live with it. Disappointment like that never really goes away. And besides, if she hadn't been let go, she would have perished with the rest of my team."

Reaching the HorVert, Atlas took Jim down to the ground level.

"We're going to the industrial area which also houses the hyper speed railway rolling stock," he explained.

As the doors slid open, they stepped into the darkness.

"It's always kind of dark down here," explained Atlas. "The lights are always on, day and night. The corridor network is located below this level and the underground bunkers are below that."

Atlas and Jim made their way past rows of sleek hyper-speed electromagnetic railway trains. Every lead car had a very pronounced wedge-shaped front end. The streamlined silver and black vehicles were now covered in dust.

"They haven't run since the last Mitel invasion almost sixteen years ago," Atlas mused. "A shame really."

Atlas brought Jim to a large incinerator plant. It was dark and foreboding. Huge recirculation tubes were everywhere, connecting one structure to the next.

"This place burns all kinds of waste," explained Atlas. "The gases are recycled, separated, and burnt over and over as heat is slowly pulled out for geothermal and other uses. The residual gas is eventually released back into the environment as cool clean air."

"Wow," muttered Jim.

"This way," pointed Atlas.

They headed to the structure where food was burned. As they entered through a side door, they saw Caden

Holder, another hologram. Atlas waved as they approached.

"Hello, my friend," smiled Caden, "how are we doing today?"

"*Caden is naturally upbeat,*" whispered Atlas. "Gets on my nerves sometimes."

Jim chuckled.

"I'm well Caden," replied Atlas.

"Who do we have here?"

"He is a travel companion that we met in Amer."

"What a tragedy *that* was. And now Altar. Maybe someday we will finally see lasting peace."

"One can only hope."

"Indeed. Well, you are free to look around. We just received a delivery. I was getting it ready to burn it."

The two engaged in small talk as Atlas picked through the food. They both showed Jim what to look for and what to avoid.

"Most of it isn't fit to eat," explained Caden. "Your best bet is to focus on the plastic food and fluid containers. They tend to be the freshest and are sanitary. We run it all through a separator first to reclaim the plastic."

"What about metal containers?" Jim asked.

"That's a good one," laughed Caden. "It's been six hundred years since we last used those. But I still remember them. My memory is still pretty good," he added, pointing to his head.

When they were done, the three men shook hands.

"Come back any time Atlas," said Caden. "Always good to see you and always nice to have visitors. Oh, and your friend here is welcome too."

"Thank you," smiled Jim.

As they exited, Atlas looked down at Jim.

"Caden served a variety of hybrids while in the HPF. He then transitioned to a computer technician at the GDC before eventually being retired."

"Don't you mean *he retired*."

"No. The HPF forced him to retire over concerns that his electric charge had declined to the point where it affected his brain functions."

"Oh."

"It's funny, and I mean that sarcastically, how Thrae never really gave much thought about what to do with holograms once they are deemed no longer able to serve. Even though there's a hologram shortage in the HPF these days, holograms can't serve indefinitely. It's just not feasible. We're not robots. We are . . . I'm not sure *what* actually. But we're definitely *not* robots."

They took the HorVert elevator up to the passageway and made their way to the original elevated walkway. As they turned onto the walkway, Jim heard Atlas make a strange noise. As he looked over, he saw Atlas fade away and eventually disappear, his backpack falling to the ground with a thud.

"Atlas? Atlas where are you?" asked Jim nervously.

A minute later, Atlas reappeared.

"Where *were* you?"

"I don't know. It was bright. I thought, I don't know."

"You thought *what?*"

"I thought I saw people. People from my past. They were trying to talk to me but I couldn't hear them."

"Are you OK now?"

"I guess so."

Atlas reached down for his backpack. He reached for the pocket containing the small screen device. He hesitated, then stopped.

I'm worried about Isak. What will he do when I'm gone? he thought.

Atlas picked up his backpack and put it on.

"Are you sure you're OK?" asked Jim.

"Yes. Let's get back. It'll be morning soon."

As they walked along, a trio of Scavengers from Amer watched silently from the shadows. They had been sent ahead after receiving a tip from a local Scavenger group.

"That's them all right," whispered one Scavenger.

"We need to get word to Big Kelan," replied a second Scavenger quietly. "He'll round up a bunch of our guys and come here."

"Not only that," added the third Scavenger, "he'll bring the dwarf electro laser. That's when we'll get our revenge once and for all."

CHAPTER TWENTY-TWO – LON'S REBUKE

A well-worn Mitel shuttle pod slowly docked with Cruiser Number 1. Lon and several other crew members climbed in and were flown back down to the space transport facility on the Arman Matrix. As he exited the shuttle, Lon was once again greeted by six heavily armed members of the elite Mitel Special Forces.

"Commander Rexx?" asked one soldier.

"Yes," nodded Lon.

"The Mitel Leadership wants to speak with you."

"I suspected as much. But is such an elaborate escort really necessary?"

"I'm sorry, Sir, we are simply — "

"Doing your job. I know."

Lon was brought by hover craft to the Mitel Leadership Complex. He was led up the wide marble staircase by several Leadership guards, their footsteps echoing loudly. Upon entering the Leadership Forum Hall, only seven men sat behind the large, curved stone bench.

That's odd, Lon thought.

Approaching the bench, one guard motioned for him to stop. As before, the several guards who had escorted him up the stairs took positions all around him.

"Commander Rexx," quipped the first Leadership member directly across from him. "We'll get right to the point. You have failed us once again!"

"I don't understand what you mean."

"*You don't understand what we mean*? Did you crush the Thraen resistance?"

"Well, I —"

"It's a yes or no answer!"

"No."

"Did you come back with most of your fleet?"

"We ran into —"

"*Yes or no!*"

Lon could sense something was different about the Leadership members. They were much more energetic, aggressive and aggravated.

"No," he replied quietly.

"You lost five of eight cruisers, three transport vessels, and nine-hundred fighters. Yet you only destroyed *one* small population center?"

Lon didn't answer.

"*Say something!*" bellowed the first member, his voice echoing throughout the hall. "We want to hear from the man who wants to be our next Emperor!"

Lon cleared his throat as he thought carefully of how to respond. *I must not agitate them any further,* he thought.

"Ana, *our* Battle Sphere. She was unable to contain the Thraen Battle Spheres."

"This meeting is not about her!" scolded member number 2. "We'll deal with her separately!"

"OK fine, but she was the lynchpin of our mission attack strategy," replied Lon defensively. "Not to mention that Thrae ambushed us with six *new* cruisers and a ring of well armed space globes. They knew we were coming. They hid their cruisers behind the dark side of Thrae's larger moon to avoid our scans. We were out maneuvered and outgunned right from the start."

"How was that possible?" asked the first member.

"Zan Liss."

"*Zan Liss*? Is that your answer to *everything*? The sun comes up every morning. Is that because of Zan Liss too?"

Lon glanced quickly side to side at the guards who stared stoically straight ahead.

"Answer me!" shouted the first member.

"With all due respect to this Leadership, the new Thraen cruisers were not only bigger, but much faster than any of their predecessors. Was that mere coincidence given the fact that Zan Liss almost singlehandedly upgraded the propulsion systems for our entire fleet? I don't think so.

The several data logs obtained from our cruiser blockade detected but failed to intercept two small spacecraft from deep space. Liss *himself* told me that he was escaping Earth in two small high-speed pods. These facts all point directly to Zan Liss."

"Understood and duly noted by this governing body Commander Rexx," replied a third member. "However, we put *you* in charge of a formidable fleet which included a Battle Sphere of our own, and one which successfully disabled one of the Thraen Battle Spheres."

"With all due respect, her abilities were somewhat limited. And besides, that still left one more, not to mention a fleet of advanced Thraen fighters, which proved to be more than a match for our own strike fighters."

"Where did all this new weaponry come from?"

"You're asking *me*? Remember, I was out on a year-long mission searching for the Thraen boy. *My* question to the Mitel Leadership is this: what was our blockade doing all that time? They obviously failed to detect any of the

Thraen development, testing and manufacturing facilities."

Lon summarized his thoughts.

"The Thraens painstakingly took steps to put themselves in a position to succeed against us. First, they destroyed our blockade. Knowing we would retaliate; they ambushed our fleet. Given all that we know, it is without question that the traitor, Zan Liss, was behind it."

"Maybe, *maybe not* Commander Rexx," replied the first member. "Regardless, you are giving Liss too much credit. The Thraen Battle Spheres played a critical role in defeating the blockade!"

"Granted, but —"

"Given our detailed mission plan, which included a Battle Sphere of our own, they should *not* have played such a critical role in defeating our fleet."

A sudden silence fell over the Forum Hall.

Once again, Lon quickly glanced side to side at the guards who continued to stare straight ahead.

"Commander Rexx," the first member began, "regardless of the mitigating facts and circumstances you have presented, the reality is that you have proven yourself incapable of leading a large-scale military operation. Zan Liss , now an enemy of the Mitel Empire, with only a *single* cruiser was able to destroy multiple Mitel cruisers and transport vessels outside Earth's atmosphere."

"But that was —"

"But *nothing* Commander Rexx! We painstakingly reviewed the cruiser logs and inter fleet communications acquired from the *only* returning cruiser from Earth. Our forces knew early on during the final engagement that Zan Liss had gone rogue. Despite this, he was able to hold a much larger force at bay until the young Battle Sphere chose to self-destruct. Those critical skills: to bravely outmaneuver and destroy a superior fighting force are skills you simply don't possess."

Lon did not respond.

Do you *disagree*?"

"As I said, there were several mitigating factors."

"We do not concur with that assessment. Accordingly, you are hereby immediately stripped of your rank of commander and placed under house arrest at the Arman military base until such time we decide your final punishment. Do you understand?"

"Yes."

"Do you have anything else you would like to say in your own defense?"

"No. Not at this time."

"Very well. Guards: take him away."

Lon Rexx was quickly escorted out of the Forum Hall. After the huge doors closed, the members looked around at each other.

"Well?" asked the first member.

"He has a following," replied the second member.

"That's what I've heard. Then I think it's time."

"Time for *what* . . .?"

"The time has come for Rexx to suffer a fatal accident at the base."

"Why not just kill him?" asked a fourth member, "As an example to those who dare to support him?"

"We don't need a martyr to contend with at this critical time," replied the first member. "And besides, now that we are immortal, we have all the time in the world to proceed cautiously when the situation merits it."

"I hadn't thought of it that way," smiled the second member.

"What is the status of the mechanical Battle Spheres?" asked the third member.

"One thousand are ready to be deployed on our command," replied the first member.

"Splendid. And the second-generation spheres?"

"They are currently in prototype testing. Initial results are better than expected."

"Excellent."

"Yes."

On the ICC of Cruiser Number 5, Zan glanced at the launch clock.

"OK," he said, "it's time to get down to the USEP."

"Let's go," replied Ard.

"Lia, I'm putting you in command," motioned Zan.

Lia stood up and nodded.

"At the first sign of trouble, I want you to withdraw into deep space, do you understand?"

"What about you?" she asked.

"We'll be in the USEP, and Chad will be in Battle Sphere mode. Hopefully we can either catch up to you or simply follow you back to Thrae."

"OK."

Ard followed Zan into the HorVert. After the doors closed, they sped toward the rear of the cruiser. Zan entered a three-digit code into the keypad.

"Rad Aarden speaking," said the voice.

"Rad. It's Zan. Time to go."

"Are you *sure* you need me?"

"Yes, in case things don't go as planned. The family may need medical assistance."

"On my way."

After the intercom beeped, Zan entered a second three-digit code.

"Markus, can you hear me?" Zan said through the intercom.

"Loud and clear my friend."

"It's time. Get Chad and meet us down in the launch bay."

"Will do."

The intercom beeped once just before the HorVert changed direction and headed down toward the propulsion area.

"How do you feel?" asked Ard.

"A bit apprehensive I guess," replied Zan. "A lot of things could go wrong."

"Isn't that always the case?"

"Maybe."

"Don't forget Zan, we'll have a Battle Sphere and the Mitel resistance backing us up."

"I'm not so concerned with that part. The big unknown is what kind of response we'll run into after we're detected."

"But you said —"

"I know what *I said*, Ard. The reality is we just don't know."

The HorVert came to a stop and the doors slid open. Dru waved from down the hall.

"It's all set to go," he said.

"Good," replied Zan. He entered launch chamber and headed directly to the USEP's open entrance door. As he approached, Zan noticed the oversized curving ring components extending from underneath the craft. Zan stepped into the pod and flopped into the pilot's console seat. Ard sat down next to him. As Zan ran through the final launch checklist, Rad stepped into the pod carrying his medical bag.

"Hey," he said before sitting down

A minute later, Chad and Markus, followed closely by his monitoring orb, entered the USEP and sat down in the third row of seats.

"Let's get this mission started," said Chad.

Dru stepped into the pod and gave one last look at the control panel before turning toward Zan.

"Please be careful," he said quietly.

"I promise," replied Zan.

Dru squeezed Zan's shoulder before exiting the pod. Once outside, he entered the keypad code, closing the USEP doors before exiting the chamber. Seconds later, the all clear light flashed on the pod's console.

Zan flipped three switches on the console which resealed the airlock doors and depressurized the chamber. Immediately thereafter, two large doors slid open at the far end of the chamber, revealing countless stars in outer space. Zan then pressed the launch button sending the pod streaking out the rear of the cruiser.

Lon walked across the Hub toward the officer's housing complex. The terms of his house arrest allowed him to move freely about the base. He was on his way to speak to Lex Golb, a well-connected Special Forces commander who supported a rebellion. Although Lex could not attend the secret meeting, Lon had received word he was very interested in the plan.

As he often did, Lon cut through a long spare parts storage hanger. It was getting late, and the facility was now idle. Lon walked along the extra wide center isle running through the hanger. Bright orange dashed lines were on either side of the shiny white center walkway which reflected the bright ceiling lights in all directions. Beyond the walkway, metal storage shelving units filled with cruiser replacement parts rose thirty feet into the air on both sides of the center aisle.

As he strode down the aisle, Lon continued to replay his recent conversation with the Leadership in his mind. There were so many things he wished he had said. Lon regretted that he did not mention he was very concerned that the Thraens had reestablished their deep space surveillance network; a concern that turned out to be true and helped doom the mission.

What's the point, he thought. *Those old fools simply don't care. All they want are results.*

Suddenly, a large bang echoed throughout the facility. Looking up, Lon saw a large section of shelving collapsing toward him. He instinctively dove forward as the structure crashed to the floor right behind him. Large spare parts tumbled in all directions. Lon scampered on all fours desperately trying to avoid them. Suddenly, a large engine cowl pinned his left leg. Glancing to his left, he saw heavy slip ring bars bouncing toward him. Lon instinctively raised his left arm to protect himself but incredibly, they all missed him before rolling to a stop. After what seemed like an eternity, it was quiet. Lon's leg hurt. Looking down, he saw blood through his pants. He pushed on the cowling as hard as he could, eventually freeing his leg. Lon staggered to his feet and drew his hand held electro laser. He looked all around. Nobody was there.

OK, he thought. *Somebody obviously wants me dead. I'm guessing it's the Mitel Leadership.*

Lon limped down the rest of the isle. Along the way, he repeatedly glanced toward the ceiling, his weapon still drawn.

Time to accelerate the implementation of my plan, he thought. Lon pushed his way through the doorway and hobbled off into the night. *I'll show them.*

Zan piloted the USEP toward the outer space commerce entry point. Directly ahead, a large commercial cargo vessel approximately three thousand feet long, was also heading toward it. Although somewhat smaller, it closely resembled, both in style and shape, its sister ship, the military transport vessel.

"OK," said Zan, "we're going to shadow that cargo vessel until we reach the high-altitude flight lane."

Zan initiated the pod's reverse thrusters as he carefully steered the USEP until it was traveling just above the cargo vessel. After passing through Mitel's upper atmosphere, Zan abruptly banked toward the high-altitude flight lane, leaving the cargo vessel far behind.

"Air traffic is pretty quiet up here," Ard mused.

"That's a good thing," replied Zan. He entered the landing strip coordinates of the old development facility before reaching for his night vision glasses. "This is where things get a little bit tricky," he added.

Zan piloted the pod down toward the surface under the watchful direction of the USEP's navigation computer. He reduced speed, pulled the nose up and banked left as the craft neared the surface.

At the Hub, a scanning and tracking specialist noticed a small unidentified object descend rapidly from the high-altitude flight lane.

Strange, he thought.

Zan's instrumentation panel flashed bright yellow indicating that they were approaching the surface. He looked out the trapezoidal front windows searching for the landing strip. The Black Mountains appeared on their left as Zan continued to scan the rugged terrain for the rectangular landing area. It suddenly appeared up ahead.

"There it is," he announced.

Zan manually raised the pod's nose slightly higher while the computer reduced the pod's speed to minimum normal. The USEP shuddered as it was grabbed by a landing-assist gravity control beam which quickly decelerated and gently landed the spacecraft.

At the Arman Matrix, the scanning and tracking specialist saw the object disappear from view near the surface. The sudden descent appeared to resemble a crash.

There's nothing out there that I know, he thought.

The specialist quickly alerted the squadron commander who, in a break from standard protocol, scrambled two strike fighters to quickly check out the area.

After coming to a stop, Zan turned the USEP around before shutting down the engines.

"Well, *that* was thrilling," grunted Ard.

"Glad we made it in one piece," added Rad.

"And that was the easy part," replied Zan. "Let's go."

Climbing out of the pod, they were greeted by a dozen resistance fighters. Zi walked over to Zan and gave him a big hug.

"Hello, Zan," he smiled. "Good to see you again."

"Same here Zi. If my memory is correct, the last time we met was *right here.*"

"Under much different circumstances," nodded Zi.

A resistance commander handed out small fiber optic headsets. "They're incredibly durable and very easy to sync," he said.

Suddenly a resistance fighter ran toward them from the largest structure.

"Two strike fighters are on their way," he yelled.

"OK. Let's get going," replied Zan. "Send Markus the target coordinates."

"We just did."

"Got them," confirmed Markus. "See you soon." His hologram returned to its orb and sped off into the darkness.

Chad walked over to an open area. He took a deep breath then raised his arms and spread his legs. Several resistance fighters stared in awe as Chad's Battle Sphere transformation unfolded. As the shiny metallic particles swirled all around, his Battle Hologram appeared near to the USEP.

Lon grimaced as he punched in the three-digit code outside the Hub's officer's living complex. As he entered, he was met by Lex who was muscular but about a foot shorter than Lon. Lex had a thick neck and since he was bald, his head seemed almost too small for his body.

"Lon Rexx?" he asked.

"Yes."

Lex quickly glanced up and down the hallway. He then noticed the blood stain on Lon's pant leg.

"What happened to you?"

"I barely escaped an *accident* on the way over. I'm guessing the Mitel Leadership has decided they no longer need me."

"Follow me, quickly," Lex motioned.

Lon hobbled into Lex's quarters. Before the doors slid closed, Lex peeked down the hall one more time.

"Can I get you something for that?"

"No, I'll be all right."

Lex's mobile communication beeped. He answered, then listened. "But there isn't anything up there is there?" he replied.

He listened again.

"I had forgotten about the old development complex. Keep me posted." His communicator beeped once again.

"What is going on?" asked Lon.

"An unidentified small craft crash landed in the Black Mountains. Two strike fighters have been sent there to investigate. It's not far from where the female Battle Sphere's family's being held captive."

Across the base, another computer specialist received an encrypted message from deep space. He wrote it down before forwarding the contents along to his commanding officer.

CN 5: We are under attack by one of our own cruisers. CN Unidentified.

Markus's monitoring orb passed above the small population center as he circled around to the far side of the heavily fortified complex. He noted the open area directly in front of the structure suitable for landing. Before entering the forest, he instructed his orb to scan ahead for motion sensing devices. After locating over two dozen, his orb intercepted and modified the wireless data to fool the central monitoring computer. One by one, Markus located and neutralized the motion sensors attached to various trees and large rocks.

Markus then headed to the tree line directly across from the complex. It was a large building, four stories high with thick granite walls and a flat roof. Scans confirmed several Special Forces soldiers stationed on the second, third and fourth levels. A half dozen more were positioned on the roof. A more detailed scan located Adria and her two daughters in connected rooms on the third floor's right side. Three soldiers were stationed directly outside in the hallway.

Markus instructed his orb to map out the entire structure. Side and rear entrances were on the ground level. There was also a large front entrance on the first floor. The structure contained three sets of stairways, one in the center and the others on each end. The orb registered ninety-three soldiers. Markus instructed his orb to transmit the information back to the resistance.

At the Hub's officer's complex, Lon explained his plan.

"I'm impressed," said Lex. "I'm also very encouraged that the Leadership guards have shown an interest in our cause. In my opinion, they will be critical to our success."

"I feel the same way," nodded Lon.

"When do you expect to receive an update from them?"

"Very soon. And given what just happened, I am very eager to get started. I must admit, the Leadership seemed different to me this last time. They had increased energy, looked different, and had an edge about them."

"Rumor has it that they are now immortal."

"*What?*"

"It's also rumored that some of them died during the process."

"That explains why I only counted seven of them."

Lex's mobile communication beeped again. He answered and listened. *"Are you sure?"* he asked.

He listened again.

"Very interesting. Let me know as soon as you hear anything else." His communicator beeped a second time.

"More news?" asked Lon.

"Yes. My contacts tell me a strange transmission was just received from deep space. It appears to be related to your recent mission to Thrae."

"What did it say?"

"It was sent from Cruiser Number 5. They were under attack from another Mitel cruiser."

Lon considered what he just heard.

"Did they say anything else?" he asked.

"No. That was it."

Lon thought for a moment.

"We were ambushed right from the start," he explained. "The Thraens clearly knew we were coming and were ready for us. We were systematically attacked on three separate fronts and suffered heavy losses. The stated mission unraveled very quickly from there. Cruiser Number 5 went missing during the battle but rejoined us on the way back. The commander was very young, a recent graduate from the Academy. Everything appeared to check out. I even spoke with him on the ICC monitors. There was no mention of being attacked by one of our own cruisers."

Zan, Zi, Jun, Chad and three Mitel resistance commanders gathered around a large computer monitor in the largest remaining structure across from the runway. They studied Markus's layout.

"OK" said Zi, "We already know there's an open field about a quarter mile from the right-side entrance. It's located just high enough above the fortress that the forest will block their rooftop view of our approach."

"Just to be safe, we should approach at treetop level," added a commander.

"Agreed," nodded Zi. "We'll land there and travel on foot through the woods until we reach the perimeter of the complex. Once Chad begins his diversion, my fighters will enter the lower level side entrance there," he pointed. "The second group will stage along the side wall to provide backup while the third and fourth groups provide cover fire from the perimeter, at least initially."

"They have a lot of firepower over there," said a second commander, "and almost one hundred specially trained soldiers."

"We can handle them," mused Jun. "We're just going to have to fight our way up to the third floor."

"That's why *you're* going in with me," grunted Zi.

The entire group let out a nervous laugh.

"One major challenge will be keeping the family safe," said a third commander. "The Special Forces soldiers stationed outside their rooms must have orders to eliminate them at the first sign of trouble."

"I think I know how to handle that," replied Zan. "Markus, can you hear me?"

"Loud and clear my friend."

"Before Chad creates the diversion, I want you to go up and secure the third floor hallway."

"Will do."

"I don't understand," said the third commander.

"Markus is a Thraen hologram," explained Zan. "That allows him to pass freely through physical structures."

"You're kidding *right*?"

"I guess you're too young to know about the Thraen *Hologram Protective Force*. They are quite formidable in this type of situation. When they want to operate in the physical world, they simply activate something called focused energy."

"The soldiers will be heavily armed."

"Trust me. It won't matter."

"Zan's right," replied Zi. "We'll extract the family and get them to a waiting hover craft which will land in front of the complex," he added, pointing to the screen. "We then get them back here as quickly as possible."

"What about the Mitel Military?" the first commander asked. "They will be on their way as soon as we begin the assault."

"Probably sooner than that," added the second commander."

"Chad will provide cover fire," replied Zan.

"Sounds good," nodded Zi. "Once back here, we load the family onto the USEP for Zan to take back to Thrae. Any questions?"

Everyone stood silently.

"OK then, we'll see you and Ard when we get back."

"What do you mean?" asked Zan.

"You need to have your guys stay here."

"Why?"

"Someone's got to fly the USEP. We'll also leave a perimeter force here just in case the Mitel military shows up before we get back.

"But —"

"No buts. Hand to hand close quarters combat is a lot different than flying a cruiser. If it's any consolation, I'd probably last thirty seconds trying to pull off the things you guys do up in space, OK? I can't even imagine what *that's* got to be like."

Zan looked at Zi for a time.

"Be careful Uncle."

"I always try. Besides, I have Jun here to protect me."

Everyone laughed nervously a second time.

"Any *other* questions?" asked Zi.

Nobody responded.

"OK, let's get going."

At the Thraen underground base, Mayla and Teri monitored the unfolding rescue mission.

"Computers confirm we have an active *twelve pack*," said Teri. "Running a systems check on them now."

Teri paused briefly.

"Solar powered signal accelerators are fully operational. Instantaneous communications and systems monitoring confirmed."

"Nolia, can you hear me?" asked Mayla.

"Loud and clear," she replied.

"Hey Teri," said Darius. "Chad has transformed, and systems are all normal. Everything is a go on this end."

"Excellent. We had great success having Chad create a diversion back on Earth. We fired a series of low energy plasma bursts all around the target area to distract the military forces long enough for Janus and Markus to complete the rescue."

"That sounds like a plan, although we should do more than just distract the Mitel Special Forces."

"Affirmative."

"Chad are you ready?" asked Nolia.

"I am," he replied.

"Zan, are we a go? Can Chad take off?"

Zan, now in front of the large computer monitor, put on his fiber optic headset.

"The hover crafts are on their way. Wait till I give the signal —"

"I don't think we can. Two Mitel strike fighters are approaching fast."

"Here we go," sighed Zan.

"Switching to free flight," said Chad, before racing skyward.

The four resistance hover craft flew close to the surface under the cover of darkness, zigzagging around the treetops. Jun adjusted his night vision glasses as he scanned the horizon for the open field.

"There it is," he pointed.

The craft landed in quick succession. As everyone jumped out, Zi reached for his ear mounted communications device.

"Markus, we've landed," he said.

"All quiet over here my friend," replied Markus. "I disabled the infrared motion sensors located along your approach route."

"Good thinking Markus," replied Zi. "OK everyone, let's go."

The heavily armed contingent followed Zi and Jun into the woods.

Chad raced along the tree tops to intercept the Mitel fighters.

"Identifying targets," said Darius. "Targets locked."

As Chad swooped skyward, two weapons specialists opened fire, obliterating the fighters in brilliant flashes of light.

"They never knew what hit them," said Nolia.

At the Arman Matrix, a scanning and tracking specialist lost contact with the two fighters. He contacted the in-flight communications specialist.

"Something's very wrong. They're not responding."

Chad circled back around and hugged the surface just above the tree tops, his Battle Hologram providing the directional coordinates.

"You are almost at the complex," said Darius. "Stop and wait until everyone is in position."

Chad immediately came to a stop and hovered above the treetops.

"Zi where are you?" asked Darius.

"We're almost at the complex perimeter," he replied. "Markus, time for you to go in and secure the third-floor hallway."

"I'm on my way."

Markus terminated his hologram just before his orb darted across the opening to the lower-level side door. When his orb arrived, Markus quickly reappeared. The reinforced steel double door had no exterior handle. He pushed on it but it didn't budge. Markus then reached inside and fumbled around for a handle to no avail. Instead, he felt a long metal bar. He slowly poked his head through the door and peered down the hallway.

Good, he thought, *nobody else here.*

Markus looked down and saw that the double door was held firmly shut by a large rectangular bar lying across two L-shaped brackets. He stepped through the door and using his focused energy, lifted the bar out of the brackets, carefully placing it on the floor against the side wall and away from the door. He pushed the double doors ajar.

"I'm in," he said quietly. "The side doors are open. I'm going up."

Markus quickly floated up to the second floor while his orb hovered silently in the hallway.

So far so good . . .

Approaching the third floor, he instructed his orb to perform an updated scan. It verified the exact location of the three soldiers standing in the hallway. It also confirmed that no other soldiers were on that side of the third floor. Markus turned and passed silently through several walls and rooms adjacent to the hallway until he reached the family's quarters. Adria and her daughters stared at Markus nervously.

"We're here to rescue you," whispered Markus. "You must remain quiet and be ready to move quickly when I give the word. *Do you understand?*"

They all nodded.

"You're a Thraen Hologram, aren't you?" asked Adria.

"Yes."

Markus pointed toward a large closet and instructed them to sit on the floor until he came for them.

"No matter what you hear," he said. "Don't move from this spot until I tell you to, OK?"

They nodded, sat down and held each other's hand tightly.

Markus quickly disappeared back through the side wall. Guided by his orb's directional coordinates, he stopped along the wall adjacent to where the soldiers were standing out in the hallway. Markus paused briefly before floating through the wall. He immediately enabled the focused energy in both arms and punched two of the soldiers in the face. They crumpled to the ground in an unconscious heap.

He then turned toward the third soldier who fumbled for his ball laser long weapon. In one motion Marcus ripped the weapon from his hands and struck the soldier in the face with its butt end, knocking him unconscious. The soldier fell back against the wall and slid to the floor on top of the others.

Markus quickly kneeled behind the fallen soldiers and pointed the ball laser weapon down the hall.

"I've secured the third-floor hallway," he said.

"And the family?" asked Zan.

"Unharmed but scared."

"We have reached the perimeter," confirmed Zi.

"OK, let's get this started," announced Nolia. "Until further notice, the entire Battle Hologram shall operate under full battle mode, no exceptions."

Chad eased forward. Within seconds, the complex came into view over the tree line. Several Special Forces soldiers could be seen standing on the rooftop.

"Identifying soft targets," announced Darius.

The soldiers pointed toward Chad. One of them frantically notified his commanding officer that a Battle Sphere had just appeared.

"Targets confirmed," said Darius.

The weapons specialists opened fire. The rooftop was sprayed with a low energy plasma energy burst, instantaneously vaporizing the soldiers stationed there. Trees all along the rear of the complex burst into flames. Soldiers on the floors below ran to the front windows and returned laser weapons fire; the bursts harmlessly deflecting off Chad's plasma shields. At the perimeter, Zi motioned two groups of resistance fighters toward the side entrance. Inside the complex, the Mitel communications specialist feverishly typed and sent a message on his computer:

We are under attack. Visual ID confirms it is a Battle Sphere, origin unknown. Repeat: we are under attack.

At the officer's complex, Lex's communications device beeped continuously. He answered once again and listened. "*What?*" he shouted. "I'm on my way."

"What's going on?" asked Lon.

"The two Mitel fighters have gone missing. Now our forces holding the hostages at the base of the Black Mountains are under attack!"

"By whom?"

"*A Thraen Battle Sphere!*"

Lon thought for a moment. He then suddenly realized what was happening.

"The traitor!" he blurted.

"*What?*"

"Zan Liss has come back to rescue the girl's family! He used the renegade cruiser and somehow disguised it as Cruiser Number 5! That also explains the unidentified small craft descending from the high-altitude flight lane and the Battle Sphere arriving here undetected! *We've got to get to the old development facility. We can ambush them there!*

"But you're under house arrest."

"I don't care! If we can capture or kill the traitor, I can redeem myself to the Leadership long enough for us to implement the plan. If we can take possession of Falon's family, *we* will control her!"

"OK, let's go."

They ran over to the base hover pads and scrambled into one of the many military hover craft headed toward the complex. Eighteen curved retractable overlapping roof sections closed tightly over them as the craft took off.

At the Complex, Chad's weapons specialists fired plasma bursts at the left side windows causing that portion of the structure to burst into flames. Zi, Jun and the two groups of resistance fighters dashed toward the side door. As they approached, Special Forces soldiers on the second, third and fourth floors open fire. Within seconds, they were forced to turn away from the windows by fierce laser weapons fire from the perimeter.

Several Mitel soldiers entered the third-floor hallway to secure the family. One by one, Markus cut them down with his ball laser long weapon. Outside, the resistance fighters reached the side entrance.

"Change of plans," shouted Zi, "everybody inside!"

With Jun out front, the resistance forces rushed down the first-floor hallway. Before heading up the stairway, Jun pulled out and activated his spray ball laser weapon. He killed the first wave of approaching soldiers. The conflict quickly turned into intense hand to hand combat. Jun wielded his longest knife with lethal precision as he led the charge up to the second floor. Zi motioned to the other resistance commander to split up to secure the lower floors. As they ascended the stairway, resistance fighters killed several Mitel soldiers fleeing the advancing flames. Many more Mitel soldiers were killed by perimeter fire as they exited the front entrance.

Jun raced up to the fourth floor followed closely by several resistance fighters. Zi stopped at the third floor and spoke into his fiber optic headset.

"Markus, its Zi. We're about to enter the third-floor hallway. I'll lower my weapon for you."

"Step out slowly," replied Markus.

Zi obliged, his laser weapon pointed down toward the floor. Markus then lowered his weapon, stood up and waved.

"Bring out the family," instructed Zi. "We need to get out of here before the fire engulfs the entire complex."

Markus opened the door and headed straight for the closet. Inside, the frightened trio were huddled together.

"Time to go," said Markus softly. "Follow me."

Markus, Zi and several resistance fighters led Adria and her two daughters down the stairs. On the way down, Zi called in hover craft from the open field. After securing the upper floors, Jun and his men raced down the stairway ahead of the advancing flames. After the first craft landed, the family climbed in, accompanied by Zi and Jun. One by one, the three remaining hover craft landed and picked up the rest of the resistance fighters. By now, the complex was engulfed in flames.

At the old development complex, Darius confirmed two groupings of Mitel fighters were descending through the upper atmosphere.

"They launched from a transport vessel passing right above us," he confirmed. "Lucky timing on their part . . ."

"I'm on my way," replied Chad.

He darted skyward.

The first hover craft landed at the old development facility followed by the other three. Everyone scrambled out of the crafts when they touched down. Seconds later, the first of the two dozen Mitel military hover craft appeared over the tree tops.

"Not good," snorted Zi.

Resistance fighters established defensive positions behind old storage containers, walls, abandoned equipment and ditches. All but a few of the Mitel hover craft landed on the runway, blocking the USEP's exit. As soon as the retractable overlapping roof sections opened, Special Forces soldiers jumped out of the hover crafts. Within seconds, an intense firefight erupted. Lon grabbed an electro laser long weapon as he jumped out the back side of his hover craft. He knelt to adjust his night vision glasses before cautiously following the soldiers into battle.

In outer space, several Mitel cruisers headed toward Zan's renegade cruiser from different directions.

Mat detected their approach and notified Lia. She immediately contacted Zan. He answered while running toward the USEP.

"What should we do?" she asked.

"Get out of there now!" he ordered.

"But —"

"*Now!*"

Lia reluctantly instructed Dax to retreat into deep space, easily outrunning the approaching Mitel cruisers.

As Zan spoke, he was spotted by Lon.

I knew it, he thought.

His heart pounding, Lon knelt and carefully aimed his electro laser long weapon directly at Zan. Several yards away, Jun saw the situation unfolding. In one fluid motion he pulled out his favorite knife and threw it. The razor-sharp weapon plunged deep into Lon's shoulder, causing him to drop his weapon, grimacing in agony.

As laser fire whizzed by in all directions, Jun sprinted straight toward Lon. Realizing that Jun was approaching, Lon yanked the knife from his shoulder and turned to face him. Jun dogged Lon's lunging stab then kneed him in the midsection. He grabbed Lon by the collar, punched him in the face several times as he pulled him into a nearby ditch.

"You murderous coward," Jun growled. "You knew our father was a resistance commander. He was murdered in cold blood, yet you *still* chose to join the military. You're nothing more than a traitorous whore for the Leadership."

"You're helping the Thraen resistance now," coughed Lon, blood pouring from his nose and mouth. "Who's the real whore here?"

Jun punched Lon twice more.

"I help anyone who supports our cause."

Lon groaned and spit out blood.

"I didn't know . . . about our father . . . until quite recently."

"I don't believe you!"

"It's true. Liss told me at the end of . . . the failed mission to Earth."

"You *never* had your suspicions?"

"No."

"You're *lying*! You are incapable of telling the truth. Not even to save your own skin. You're an embarrassment to our family and our people."

"Spare me your lecture," Lon replied, gasping for air while blood streamed from his shoulder. "Your resistance movement is futile. Regardless of how I feel or what you do to me or the Mitel military, the Leadership is about to unleash an army of mechanical Battle Spheres that will crush all who oppose them."

"Not if I can help it."

Jun pulled out his largest knife and placed it firmly against Lon's throat.

"Goodbye my brother."

Suddenly, a small high energy disk exploded close to the ditch. The force of the blast knocked the twin brothers to the ground. As Jun sat momentarily stunned, Lon staggered out of the ditch clutching his shoulder. He quickly disappeared into the woods.

Chad raced toward the upper atmosphere scanning his mini screens for signs of the Mitel Fighters.

"Identifying targets" confirmed Darius. "Eighty-eight fighters locked."

Within seconds, Chad's weapons specialists opened fire in all directions with incredible proficiency, vaporizing every last strike fighter. Chad quickly circled back down toward the old development facility.

On the planet surface, the firefight raged on. Jun looked around for Lon. *He's gone,* he thought angrily. Jun pulled out his spray ball laser weapon and climbed out of the ditch. He fired toward the approaching Special Forces with devastating results. Seeing Jun's remarkable bravery inspired Zi and the rest of the resistance fighters to rush forward with a barrage of ball laser weapons fire. The intense assault forced the Mitel Special Forces to retreat. Zi ran up to Jun and grabbed him.

"Now's our chance!" he yelled. "Let's go!"

Running directly behind Zi was Adria and her two daughters. The group hurried toward the USEP while Jun provided cover fire with his spray ball laser weapon. When they arrived, Rad lifted Adria and each of her daughters to Ard's outstretched arms. Zan, having climbed in, then pulled Rad's huge body through the USEP door while Zi and Jun continued to provide cover fire.

"Get in!" yelled Zan. "There's nowhere else to go!"

Jun, who was closest to the door, hesitated. Zi reached out with his free hand and shoved him closer.

"Hurry," he barked.

Jun reluctantly climbed in. An instant later, Zi was hit by a ball laser blast. He fell in a heap on the runway, his torso smoldering slightly.

"NOOO!" roared Jun. He lunged toward the door. Before Jun could exit, Rad dove across the USEP, pushed him down, before falling on top of him.

"Get off of me!" yelled Jun. "*Get off*! I need to save Zi!"

"You'll lose your life in the process," grunted Rad.

Zan jumped into the pilot's console and initiated the propulsion system.

"Ard, close the door!" he ordered.

Ard glanced down at Zi before reaching toward the keypad.

"We've got to help him!" yelled Jun. "Get off me or *I'll kill you*!"

Suddenly, out of the corner of his eye, Ard saw a huge being emerge from the darkness. He was dressed in black from head to toe with a black face cap. A second being appeared, then several more, all dressed the same. The first one stepped over Zi and in a single motion, kneeled down and pointed a large long weapon toward the Mitel forces. It looked like a spray ball laser, only much bigger. He pulled the trigger, emitting a continuous beam of superheated plasma energy. The entire tree line burst into flames. Two more beings kneeled down next to the first one and fired the same weapon.

"Load him in!" the first being growled.

Rad immediately recognized the voice. He released Jun and jumped back up toward the door. Jun quickly followed. Three of the beings carefully lifted Zi up to Rad and Jun's outstretched arms. After carefully placing Zi on the USEP's floor deck, Rad turned back toward the door.

"Tor? Is that *you*?"

"Go my brother!" Tor replied.

"But —"

"*NOW!*"

Ard entered the keypad code and the USEP doors slid closed. Under intense protective cover fire from the rest of the resistance forces, Tor and his men continued to torch the area. Zan surveyed the runway. Several Mitel hover crafts were parked there.

"We're blocked!" he shouted.

The Mitel military scrambled to regroup. They took positions in trenches, ditches and behind anything that provided cover. They returned fire at both the Nomas warriors and the USEP. Inside the pod, Janus could hear laser bursts glancing off the pod's outer skin surface.

"If they hit a window," said Markus, "there's no way you can take this USEP into outer space."

"Understood," replied Zan. "Chad! Where are you?"

"I'm on my way!" he replied, streaking down toward the old development facility.

"We need you to clear the runway!"

"Understood," replied Nolia.

Outside the USEP, Tor realized what happening. He motioned his men to move forward as they continued to fire their continuous beams of superheated plasma energy. Tor was suddenly grazed in the left arm by a laser burst.

"Arrghhh!" he grimaced, falling to one knee. Despite the searing pain, he continued to return fire.

There are too many, he thought. Seconds later, two Nomas warriors were cut down by Mitel laser fire.

"Chad!" blurted Zan.

"I'm almost there," he said.

"Identifying targets . . . and locked," said Darius.

Chad's weapons specialists obliterated the hover craft parked along the runway. His weapons specialists then fired at the pockets of Mitel soldiers.

In the USEP, Ard ran a quick scan of the tarmac. "All clear," he confirmed.

Zan accelerated the pod through the smoke, took off and banked hard right before racing skyward. Rad knelt over Zi, struggling to maintain his balance during the steep ascent.

"Give me my bag," he instructed.

Ard quickly complied. After cutting open Zi's jacket, Rad pulled out a clear plastic pouch and ripped it open. Inside was a large circular patch of synthetic skin soaked in Nomas herbal healing compounds.

"What are you *doing*?" asked Jun.

"Rad's our Chief Medical Officer," replied Ard. "He's trying to save Zi's life."

Rad gently applied the patch over the open wound. He then rummaged through his bag and pulled out a rectangular device. He activated it, causing one end to glow bright red. Rad administered concentrated absorption vaccinations around the perimeter of the patch.

"To reduce the pain and shock," explained Rad.

"Is he going to . . . ?" asked Jun quietly.

"Die? I don't think so. A few inches more toward the center of his torso and he would be dead already."

"Look, I'm sorry . . ."

"Don't be. We're all in this together, doing the best we can."

Before racing skyward, Chad's Battle Sphere unleashed a devastating barrage of laser cannon bursts at the rest of the Mitel ground Forces. After that, the firefight quickly turned into a rout.

Zan piloted the USEP through Mitel's upper atmosphere into outer space. Suddenly, the three-dimensional displays detected a cluster of small objects approaching.

"We've got company," said Zan.

"Who?" Ard asked.

"Mitel strike fighters. Looks like an entire grouping."

Ard rushed over and sat down next to Zan.

"We don't have time to energize the slip rings and make a run for it."

"Unfortunately not. We'll have to try to outrun them at normal speed."

Zan pushed the second console button initiating maximum normal speed. The USEP lurched again as it accelerated.

"They're still gaining on us," he said.

"Can we out maneuver them?" Ard asked.

"There's too many."

"They're within firing range," confirmed Ard.

"Where's Chad?"

"Wait . . . now they're gone."

"Sorry I'm late," announced Chad over the encrypted communications system."

"What a relief!" sighed Ard. "Thanks boss!"

"No problem, guys. I'll wait here to make sure you're not being followed. I'll catch up with you later."

"Many thanks Chad," replied Zan. He then contacted Lia. "Lia. It's Zan. Where are you?"

"We just passed Gliese, the big planet."

"Zan," said Rad. "We need to get Zi to the cruiser's medical facility right away. I don't think he'll survive the trip back to Thrae without better care."

"Understood," nodded Zan. "Lia —"

"I heard him. We're turning around."

Once Chad's Battle Hologram confirmed the USEP was not being pursued, he raced back down to the planet surface.

"Several strike fighters from the Arman Matrix are headed toward the old development facility," confirmed Darius.

"They're going to cluster bomb the resistance fighters," replied Chad. "We can't let that happen." He accelerated straight toward the fighters. When they detected his approach, they split off in several directions. But it was too late. The weapons specialists opened fire and quickly eliminated them.

"Nice work everyone," said Chad. "I want to make sure the resistance fighters won't come under attack fire while they withdraw from the facility."

"I have an idea," replied Nolia. "Let's head to the base and take out the rest of the fighters and hover craft before they take off. Dealing with that mess should keep the Mitel military busy."

"Let's go!"

In the deep woods, Lon stumbled across Lex and eleven Special Forces soldiers. As the medic sanitized and bandaged Lon's shoulder, he vented his frustration.

"The traitor," snarled Lon. "I *knew* he was behind the family's rescue. I swear I'll kill Zan Liss *if it's the last thing I do*!"

"Did he do this to you?" asked Lex incredulously.

"No, it was . . . a resistance fighter. He knifed me just as I was about to blast Liss with my electro laser long weapon. I had him dead to rights . . . arrggh!"

"Too bad. Like you said earlier, that would have been helpful. What now?"

"I can't go back to the base, that's for sure. And at this point, I wouldn't want to anyway."

"Probably not an option . . ."

"It's time to put the plan into action. We're running out of time. Once the Leadership launches their mechanical Battle Spheres, things will only become much more difficult."

"True. But where do we go in the meantime?"

Off in the distance, several large explosions lit up the night sky.

"It sounds like the Battle Sphere has turned its attention on the base," said Lex.

"I guess they won't come searching for us anytime soon," grunted Lon.

"Attacking the Hub will further deplete the Mitel military which can only help our cause."

"I tend to agree."

Lon then thought for a moment.

"I think Adrian Sidd's compound is within a day's trek from here," he said. "We can stay there until things settle down."

"Good idea," replied Lex. "Let's get moving."

As the USEP sped toward the cruiser, Jun thought about his conversation with Lon. He then remembered the mechanical Battle Spheres. He immediately told Zan and the rest of the group.

"Did you kill him?" Ard asked.

"No. I was about to. There was an explosion and he got away."

"I assume it's not that easy to kill your twin brother," replied Zan.

"It makes no difference to me. He is an enemy of the resistance."

"Well, at least he told you that the mechanical Battle Spheres are close to deployment."

Seconds later Chad's Battle Sphere streaked past their pod on its way back to Thrae.

"*Showoff*," said Ard.

When the Mitel Leadership receiving the news of the rescue, they convened an emergency meeting in the Forum Hall. The seven immortals sat behind the large, curved stone bench.

The rescue of Falon's family was most unfortunate," said the first Leadership member.

"It certainly was," nodded a second member. "Several witnesses confirmed that a Thraen Battle Sphere was instrumental in the rescue. It destroyed one hundred-thirty-two airborne strike fighters during the raid. It then obliterated another one hundred-ten fighters parked at the Arman military base along with dozens of hover craft."

"The Base itself was also heavily damaged," interjected a third member.

"Although disappointing, the Thraen Battle Sphere's days are numbered," replied the first member. "Our mechanical version will see to that!"

"What about Lon Rexx?" a fourth member asked. "I hear he's missing?"

"He was spotted at the old development facility. As was Zan Liss."

"Rexx was right for once," snorted the second member.

"Indeed. For once."

"Is Rexx *dead*?" asked the third member.

"We think so. Very few soldiers and their commanding officers survived the encounter. We confirmed the location of his tracking device. It's in the woods beyond the development complex. It's not moving."

"He's either dead or he abandoned it."

"A third possibility is that his body armor was taken off by force before he was taken prisoner."

"We'll soon confirm the first possibility since a large Special Forces contingent is gearing up to sweep the area."

"Good."

The members sat in silence for a time.

"What are we going to tell Falon?" asked a fifth member eventually. "I mean about her family?"

"Other than the exterior walls, the heavily fortified complex burned to the ground during the attack," replied the first member.

"I understand, but —"

"Given the level of damage, we'll regrettably inform her that the Thraen Battle Sphere *killed* her entire family."

At the old development facility, Tor and his men hastily constructed a makeshift raised platform. They carefully placed the bodies of the two dead warriors on top before setting the structure on fire. The remaining Nomas watched somberly as the bodies were engulfed in flames.

Goodbye my brothers, Tor thought. *I can't thank you enough for your selfless courage. I hope that one day we see that your sacrifice was not in vain.*

He then turned toward the rest of his men. "Let's go home."

Upon his return, Tor is immediately called in front of the elders. He walked into the Chamber, his left arm in a sling.

"We voted," barked one elder. "You were *not* to get involved!"

"I understand," replied Tor.

"Yet you did anyway?" asked a second elder tersely. "We lost two brave warriors!"

"The mission was successful," replied Tor defensively. "Ana's family was rescued unharmed. The Mitel and Thraen resistances worked side by side together —"

"That's not the point!" shouted a third elder.

"Then what *is* the point?" boomed Tor. "Our future is at stake and all you can do is come here and act like nothing is happening!"

"Don't take that tone with us," replied a fourth elder.

"With all due respect" replied Tor, "the warriors who accompanied me volunteered for the mission. They knew the risks. They also knew the consequences for their inaction. If it wasn't for them, Zan Liss and the others would not have escaped alive."

"We appreciate their bravery," replied the first elder. "And yours as well . . ."

"Feel free to replace me," replied Tor. "I for one am tired of all of this. Either we do what is right, or you can choose to go in another direction. It's up to you."

Once again Nya, the oldest elder, slowly stood up and looked at Tor.

"I've been thinking a great deal about this ever since our last meeting," she began. "I have since concluded that you were right all along. In retrospect, I am truly sorry for not supporting you."

She then glanced around the Chamber before continuing.

"We as a people have sacrificed *too* much and worked *too* hard to let outside forces dictate what we do. What Tor and others did was *very* brave. More importantly, it was the right thing to do which proves to me that Tor is the right person to lead us through this crisis."

She paused before motioning toward Tor.

"Tor should not reach the point where he feels he has no other alternative but to risk his life doing things *on his own*. He should be able to come to this governing body and know that we will listen to his concerns and give them the thoughtful consideration they deserve."

Several elders shook their heads in agreement.

"We all know our history," Nya continued. "A road filled with adversity and seemingly never ending challenges. But along the way, we have assimilated many outsiders into our culture. They came here in search of us, most of them with preconceived notions that we were nothing more than vicious animals. Cautiously and in some cases unconventionally, we accepted each and every one of them. Unsurprisingly, they all stayed and lived out the remainder of their lives very happily. Many of them took Nomas partners and raised a family. Tor's grandfather was an outsider. Maybe that's why your brother Rad was drawn back to the Atreus. Who knows?"

Nya paused.

"Tor has been a courageous and noble leader. I personally do *not* want to see him replaced. My advice to this Chamber is that when he comes to us in advance with a difficult request, and there will be *many* going forward, that we truly listen before rendering a decision."

The oldest elder smiled and then sat back down. As the elders looked around at one another, another elder slowly stood up.

"I really don't have much more to add. I agree wholeheartedly with what Nya just said. We must face our uncertain future together and without hesitation. That is the only way we will persevere, not only as a people, but as a global society. We must follow the path that Thrae followed, one of mutual support and acceptance. Otherwise, we are doomed to repeat our mistakes."

As he stood there, a single elder clapped. He was joined by another. A third elder stood up and clapped. Within seconds, the rest of the Chamber stood up and gave Tor a standing ovation. But it wasn't just for him. The applause was also for the unity and courage of the

Nomas people. It was the sound of strength and determination that echoed throughout the Chamber.

There is hope, Tor thought.

Lon, Lex and the eleven Mitel soldiers approached the gates of Adrian's sprawling compound. They were tired and hungry after their day and a half trek on foot. Lon was also in a great deal of pain from his shoulder wound. Upon entering, he was quickly attended to by the medical staff while everyone else bathed and ate. After Lon did the same, the group rested overnight. The next morning, two guards appeared.

"Director Sidd would like to speak with you," said one guard.

Lon was transported to the huge multi-level glass and stone structure. He followed the guards up the stone steps, through the large sliding front doors, before being scanned, and then upstairs to the three story room. Upon entering, Adrian's head was once again visible above his silver and black chair as he stared out the windows.

"Lon Rexx to see you Sir," said the guard.

Adrian spun around quickly.

"Thank you. Commander Rexx, please sit down."

As the guards took positions in the back of the room, Lon sat down in the same chair as before. He suddenly felt strange, almost as though he was in the Mitel Leadership Forum Hall.

I don't like this, he thought.

"I hope you are feeling better today," nodded Adrian.

"Somewhat," replied Lon. "The last few days were pretty grueling."

"Understood, but things are only going to become more difficult from here, wouldn't you agree?"

"My intentions are not to be on the front lines on an ongoing basis."

"But you were there this time. Why?"

"I went to speak with Commander Lex Gold. On the way over, I narrowly missed being crushed by a falling shelving unit filled with cruiser spare parts. I don't think it was an accident."

"The Leadership."

"Yes. While we were talking, Lex received a series of seemingly unrelated communications. As events began to unfold, I realized what was really happening. We then raced over to the base hover pads. I thought if we could capture Zan Liss, it would restore the Leadership's faith in me and buy us some more time with them. And if we could capture Falon's family, that would be even better. We arrived at the old development complex right after they did. Unfortunately, the ensuing firefight didn't turn out as I had hoped."

"No, it didn't," replied Adrian. "Falon's family was apparently rescued. Now I fear we've lost her as an asset."

"I don't view her as much of an asset anyway."

"We need *all* the help we can get commander Rexx," snapped Adrian. "I'm sure you would agree with that."

"Yes of course," replied Lon defensively. "I risked my life trying to stop the rescue."

"Understood, and it was a brave effort on your part," replied Adrian. "And I guess you could also make the argument that the Leadership lost Falon's allegiance also. One less asset at their disposal."

"Agreed," nodded Lon. "Oh, before I forget. As I looked back from the woods, I noticed a series of blinding flashes that caused the entire tree line on the far side of the development complex to burst into flames. I've never seen anything like it."

Adrian stiffened.

"Do you know what it was?" asked Lon.

"It must be a new type of laser weapon," replied Adrian. "Did you see who was firing it?"

"No. But I assume it was the resistance," replied Lon, "I was wounded and trying to withdraw to a safe location and regroup. That's when I met up with Lex and his men. After talking it over, we decided to come here."

"And you're *sure* the Mitel Leadership didn't track you here?"

"We disposed of our communications devices in the woods. We also left all our body armor and helmets with their imbedded tracking devices there as well. There is no chance they could have tracked us here."

"Let's hope not. If they did, they will likely wipe this place off the face of the planet before much longer."

"Well, like I said —"

"They will eventually find your equipment. When they do, they will know you aren't dead."

"Well, it wasn't like we had a lot of options," replied Lon, trying unsuccessfully to hide his growing annoyance.

"Understood," replied Adrian, forcing a smile. "We need to be extremely careful going forward. We cannot tip our hand to the Leadership. They are too cunning and ruthless."

"I agree completely."

"OK, listen," said Adrian. "You're tired, injured and need rest. The guards will see you back to your quarters. We can discuss plans going forward once our intelligence network fully apprises us of the fallout from the rescue."

Sounds good," nodded Lon. He stood up favoring his shoulder and slowly followed the guards out of the room. As the doors slid closed, Adrian looked out the windows.

Lon's temper and his desire for revenge will be his undoing, he thought. *However, his news of the broadband plasma spray weapon is very intriguing. I wonder how it compares to the version I've been developing.*

As he surveyed the horizon, Adrian could feel his excitement rising.

The Nomas people have entered the conflict. This could be the opportunity I've been hoping for!

CHAPTER TWENTY-THREE – REVELATION

Janus awoke in the underground base medical facility. He had been placed in a medically induced coma for six days as a precautionary measure. When he awoke, Mayla was sitting next to his bed.

"Well hello stranger," she said softly.

"How long have I been here?" asked Janus.

"Six days."

"*Six*?"

"You hit that ledge pretty hard. How do you feel?"

"OK, I guess. A little weak . . ."

"I'll find a medical technician and get you some food. Is it OK if Molly comes in to see you? She has come here to sit with you every day."

"Of course."

Mayla stood up.

"Is Chad OK?" asked Janus.

"Chad's fine. He just arrived back from Mitel."

"*What*?"

"Along with Zan, Ard and the *renegade* cruiser. They successfully rescued Ana's family."

"Whose idea was *that*?"

"I'm sure you can guess."

"Zan."

"You are correct."

"I continue to underestimate him."

"True. Make sure you remember that when he asks us to help free his people. And you *know* someday he will."

Janus smiled as Mayla left the room. A minute later, Molly walked in.

"Hi Janus. It's good to see you awake."

Janus noticed that Molly looked very tired. She was struggling with losing Jim and he didn't know what to say, so he decided not to bring it up. He also noticed that she was wearing a streamlined Thraen outfit: tight fitting breathable pastel-colored pants and shirt with slight v-neck collar, short sleeves and hip pockets.

"Thanks for coming Molly. I see you are assimilating quite nicely into Thraen culture," he replied. "You look very stylish."

"Oh this?" asked Molly. "Thank you. The outfits are very comfortable."

She sat down in a chair. She eventually mentioned there was no new news about Jim. Suddenly, Adria appeared in the doorway.

Janus stared at her intently causing Molly to turn around and look.

"I'm sorry Molly, could you excuse us please," asked Janus.

"Sure, no problem," replied Molly.

After she exited, Adria approached Janus.

"Hi," she said.

She is as beautiful as I remember, he thought.

"I came here to see how you are doing and to thank you for rescuing us from the Mitels."

"*You* were the family that was rescued?"

"Yes."

"I had nothing to do with that," replied Janus, looking somewhat confused.

"Modest as always . . ."

"This time it's true."

Adria smiled. "OK, well, how are you doing?"

"I'll be fine. What brings you to see me here today, after all this time?"

"I wanted to talk to you. To tell you — "

"What else is there to tell? *You* broke up with *me*, remember?"

"I do. But we never really talked about it. I never told you how sorry I was for hurting you."

Janus looked away.

"Listen, Janus," Adria began. "It wasn't easy for me either. I just didn't see a future for us together. You're an immortal and I'm a terminal. There was never any realistic hope for us to have a long-term relationship. One day I'll begin to grow old and frail. At that point, I'd probably resent your immortality and you'd probably pity me and feel guilty or sorry for me or both. We would have been miserable."

"I'm not sure that I'm still immortal, actually."

"*Really*? How is such a thing even possible? You are a natural immortal. You were born without needing to take the serum."

"True. But right before I left Thrae helping Chad escape the Mitel invasion, I transformed myself into a Thraen hologram. Fifteen years later, I was released from that physical form by the miracle of life event."

"I remember you telling me all about the reverse transformation process. You said it was just a story."

"I was wrong."

"Have you been tested? I mean to confirm whether or not you are still immortal?"

"No."

"Are you going to?"

"I don't know. Part of me doesn't want to know."

"If it was me, I would like to know."

"I might at some point. We shall see."

"If you do, please let me know."

"If I do, I will. But you wanted to tell me something?"

"Yes. But I wanted to say something else first."

"OK. What?"

"Just so you know, you weren't always the easiest person to talk to. At times you were unapproachable and sullen. It was like you were carrying the weight of the world on your shoulders. Sometimes I felt like you hid behind an emotional wall. And as hard as I tried, I just couldn't break through it."

Janus listened quietly.

"There were things I wanted to tell you, really important things, but I couldn't. It seemed as though you didn't have the emotional energy to devote to things beyond the problems of our planet. I still wanted to tell you something very important after we broke up. Then the invasion came and you disappeared . . ."

"I'm sorry that you felt like you were unable to talk to me," replied Janus softly. "I knew I was somewhat distant emotionally. It's just that when we met, I was GDC Commander and very busy — "

"It was more than that."

"You're right," Janus sighed. "I became detached after Liana's death. Losing my two daughters Zeya and Mistil to the ravages of the serum also affected me deeply. I seem to have always been deeply affected by tragic events throughout my immortal life. When I was only 15 years old, I witnessed a transportation accident unfold in front of me. A small altitude transport vehicle lost control and crashed as it transitioned from the antigravity skyway to the surface. My father and I tried to help. I never forgot the look on the face of the young girl who died in his arms. We were powerless to help her. As I stared down at her, I felt her eyes look deep into his soul as she passed away.

Going forward, I decided to dedicate my existence to helping and improving the lives of all Thraens and for a long time, I spent my entire waking existence focused on just that. But it obviously came at a cost. I witnessed profound tragedy over and over again. It was during those times that I wondered if immortality was simply a curse."

"Maybe it is. It probably depends to a large extent on your life experiences and your reaction to them."

"Maybe, but regardless of my deep involvement in the welfare of Thrae, when you live such a long life, it's impossible not to live through many historically bad events and suffer repeated tragedy. And even though I was able to help our planet overcome several challenging obstacles, I grew disillusioned and weary of chronicling all the human pain and suffering that repeated itself over and over again."

Janus paused.

"You begin to see patterns," he continued. "You can almost sense a tragic incident approaching as events unfold, but you find yourself powerless to stop it. I also became disheartened how humans appear incapable of breaking the cycle of intolerance and violence. The discovery of immortality almost ruined Thrae's harmonious balance that was so painstakingly achieved, and it startled me to see just how fast everything could unravel."

Janus paused again.

"At this point, I don't know if I *want* to be immortal anymore. While I don't think I'm the same person who left Thrae fifteen years ago, part of me is very tired. And quite honestly, part of me is very curious to see what lies beyond the human life form."

"What if there's nothing?"

"Then I won't know any different, will I? But, if something does exist, maybe in another plane or dimension, or even universe, just think how new and wondrous that something might be."

"I don't disagree," smiled Adria somewhat amused.

There was a brief silence.

"Janus, listen," said Adria. Because of the invasion, I didn't get to tell you about something *very* important. After the attack was over, I tried to find you, but you had disappeared."

"What did you want to tell me?"

Adria looked at Janus intently. She sat down on the side of his bed, took his hand, and held it tightly.

"That I was pregnant."

"*What?*"

"Before we broke up, I became pregnant. When I found out, I wanted to tell you but initially I was afraid to. I didn't know how you would react to the news. When I finally got up the courage, you were gone. Later, on the way back from Mitel, they told me that you'd met her. I mean in her hybrid form. Her name is Ana.

The Battle Sphere Ana?"

"Yes. Her full name is Ana Stone."

Janus sat stunned for a moment.

"Somehow, I knew," he replied eventually. "For reasons I can't explain, I refused to attack her when we were in Battle Sphere mode. Not just because she was Thraen. There was something else stopping me, something deep down inside that told me not to. It's like she was a part of me."

"And she is," smiled Adria. "I knew something was different about Ana at a very young age. I had her tested and confirmed that she was a natural immortal just like her father. That part was fine. As her parent, I'm supposed to die before her anyway right? Well, at least in the terminal society."

Janus, still holding Adria's hand, studied her face.

"Others confirmed she had extraordinarily high levels titanium, aluminum, beryllium, cobalt, manganese and cadmium in her bloodstream. At the time, nobody would tell me why. I wanted answers as to why she was still so healthy. I didn't challenge the medical staff. In retrospect, I should have. After that, I began to notice her powers. As a 1-year-old, she turned silver after becoming angry because she couldn't pull herself up on a chair. I started researching Thraen history and human hybrids. I realized that she had to be a Thraen Battle Sphere, just like her father. But I still didn't know what to do, or who to turn to. I was scared and didn't trust anyone at that point. I guess the word got out about her human hybrid abilities, which probably explains why we were eventually kidnapped by the Mitels. She was a pawn in a power struggle and still is. I feel very bad for Ana. She has suffered through a lot. Her sisters have too. None of them had anything close to a normal childhood."

"I'm truly sorry, Adria."

"It's not your fault Janus. Life can be very unfair and exceedingly cruel. But it can also be so wondrous and beautiful. I just wish I had known what happened to you. I wanted very much for you to know about Ana."

Adria and Janus suddenly felt someone watching them. They looked to see Mayla standing in the doorway, her arms crossed against her chest.

"Mayla, how much did you hear?" asked Janus.

"Pretty much everything, I think."

"Listen, Mayla —"

"I've got to get going. As acting resistance co-commander, I need to begin preparations for the impending attack."

"What attack?"

"The mechanical Battle Spheres."

"The mechanical Battle Spheres? Mayla, listen," urged Janus.

"Janus, my allegiance is to Thrae, first and foremost. That's why I joined the Hologram Protective Force."

"But Mayla —"

"As I said, I must be going."

Mayla turned and walked down the hall.

On Mitel, Ana was pacing in her quarters. She was nervous and agitated. She had heard rumors there had been an attack at the secret location where her mother and two sisters were being held captive. She also heard there were many casualties and that the building had been destroyed by fire. Unconfirmed reports said a Thraen Battle Sphere inflicted most of the destruction. Suddenly her communicator beeped. Ana lunged forward and pushed the button.

"Hello?"

"Falon Ross?"

"Uh, speaking . . ."

"This is Leadership Member Kye Lindar speaking," said the voice.

"Hi," she replied, her heart now pounding.

"I must regrettably inform you that your family has been killed."

Ana did not answer.

"Witnesses at the scene confirmed that they were brutally murdered by a Thraen Battle Sphere. We believe this atrocity was in retaliation for our recent attack on the Thraen planet."

Ana stared off into space and speechless.

"Falon? Can you hear me?"

Tears streamed down her face. She reached over, pushed the communications button ending the conversation with a beep.

Ana stood alone, in total shock. As she stood there shaking, she became filled with a wide range of emotions including sadness, anger, loss, loneliness and despair. She cried for hours before falling asleep.

CHAPTER TWENTY-FOUR – THE CONFRONTATION

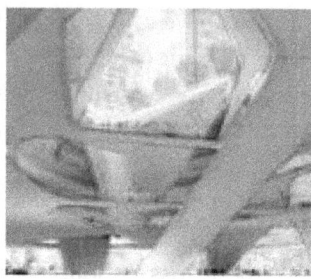

Atlas grabbed his backpack to go out looking for food. Jim jumped up from his cot and approached him.

"Can I go with you tonight?" he asked.

"Probably not a good idea," replied Atlas.

"The places I'm going to require me to pass through walls. I'd rather not leave you alone out in the passageways for long periods of time. I just don't think . . ."

Atlas's voice trailed off.

"Don't think what?"

"I don't think you or Isak should be out alone. I am concerned that Scavengers will try to do something."

"You worry too much."

"I don't, actually. Please promise me that you won't go out alone."

"Ok, I promise."

"Good. See you when I get back."

Atlas floated to an underground enclosure door and quickly exited.

An hour later Isak woke up.

"Hey Isak," said Jim. "I'm bored. You want to go outside and get some fresh air?"

Isak shook his head yes.

They grabbed a bite to eat from a few containers before heading down the same long corridor as Atlas. When they came to the large, blackened door, Isak turned the inside handle and pushed the door open. They made their way up the two flights of stairs and down the passageway to the elevated walkway. It was a nice warm night. A gentle breeze was blowing.

"Hey," said Jim. "You want to go see if Finch is at work? I think I remember the way there."

"OK," mouthed Isak.

They walked along the elevated walkway. It was late and nobody else was out and about. Atlas followed Jim to the passageway.

"I'm pretty sure we go this way," pointed Jim.

At the end of the passageway, Jim saw the HorVert elevator. "We go up that," he said.

As the doors slid open, the two men stepped inside. "Level four, fifth stop please," said Jim.

As the HorVert rose up into the air, Jim again stared out at the population center in awe.

Looking out at the brightly lit sky structures, Isak glanced at Jim, shook his head and smiled.

At the fourth elevated walkway, the HorVert changed direction and headed horizontally past four exit ports. At the fifth port, the HorVert stopped, and the doors slid open.

"Let's go," Said Jim.

Isak followed Jim to the narrow passageway which brought them behind the food establishment.

"This is it," smiled Jim. He knocked three times on the rear door. Several seconds later, the door opened.

"Well, look whose here," grinned Finch. "And you brought Isak with you." She jumped past Jim and gave Isak a big hug.

"You guys here looking for food?" Finch asked.

"Uh, no, we came by to see you and say hi," replied Jim.

Finch looked at Jim and smiled. It looked like she was blushing.

"Well, that's really nice of you. Wait here, it's almost my break."

A few minutes later, Finch reappeared with a few protein bars and handed one each to Jim and Isak. "Let's go for a walk," she said.

They walked back down the passageway and then along the pathway for a while. Isak dropped back several feet to allow the two some privacy while he surveyed the shadows closely for any signs of Scavengers. Jim and Finch talked and laughed as she described her life before becoming a hologram. She eventually turned serious when she talked about her life after becoming one.

"Atlas told me what happened," said Jim. "I'm really sorry."

"Thanks. If I had the chance to go back in time, I'd probably do it all over again," replied Finch. "And anyway, the past is the past. I finally decided that it does no good to dwell on the past." She then crossed her arms across her chest as she walked.

Sensing that Finch didn't want to talk about it too much, he quickly tried to change the subject. "Finch, what do you know about the Scavengers?"

"The *Scavengers*? I know a lot."

"Really?"

"When you've lived as long as I have, you learn about a lot of things," she smiled.

"I'll bet. What can you tell me?"

"Well, the Scavengers are certainly misunderstood."

"You mean by the surface dwellers?"

"Yeah," laughed Finch, "although we don't refer to ourselves by that name."

Jim suddenly felt embarrassed.

"They simply wanted to be left alone," she continued. "A long time ago, they rejected the direction that Thrae's technology was going. But they weren't the only ones who were concerned. As a global society, Thrae went through a very tumultuous time. Immortality turned out to be more of a curse rather than the euphoric discovery it was originally touted as. We struggled to control human hybrid transformations which eventually became uncontrollably tainted by immortality as well.

Back then, Chancellor Sejus Theron, head of the World Council, did his best to solve our planet's complex technological adverse effects. But they were bigger than any one person or a group of people could fix. We eventually realized that our technological advancements were outpacing our ability to control them. Things got scary. Millions and millions of people were dying from the toxic immortality serum. Unfortunately, we as a people collectively allowed it all to happen although Theron was blamed for everything. And he took that hard. I still remember to this day how much he cared for Thrae. It was almost as though cared for our planet and people even more than he cared for himself. He eventually just went away . . ." Finch's voice trailed off as she thought about it more.

"Wow," said Jim quietly. "Atlas said the Mitel invasions changed the Scavengers, made them more aggressive."

"Yeah, that's his opinion," she replied. "He's right to a point, I guess. But life became harder for all of us."

She then looked at Jim.

"You want my take on it?"

"Definitely," smiled Jim.

"I think that selfish, short-sighted individuals started to take over some of the groups. It's not a surprise to me that those groups are the ones that are causing most of the problems. What worries me is that their violent actions are starting to turn public opinion against the Scavengers as a whole."

Finch then chose her words carefully.

"To me," she continued, "it's no coincidence that the *men* in leadership positions are creating most of the problems since the Scavengers are for the most part a male dominated society. Change and progress in that regard has been very slow. I've met some very strong and smart Scavenger women who are eager for change, but they have been denied leadership positions for the most part. What the Scavengers need is a smart, fearless woman who is a visionary and not afraid of change. But she will need special men to support and protect her as she takes action to unite the entire Scavenger society behind her. As it stands now, trust between groups is at the lowest levels I can ever remember."

"That's very insightful," replied Jim.

Finch laughed again.

"Hey," she said, "I want to hear about you."

Jim paused.

"What's wrong?" asked Finch.

"I don't know anything about my past," replied Jim quietly. "Isak found me wandering about in Amer just before the missile hit. I don't remember anything at all. I don't even remember my name. All I know is that Atlas said I'm an alien."

"*What?*"

"He did a scan of my insides and said I'm different."

Jim then raised his left hand and showed Finch his five fingers.

"*Wow,*" whispered Finch.

She then raised her right hand and placed it against Jim's palm, her focused energy sparkling brightly. Feeling her hand against his felt good.

"Look, they still fit together," she smiled.

This time Jim blushed.

"Listen, maybe I can help you figure out who you are?"

"That would be great," replied Jim.

"But in the meantime, I've got to get back to work. I'm supposed to close up the place."

Isak and Jim walked Finch back to the rear of the food establishment.

"Thanks for coming by," she said.

"You're welcome," grinned Jim.

Finch kissed Jim on the cheek before closing the door behind her.

As the two men turned toward the walkway, Isak elbowed Jim softly and winked at him.

"*What?*" Jim asked defensively.

They made their way back down the HorVert elevator and through the long passageway. As they turned onto the elevated walkway, Isak stiffened.

"What's wrong?" asked Jim.

Isak looked down at Jim, his metallic green eyes flashing. He then placed his finger against his lips before cautiously stepping forward while looking side to side. Suddenly, nine Scavengers stepped out onto the elevated walkway several yards up ahead, blocking their advance. Sensing something behind him, Jim spun around to see ten more Scavengers standing about twenty yards behind them.

"This is not good," muttered Jim.

Two levels above, two heavily armed hologram soldiers were out on patrol. One of them noticed the two groups of Scavengers on either side of Jim and Isak. He tapped his buddy on the shoulder, and they stepped toward the acrylic railing and looked down and watched.

Big Kelan stepped out from the first group of Scavengers and stared menacingly at Jim and Isak. He stood about seven feet tall and weighed three hundred and seventy pounds. He was not particularly fit looking or muscular but intimidating.

"Where's Atlas?" he asked loudly.

Isak glanced down at Jim and mouthed instructions.

"Stay calm and remember what I taught you. It will see you through this alive."

"I'll do my best," muttered Jim.

Isak squeezed Jim's shoulder.

"I'll take on the front group and you deal with the rear," he mouthed, "OK?"

"Got it."

"I said, where's Atlas?" asked Big Kelan.

"We don't know," replied Jim.

"He hurt two of my men very badly and one of them died eventually. He shouldn't have done that."

Jim didn't answer.

"We need to make it even," said Big Kelan. He waved his hand forward signaling the Scavengers on both sides to run toward Jim and Isak. Big Kelan stood and watched.

Jim stepped forward and kicked the first Scavenger in the groin. He fell to the ground screaming in agony. Jim silenced him with a kick squarely in the face. He then deflected punches from a second attacker before counterpunching him hard in the throat, dropping him. A third attacker grabbed Jim by the shirt. He contained that arm, lowered his head in time to receive two blows to his forehead. Jim deflected the next punch with his left arm. A fourth Scavenger punched him in the back of his head while a fifth tried to shove Jim off balance. He held firm. Jim deflected several more punches from all three men. Seeing an opening, he punched the third Scavenger squarely in the nose with his open palm, causing him to release his grip. Jim quickly punched him in the nose several more times, dropping him to the ground. He used the same open palm thrust to punch the fourth Scavenger in the face, staggering him backward. Jim stepped forward and kneed the Scavenger in the groin, collapsing him to the ground, withering in pain.

A sixth Scavenger punched Jim squarely in the side of the head. The pain was intense, but Jim kept his balance. As the Scavenger's momentum carried him forward, Jim countered with an elbow chop to the neck. The Scavenger doubled over in agony. Jim elbowed him a second time causing the Scavenger to collapse in a heap. Refocusing, Jim quickly deflected wild roundhouse punches from the fifth Scavenger before countering with open palm thrusts to his face. Jim finished the Scavenger off with a closed fist punch to the throat.

Out of the corner of his eye, Jim saw a seventh Scavenger lunge forward swinging a metallic bar toward his head. He instinctively raised his left arm up along his body and blocked it. Jim heard a loud *crack* as the bar splintered both the ulna and radius bones below his elbow. The pain was like nothing Jim had ever experienced before. The Scavenger stepped back quickly as he prepared to strike Jim a second time. As Jim pivoted toward the Scavenger, he swung the bar, striking Jim's raised arm a second time. The force of the blow shattered Jim's humerus bone above his elbow.

"Uhhhh," grunted Jim in anguish. Despite the pain, he remembered what Isak had taught him.

Always counterattack. Always.

The Scavenger stepped back and prepared to strike Jim a third time. With his arm hanging motionless against his side, Jim lunged toward the Scavenger as he swung the bar a third time, shattering Jim's shoulder socket.

The Scavenger tried to step back again, but it was too late. Jim was now right in front of him.

With his good arm, Jim punched the seventh Scavenger repeatedly in the face, fracturing both orbital bones around his eyes. Blood was everywhere.

"I can't see, I can't see!" shrieked the Scavenger.

Jim yanked the metallic pole out of the Scavenger's hand and clubbed him over the head with a thunderous *crack*. The attacker fell to the ground in an unconscious heap.

As Jim stood over the motionless Scavenger, the three remaining attackers prepared to rush him. With his left arm hanging limp, Jim reestablished his defensive position, firmly clutching the bar in his right hand.

Isak had systematically overpowered his group of attacking Scavengers. He shoved the last one to the side before punching him into unconsciousness. Turning to help Jim, he saw Big Kelan pull out a dwarf ball laser weapon. He pointed it directly at Jim, waiting for a clear shot. Using the metallic bar, Jim dropped the first attacker with a blow to the head.

Isak waved at Jim and mouthed a warning, but Jim couldn't hear him. Isak glanced back at Big Kelan who had become impatient. He mouthed a second warning, but it was no use.

Isak then rushed Big Kelan. As he did, he blurted "*Get down!*"

Jim instinctively dropped to the ground just before Big Kelan opened fire. The laser blasts hit and killed the remaining two attacking Scavengers.

Noticing Isak approaching, Big Kelan pointed his dwarf laser weapon at Isak's legs. He fired repeatedly. To his astonishment, the blasts deflected harmlessly away. Isak kept coming. Now frightened, Big Kelan fired his laser weapon directly at Isak's chest. The result was the same. Big Kelan froze in fear.

Isak snatched the weapon from big Kelan's hand and squeezed it into pieces. He then punched the frightened man directly in the face with all his strength, killing him instantly.

Along the raised walkway, Atlas approached through the air with a loud shriek. The Scavengers who were still conscious staggered to their feet and stumbled past Isak, disappearing into the night. When Atlas arrived, Jim was hunched over holding his badly shattered arm. His hair matted with blood.

"Are you both OK?" asked Atlas.

"Yes," replied Isak.

"Thank goodness . . . wait . . . you're *talking*?"

"I am," replied Isak.

"What? I mean . . . *how*?"

"I tried to warn him," explained Isak pointing toward Jim. "It just came out."

"After all this time . . . and it took a complete stranger, not to mention an alien, to do it."

"He's *not* a stranger. He's, our friend."

The two hologram soldiers floated down from the upper walkway. They surveyed the several Scavengers lying motionless on the ground before approaching the trio.

"Don't move," ordered the first soldier." Their electro weapons were drawn and ready.

"OK," replied Atlas. "But this man requires urgent medical attention," he added, pointing toward Jim. The first soldier studied Atlas intently. He knew he had seen his face before.

"Wait, I know you. You're Atlas Root, *the Battle Hologram commander*," he said.

"Yes. Or at least I was."

"It's an honor to meet you Sir. I've read a lot about you and your accomplishments."

"I'm humbled. Then you should also know Isak Sone. He was the Battle Sphere that I served."

The two soldiers stared at Isak in disbelief.

"*You're Isak Sone?*" asked the second soldier.

"Yes," nodded Isak.

"You're a legend."

"I might be to hybrids and holograms. Otherwise, Atlas and I have long since been forgotten."

"And who's *this*?" the first soldier asked, pointing toward Jim.

"He's our travel companion," replied Atlas.

The second soldier studied Jim closely.

"Are you OK?" he asked.

"I'm pretty sure my arm is broken," groaned Jim. "I heard loud noises when I was being beaten with this." Jim held out the metallic rod with his right arm.

"You *think* it's broken?" asked the second soldier. "I can tell that it is just by looking at it. And it looks *bad*."

"By the way," added the first soldier, "you're both very impressive hand to hand fighters."

"Thanks," grunted Jim. "Isak taught me everything."

"He needs *immediate* medical attention," repeated Atlas.

The soldier thought for a moment.

"Listen," he said. "I want the three of you to get out of here before backup arrives. There's a medical facility not too far in that direction," he pointed. "Ask for Evan Lennac. Tell him Anton sent you."

"OK thanks," replied Isak. "What are you going to tell the authorities about all this?"

"We'll tell them we found these Scavengers during a routine patrol. We'll conclude it was probably the result of a territorial dispute. Now hurry, you need to get going."

"Thank you," nodded Atlas.

"It's the least we could do," smiled the first soldier. "We holograms never forget the bravery of hybrids and holograms from the past."

Isak smiled and waved as he helped Atlas steady Jim as he shuffled down the walkway into the darkness.

"Jim, how's your arm? Can you move it at all?" asked Isak.

"No," mumbled Jim.

"Does it hurt?"

"Yes,"

"A lot?"

"*Yes*," said Jim, trying not to laugh.

"What could *possibly* be funny?"

"I don't know. I'm just happy to be alive I guess."

Atlas looked at Isak.

"What are we going to do?" he asked.

"He needs some painkillers," replied Isak. "Then he needs to lie down for a while before we bring him to the medical facility."

"Where?"

"Can you contact Finch?"

"Yes, *why*?

"We can bring him to her quarters for the time being."

"Do you think she will be OK with that?

"I'm *pretty* sure," smiled Isak.

"Now what are *you* smiling about?"

"Oh nothing . . ."

"You're both acting very strange. This is the last time I leave the two of you alone, I can promise you that."

As they kept walking, Isak patted Jim on the back.

"You did great back there by the way."

"Thanks," winced Jim proudly.

Word of the late-night brawl spread quickly. Seven Scavengers including Big Kelan were pronounced dead at the scene. It would change the complexion of the late-night Scavenger activities in Amer and Pisco for many years to come.

"It's a horrible tragedy," said a member of the local Ruling Advisory Panel. "Off the record, it was long overdue."

The next day, the first hologram soldier saw Jim's picture on the news feed. He spoke with his colleague at the GDC who notified Arius who in turn told Mayla. She immediately contacted Molly.

"We've received word Jim was spotted in the population center of Pisco," she said.

"What?" Molly asked. *"Are you serious?"*

"Yes. A Thraen hologram soldier said he saw Jim. It's not far from Amer.

"Let's get out there right away."

Molly, Chad, Luna and Markus quickly traveled by hover vehicle to Pisco. They were put in touch with the hologram soldiers who were at the scene of the fight. The soldiers agreed to meet them at the elevated walkway.

"The fight took place right about here," said the first hologram soldier.

"What was it like?" asked Markus.

"It was pretty intense, two against about twenty."

"Ask him why he thinks one of them was Jim," asked Molly.

Markus complied.

"I got a real good look at him after the fight was over. When I saw his picture on the news feed the next day, I said *that's him.*"

"Are you *sure?*" Luna asked.

"I'd stake my life on it."

"Did he tell you his name?"

"No."

"Tell us more about your encounter," said Markus.

"We watched the fight unfold from up there," the soldier pointed. "He is an excellent hand to hand fighter."

Markus explained to Molly what the soldier said.

"Jim can't fight," said Molly shaking her head.

Markus turned back toward the soldier.

"What else can you tell us?" he asked.

"When we came down, I asked him if he was OK."

"And?"

"He said he thought he broke his arm."

"He told you that?"

"Yes."

"In Thraen?"

"Yes. He spoke perfect Thraen."

When Markus explained the details to Molly, she shook her head again.

"He couldn't speak or understand anything more than rudimentary Thraen. It can't be him."

"Molly, I —"

"I'm sorry Markus."

Molly then turned and walked away, crushed. Chad and Luna headed after her.

"Thank you for your time," said Markus. "It's a difficult time for the family right now."

"Understood."

As Markus walked away, he heard the soldier say something else. Markus turned around. "*I'm sorry, what?*" he asked.

"It was him," repeated the soldier.

"OK, thank you again."

"His friend was there, the hologram Atlas Root."

Markus thought for a moment.

"*Atlas Root was there?*" he asked eventually.

"Yes."

"Are you *sure*?"

"I'm sure. Why, do *you* know him?"

"Yes. Atlas Root was a Battle Hologram commander a long time ago," replied Markus.

"That's right," smiled the soldier. "How'd *you* know that?"

"Because I was once a Battle Sphere."

"*What*?"

"I'm Markus Kilmar."

The soldier was astonished.

"Listen," said Markus. "I know it's probably a long shot. This person has skills and abilities that Jim didn't have. If you or one of your colleagues comes across either of them again, could you *please* let me know as soon as possible? I can be reached through GDC command. I don't want to get their hopes up again until I know for sure."

"I will, Sir. Right away."

CHAPTER TWENTY-FIVE – ANA'S RAGE

Zan entered the base's underground medical facility. He walked past the central station and down a long hallway to the emergency care section. A Thraen Special Forces soldier was standing guard outside the unit. He eagerly shook Zan's hand and escorted him to Zi's room. Zi was sitting up in bed while Jun, heavily armed, was seated in the corner.

"Hello gentlemen," smiled Zan. "Zi, they tell me that you are making remarkable progress."

"I am indeed," Zi grinned. "Thank you."

"The thanks go to Rad. He's exceptional at what he does."

"I should be thanking your whole team. If it wasn't for all of you, I wouldn't be here right now."

"It's funny how things work out," Zan replied. "If the Thraen resistance hadn't spared my life at the old Thraen defense fortress years ago, none of this would be happening."

"Is that when you located the high-speed pods?"

"Yes. We scaled up the technology then retrofitted the entire Mitel fleet. And thanks to Dru and his mechanics, we enhanced that technology and upgraded the entire Thraen fleet."

"The technology didn't help the resistance. But if it can be used against the Leadership and the Mitel military, then so be it."

"That's the plan eventually."

"So, what's next?"

"I'm about to meet with resistance co-commander Mayla Tallis. We need to be ready for the inevitable attack of the mechanical Battle Spheres. It will be a formidable challenge."

"That's for sure," nodded Zi. "When can Jun and I go home?"

"Good question." Zan then turned to Jun. "I think the two of you should use this time to get to know the Thraen people and culture. In many ways, they are just like us, other than the aggressor part. I could introduce you to several resistance commanders. You could share ideas and begin to form ties to help move forward our common future."

"I'd welcome that," replied Jun. "I may even come across a new weapon or two."

"Speaking of that," pointed Zan. "You don't need to load up with as much weaponry here. Your joints will thank you when you're older."

"I'll keep that in mind," grinned Jun, "force of habit."

When Ana awoke, it was still dark. She was anxious and lonely. Ana eventually forced herself out of bed, slowly making her way to her desk. Inside the top compartment was a small computer chip which contained several three-dimensional still and moving holographic images of her family. She inserted it into her computer.

Ana sat in the dark as the images appeared in the room. She watched them repeatedly, slowly wiping the tears from her face.

Ana eventually turned off her computer and sat in the dark for a long time. She tried to make sense of everything but just couldn't. Instead, Ana became increasingly agitated. That anger slowly grew into a simmering fury. She quickly rushed out of her living quarters, down a flight of stairs and through a side door to an open area.

I don't care who sees me, she thought.

Ana moved her feet apart and raised her arms. The silver shard mesh spread down her neck and torso until her body was covered. A few minutes later, she was hovering in place, having transformed. Ana surveyed her diagnostic mini-screens. Everything looked normal. She then programmed a course to Thrae.

One last trip, she thought.

Ana turned off her communications system.

I won't need that anymore, she thought. *And soon I won't need anything anymore . . .*

Ana darted skyward.

Sitting in his bed, Janus replayed recent events in his mind, trying to figure out what to say to Mayla. He wanted her to know how much he loved her. But he also wanted to tell her so many other things which he had kept pent up in his mind for a long time. He repeatedly tried to contact Mayla, but she didn't answer.

The following day, deep space surveillance detected Ana's Battle Sphere entering Thrae's solar system, having passed through the shared asteroid belt. Communications specialists continually contacted her without success.

"She either refuses to answer or she has turned off her communication systems," offered the specialist.

"She probably turned it off," replied Zan.

"Agreed," nodded Mayla, her arms crossed.

Then it occurred to her.

"Do you think the Leadership may have told Ana her family was killed during the rescue?"

"That would explain why she's coming here in Battle Sphere mode *but not responding*. Pinning the blame on Thrae using *that* fake story would take the heat off the Mitel Leadership. I'll have Rad reach out to his people to see what they know."

"His *people*?"

"The *Nomas*."

"They really exist?"

"Yes. Located somewhere deep in Mitel's Stone Forest, so I've been told. For proof, just look at Rad. If he doesn't fit the description of a Nomas warrior, nobody does. He's a walking, talking mini-living structure all covered in hair."

"I'll take your word for it," replied Mayla.

An hour later, Rad sat down in front of his computer and typed an encrypted message.

Hello Tor. It's Rad.

He hit the transmission key and then stared blankly at the computer for a time.

Hello brother. It's good to hear from you. Did everyone make it back OK?

Ard grunted and smiled. He then typed more.

469

Yes, thank you. We would not have escaped without your help. It was a most pleasant surprise at a critical moment. I'm also very glad you made it out alive.

You are most welcome. Unfortunately, some of my volunteers did not. But that possibility was known going in.

Volunteers?

Yes. Several Nomas warriors volunteered to come with me after the elders refused to authorize our direct involvement. They have since come around. After that mission, the Nomas people are steadfast in their commitment to defeat the Mitel Leadership.

That is very welcome news. We must all talk in greater detail soon. In the meantime, it appears the female Battle Sphere is on her way here. Do you have any Intel as to why?

Yes. She was told by the Leadership that a Thraen Battle Sphere killed her family as revenge for attacking Mitel. She departed before we could speak with her. We have since tried to reach her but it appears she may have disabled her communication system.

Understood and thank you.

Be safe my brother.

Over the next twelve hours, underground base communications personnel tried to reach Ana over a wide range of encrypted and unencrypted channels.

"She just isn't responding," sighed the communications specialist.

"We need to talk to Janus," said Markus. "He needs to know what's happening."

Mayla didn't respond.

"You go Markus," said Teri. "Take Chad with you."

"Will do," replied Markus softly.

Markus and Chad traveled via a small base hover craft from the command center to the medical facility. As they entered his room, Janus was sitting in a chair. Adria, who had come again to visit, was standing nearby.

"Hi Janus," said Chad.

"Hello my son. Hi Markus. Any update on Ana?"

"She's now only a few hours away."

"And she's still not responding," added Markus.

"Maybe she'll respond to me," said Adria. "Maybe she is listening, but thinks it is just another lie."

"It's worth a try," replied Markus. "Let's get over to the command center right now."

"I'm coming with you," said Janus.

"You need more rest Sejus. We can conference you in from here, OK?"

Janus reluctantly agreed.

Markus brought Adria to the underground command center. Over the next hour, she tried to contact Ana over a wide range of communications channels. There was no response.

"She's nearing the planet, Sir," confirmed the scanning specialist.

"She could do some real damage," replied Teri.

"Yes, she could," added Mayla. "Chad, can you be ready to go at a moment's notice?"

"Yes."

"To do what?" asked Adria.

Mayla shot a quick glance at her. "To defend Thrae," she replied.

"But she thinks her family is *dead*! She is hurt, angry and confused."

"I understand. It's all the more reason we must be ready to confront her. Her Battle Sphere has incredible destructive capability. We *cannot* allow her to harm innocent Thraens."

"We *must* find some way to tell her we're OK."

"We've been trying Adria. And we will continue to do so. But we *cannot* allow her to hurt others."

Adria's eyes filled with tears. She then nodded that she understood.

Sitting in his chair, Janus got an idea. He grabbed his portable computer, logged into the confidential data base, and accessed the command center scanning database. He pulled up Ana's tracking information. Janus ran a search for time anomalies. He located one two hour pause just inside Thrae's side of the shared asteroid belt.

That's it, he thought.

He ran numbers in his head. He then ran them a second time.

It might work.

Janus slowly got up from the chair, made his way unnoticed down the hall and out of the medical facility. Once back in the main underground base, Janus walked across Bay Number 1 and out the now open stone-faced doors onto the shelf. He strode along another one hundred yards and stopped. Janus took a deep breath and focused intently. At first nothing happened.

Don't fail me now, he thought.

He tried to relax. Janus looked out at Lake Victoria and closed his eyes. He focused on his transformation. He breathed a sigh of relief as he felt the metallic shard mesh spread down his body. Minutes later he was hovering in place about twenty feet above the shelf.

"Hello commander," said Lucian. "How are you feeling?"

"Fine," replied Janus.

"Your energy levels are only twenty-five percent," confirmed Martin, "You need to recharge before —"

"There isn't time."

"Why not?" asked Lucian.

"Ana is about to pass through our upper atmosphere. As you know, she is operating *without* a Battle Hologram and has apparently turned off her communications system. She incorrectly believes that her family was killed by a Thraen Battle Sphere. I assume she has returned for revenge."

"*Is that all?*" replied Martin sarcastically.

"There is something else she doesn't know."

"*What?*"

"She's my daughter."

"Ohhhh . . ."

Lucian looked around at his Battle Hologram command cube. Everyone stared back at him stoically.

"Commander, you must recharge," urged Lucian.

"As I said, there isn't time. We need to intercept her before she hurts innocent civilians. Hopefully we can preoccupy her long enough to get a message to her that her family is safe and back on Thrae."

"If you don't defend yourself, it's going to be risky given her concentrated firepower capability."

"I fully understand. Martin, how much energy do you calculate a Battle Sphere would expend from here to the shared asteroid belt?"

"You mean at all out speed without stopping to recharge?"

"Yes."

Martin typed quickly. He studied the results and then typed again.

"Approximately sixty-five percent give or take."

"That's the number I came up with too. OK let's go."

"But —"

"*Let's go.*"

"OK. Target identified at sixty thousand feet," said Martin, "approximately one thousand miles southwest of here. Initiating all out-speed intercept in three, two and one. *Launch.*"

Janus's Battle Sphere streaked skyward.

In the underground base's control center, the scanning specialist stared at his monitor.

"Something just launched from the shelf. It's headed incredibly fast straight toward Ana."

"*Janus,*" mumbled Mayla.

"What's he doing?" asked Markus.

"Risking his life for his daughter," replied Mayla. "He hasn't fully recovered from their last encounter. Chad, please get ready."

"I'm heading onto the shelf now," he replied.

On her diagnostic mini-screens, Ana registered Janus's Battle Sphere approaching.

"You're going to pay for what you did," she muttered, "with your life."

Ana darted straight toward Janus's oncoming Battle Sphere. Before she could open fire, he turned and sped down toward the planet surface.

"Coward," she muttered. She raced after him.

Janus headed toward a large open expanse of lightly populated terrain. He slowed down just enough to allow

Ana to catch up. The instant Janus was within range, she opened fire with a barrage of concentrated plasma canon fire. The force of the blows pushed his Battle Sphere downward. He could hear the tops of the vegetation snap and crack as he struggled to remain airborne.

"She's already beginning to weaken his outer defense shields," said Martin.

"She's going to kill him if we don't intervene," said Mayla anxiously. "Chad, head over there now."

Out on the stone shelf, Chad was having trouble transforming.

"Just relax Chad," said Darius. "Think of something peaceful."

"I'm trying," replied Chad. "I'm worried about Janus and I keep thinking about my Dad. I just . . ."

"What?"

"I can't lose both of them!"

Janus weaved back and forth trying to avoid Ana's weapons fire. Ground vegetation exploded all around him. Janus swerved hard left over a large lake and flew just above the rippling waves. When Ana caught up to him again, She opened fire causing huge columns of water to rise into the air along either side of Janus's Battle Sphere. He then darted right and headed inland toward the enormous Tatura desert, with its dunes over two hundred feet high.

"Janus," Lucian cautioned, "your reserves are down to fifteen percent. You need to withdraw and recharge."

"No," he replied.

Janus hugged the dunes, darting up and down, pockets of sand exploding all around him. After the tenth dune, Ana got an idea. On the next peak, she timed her cannon fire to shoot directly through its peak just as Janus disappeared from view.

Chad continued to concentrate. He tried to transform repeatedly without success.

"Chad," said Mayla.

"*What?*"

"Your father would have wanted you to save Janus. Concentrate on that."

Chad didn't respond. He took a deep breath and thought about Jim. He remembered the camping trip on Lake Edward and how happy his father was."

Suddenly he felt the silver metallic mesh working its way down his body. He glanced down to see that his arms were now silver.

Finally, he thought.

Ana's first attempt shooting through the dune was high, her Battle Sphere darting through a plume of sand. At the next peak, her plasma pulses were much too low.

Chad's Battle Hologram waited patiently as he completed his transformation. He listened to the background chatter as the Command Cube completed their preflight checklist.

"Propulsion systems on-line . . ."

"Core patterns normal . . ."

"Laser cannons fully operational . . ."

"Energy levels normal . . ."

"All systems normal," confirmed Darius, "Initiating all out-speed intercept in three, two and one. *Launch*."

Chad's Battle Sphere streaked skyward.

At the third and fourth peaks, she fired again, just barely missing Janus's Battle Sphere. At the fifth dune, she struck his Battle Sphere several times causing his shields to weaken even more. At the next peak, she fired again, hitting Janus on the left side. His shields failed completely as his Battle Sphere stopped spinning and arched out of control.

"Commander!" shouted Martin.

At the command center, everyone stared at the wall monitors replaying Janus's mini-screen readouts and visual displays.

"Janus, *no*," whispered Mayla.

Janus's Battle sphere plowed through the upper portion of the next dune, sending a huge plume of sand high into the air in all directions. His sphere skipped down the backside of the sand dune before rolling to a stop.

When Ana arrived, Janus was sitting upright. He had returned to human form, although still covered in his silver shard mesh. Ana slowly moved her spinning Battle Sphere forward until she was within twenty yards of him. By now Janus's mesh had completely receded. He was sitting in the sand naked and vulnerable. Janus raised his arm to shield his eyes from the sand being whipped up all around him. He sat helplessly as Ana prepared to fire her plasma cannons at him.

Chad raced toward the desert at all out speed.

"He's not going to make it in time," said Markus.

Mayla watched Chad's progress as tears welled up in her eyes.

Ana stared down at Janus in disgust as she readied a lethal plasma burst.

"This is for my family," she muttered.

Suddenly, Ana's primary screen and surrounding diagnostic mini screens dissipated. So did the rest of her Battle Sphere.

What's happening? She thought.

Before the last mini screen disappeared, Ana saw that her energy reserves had reached zero.

Oh no, I wasn't paying attention.

Having morphed back to her silver shard covered human form Ana fell to the ground, hitting the sloping sand dune with a thud.

"Ouch!" she shouted.

She sat motionless for a few seconds before springing to her feet. She walked straight toward Janus still lying in the sand.

"You are going to pay for what you did!" she shouted.

"Ana, listen to me. My name is Janus Stone. I am here to tell you that your mother and sisters are alive and well and that I'm your father."

"My mother is dead. So are my sisters. *You killed them!*"

"No, your mother and sisters are alive. They are back on Thrae. They were rescued by your *brother* Chad, along with a coalition of Mitel and Thraen resistance forces and Nomas warriors."

"But the Leadership said —"

"They lied to you Ana. That's what they do. We tried to tell you on your way here, but you apparently turned off your communication systems. If you check your data logs, you'll see that your mother tried to reach you too."

Ana paused and stared at Janus intently. It then suddenly dawned on her who she was talking to.

"Wait . . . *you're my father*?"

"That's what your mother told me after she returned. Given your similar looks, your stubborn streak, not to mention the fact that you are an immortal Battle Sphere, I have no reason to doubt it."

"I don't understand. How is that possible?"

"After the death of my wife, your mother and I dated for a time before the second Mitel invasion fifteen years ago. We cared about each other very much. But unfortunately, I am not always the easiest person to be around. I can be intense, moody and tend to take on a lot of responsibility for the welfare of others. I have known about these traits pretty much all my life. But it's hard to try to change who you are, at least some things. On top of that, your mother ultimately concluded that me being an immortal while she a terminal, gave us little hope of having a happy relationship in the long run. She broke up with me and before she could express her true feelings, I left for Earth with your infant brother. After she was rescued, she came and told me."

"I don't know what to say," she mumbled. "I almost killed my father . . ."

"I'm glad you didn't."

"You intentionally put yourself at risk to deplete my energy reserves, didn't you?"

"Yes."

"Wow . . ."

"I know it's a lot to take in, but the good news is that your mother and sisters are back on Thrae, safe and sound."

Seconds later, Chad's Battle Sphere appeared over the sand dunes and slowly descended toward them.

"Now I understand what you were doing Janus," said Chad.

"Ana," said Janus. "This is your brother Chad."

"Hi Ana!" said Chad.

"Hello," replied Ana meekly.

"Are you both OK?"

"Yes," Janus and Ana replied in unison.

"OK, great," replied Chad. "I'll tell Mayla to get some hover craft out here right away to pick you guys up."

"Will do. In the meantime, I'll stay nearby until they arrive. I assume you guys have some catching up to do."

Chad then disappeared back over the sand dunes.

In the Mitel Leadership Forum Hall, seven immortal men sat behind a large, curved stone bench. With each passing day, their bodies slowly morphed into younger, stronger, and more aggressive versions of their former selves. Thanks to the immortality serum, they felt invigorated and excited about a wide range of future possibilities.

"Our percentage of trade revenues have been at their lowest levels in years," said the first member.

"We can thank the black market for that," replied a second member is disgust.

"And the resistance," added a third member. "They are funneling an ever-increasing amount of goods through their distribution network. We are unable to stop it or tax it."

"And don't forget about the Sidd family," said a fourth member. "We decided to leave them alone for the time being in order to deal with the resistance."

"Not to mention their popularity and loyalty among our former military personnel," added a fifth member.

"That too," acknowledged the fourth member. "And as a result, they are generating tremendous revenues from their black-market weapons sales. And now those weapons are being used against us!"

"Ah yes, the Sidd family business," replied the first Leadership member. "They will be one of our first targets."

"You mean by the mechanical Battle Spheres?" asked the second member.

"Yes."

"How many are ready for deployment?"

"We have almost twelve hundred."

"Excellent," nodded the third member, "how should we deploy them and when?"

"The answer is obvious," replied the first member. "Thrae."

"*Thrae*? Why Thrae?"

"For the first time in their history, Thrae has *three* fully functioning Battle Spheres at the same time. With Falon's rescue, we now know they are working directly with the Mitel resistance. This unprecedented alliance poses the most significant threat our authority has ever faced. We cannot allow them any time whatsoever to plan an attack against us. We *must* strike first."

"With all due respect, the expedited design, fabrication and testing of both the first and second generation mechanical Battle Spheres has placed an incredible strain on our finances."

"We shall demand an increase in our share of trade revenues."

"That will fuel more resentment against us, and more support for the resistance."

"If we *cannot* maintain power," the first member growled, "we won't have to worry about our finances!"

"What do you propose?" asked a fourth member.

"We send One Thousand mechanical Battle Spheres to Thrae, preprogrammed to destroy the three Thraen Battle Spheres and as much of their infrastructure as possible."

"And if they fail?" asked a fifth member.

"Given the results of their developmental testing, one thousand mechanical Battle Spheres should represent an overwhelming attack force."

"In theory I don't disagree. But we've been wrong before."

"*If they fail,* we will quickly analyze the data, determine what went wrong, and program that information into the second-generation battle spheres," explained the first member. "The second-generation spheres are about to undergo initial testing. They represent a significant upgrade over their predecessor in both firepower and maneuverability. By incorporating the combat data from the first attack, we can eliminate any Thraen advantage. The attack should also buy us enough time to bring the second generation on line before the Thraens can launch a counter attack. It's only a matter of time before they attack us anyway."

The other Leadership members nodded silently.

"All in favor of launching the assault raise your hand," asked the third member.

All seven leadership members raised their right hand.

"Good," smiled the first member. "I will notify our scientists to prepare the attack."

CHAPTER TWENTY-SIX – MOVING ON

Atlas and Isak brought Jim to Finch's living quarters where she administered multiple painkillers and tried her best to make him comfortable. She also told Jim more stories about her long life. Finch knew he was a friendly and caring soul. She also knew Jim was getting worse. His temperature was now 104 degrees. Although Atlas and Isak did not trust many surface dwellers, they also knew there was little they could do to help him.

"We need to get him to the medical facility tonight," she told Atlas. "That way we won't be noticed."

Late that evening, Finch helped Jim get dressed. The three then assisted him to the HorVert elevator. Jim was getting weaker by the hour and was now having trouble walking. They traveled along several stops before heading up to the raised walkway. Entering the medical facility, they were greeted by three hologram staff members who immediately recognized the severity of Jim's injury.

"We were told to ask for Evan Lennac," Atlas explained, "and to say that Anton sent us."

"Please follow me," replied the lead staff member.

As they walked down the hall, Isak looked at the staff members, his eyes flashing metallic green.

"Who is Evan Lennac?" he asked.

"He's just the best medical surgeon in Pisco."

"How does he know Anton?"

"Anton saved Evan's life during the second Mitel invasion."

They walked through a set of sliding doors and down a brightly lit hallway.

"Let's put him in here," said the lead staff member.

Jim was placed on a cot surrounded by computers and medical equipment.

"Evan is on his way," replied a second staff member.

A few minutes later, Evan walked into the room.

"Hello everyone," he said.

Evan stood six feet seven inches tall. He had a lean build and appeared fit for his advanced age of 76. He was bald and had long scars across his forehead and right cheek. He produced a large handheld scanner from his long lab coat. He ran scans of Jim's arm.

"OK," Evan sighed. "His arm and shoulder socket are damaged beyond repair. They will have to be removed and —"

"*What?*" Jim blurted.

"Replaced," Evan added.

"I just . . . I don't . . ."

"Listen," said Isak. "My arms, legs, eyes, shoulders and chest muscles are all robotic replacements."

"Atlas told me," mumbled Jim.

"OK good. So you know its routine surgery."

"*Routine surgery . . . ?*"

"In a manner of speaking," replied Evan. "Regardless, your arm and shoulder cannot be saved. The bones are shattered beyond repair. The arm itself is badly infected and is beginning to contaminate the rest of your body. By putting it off, you are risking your life. The choice is yours."

Jim thought for a moment.

"Will it hurt?"

"You'll be under sedation. You should be able to walk out of here tomorrow."

"*Tomorrow*? OK, let's do it."

The last thing Jim remembered before the surgery was counting backward from twenty as Finch held his left hand.

When he awoke, Isak was sleeping in a chair in the corner. Finch and Atlas were gone. Jim looked down at his right arm. Healing accelerator patches were located completely around his shoulder and across his chest. He raised his arm and wiggled his fingers.

It seems just like it was before, only the skin is smoother and has no wrinkles, he thought.

Just then, Evan entered the room.

"How do you feel?" he asked.

As he spoke, Isak awoke and sat up in his chair.

"I feel fine," replied Jim somewhat surprised.

"It was a bit of a challenge, but we played with the three-dimensional accessory generator until it created the internal components for your fifth finger."

"But how did you . . ."

"We scanned your good arm and flipped it before inputting the data into the generator. That part was easy. As I said, getting the internal components working properly for the additional finger was the difficult part. But that came out very nicely as well. We eliminated the infection and returned your body temperature back to normal."

"Thank you," nodded Jim. "What's my arm —"

"Made of? Your friend Isak would only let me make it out of graphene for some reason. The same is true for your shoulder. We replaced that in its entirety due to the extent of your damage."

Isak smiled and winked from his corner seat. "Now you really *are* one of us."

"I must say," continued Evan. "A graphene appendage of any type is incredibly expensive. However, Anton assured me that the entire cost would be paid for by the HPF veteran's fund.

Jim looked at his arm again.

"Whatever was used to inflict such catastrophic damage to your original arm will be quite ineffective the next time around. As will just about anything else. The increased strength on your left side will be very noticeable."

"I see."

"You will need to keep that patch around your arm for one week. Do not attempt to take it off. The patch also contains an anti-rejection serum that is being introduced into your body during the one-week period. After that, you should be better than new. Any questions . . . ?"

"I don't think so."

"OK. A staff member will bring you some food. If continued monitoring goes as expected, you should be free to go later today."

"That's great. Thanks again."

"You're quite welcome."

Evan then turned to Isak who quickly stood up.

"It was an honor meeting you Isak. I can't thank you and Atlas enough for what the two of you have done for Thrae. If you ever change your mind, Anton and I would be more than happy to reach out to the GDC and press for the recognition you both deserve."

"Maybe someday . . ."

"Then I'll wait to hear from you."

"OK," smiled Isak.

"Oh, before I forget. I told Atlas that I heard of an experimental program that infuses holograms with a second gamma ray energy burst. It hasn't been perfected and as a result, appears to be a bit risky. But it may be his only option to try to replenish his electrical reserves."

"What did he say?"

"He laughed and said *let me know when it's perfected*."

"That sounds like Atlas," Isak grunted.

"You know him much better than I do. But he needs to decide on his own. If the infusion goes wrong, he will cease to exist."

"Understood and thank you."

It took longer than expected for Jim to be cleared by the medical staff. Meanwhile Jim and Isak ate everything in sight.

"I thought medical food isn't supposed to be good," said Jim between bites.

"Where did you hear that?" asked Isak.

Jim thought for a moment.

"I don't remember."

"Well you haven't eaten anything for a few days. Eat what you can now. The food back at the enclosure has all gone bad by now."

Later that night, Jim, Atlas and Isak walked out of the medical facility.

"What now?" Jim asked.

"I think we should continue on to Timad," replied Atlas.

"Why?"

"I'm not sure the Scavengers are done with us yet. And I don't want to hang around to find out."

Jim thought about Finch.

"But I like it here," he said.

"We can always come back," replied Isak.

"But . . ."

"I think Finch likes you too," smiled Isak.

"I need to at least say goodbye to her."

The trio headed up the HorVert elevator and down the passageway to the back of the food establishment. Isak and Atlas stayed back while Jim knocked on the door. When Finch opened the door and saw who it was, she floated toward Jim and gave him a big hug and a kiss. Jim showed Finch his new arm and shoulder before explaining that he, Isak and Atlas would move on to the next large population center. Finch grew silent as glistening tears rolled down her hologram cheeks. Jim reached up and wiped them away with his new hand. He was surprised to feel the sensation of wetness.

"Listen, I'll be back soon," said Jim. "Atlas thinks its best we keep moving until we're sure the Scavengers are going to leave us alone."

"What if you *don't* come back?" asked Finch. "What if you forget about me?"

"I'll never forget about you, ever."

"Promise . . . ?"

"I Promise."

Finch grabbed Jim firmly by his shirt and stepped up against him. She then hugged him tightly and kissed him again. The entire passageway sparkled brightly. She eventually stepped back and looked him in the eye.

"I'll be waiting for you," she said almost in a whisper.

Jim smiled and nodded.

"I'll see you soon. I promise."

Finch then waved goodbye before closing the door behind her.

The trio headed back to the circular enclosure and packed up their belongings. Atlas and Isak put on their backpacks and headed toward the perimeter wall. As Jim lifted up his backpack with his new arm, it felt light as a feather. *Wow,* he thought. He then hurried to catch up.

"That door," Atlas pointed.

As they approached, Atlas reached through the door and opened it. He quickly peered down the long corridor. It was empty. Atlas motioned Isak and Jim to follow.

"Are we going back to the hyper loop tunnel?" asked Jim.

"Yes," nodded Atlas.

Twenty minutes later, they exited the corridor into the more dimly lit hyper speed tunnel. Jim and Isak swung themselves down onto the high speed channel while Atlas floated down.

"This way," he pointed.

The tunnel was long and straight. Moonlight was visible through the tunnel opening a few miles off in the distance. As Jim walked in silence, he thought about Finch. He then felt that nagging feeling he was part of something else, something special.

Who am I? he thought. *And why can't I remember?*

As they headed down the tunnel, a Scavenger quietly stepped through the passageway door. He kneeled down at the top of the eight-foot-tall rectangular side structure and watched the trio depart.

CHAPTER TWENTY-SEVEN – THE MECHANICAL INVASION

A hover craft entered the underground base through one of the many launch tunnels and landed on the tarmac. After the curved retractable overlapping roof sections opened, Janus and Ana climbed out dressed in one piece military jumpsuits. Adria and her daughters ran as fast as they could toward the hover craft. When Ana saw them, she immediately ran toward them. The family hugged Ana for a long time. There were plenty of tears, some shed out of joy and others simply released the pent-up pain, frustration and fear they had held for so long.

After grabbing a meal at the base cafeteria, Ana suggested the entire family go on a long vacation to relax and spend time with one another.

"I'm sorry Ana, but that's going to have to wait," said Mayla. "We need your help."

"What?" asked Ana. *"Why?"*

Mayla glanced over at Janus before responding.

"The Mitel Leadership is about to launch a fleet of mechanical Battle Spheres to attack our planet. Although we suspect they may not be as agile, proficient or possess as much firepower as Thraen Battle Spheres, they will still represent the most formidable force our world has ever seen. We need everyone to be available and ready at a moment's notice."

"OK," replied Ana quietly.

She then thought for a moment.

"But I'm already ready. Why can't I just spend a little time with my family?"

"You *aren't* ready," replied Mayla. You need to practice with your Battle Hologram team. They will show you your true potential as a Battle Sphere."

"But I figured all that stuff out on my own."

"Yes you did," smiled Mayla. "A lot of it, anyway. And that was truly remarkable. But your Battle Hologram can help you fly faster, shoot all two hundred of your laser cannons at once with pinpoint accuracy, track your energy reserves and support you along the way."

"What about the Thraen space fleet and outer space globes? Why can't they defend our planet?"

"We're making great progress rebuilding our cruiser fleet, but we still have a long way to go. We also lost several outer defense globes during the last Mitel attack. If our relatively small fleet suffers significant losses confronting the Mitel Battle Spheres, we would be vulnerable to another blockade or even worse. We must hold them back for now."

"But won't they still be vulnerable to attack?"

"We plan to send them out into deep space as soon as we detect the approaching spheres. It will be up to you, Chad and Janus to defend Thrae this time."

Ana looked at Adria who nodded and smiled that she should do this for her people.

"OK," replied Ana. "When do we start?"

"How about tomorrow morning?" asked Janus. "In the meantime, why don't you spend today with your family? I'm sure Mayla can locate living quarters here on the base for the four of you."

"No problem," replied Mayla. "Come with me."

Janus watched silently as the five women disappeared through a side entrance.

Early the next morning, Ana was awoken by intercom beeps. She pushed the button. "*Hello?*"

"Ana, it's Chad. Time for training," he replied. "Are you awake?"

"*I am now,*" she responded, rubbing her eyes. "Give me twenty minutes to shower and get dressed."

"OK," Chad sighed.

Forty minutes later, the doors slid open to Ana's quarters. Chad was sitting with his back against the wall on the hallway floor. "Let's go," she smiled.

Chad led Ana across the main underground base to Bay Number 1, through the open stone faced camouflaged doors out onto the shelf. Janus, Zan, and a sizeable crowd including several technicians, mechanics and soldiers were waiting there.

"Does everyone need to be here?" whispered Ana.

"Most of them have never seen a Battle Sphere before, why?" asked Chad.

"You know," blushed Ana. She pointed down toward her clothes.

"Oh, that. Don't worry. You kind of get used to being mostly naked in front of strangers. You'll still be covered by your silver mesh."

Noticing Ana's frown, Chad thought quickly.

"I'll go first," he offered. "Everyone will be focused on me. Then you can begin, OK?"

"I'll give it a try . . ."

"Great. But before we start, I want you to stand about twenty yards away from me and just follow my lead."

"OK," Ana sighed.

Ana and Chad took positions sixty feet apart on the shelf. As Ana watched, Chad glanced out toward Lake Victoria before closing his eyes to concentrate. A minute later, the silver metallic mesh pattern, resembling shards of glass, quickly spread from his eyes to cover the rest of his body. His eyes turned bright white before he levitated up into the air. Heavy metal trace elements and helium-4 were drawn from the surrounding atmosphere and ground area from every direction. Swirls of shiny particles of titanium, aluminum, magnesium, cadmium, iron and beryllium whirled around Chad's blue plasma sphere.

Feeling more comfortable, Ana stared out at the lake and closed her eyes. She concentrated until she felt the familiar feeling of the metallic mesh working its way down her body. She liked the feeling as it made her feel safe and in control. As she rose into the air, beams of white light streamed from her eyes toward the ground across the Mesa and toward the cliff. The same shiny particles appeared from all directions and swirled at that location like a large dust devil. Seconds later, her Battle Hologram appeared in the center of the whirlwind and grew from the ground up to form the three-dimensional hologram cubes. Hologram personnel could be seen moving back and forth inside her Battle Hologram.

Team Commander Hayden Colten appeared at the Battle Hologram entrance. He exited and made his way toward Ana's hovering Battle Sphere. He glanced at Chad's Battle Sphere and the crowd as he approached. Hayden was surrounded by the same blue translucent haze as the Battle Hologram itself. He stopped about twenty feet in front of Ana and looked up at her.

"Hi Ana," he said. "Do you remember me?"

"How could I forget?" she replied.

"I'm glad I made an impression on you," he smiled. "Are you ready for some training?

"Yes. Listen, I'm sorry for last time. I was angry and hurt."

"Not to worry. I'm glad you're finally home. I'm also very happy to hear that your family is safe and sound."

"Thank you."

"You're quite welcome. We're hoping to familiarize you to a point where you are comfortable and trust your Battle Hologram."

"I've taught myself to do a lot already," replied Ana proudly.

"You have," grinned Hayden, "and we've been monitoring that progress from afar, so to speak. But I think you'll be surprised what your Battle Hologram can do for you if you let them."

"I'm ready to try."

"Great. Let's get started, shall we?"

"Ready when you are."

Hayden gave the thumbs up and headed back toward his Battle Hologram.

Darius looked across from his station inside Chad's Battle Hologram toward the neighboring hologram structure. "Hello, Darius speaking," he said over the encrypted communication system.

"Hello Darius," replied a female voice, "Raya Stone speaking. I've gone ahead and patched in both Battle Spheres."

Raya stood six feet two inches tall with a dark complexion, white hair and haunting gray eyes.

"*The* Raya Stone?" asked Darius.

"Since when did I become famous?" she chucked.

"Oh, come on, you *know* you are."

"What's he talking about?" asked Ana. "Wait. Raya *Stone*. Are we related too?"

"I'm Janus's ascendant cousin, five generations prior. You?"

"I'm his daughter . . ."

"That makes me your aunt, maybe *forty-five* times removed."

"How old are you?"

"Almost 1,350 years old. I joined the HPF when I was a teenager. At first my parents were unhappy about it. But they eventually came to realize how critically important the HPF was. I've served five, now six Battle Spheres. I became human again when Val Rand self-destructed in deep space to destroy an interstellar attack force. I lived as a human for a year after that. But since my immediate family had died long before then, I rejoined the HPF. If I had known Janus was so interested in the reverse transformation process, also known as the *miracle of life*, I would have told him all about it. He never asked me."

"You're 1,350 years old?"

"Yes. I've seen a lot of things change over that time. I've also watched many people that I cared about a great deal die. Sometimes it seems like time almost becomes a blur. But I still remember when Janus was born. He was a little brat as a kid, but he grew up to be one of our greatest leaders, probably the greatest."

"Wow . . ." whispered Ana.

"You're not too shabby either," said Darius. "You've helped guide some of Thrae's greatest Battle Spheres including Markus Kilmar."

"Oh, I love Markus. He's the best."

"He's here. He's a hologram now too."

"*Really*? I've got to talk to him! He refused to listen to me when I told him repeatedly to withdraw and recharge during the Mitel invasion. He's stubborn, just like Janus. I think it might be a man thing."

"Uh, maybe not," replied Ana.

"You're stubborn too huh? I stand corrected. I guess it runs in the family."

"Uh, hey everybody," said Teri, "don't mean to interrupt the family reunion, but we think it's time for Chad to take Ana to the shared asteroid belt. She and her Battle Hologram need to get in some target practice together."

"Sounds good to me," replied Nolia.

"I'm ready," added Raya.

"Solar powered signal accelerators are fully operational," confirmed Darius.

"Instantaneous communications along the mission route has been confirmed," said Raya. "Systems monitoring verified."

"OK great. I think we're good to go," replied Darius. "Chad, are you ready?"

"Yes."

"All set on my end," confirmed Raya. "Ana?"

"I think so."

"Shields confirmed as fully operational," said Darius, "and energy reserves still at maximum."

"Same here," added Raya. "Prepare to initiate *all-out* speed mission launch."

The Battle Holograms sped up Chad's and Ana's variable speed flywheels causing their Battle Spheres to spin faster and faster. Ana tracked her rpm surge on a diagnostic mini screen until it leveled off at one hundred twenty thousand.

"Launch sequence activated," confirmed Darius. "Initiating all out speed in three, two and one. *Launch*."

One by one, the two Battle Spheres sped away from the Shelf, through the upper atmosphere and toward the shared asteroid belt. When they arrived, Chad positioned himself about a quarter mile behind Ana while her Battle Hologram searched for dense pockets of asteroids.

"Three dense asteroid pockets are approaching on our left," announced Raya. "This looks like a good place to start."

"Laser cannons energized and ready to go," announced Ana's weapons coordinator.

Ana scanned his mini screens. Yellow dots with small identification labels appeared on several screens as her Battle Hologram identified and tracked the approaching targets. Within seconds, the yellow dots on her screen multiplied, until they appeared as a swarm.

There are so many, Ana thought.

"Identifying targets," said Raya. "Targets locked."

As Ana's Battle Sphere converged with the enormous asteroid field, her 200 laser cannons fired rapidly in every direction. The light pulses curved away before streaking ahead to intercept the approaching metal, ice and rock. Seconds later, hundreds upon hundreds of bright white flashes caused the approaching asteroids to disintegrate. She easily weaved her way around the oncoming debris.

"You are doing great, Ana!" encouraged Chad who had dropped further back.

A quick glance across her mini screens told Ana that the second of the three large fields was approaching. Like the first, her weapons specialists quickly destroyed the oncoming targets.

"Wow," she said out loud. "I had no idea my cannons could destroy so many targets at once."

"Your weapons specialists are very good at what they do," replied Hayden. You need to learn to trust them."

"Understood," replied Ana.

"The third wave is approaching," announced Raya. "Locking tar . . ." her voice trailed off.

"Raya, what's wrong?" asked Hayden.

"The asteroids. Something's wrong," she replied.

Suddenly the asteroid field swerved in all directions, the lead objects opening fire at Ana.

"They are mechanical Battle Spheres!" blurted Raya.

"Entering free flight," said Chad. He darted forward.

Within seconds, the mechanical Battle Spheres were everywhere. Both Chad and Ana's weapons specialists returned high energy plasma bursts as they cycled through their series of five targets.

"There must be a thousand of them," said Chad.

"They're moving too fast to lock onto," added Darius.

"We need a plan," said Nolia. "I propose we split up to avoid friendly fire."

"Sounds good," replied Hayden.

"I'm on my way," said Chad. He quickly accelerated to his left. He was immediately chased by hundreds of mechanical spheres.

Now surrounded, Ana resisted the urge to take control of her plasma cannons. Now she knew that to do so would greatly reduce her effectiveness. Instead, she used the skills she acquired in the Stone Forest to dodge back and forth to avoid the multitude of spheres and their weapons fire. Despite her efforts, her protective shields were still hit repeatedly by incoming plasma bursts. She kept telling herself not to override her Battle Hologram.

"Shields are weakening," said Raya.

"Reserves are down to thirty-three percent."

Chad, now twenty miles away, also labored to hold his own against the swarming mechanical spheres.

"They're everywhere," he said. His Battle Hologram feverishly executed evasive maneuvers, jerking his Battle Sphere in all directions.

After several punishing hits, Ana's shields were failing.

"Commanders, we need to withdraw," urged Nolia. "*Now!*"

Chad, sensing the urgency in her voice, darted through an opening in the swarm back toward Ana. Seconds later, her outer defense shields went off line. Ana desperately searched for an opening in the swarm.

"Ana!" shouted Raya, "you must withdraw *now!*"

"*I'm trying,*" she shouted.

As he closed in, Chad focused intently on Ana's Battle Sphere. He placed a translucent blue protective plasma shield around her Battle Sphere just as the swarm unleashed another round of plasma bursts. They deflected harmlessly off the temporary shield.

Thank goodness, he thought. "Ana, follow me!"

Chad accelerated away from the mechanical spheres. Ana raced after him, colliding with one, then a second sphere, obliterating both on impact.

"Where are we going?" she asked.

"Back to Thrae," replied Chad. "We need to regroup before they arrive." Streaking away at all out speed, they left the mechanical Battle Spheres far behind.

Nolia and Hayden immediately alerted Arius, Mayla and Teri about the sudden encounter.

"We don't have much time to prepare," concluded Arius. "Instruct all of our space cruisers to withdraw into deep space. That includes Zan's cruiser. Notify the general population to head to underground defense shelters as quickly as possible. I realize that withdrawing our cruisers leaves our people and infrastructure more vulnerable to attack, but we simply can't risk losing them at this time. In my opinion, that would be even more catastrophic to the security of our planet. Hopefully our Battle Spheres and upgraded outer defense globes will be enough. The globes were designed to neutralize Mitel cluster pod warheads. The mechanical Battle Spheres should represent comparable targets. As of now, we are on *high alert* until further notice."

Upon receiving the news, Zan and Ard took a shuttle pod into outer space and docked with the renegade cruiser. Everyone turned to look at Zan as he entered the ICC.

"Welcome back," said Lia. "We didn't expect to see you so soon."

"He just can't stay away," replied Ard. "He's addicted to all the excitement but won't admit it. They say that's the first step toward recovery."

"Yeah, that *must* be my problem," Zan grunted as he flopped into the command console.

"The other cruisers just left," announced Mat. "Should we plot a course to follow them?"

Zan thought for a moment.

"No."

"*No?*" asked Ard. "Why don't I like that answer?"

"Ard, do you believe in destiny?"

Ard paused.

"I really haven't thought about it much. But if I had to guess, I'd be inclined to say that *if you keep taking unnecessary risks, you are destined to get killed eventually.*"

Zan shook his head.

"I'll take that under advisement. For now, I propose that we relocate behind the larger moon. If it looks like the Battle Spheres need help, we step in."

"If three Thraen Battle Spheres need help, that's not a good sign."

"Probably not Ard, but what else do you suggest we do? Let them all get *destroyed*? Remember, I'm counting on them to help free our people when the time comes. Think of it as an insurance policy."

"I know that's what you're hoping, but —"

"I'm in," interrupted Lia.

"I am too," replied Mat.

"Me too," added Dax.

Zan then entered a three-digit code on his console communications system. It beeped once.

"Dru here," the voice answered.

"Dru, it's Zan."

"Good to have you back on board."

"Thanks. Listen, would you be willing to help —"

"Yes. We've been tinkering with the propulsion system to get a little more speed out of it. I think you'll notice the difference. We also made sure both weapons tubes are fully loaded with the newest Thraen built cluster pods. We had a hunch you might want to help the Battle Spheres out if necessary. We also spoke with Rad. He's not thrilled, but he supports helping out where we can."

"Thank you all," Zan replied. The intercom beeped again. He then looked toward Ard.

"OK, OK, I'm in too," grumbled Ard. "It's not like I had anything else planned for tonight anyway."

"I knew I could count on you Ard. Dax let's get this cruiser behind the moon," instructed Zan.

"Doing it now."

Seconds later, the vessel sped away from Thrae.

Chad and Ana slowed down as they approached Thrae, eventually coming to a stop five hundred miles above the planet surface.

"OK," said Mayla over the encrypted communications system. "You both need to recharge immediately."

Markus stood silently off to one side in the underground command center, watching events unfold. Janus walked out onto the shelf, looked out at Lake Victoria and took a deep breath. He then raised his arms and moved his legs apart.

Hopefully someday this will no longer be necessary, he thought. *But until then . . .*

He closed his eyes. They reopened seconds later as the silver shard mesh worked its way down his body.

In the GDC Arius stared intently at the three-dimensional images and data fields throughout the command center. On the deep space scanner, the mechanical Battle Spheres abruptly appeared as a large cloud-like disturbance.

Here we go, he thought.

"The mechanical Battle Spheres are due to arrive in approximately two hours," announced a hologram scanning specialist.

Arius activated the worldwide military communication system. "This is GDC Commander Court. We have detected the approach of the Mitel Battle Spheres. They are currently two hours away. As you know, our people are counting on all of us to defend our planet with determination and courage. Good luck."

Janus, having transformed, hovered above the shelf. While Ana and Chad recharged in outer space, Mayla patched them in with Janus, Teri and Arius. All three Battle Hologram Command Cubes listened in.

"They're not as fast, but very agile," explained Chad. "They also don't appear to have outer defense shields."

"Chad's right," replied Ana. "He placed a small plasma shield around me when my own shields gave out in the middle of a swarm. When I flew out, I collided with two of them. His shield destroyed them."

"I see the Mitels still like to use the swarm maneuver," mused Mayla. "Maybe we can use that technique to our advantage."

"How?" asked Arius.

"If the mechanical battle spheres are agile enough to avoid target locks, the weapons specials could fire a wide barrage at the swarm. If the spheres don't possess outer defense shields, the barrage *should* destroy many of them."

"That's too inefficient," replied Arius. "I want our three Battle Spheres to spread out in a row beyond Thrae's atmosphere. It will allow them flexibility to quickly move back and forth to the planet surface if needed. Our spheres will open fire at the Mitel spheres the very second the come within range. Hopefully we can eliminate most of them during that initial barrage which would also reduce the risk of a surface attack."

"That assumes they fly right at us," Teri pointed out.

"They will still be on an approach trajectory. And if they start to deviate from that, we will adjust the location of our defense row. We are also repositioning ten of the thirteen remaining outer space defense globes to the approach side of the planet. They will be stationed at twelve hundred mile intervals, which should allow us to maintain concentrated firepower over a *very wide* approach angle."

"That leaves only three globes covering the back side of the planet."

"Understood," replied Arius quickly. "We have no choice but to commit our resources based on the known threat."

"We must be prepared to change and adapt to a changing attack plan," said Nolia. "We were very fortunate in the last two Mitel confrontations. In each case, we had the element of surprise. We don't have it here. If anyone does, it's them."

"At least until we get some baseline performance data on their spheres," replied Lucian. "We don't know how they recharge, how long it takes, or their weapons capability. We also don't know how long they can sustain a weapons barrage. We'll find out soon enough."

"I agree with both of you," added Mayla. "We need to adopt a defensive approach, at least initially. That is why I feel Arius's plan makes sense."

"I agree," stated Janus.

"Then, it's settled," replied Arius. "Now if you'll excuse me, I must turn my attention to monitoring the status of the worldwide civilian sheltering."

Janus darted skyward from the shelf to join Ana and Chad in outer space.

"OK," said Hayden, "I suggest we establish a frontline position four hundred miles apart at an altitude of seven hundred and fifty miles."

"Sounds good," replied Janus.

The three spheres headed another two hundred-fifty miles into outer space toward the equator before turning east. Four hundred miles before the center coordinates, Janus instructed Ana to stop. Janus stopped at the center point while Chad continued another four hundred miles east.

"What now?" Chad asked.

"Now we wait," replied Janus.

As he hovered silently, Chad's thoughts turned to Jim and then Melissica. *I miss them so much. I sure wish I knew that he is OK*, he thought. *I also wish Melissica was here with me on Thrae. She always knows just what to say to calm me down.*

On the ICC of the renegade cruiser, Mat tracked the approaching mechanical Battle Spheres.

"They are almost within range," he confirmed.

"Zan," said Lia, the rest of the Thraen fleet is wondering where we are. What should I tell them?"

Zan thought for a moment.

"Tell them we've been delayed," he replied. "That's not *technically* lying is it?"

"Depends on your definition of lying," Ard mused.

High above Thrae, Janus, Ana and Chad kept a close eye on their diagnostic mini screens. In the underground base command center, Mayla studied the wall mounted monitors tracking the approaching swarm.

"The outer space defense globes are ready," muttered Mayla. "Hopefully things go as planned."

Across the room, Teri tracked the performance and diagnostic status of the Thraen Battle Spheres.

"Is everyone ready?" asked Hayden.

"Yes," replied Darius and Raya in unison.

"They are just about within range," confirmed Martin.

Suddenly, the mechanical Battle Spheres abruptly came to a stop.

"They've detected us," said Janus.

The mechanical spheres opened fire. Within seconds, plasma blasts deflected off Janus's Battle Sphere. Chad and Ana were also hit. There were reports that the outer space globes were also experiencing incoming fire.

"What is going on?" asked Nolia.

"Apparently, they have a longer firing range then we do," responded Janus.

"Not a good start," stated Teri.

"Start moving side to side to avoid their laser bursts," instructed Janus. "That may force their hand."

After ten minutes of dodging laser bursts, the incoming Mitel laser fire ceased. The mechanical battle spheres then spread out.

"OK," said Janus. "They appear to be preparing their assault. Is everyone ready?"

"Yes," replied Chad.

"Me too," said Ana.

The mechanical Battle Spheres raced forward before dividing into five groups of one hundred ninety-six spheres each. The groups on either end headed toward the outer defense globes on both sides of the three Thraen Battle Spheres. The other three headed directly toward Janus, Chad and Ana. As they approached, the mechanical spheres rotated through a random dodging pattern. Raya, Darius and Martin quickly realized they could not secure a weapons lock onto the approaching spheres.

"Running the attack pattern through our computers," said Hayden. He stared at the screen for several seconds.

"It doesn't appear to repeat itself. But I've got to assume it will reduce their energy reserves eventually."

"Probably not enough to make a difference during their approach," replied Nolia.

"They are within firing range," announced Darius.

"Weapons specialists, fire at will!" instructed Lucian.

The weapons specialists for all three Thraen Battle Spheres rotated through their battery of five laser cannons.

"Got one," announced a weapons specialist.

"Me too," said another.

One by one, the weapons specialists modified their firing patterns to coincide with the random patterns. Their kill rate increased.

That appears to be the only way, thought Mayla. She tracked the approach on the three-dimensional displays. *They will still not get enough of them before being overrun.*

"Janus, Chad and Ana, you need to take evasive action!" she shouted.

But it was too late, as Mitel spheres swarmed around all three Battle Spheres. At the same time, the two outer groups of mechanical spheres overwhelmed and destroyed the two closest outer space defense globes.

While the weapons specialists struggled to destroy the darting spheres, Martin, Raya and Darius kept a close eye on their energy reserves.

"Shield levels are decreasing rapidly," confirmed Lucian, "but they're still holding up."

On the ICC of the renegade cruiser, Zan and the rest of the group listened intently to the unfolding attack.

"There are just too many of them," said Zan. "Let's go lend some help."

"Weapons tubes activated," confirmed Ard. "Pods ready to launch."

"Let's see how well they dodge a concentrated barrage of our cluster pods."

The cruiser accelerated out from behind Thrae and raced toward the spheres.

"Activate the high-speed defense shields," instructed Zan.

After destroying the outer space defense globe closest to Chad, the group of mechanical spheres darted toward the planet. Nolia noticed immediately.

"Chad, the cluster of spheres to your left is heading toward the planet surface!"

"Got it," he replied. Chad focused intently and projected a partial shield across that portion of the planet. Before they could register its existence, the entire group of mechanical spheres flew into the shield and disintegrated. From his position, Chad noticed the small flashes of light propagating along the shield.

"Nice work Chad," said Darius. "But that drew down your energy reserves substantially. You are now down to thirty-one percent. You will need to withdraw and recharge soon."

"We need help over here," requested Raya. "Ana's shields are about to fail."

Chad switched to free flight, darted through an opening in the swarm and raced toward Ana. As he approached Janus, he could see he was holding his own.

"Get over to Ana," urged Janus.

"On my way," replied Chad, streaking past the second swarm. Glancing at his diagnostic mini-screens, Chad noticed that his swarm of mechanical spheres was right behind him.

"Ana," said Hayden. "You need to escape the swarm *now!*"

Ana instinctively took control of her propulsion and weapons systems, desperately looking for an opening.

I won't get there in time, Chad thought. He then noticed dozens of incoming cluster warheads.

"They're from Zan's cruiser," confirmed Hayden.

Chad abruptly stopped and concentrated on Ana. Just as the warheads arrived, Chad once again placed a small protective shield around her Battle Sphere. Brilliant flashes erupted all around Ana as dozens of mechanical spheres were hit and destroyed. A second round of incoming warheads set off another wave of explosions.

"Chad," warned Darius, "Mitel spheres are right on top of you!"

Chad reflexively darted forward, right in the path of Zan's oncoming cruiser.

"*Chad!*" shouted Darius.

Chad swerved at the last second, narrowly missing the cruiser. The pursuing swarm of mechanical spheres plowed into the side of the cruiser in rapid succession, their impact mostly blunted by the high-speed shields. As the spheres disintegrated, several large shards pierced the cruiser's outer hull, setting off alarms throughout the cruiser. The emergency environmental monitoring system automatically closed several bulkhead doors.

Lia quickly made her way to the auxiliary wall cabinet and retrieved several oxygen masks and backpack units.

"Everyone, put one on," she motioned.

"I don't think they teach that maneuver at the Academy," said Ard. "But it sure did the trick."

Zan reached down to his console communicator and entered a three-digit code. It beeped once.

"We already have them on," said Dru. "We eventually decided to start carrying them around with us every time you come on board."

"Good to know," replied Zan. "Are the propulsion units —"

"All three units are fine. At least for now . . ."

"OK thanks." Zan then entered a second code. After a beep Rad answered.

"Thanks for checking," he said. "Dru recommended that we carry them around with us —"

"When I come on board," interrupted Zan.

"Correct. Are you going to keep us in one piece?"

"We're trying."

"OK thanks." The system beeped again.

Ana sped out of the swarm destroying three more mechanical spheres with her temporary plasma shield before it dissipated. She then darted down toward the planet surface to hide and recharge. The swarm quickly chased after her. Janus found an opening in his swarm and darted down after Ana, his mechanical battle sphere swarm racing after him.

After destroying the second outer space globe, the remaining group of mechanical spheres headed toward the surface to attack population centers. From outer space, Chad hovered in place momentarily.

"I've got to help them," he thought aloud.

"Your energy reserves are down to twenty-four percent," replied Darius. "You must recharge first, even if it's just for a few minutes."

"There isn't time." Chad then raced at all out speed down through the upper atmosphere.

Approaching the planet surface, Ana looks for somewhere to hide. She then remembered the underground base entrances. *No, it would give the base away*, she thought. Ana then darted across a long but narrow lake, the waves below her appearing as a blur.

Janus quickly closed in on the mechanical spheres chasing Ana.

"Identifying targets," said Martin.

Before he could lock onto the targets, the mechanical battle spheres opened fire, striking Ana multiple times. She lost control and plunged into the water.

"Ana!" shouted Janus as he streaked past. As he overshot the lake, his pursuing mechanical spheres opened fire. Janus could feel the blasts piercing his weakened defense shields. Several weapons cubes went black as they were destroyed along with their laser cannons. As the barrage continued to pummel his Battle Sphere, Janus swerved out of control. He narrowly missed a large stone outcropping before plowing into a hill made of relatively soft surface soil. The force of the impact sent dirt and debris high into the air in all directions. Janus' Battle Sphere was now buried in a shallow crater.

Dozens of Mitel mechanical spheres slowed down and hovered over both crash sites. Ana, having transformed into her silver mesh, struggled to the surface. There was no sign of Janus. As the mechanical spheres prepared to fire at Ana, Chad swooped down on them.

"Identifying targets," said Darius, "and locked." Chad's weapons specialists opened fire.

At the underground base, Markus was growing increasingly upset. He felt useless and helpless. To vent some of his frustration, he walked out of the command center. He then headed through Bay Number 1 toward the shelf. Along the way, he listened to the chatter through his monitoring orb hovering close behind him.

This is simply horrible, he thought.

Chad's continuous laser cannon fire caused the mechanical battle spheres to scatter in all directions. Nolia then noticed a cloud of incoming objects on her monitor.

"We've got more company," she announced.

The almost two hundred remaining Mitel mechanical spheres, having registered the skirmish, had all changed direction to assist in the attack.

"Chad," urged Mayla, "you must withdraw and recharge!"

"If I do, they'll kill Ana and Janus for sure!"

"If you don't, they will kill you also!"

"Not if I can help it!"

Markus made his way onto the shelf. Now in a rage, he yelled toward the sky. *"This can't be happening!"*

He then heard a faint humming noise. Feeling strange, Markus looked all around. He saw nothing.

Without warning, his eyes turned bluish white. Before Markus could react, he levitated in the air, encircled by an electrically charged brilliant white hologram sphere twenty feet in diameter. Naturally occurring electric charges from Thrae's upper and lower atmosphere were immediately drawn to the sphere from all directions. As the charges were absorbed, Markus's transformation accelerated. A powerful electromagnetic field surrounded and intensified around the transforming sphere. The transformation itself followed the Battle Sphere blueprint embedded in his hologram architecture. The only difference was that the hologram sphere itself was not limited by the physical world.

The brilliance of his transformation caused a bright light to shine through the large door opening of Bay Number 1. Several technicians ran over to see what was happening. Looking up, they couldn't believe their eyes. Markus's bright white hologram Battle Sphere hovered above the shelf. Across the way appeared a fourth Hologram Matrix.

"This is *incredible*," said Darius.

"Yeah," whispered Martin. "His electromagnetic field is *off the charts*."

Before anyone else could speak, Markus switched to free flight and took off toward Chad and the others.

Chad hovered for a second above Ana. Looking all around, he noticed that the first swarm of mechanical battle spheres had disappeared from view. Chad turned and raced toward the sky to confront the descending swarm of mechanical spheres. As they approached on another, the spheres once again rotated through a random dodging pattern.

"It makes it pretty hard to hit them," said a frustrated weapons specialist.

In a matter of seconds, Chad was once again surrounded by a swarm. His weapons specialists feverishly rotated through their laser weapons cluster, firing at will.

"Chad, you are down to *sixteen percent*," warned Darius.

But Chad wouldn't listen. He would not abandon Ana and Janus under any circumstance. One by one, his weapons cubes went dark as the incoming plasma bursts penetrated Chad's weakened defense shields.

If I can draw them away, he thought. *That may allow Ana and Janus to escape.*

Chad looked for an opening in the swarm. Seeing one, he darted into the clear. As he looked at his mini-screens, Chad was hit by incoming bursts. He lost control of his Battle Sphere and plummeted toward the surface. Seeing the rocky terrain below, Chad focused on trying to place a small plasma shield around his Battle Sphere. A light blue hue appeared in front of him.

It's weak, but it's all I've got, he thought.

"Chad!" shouted Mayla.

Chad's Battle Sphere narrowly missed a large, jagged granite ledge before glancing off an adjacent face. The blunt force of the impact dissipated his plasma shield and knocked him unconscious. His Battle Sphere bounced off two more stone formations, tearing open portions of his outer skin surface, exposing his inner architecture. His Battle Sphere hit the ground with a loud thud. Lying in a heap, his reverse transformation had begun.

At the lake, Ana struggled to shore. Now exhausted, she crawled out of the water on her hands and knees, rolled over onto her back and passed out.

A few miles away, Janus thrust his silver shard covered left hand out from under the dirt at the bottom of the shallow crater. With his remaining strength, he freed himself from the surrounding soil before lying down, fatigued. He then lost consciousness.

All but six of the three hundred fifty remaining mechanical spheres split into smaller groups as they prepared to launch their preprogrammed attacks on Thraen population centers. The other six mechanical spheres split up into groups of two to circle back to inspect the three Thraen crash sites and make sure the Battle Spheres had all been destroyed. Noticing Ana, Chad and Janus lying on the ground, they prepared to fire.

As Markus approached, the six mechanical spheres registered his powerful magnetic field. They stopped and turned to confront him. One by one, the other groups also detected the approaching anomaly and doubled back to provide support.

Markus slowed to a stop over the lake. He was quickly surrounded by the returning spheres. He silently hovered in place for several seconds while the mechanical spheres scanned his Battle Sphere. Their databases did not register his hologram configuration or energy profile. After performing several scans, the mechanical spheres hovered silently in place as they weren't programmed to deal with this kind of Battle Sphere.

Without warning, they opened fire on Markus. The continuous and relentless barrage lasted for almost a minute. The plasma pulses passed harmlessly through Markus's hologram sphere while he hovered silently. As the onslaught continued, the mechanical spheres began destroying their counterparts hovering on the opposite side of the swarm. Once the spheres registered that they were destroying each other, the entire swarm ceased firing and continued to hover in place.

"OK, now *it's our turn*," said Battle Hologram Team Leader Jayden Dalton, "open fire."

Markus's two hundred hologram cannons simultane-ously emitted modest laser pulses lasting only a fraction of a second. Exiting his Battle Sphere, the intense electro-magnetic field caused electrons to be torn off air mole-cules creating high energy plasma lightning bolts. Con-taining twenty million watts each, the bolts flashed in all directions followed by a thunderous sonic boom. The me-chanical spheres, their circuitry burnt to a crisp, dropped into the water. In a matter of seconds, all three hundred fifty-six remaining spheres sunk to the bottom of the lake, ruined.

"Excellent job everyone," said Jayden.

Markus turned his attention to Ana and Janus. His Battle Hologram quickly ran scans on both.

"They are going to be OK," confirmed Jayden. "We'll get hover crafts out there immediately to pick them up.

Markus then glided ahead looking for Chad. Passing over a stone ridge, he saw Chad lying down below, hav-ing transformed back to human form. As Markus moved closer, he could see that Chad's left arm and legs were horribly mangled.

Oh no, he thought.

"I need help and I need it fast," said Markus.

Mayla could tell by the emotion in Markus's voice that something was horribly wrong.

"Markus, what's wrong?" she asked.

Markus did not immediately answer.

"Markus — "

"I don't know if he's even alive," he replied almost in a whisper.

"He's alive," replied Jayden. "But I don't know for how much longer."

Three medical hover crafts took off from the under-ground base and raced to the crash site. A special Incubator device mounted inside one of the craft, levitated Chad into its emergency tube. The craft turned and sped back to the base. As a precaution, Ana and Janus were retrieved the same way flown back in separate hovercrafts.

When Janus awoke, he looked around the room. *Where am I?* he thought.

Realizing that he was back in the medical facility, it all came rushing back to him.

"Where's Ana and Chad?" he asked the technician next to his bed.

"Ana's down the hall," replied Zan, seated in the far corner. He stood up and approached Janus. "She's doing fine," he added.

"What about Chad, and the mechanical Battle Spheres?"

"The mechanical spheres have all been destroyed."

"What? *How?*"

"Markus Kilmar."

"*Markus?* I'm sorry, I don't understand."

"Markus became so agitated that he transformed into a Battle Sphere."

"*A Battle Sphere?* Markus?"

"A *hologram* Battle Sphere no less. And it appears he has significantly more firepower capability than a traditional Battle Sphere, *at least* under atmospheric conditions."

"How is that possible?"

"Scientists are still trying to evaluate the data. But it appears that he can throw incredibly powerful lightning bolts through his cannons. It has something to do with his magnetic field that amplifies an extremely short and modest plasma charge. He completely fried the last three hundred and fifty-six mechanical spheres in a matter of seconds."

"Unbelievable. What about Chad? How's he doing?"

Zan didn't answer.

"Zan, *what's wrong*?"

"Chad was hurt very badly Janus. They're not sure if he's going to survive."

Janus could feel his heart racing.

"I'm very sorry," said Zan. "He's being treated by Rad along with a staff of the best medical personnel on Thrae."

Janus Nodded.

"Listen, I'll go check on his status, OK?"

"Thank you," Janus nodded.

Zan headed toward the door. He stopped and turned around.

"Your son is the bravest person I've ever met. It's an honor to serve alongside him."

Janus nodded again before Zan walked out of the room, the doors sliding closed behind him.

Janus covered his face with his hands and cried.

CHAPTER TWENTY-EIGHT – SOUL SEARCHING

Janus watched silently through large windows as medical personnel attended to Chad. Several memories drifted across his mind's eye as he did. Janus felt helpless, useless and empty. He found himself starting to go to a dark place emotionally and knew that would not solve anything. Janus eventually decided to take a short hovercraft ride to clear his head.

He left the top open as he flew along, trying to both relax and relieve the stress he was feeling. Janus suddenly found himself headed toward Liana's vault. Realizing where he was going, Janus didn't fight the urge. Deed down, he felt as though he was being drawn there. He landed the hovercraft in a field behind a row of trees not far from the complex, exiting the craft through a sliding side door.

Janus walked toward the sixty-foot-tall circular marble building. As he approached, he glanced up at the spiral design atop the structure. He stopped for a time to stare at the millions of stones in the circular meditation pond. Janus secretly wondered which ones might actually belong to his wife and daughters although he knew none were individually designated that way.

Janus eventually entered the brightly lit building. He looked up at the translucent spiral ceiling before making his way to the black doors at the center of the structure. He peered into the retinal scanner and entered the dimly lit viewing room as the doors slid open. Janus tried to remember the last time he had been there, and given what Chad recently experienced, he was nervous.

Janus's thoughts then turned to Molly. He wished there was something he could do to take away her pain. Janus took a deep breath before repeatedly trying to activate Liana's hologram program.

Nothing happened.

He was disappointed, but not surprised. Janus still wanted to use the opportunity to talk about things. He took another deep breath before speaking.

"Hi, Liana. It's Janus."

His words echoed ever so slightly around the room.

"I've come to talk."

He gathered his thoughts.

"You were always there for me. You listened to my seemingly endless stream of complaints, problems and emergencies, some of them self-inflicted. You offered wise counsel, love, and support. Most of all, you weren't afraid to tell me when I was wrong. In retrospect, I was wrong quite often."

Tears started to well up in his eyes.

"Liana, I miss you more than I can put into words. I miss Zeya and Mistil too."

Janus wiped the tears away.

"You'd be interested to know that I've recently found out that I have another daughter. Her name is Ana. She has my eyes and nose, and my stubborn streak. She's also a natural immortal and a Battle Sphere. You probably wouldn't have been surprised by any of that."

Janus looked around the room for a time.

"Liana, we recently had a series of confrontations with the Mitels. Although we did very well, Chad was critically injured near the end of the most recent encounter. The medical staff doesn't know whether he's going to live or die."

Janus put his hands over his face and cried. His shoulders heaved as he let out all his emotions. It felt as though he was releasing a thousand years' worth of pain, frustration and sorrow. After a time, Janus composed himself.

"I'm tired Liana, so very tired. I don't know if I'm still immortal and quite frankly, I don't care anymore. In some ways, it has been a curse."

Janus paused.

"I think that I'm starting to lose my will to fight, Liana. I have grown weary of all the death and destruction. So many innocent children killed during the Mitel attacks, not to mention all the world wars that came before that. Sometimes I just want to go to sleep and not wake up. Then I won't have to face this reoccurring cycle of human violence. I'm tired of killing others in the name of lasting peace, a peace that I fear is unachievable. It seems like humanity is caught up in an endless cycle of violence. Quite honestly, the face of death is probably something I recognize better than anything else. I saw it again when I went to visit Chad. He lay there in a critical care tube, all bent and broken, his face badly lacerated. He just laid there, motionless, barely clinging to life. He's only 16 years old. To an immortal, that is just the blink of an eye. Before that, you died. Before that our two daughters . . ."

Tears streamed down his cheeks again.

"I just don't know what to do anymore. I feel lost and all alone."

Suddenly, a blinding bright white filled the room. Janus raised his arm to shield his eyes. When the brightness subsided, he cautiously lowered his arm. Standing right in front of him was Liana's hologram, sparkling brightly.

"Hello my love," she said.

"Liana? Is that really *you*?"

"Yes."

"But how is this possible?"

"I exist now in another form and dimension, one that isn't constrained by time. I still don't understand much of it as it is all still new to me."

"But you died sixteen years ago."

"To me, it seems like only yesterday. All I can tell you Janus is that I can't maintain this appearance very long. As it is, I commandeered another hologram program from this facility. I fear that I've corrupted it also."

"OK then, tell me: what is going to happen to Chad?"

"I have no more ability to tell the future than you do."

"He is so young. He can't die. Not now. Not yet."

"We all receive one human life Janus. It's what we do with that time that's truly important."

"What should I do Liana? Mitel will not leave Thrae alone."

"You already know the answer to that. It's something both you and Markus regret doing previously."

"Attack Mitel and free their people once and for all?"

"Yes."

"And then you think there will be lasting peace?"

"I don't know. But it appears to be the only way Thrae will break the cycle of Mitel aggression."

"If we are successful, who will lead the Mitel people?"

"It must be led by someone who has uncompromising courage, compassion, ethics and morals."

Janus thought for several seconds.

"OK," he nodded. "Then I will dedicate my remaining time to achieving just that."

Liana smiled. She then changed the subject.

"I am happy to hear about Ana," she said. "You need a daughter in your life. She is so much like you."

Liana paused.

"Do you love her?"

"*Ana*? Of course —"

"No, I'm talking about Adria."

Janus stared at Liana. "I don't know," he replied.

"I think you *do* know."

"Why are you asking me this Liana? You know I love you and always will."

"I know Janus, and so shall I. But I am in your past now. There is a woman who loves you with all her heart," Liana continued.

"*Mayla*?"

"Yes. And you know that you love her too."

Janus nodded.

"Then go tell her. Be with her. Live and love with her. Cherish her."

"OK," whispered Janus. "But —"

"No *buts*."

Liana stepped forward and embraced Janus tightly. As she did, the room filled with an incredible brightness. He felt her loving spirit flowing throughout his body. It was peaceful and calming. Liana then stepped back and gazed at Janus intently.

"Please go to Chad's side. He can't talk but he needs you desperately."

"What if he dies Liana?"

"As I said Janus, we only get one human life. But that life can take different forms."

"What do you mean?"

"I must go now. Goodbye, my love."

"Wait —"

There was another blinding flash and just like that, Liana's hologram was gone. The room was now suddenly dark and empty. Janus stood silently for a time, thinking about what she said.

"Thank you, Liana," he said loudly, his voice echoing throughout the chamber. "I will always love you."

Janus exited the structure and headed straight for the medical facility. When he entered the waiting room, he saw Mayla and Molly sleeping in chairs in the corner. Janus walked quietly toward Mayla and kneeled beside her chair. He reached out and touched Mayla's hand, awakening her. Mayla looked at Janus and smiled.

Janus then reached over and hugged her tightly.

"I love you," he whispered.

"What about Adria?" she asked quietly.

"She's Ana's mother. That will never change. A small part of me cared for her deeply at one time. But I don't love her. I love *you*, Mayla."

Mayla's face lit up.

Just then, Rad walked in. Molly woke up and rubbed her eyes. Janus sprung to his feet. "How's Chad?" he asked, "Any improvement?"

"I'm afraid not. Janus, the prognosis is not very good. He has suffered severe blunt force trauma throughout his body. Unfortunately, we can only do so much."

"There must be something —"

"The next 48 hours will be critical."

"What are his chances of survival?"

"I don't think you want me to answer that question right now."

"Is there *anything* we can do?"

"Yes. Hope for a miracle."

After Rad left, Janus hugged Molly for a long time.

"I'm so sorry," he whispered. "I'd do anything to help him."

"So would I," replied Molly, tears streaming down her cheeks.

Janus sat with Chad all night. Molly stayed with him for most of the evening before going to her quarters to get a few hours' sleep. During the middle of the night, he sent out a broadcast message from his portable communications device to Zan, Ard, Jun, Zi, Arius, Ana, Markus, Mayla, Teri and Rad. He requested that they meet him at the underground base's smaller forum hall at 8:00 a.m. to discuss the growing Mitel threat. Janus sat with Chad until sunrise at which time Molly returned. He hugged Molly tightly before leaving.

"Please let me know if his condition worsens," Janus whispered.

"I will," she replied. "You need to get some sleep."

Janus made his way up to the forum hall. When he entered, everyone was already there. They all noticed the haggard look on his face.

"Thank you all for coming," said Janus.

"Any update on Chad?" asked Arius.

"I'm told things aren't looking very good."

"I'm truly sorry Janus . . ."

Janus sat down slowly in a chair near the front of the hall. He rubbed his face with his hands before continuing.

"Sitting and watching Chad, I've thought about many things," he began. "I've come to the conclusion that we *must* now attack Mitel and eliminate the Leadership and their allies once and for all. That course of action, although very challenging and risky, will be our only hope of facilitating a lasting peace. We have tried everything else."

"I don't disagree," replied Markus. "We should have brought the fight to them long ago. But that was then. Our current military capabilities are at their lowest levels in recent history. That would make such an assault all that more risky."

"Understood," replied Janus. "But we have no choice. The Mitels keep raising the stakes. They relentlessly continue to develop more sophisticated and powerful weapons of war. Enhanced cluster warheads and now mechanical Battle Spheres. Thrae must act before it's too late."

"Agreed," nodded Zan.

Janus looked down at the floor.

"The World Council discussed invading Mitel more times than I can remember. There are many arguments for and against. In the end, the Council always concluded that the risk of failure far outweighed the likelihood of success. Their rationale: in the event of failure, Thrae would be more vulnerable than ever."

Janus paused before looking back up.

"As I sat there with Chad, I realized that for the first time, we appear to have established a coalition that has a better than even chance of defeating the Mitel Leadership and their allies . . ."

"The people of Mitel are hungry for change," interjected Zi. "But they are not stupid. If they see that there is a fighting chance for victory, they will rise up and join our cause. That is why we have painstakingly, at great personal sacrifice, infiltrated the Mitel military. We now have that chance."

"And for all of those reasons," added Rad, "The Nomas people have agreed to fully support the Thraen and Mitel resistance forces."

"We must also go to great lengths to avoid killing innocent men, women and children," said Zan. "If we don't, we will be viewed as being no different than the Mitel Leadership, their military or their allies. If, by our actions, *that* perception spreads throughout the general population, then the mission will fail."

"You're right," acknowledged Zi. "And that will be an ongoing challenge. And if we begin to prevail, the Leadership will become desperate. There's no telling what they may try to do to their own people while blaming it on us."

"That is a concern," added Janus. "But if we are successful, this is also the first time I can recall having confidence in a successor leadership team."

"Assuming that we are successful," replied Mayla. "Who can we count on to lead the Mitel people in a productive and peaceful direction?"

Janus pointed directly at Zan.

"*Him.*"

He then pointed at Rad.

"And him."

Janus then pointed at Zi.

"And him. Between the three of you, I have complete confidence that Mitel will embark down the road to peace and prosperity, the likes of which your world has never seen."

"What about me?" Jun asked.

"Your job will be to protect all of them from the pockets of resistance looking for revenge."

"That I can do," nodded Jun.

"How do you see the mission unfolding?" asked Arius.

"For starters," replied Janus, "we must accelerate our cruiser construction efforts to unprecedented levels."

"I will get on that right away," replied Zan.

"Good. And let's not forget, we still have Ana and me as Battle Spheres."

"That's right!" replied Ana.

"We also have a new secret weapon. Markus Kilmar, the *hologram Battle Sphere*. He will operate within Mitel's atmosphere with his high energy plasma bolts to help us control the skies."

"Indeed," acknowledged Markus.

"We will also have the Mitel resistance and the Nomas people providing both air and ground support."

"My brother Tor and the Nomas people will do whatever you ask of us," replied Rad.

"So shall we," replied Zi and Jun in unison.

The room was quiet for a time.

"What's our timeframe?" asked Ard.

"Within the next six months," replied Janus. "A year at the most."

"That is a pretty tall order," mused Arius.

"I don't think we have any choice. In my opinion we are on borrowed time already."

"You are probably right."

"I calculated we will need twenty state of the art cruisers, two thousand advanced tactical fighters and transport vessels to deliver them to Mitel."

"We have seven hundred advanced fighters already," Zan pointed out, "along with five new cruisers plus our upgraded renegade cruiser. Six more cruisers are well under construction as are four oversized transport vessels capable of carrying five hundred fighters each. Modules for six more cruisers are also being fabricated."

"They will all be equipped with our advanced cluster pods and propulsion systems," added Ard. "That should surprise more than a few Mitel cruiser commanders."

"But again," replied Arius, "how do you see the mission unfolding?"

"Ana and I would arrive first to attack their space cruisers and Transport vessels," replied Janus. "At the same time, Zan will pilot a USEP to the planet surface where Markus can transform. Ana or I will provide protection for the landing if necessary. From there, Markus will focus on destroying Mitel strike fighters and military infrastructure. Our fleet would subsequently arrive to join in on the assault. If all goes as planned, we will control the skies and outer space. Our ground forces will then seize control of the Leadership complex and all strategic installations such as the power and transportation grids before they can be destroyed."

"I see."

"We also have time to fine tune our attack plans."

"I'll instruct our battle operations team to start running mission computer simulations," said Teri.

There was a brief silence.

"The mission's success will also hinge on our ability to finally deploy large high speed invisibility shields," said Janus. *"It must be a surprise attack."*

"That's for sure," nodded Arius. "Our scientists have been working around the clock developing large invisibility shields. Although they seem to be getting close, they're still struggling with some technical hurdles."

"I'll reach out to Tor on that," said Rad. "The Nomas may be able to provide some technological assistance."

"We've also recovered several of the least damaged mechanical Battle Spheres," interjected Teri. "Maybe we can reverse engineer our own version to neutralize the Mitel spheres."

"All good suggestions everyone," replied Janus.

"Well," said Zan. "I guess we —"

"Have a lot of work to do," interrupted Ard.

"Yes," Zan smiled.

"Then let's get started."

"Not so fast," replied Janus. "We still need the approval of the World Council."

"Do you want me to approach them?" asked Arius.

"I'd like us to go together."

"Good idea. It's not going to be easy convincing them to authorize such a mission at this time."

"I agree," replied Janus. "I've decided that I am going to make them feel very guilty and uncomfortable to consider saying no."

"What will be your rationale?"

"I will tell the Council the truth. To deny the mission will lead to the death of countless more innocent Thraens if Mitel is given the opportunity to attack us one more time."

"And I will reinforce that message when I am given the opportunity to speak," added Arius. "I'll schedule the meeting right away."

By now, Janus had a faraway look in his eye. He was thinking about the lecture he gave Teri in front of Chad in Chad's Battle Hologram back on Earth. Back then, he clarified that a hybrid fighting machine's duty was to protect and defend its people at all costs. For a hybrid to end one's existence would be to neglect one's duty to protect and defend the innocent men, women and children who cannot otherwise protect and defend themselves.

After Chad had reversed his core back on Earth and given the recent events, Janus knew he had changed his thinking on the matter. After the meeting, Janus walked out of the small forum hall with Mayla.

"Are you OK?" she asked. "You seemed distracted in there toward the end."

"So much is happening so fast," he replied. "I just need time to process everything and . . ."

"And *what*?" asked Mayla.

"Hope for a miracle."

"We're all hoping for that."

"I know," Janus nodded. "Listen, I'm going to go for a short walk to try and clear my head. See you back at the medical facility?"

"OK," replied Mayla. She squeezed his hand before walking down the hall.

Janus walked through Bay Number 1 and out onto the shelf. He stared at Lake Victoria for a time. His thoughts eventually came back to Chad. He remembered Chad when he was just an infant and bringing him across the universe in the cramped USEP. He recalled watching Chad from afar as he ran around Jim and Molly's back yard as a boy; and talking to him in Randall Park several years later for the first time.

You were forced to grow up fast, he thought.

Janus then contemplated his upcoming meeting with the World Council. After all this time, and despite being at a relative low point in their military capability, Janus was confident that the Council would finally authorize the invasion of Mitel. Given what has transpired between the two worlds over the last fifty years, there isn't another legitimate option to achieving lasting peace.

I'll do whatever I can to help you my son, he thought. *And I'll do whatever it takes to stop the Mitel Leadership once and for all.*

CHAPTER TWENTY-NINE – TRANSFORMATION

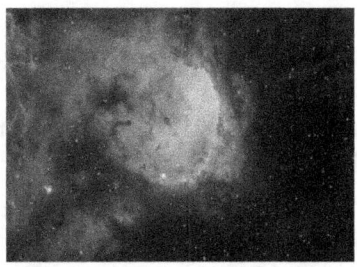

The next morning, Janus headed to the medical facility where he received news that Chad's condition was deteriorating rapidly. Feeling helpless, he went for another short walk. Janus again made his way onto the shelf and stared out over Lake Victoria. It was a beautiful sunny day. A gentle breeze blew against his face as his mind wandered. He thought about Liana and replayed their recent conversation in his mind. It suddenly occurred to him what she might have been trying to tell him.

Janus rushed back into the underground base. He climbed into a base hover craft, powered it up and exited through one of the auxiliary tunnels. Janus banked right and sped toward the old GDC defense fortress.

As it appeared over the tree line, it was obvious that the facility was closed. He landed the hover craft next to the large stone structure and headed straight for the entrance.

I've got to get in, he thought.

On a hunch, Janus entered the voice recognition security codes before stepping ahead for an eye recognition scan. The sliding doors opened and motion sensors activated hallway lights as he entered the facility.

Janus walked down the hallway to three HorVert elevators. Entering the middle one, he quickly instructed it to head directly to the USEP facility. The elevator hummed downwards and then diagonally across the command facility. When he arrived, Janus stepped out into relative darkness. As his eyes grew accustomed to the reduced light, he walked down a hallway to a large open room containing four rows of computer stations. The room itself was much brighter. Looking up, Janus noticed the large opening cut through the ceiling now covered by temporary Plexiglass panels.

Janus quickly walked over to the far wall. He entered a code into a wall mounted keypad which immediately powered up the facility. As he listened to the hum of the systems coming back online, Janus walked over to the last row of computer stations and sat down. He stared at the five USEP pod storage bays located beyond the computers along a long, curved wall. The memories of his escape with Markus and his infant son all came rushing back to him.

Janus sighed deeply.

Hearing a loud beep, he then made his way to the third row of computers. Janus entered a series of instructions and the doors to bay five slid open. Still inside were several silver monitoring orbs about a foot and a half each in diameter with three black or blue stripes, one along the top and on each side which met in the back to form an oversized arrow. Directly in the front was a shiny oblong screen.

The small orbs used a time-tested Thraen technology to achieve their antigravity propulsion: a spinning superconductor ceramic disc in its center, surrounded by a hermetically sealed film of frictionless helium-4 super fluid sonically stimulated with electromagnetic energy to produce *gravitational propulsion*. The angular momentum of the spinning disc controlled the direction and speed of the orb. Later, scientists developed electromagnetically charged plasma fluid chambers surrounding a solid superconductor sphere to achieve the same result.

Janus moved over to another computer at the end of the second row. He entered a few commands causing an overhead panel to slide open. A large black L-shaped tubular machine with a complex array of cables and control boxes descended from the ceiling. On either end was a large convex shaped perforated cap that resembled a very large microscope. The machine had only one purpose: to transform whatever it scanned into an identical and similarly functioning three-dimensional hologram.

Does it still work? There's only one way to find out.

Looking around, he noticed a large empty storage bin on wheels across the room. He pushed it directly under the shorter vertical cylinder.

Janus returned to the computer panel and hit another button. There was a loud humming sound. Seconds later, the storage bin disappeared. The machine quickly powered down and went quiet. Only a hint of gray smoke remained where the storage bin had once sat. Janus shifted his attention to the longer horizontal cylinder. A blue translucent three-dimensional hologram copy of the storage bin suddenly appeared. It slowly floated across the room, eventually disappearing through a side wall.

It works, he thought excitedly.

Janus hurried back to the hover craft and quickly returned to the underground base. Re-entering the medical facility, he was greeted by Markus.

"Where have you been?" he asked. "We've been looking all over for you. Rad said Chad doesn't have much time left."

"Sorry Markus. I went over to the old GDC defense fortress."

Markus paused. "I think I know what you're up to," he replied.

"The hologram transformer. *It still works*. We need to get Chad over there right away."

"But how? The medical staff won't allow his release."

"We'll get Rad to authorize it."

"He doesn't have that kind of medical authority here Sejus."

Janus thought for a moment.

"Where's Molly?"

"She was outside Chad's room with Rad."

"Let's go."

Janus and Markus hurried over to Chad's room. Rad and Molly were still standing outside.

"There you are," said Molly sadly. She looked haggard and exhausted.

"I'm sorry Molly," said Janus. As he hugged her, Molly cried.

Janus stepped back, held her shoulders and looked at her intently.

"I think I have an idea that will save Chad's life."

"*What?*" asked Molly, wiping away her tears.

Janus quickly explained his trip to the old GDC fortress. He also explained how Markus had been transformed into a hologram before their departure to Earth;

and that his hologram was created based in part on his DNA profile rather than his crippled physical self.

"It sounds too good to be true," said Rad.

"It will work," replied Janus resolutely. "I'm sure of it. Molly, as his legal guardian, you need to authorize his release."

"Of course," she replied hopefully.

"Markus, Rad, I want you to formalize Chad's release with Molly as quickly as possible; request an Incubator craft and begin the preparations to transport him. In the meantime, I'm going to try to communicate to Chad what is happening."

"Rad, Markus, let's go," said Molly firmly.

As they rushed off, Janus entered Chad's room and sat down next to him. He reached over and gently took his hand.

"Chad, it's me, Janus. If you can hear me, squeeze my hand once."

Chad squeezed Janus's hand weakly.

"You were critically injured. Do you understand your medical prognosis? Squeeze once for yes and twice for no."

Chad did not respond.

"What I am trying to say is, do you fully understand that your body is injured beyond repair and that . . . *you are dying*?"

Chad squeezed Janus's hand once.

"OK. I want you to listen carefully. I can turn you into a hologram just like Markus. I am confident that you will be fully functional, but no longer human. If that's something you want us to do, we need to act quickly."

Chad immediately squeezed Janus's hand once.

"OK great. Just hang in there a little bit longer for us, promise?"

Chad squeezed Janus's hand once.

In less than an hour, Chad was transported by Incubator craft to the old GDC fortress. Janus, Markus and Zan had arrived and removed the Plexiglass panels covering the large opening. Chad was slowly lowered through the opening before Markus instructed his orb to use its modest antigravity beam to guide him under the short vertical cylinder.

Just as Rad and Molly entered the room, Janus entered instructions into the computer. In a matter of seconds, a silver and blue monitoring orb activated and slowly rose above the floor. Janus directed the computer to locate the orb directly in front of the longer horizontal cylinder. Once there, the orb hovered silently. Janus quickly programmed the orb to accept the Thraen hologram technology.

"OK Chad, here we go," said Janus. He hit the activation button. There was a loud humming sound. Seconds later, Chad disappeared. Only a hint of gray smoke remained.

Molly gasped.

The machine quickly powered down and went quiet. Seconds later, Chad's orb darted around the room before coming to a stop in front of everyone.

"So, *this* is what it's like," announced Chad from inside the orb. "OK, now let me see if I can do it."

A bright beam of light projected down to the floor from a small lens located just below the horizontal blue stripe on the side of Chad's orb. A life size three-dimensional hologram of Chad rose up from the ground.

Janus sighed with relief at the sight of his son looking just like he did before the crash.

Chad looked down at himself.

"You were right Janus," he said. "I look the same as before."

The opaque hologram glowed brightly, surrounded by a light blue hue. Everyone stared at Chad's hologram. Molly and Rad were amazed at how detailed and accurate the image was.

Molly rushed over to Chad and gave him a big hug. Sparkles were everywhere. To Chad's surprise, his sense of feel was essentially unchanged.

"Oh honey," sobbed Molly. "I'm so glad you are OK."

"Don't cry Mom," replied Chad softly. He rubbed her cheek gently and then looked at Janus. "Thank you for saving my life, Janus."

Janus smiled and nodded.

"I guess we've now come full circle," Chad continued. "Now I'm a hologram and you're human."

"I hadn't thought of it like that," replied Janus.

"It'll take some getting used to lad," said Markus. "And you'll come to find out that there are actually several benefits to being a hologram."

"Understood," smiled Chad before turning serious. "I'm just sad that I'll no longer be able to transform into a Battle Sphere."

"That's not necessarily true lad."

"*What do you mean?*"

"When you, Ana and Janus all got shot down fighting the mechanical Battle Spheres, I got so upset that I transformed into a *hologram* Battle Sphere."

"His firepower is extraordinary," said Zan, "at least within a planet's atmosphere. He wiped out the entire fleet of mechanical Battle Spheres almost instantaneously."

"*Wow,*" replied Chad.

"And who knows," added Markus. "Given your abilities to project the plasma shield, we may find out that you have other powers that I don't."

Chad's face brightened.

"Let's find out," he replied.

Chad then thought about Melissica. *I hope she doesn't want to break up with me now*, he worried.

CHAPTER THIRTY – LON RETURNS – PART II

Lon Rexx walked toward the heavily fortified Mitel Leadership Complex. Dressed in a black military uniform, and wearing graphene handcuffs, he was surrounded by a dozen heavily armed Mitel Special Forces. Two soldiers had their electro lasers pointed toward Lon. As the group approached the initial entry checkpoint, Two Leadership guards walked out to greet them.

"Who do we have here?" asked the first guard.

"The traitor Lon Rexx," replied the commander. "We caught him hiding in the Black Mountains. We have been instructed to bring him in front of the Mitel Leadership so they could impose swift punishment."

"Can I see your orders please?" asked the second guard.

"Certainly," replied the commander. He pulled out a small black device that activated a hologram document. The guard pulled out a small device from his utility belt and scanned the document. The device beeped twice.

"Everything appears to be in order," said the guard. "You know where to go from here, right?"

"Yes," nodded the commander.

"And hey, what's with the gray pants and brown long sleeve shirts?"

"Experimental uniforms. We were the lucky ones who got to try them out," winked the commander. "If nothing else, they're comfortable."

"Ha," replied the guard. He then waved them along.

The group walked across the complex grounds, past the large administration structure toward the imposing stone and glass Leadership building. Glancing up toward the twenty-foot-high stone walls, they noticed several snipers keeping a close eye on them.

"So far so good," whispered the commander.

"Yes," replied Lon softly.

Several huge security guards surrounded the group as they entered the Leadership building.

"We were informed by the checkpoint guards that you captured Lon Rexx" said a security guard.

"Yes," replied the commander proudly. "We caught him hiding in the Black Mountains," he added, pointing toward Lon. "We're here to deliver him to the Leader —"

"The Mitel Leadership was *not* expecting you," interrupted a second guard. "They usually punish anyone who attempts an unannounced visit. But you are in luck *this* time. Given the identity of your prisoner, they are willing to meet with you. Follow us to the Forum Hall."

"My apologies and thank you."

"First we still need to document his identity."

A third guard pointed a hand-held scanner at Lon before motioning him to confirm his identity on the retinal scanner. Lon stared at the machine. A light on the left side of the device quickly flashed green.

"Follow us, please," said the first guard.

The group followed three security guards up the wide marble staircase while four heavily armed guards followed closely behind, their footsteps echoing loudly. On the second floor, the first guard motioned the group into the Forum Hall. The seven Leadership members were seated behind the curved stone bench. Lon immediately noticed that they looked different somehow. As the group approached the bench, they were instructed to stop by four more heavily armed guards.

"*Lon Rexx*, we initially thought you had been killed," said the first Leadership member sitting directly across from them. "Once your deactivated helmets and body armor were located, we knew you had survived and likely gone into hiding. I must admit, we are quite surprised you were caught so quickly."

"Me too," quipped Lon.

"It looks like your luck has *finally* run out," replied the first member.

Outside the complex, dozens of Mitel Special Forces dressed in the brown and gray uniforms rushed the initial entry checkpoint. They quickly overwhelmed and killed the checkpoint guards and entered the complex grounds. Rebellion snipers, having taken off their camouflage shirts to expose their brown shirts, shot and killed loyalist snipers as they prepared to fire at the incoming soldiers down below.

Inside the Leadership building entrance, rebellion guards shot and killed the remaining loyalist guards. The sound of ball laser fire echoed up the stairway.

"*What is going on?*" asked the first member.

On cue, the Special Forces soldiers and rebellion guards opened fire on the remaining loyalist Leadership guards.

When it was over, Lon pulled off his fake handcuffs and tossed them aside. Approaching the bench, he stepped over the dead, smoke rising from their bodies.

"*What is the meaning of this?*" a second leadership member demanded.

Reaching under his shirt, Lon pulled out a dwarf electro laser.

"I think it's pretty obvious," he replied.

"You can't do this!"

"I just did."

The second member shook his arm in defiance.

"We must unleash the second-generation mechanical Battle Spheres to protect us!"

Lon pointed his electro laser at the member.

"Too late for that," he replied.

Lon fired a laser burst at the member, hitting him squarely in the chest. The impact staggered the member backward. He stared at Lon in astonishment before collapsing dead on the floor.

"Anybody else want to tell me what I can't do?"

"What do you want Rexx?" asked the first member.

"I didn't come here this time to *ask* for anything. I came here to take. I came here to seize power."

"I see."

"I don't think you do," replied Lon, his temper rising. "*All of you* have a self-centered attitude and a pompous behavior. Every time I came before you, you belittled me and talked down to me. You never served in the military, yet you put the lives of others at risk without a second thought. You criticize everyone and treat people like inanimate objects."

"*And you don't, Rexx?*" the first member asked.

"No."

"We have heard many stories about you."

"Are you going to try to lecture me *again*?"

"No. But you have always lied and cheated and sacrificed the lives of others to preserve your own."

"That's preposterous."

"*Really*? To satisfy my own curiosity, I spent hours reviewing cruiser logs from the failed mission to Earth. I came across a series of entries received from your crippled cruiser. You fled to the only cruiser that made it out. You sacrificed your entire crew to save yourself. So how are you any different? How are you any *better* than us?"

"You're lying!"

"No, it's the truth. The last transmission sent by your communications specialist seconds before the annihilation event. It read: *Rexx, Cmdr. Departed cruiser ahead of crew in violation of evacuation protocol. Stated reason: to coordinate fleet withdrawal. He departed before rescuing us. He left us for dead.* End of transmission."

Lon was now furious. He could also feel the soldiers and guards staring at him.

"You will say anything to push your own agenda!" he bellowed. "You and all the other Leadership members put the fleet in an untenable position by sending it across the universe in search of the secrets of immortality; secrets that were going to be used *just for you*. I did what I could at the time under very difficult circumstances. You, on the other hand are selfish, pompous and arrogant!"

The first Member knew that his life now hung in the balance.

"I am sorry Rexx," he replied quietly. He then struck a conciliatory tone. "What I was trying to say was that self-preservation is the only way to survive life on this planet. We can work together."

"It's too late for that."

Lon systematically opened fire at the members as they desperately tried to flee.

Outside the Leadership complex, more Rebellion soldiers streamed through the entry checkpoint. They searched the remaining buildings for Leadership loyalists. Soon thereafter, Adrian Sidd and Lex Golb entered the complex surrounded by several Special Forces personnel. The two men walked confidently straight toward the Mitel Leadership building. Up in the air, Adrian's strike fighters streaked by overhead.

In the Forum Hall, Lon walked up to the first member as he lay dying on the floor. He kneeled and stared at him in disgust.

"A pretty short immortal life, wouldn't you agree?"

The Leadership member moved his lips as he tried to speak. Lon stood back up and shot him again. Seconds later, Adrian and Lex entered the Forum Hall still surrounded by Special Forces personnel.

"We did it!" shouted Lon triumphantly.

"Yes, we did," nodded Adrian.

"Before I killed them, one member yelled something about a second-generation Battle Sphere," explained Lon.

"That's very good to know. Did he say more?"

"No."

Adrian looked around the hall briefly.

"It's a pity we didn't take any of them prisoner."

"Why?"

"So, we could interrogate them, Lon. It's much easier being told where everything is rather than having to go searching for it."

"I guess so . . ."

"*You guess so*? They could have told us a great deal about their mechanical technology, immortality serum and where the riches are hidden. That's just for starters."

Lon didn't respond.

"It's your temper Lon," Adrian continued. "It keeps clouding your judgment. Today is a prime example. I'm afraid you have become too much of a liability."

Lon glanced around the Forum Hall. Everyone there was staring at him. Adrian stepped forward and raised his left arm toward Lon as he prepared to fire an arm-mounted laser weapon.

"Arrgh!" growled Lon. He dashed toward the stone bench as he fired his dwarf laser at Adrian, striking him between the chest and shoulder. The force of the blow caused Adrian to stumble backward ever so slightly. Lon glanced out of the corner of his eye in disbelief as Adrian raised his arm a second time. He then shot Lon several times in the back as he tried to flee over the stone bench; the force of the pulses shoving him over the top surface and down to the floor with a loud thud. Lon laid there motionless, his eyes open, blood oozing from his mouth as smoke rose from the back of his torso.

"That's that," said Adrian calmly.

"Are you OK?" asked Lex incredulously. A large hole had been burned through Adrian's shirt near his shoulder. Lex was at a loss as to how he was still standing.

"Robotic appendages," explained Adrian matter-of-factly. "You could call me a cyborg at this point."

Suddenly uncomfortable, Lex changed the subject.

"We're in charge now," he said.

"Not quite," replied Adrian. "First, we must secure the Complex. Next, we seize control of both the skies and outer space. I've ordered fifteen hundred of our strike fighters into the air from our underground bases. They have been instructed to shoot down any military craft attempting to take off. Initial reports from outer space are excellent. We appear to be in control of the space cruiser fleet thanks to our loyal commanders."

"That's great news," replied Lex.

"It's a very promising start," acknowledged Adrian. "But we must be prepared to put down any counter rebellions from those loyal to the Leadership. We will also have to deal with the Mitel resistance. But we are far from being *in charge*."

"You're right. Sorry, I spoke too soon. And what do you propose we do about the Thraen resistance?"

"We'll deal with them in due time. But first things first: we must locate and take control of the second-generation mechanical Battle Spheres. We need to make sure they are ready to go and re-programmed to serve *us*."

"Good idea."

"But for now, let's go outside and see how our purge of the complex is coming along. It should be just about complete. After that, I want you to order a final sweep of all the buildings and then arrange for a group of soldiers to come back here and clean up this mess."

"Will do."

Adrian walked out the Forum Hall followed by Lex, the Special Forces soldiers and Leadership guards. Walking down the stairs, Adrian clenched his robotic fists.

I have a big score to settle with the Nomas people for what they did to me, he thought. *I'll find their hidden city and take their technology for my own use. After that, I'll eradicate them.*

CHAPTER THIRTY-ONE – DREAMING

Molly walked through the opening between the huge stone-faced doors onto the shelf. The sun was setting beyond the mountains across Lake Victoria. Orange and red reflected off the long thin rows of clouds. The lake's gentle waves glistened as they reflected the sun's rays. It was simply beautiful. As she walked further away from the huge cavern, the sound of construction faded. Looking out at the lake, Molly thought about everything that has happened during the relatively short time she, Chad and Jim had spent on Thrae. Even though she refused to give up hope, Molly knew deep down she might never see her husband, who was also her best friend, ever again. Her teenage son is now a living hologram, who now has a Battle Sphere for a sister.

She crossed her arms and took a deep breath.

Susan, having just finished her end of the day debriefing, stepped out through the opening for some fresh air. Seeing Molly standing alone in the distance, she walked over to her.

"Hey," said Susan stopping next to Molly. "OK if I join you?"

"Sure," replied Molly quietly.

"It's a beautiful sunset, isn't it?" offered Susan.

"It really is," acknowledged Molly. "Thrae is truly an incredible place. Here we are, the first of our kind to visit another inhabitable planet, but all I can think about is Jim."

Molly sighed deeply.

"Is it wrong of me to keep hoping that he's still alive?"

Susan paused before answering.

"Molly, I've been in love a few times anywhere from for a few months to a few years," she replied. "But it was *never* the kind of relationship that you and Jim have. I mean, I can't begin to comprehend what that's like. You raised a son and shared your lives together. Through good times and bad, you guys are able to count on each other. You're a *team*, you know?"

"Yeah," replied Molly, wiping away the tears.

Susan turned toward Molly and looked at her intently.

"Never give up hope Molly. *Never*. If Jim is out there, we'll find him."

"And what if he isn't?" asked Molly almost in a whisper.

Susan stepped forward and hugged Molly.

"Don't think like that, OK? If there's one thing I've learned from being in the military is that there is a time and place for everything. Losing colleagues who were also special friends and special people happened more times than I care to admit. But despite all odds, people sometimes do make it through."

"But Jim isn't like those people. He was never trained like that."

"You'd be surprised how resourceful people can be, especially when they're in danger. I don't know Jim very well, mostly from the time hurtling across the universe in tight quarters, but he seems to me to be the kind of person who just might surprise you that way."

"I hope you're right," sniffled Molly.

"*Listen*, if the time comes for you to accept that Jim is gone, you'll know it. You'll work your way through it, no matter how painful it might be."

Susan stepped back and looked at Molly again.

"But that time *isn't now, OK?*"

Molly shook her head and wiped away more tears.

"Listen," said Susan, "over the next few days, let's put together a plan to search for him in ways we haven't tried yet, OK?"

"OK," replied Molly.

"In the meantime, you have your son to worry about. Chad's an incredibly brave and mentally strong kid, but transitioning to his new life as a hologram is going to have its ups and downs. He needs you now more than ever."

"You're right," replied Molly resolutely. "Susan, thank you so much. If, you'll excuse me, I'm going to check on him right now."

"You're welcome," smiled Susan. She watched Molly walk back toward the huge stone-faced doors for a time before turning back to gaze at the end of the sunset.

Atlas, Jim and Isak settled into the circular enclosure at the center of the underground hallway network below Timad. Like Amer, the enclosure had a stream running through it with well-developed ground foliage. Jim felt right at home. They were unaware that Scavengers had observed them entering the population center. Word quickly spread. Several Scavengers vying to fill the void left by the death of Big Kelan gathered their best fighters and headed to Timad. They knew full well that whoever

received credit for killing Isak, Atlas and Jim would replace him as the new Scavenger boss. As soon as the Scavenger groups arrived, they bickered. The leaders finally
agreed to assign search areas to each Scavenger group.
Search patrols were to commence after dusk.

In their circular enclosure, Isak and Jim ate the last of
the food they brought from the medical facility before the
trio retired for the night. Lying on his foam cot, Jim gazed
up through the foliage at the filtered light shining down
through the top of the enclosure. He eventually drifted off
to sleep. Over the next several hours, Jim had several
dreams. In the first one, he was fighting several Scavengers in the dark all by himself. In the second dream, he
was being chased by angry holograms down an underground passageway. When he reached a large, blackened
door, it was locked. When he turned back around, Atlas
was standing right in front of him, smiling. The last dream
involved Molly and Chad. In it, the three were camping
out on Lake Edward. Jim and Chad went fishing near several large rocks. Afterward, they all went for a peaceful
walk around the island. As Jim hopped into their motor
boat to go for supplies, he saw storm clouds gathering. He
knew something bad was about to happen. He suddenly
woke up, his heart racing.

Jim sat up and glanced around the enclosure. Isak was
fast asleep nearby and Atlas was nowhere to be found,
presumably out looking for food.

I have a family, he thought.

Unable to sleep, he stared up at the lights waiting for
Atlas to return. Early the next morning, Atlas entered the
enclosure carrying his backpack filled with food. As Jim
jumped up from his cot, Isak awoke. Jim described his

dream to Atlas while Isak listened quietly. As he spoke, Jim noticed that Atlas had a guilty look on his face.

"What's wrong, Atlas?" he asked.

Atlas lowered his backpack to the ground and rummaged around the bottom of the bag until he found a small black hand-held device. He looked at Jim.

"I'm truly sorry," he began. "I've been holding back information about you."

Atlas activated the device and handed it to Jim.

"Your name is James Johnson," he explained.

Jim watched the missing person message intently. Memories of his life rushed back to him like a raging river.

"Oh my god," he muttered "I'm *Jim Johnson*. I have a wife Molly and son Chad. We came to Thrae recently. We traveled with others six hundred light years from planet Earth in two small high-speed pods. We came here with Janus Stone to try to help free Thrae from the Mitels."

"That's quite a distance," replied Isak. "The name *Janus Stone* sounds oddly familiar . . ."

"I'm guessing you want to return to your family right away," said Atlas glumly. "I knew it was just too good to be true."

"What do you mean?" asked Jim.

"That you were our friend . . . and would help us."

"I *am* your friend, and I would do *anything* to help the two of you."

Jim paused.

"Listen to me carefully," he continued. "I think getting hit on the head allowed me to understand and speak your language. Now that my memory is returning, I don't know how much longer that ability will last."

"Understood," nodded Atlas.

"My adopted son Chad Stone is from Thrae," Jim continued. "He is also a Battle Sphere just like Isak was. He is also Janus's natural born son. They came to Earth over fifteen years ago to escape the horrific Mitel attack."

"That attack was really bad," replied Atlas. "But I don't recognize this *Janus Stone* person."

"He is or *was* immortal. He is also known as Zebulon Park."

"The *Battle Sphere*?" asked Isak skeptically. "I thought he was dead."

"No, he isn't" replied Jim. "And now he can transform again."

Jim thought for a moment.

"He was also known by another name," he said. "One which I think is very important to the both of you."

"*Who*?" asked Atlas.

"A long time ago he was known as Chancellor Sejus Theron, head of the World Council."

Atlas grunted and rolled his eyes.

"No, listen to me," pleaded Jim. "I don't know what he was like back then, but I'm pretty sure he's changed a great deal. He's changed quite a bit in the short time I've known him. He would be the first to admit that he has made many mistakes in his life."

Atlas and Isak glanced at each other.

"I think he can help both of you clear your names now," added Jim. "And I'll be with the two of you every step of the way. I promise you."

Isak and Atlas didn't respond.

"Since Janus is able to transform again after so many years," continued Jim, "maybe there's hope for you too, Isak. And Atlas, I've heard that Thraen scientists can boost your electric charge."

Isaac and Atlas again stared at each other.

"We don't trust the surface dwellers," replied Atlas eventually. "Too much time has gone by, and we don't want to be disappointed again, or even *worse*. At least down here, we have our freedom."

Jim looked at Isak intently.

"Is that the way you feel too?"

Isak looked away.

"I must defer to Atlas," he replied quietly.

Jim thought for a moment.

"OK, fine," he said. "But I owe it to myself to find my family. I'm going to leave after dark."

He then paused.

"Listen, I want to thank the both of you. You saved my life and then taught me a level of courage I never thought I could ever be capable of."

Atlas and Isak listened silently.

"You showed me how to be mentally and physically tough. You also taught me how to defend myself. I know now that if given no other choice, I could use those skills to help others who can't protect themselves."

Jim paused again to gather his thoughts.

"I really want to use my new skills to make a difference somehow. I never told you this, but I snuck out early one night when Isak was sleeping. Atlas, you were out somewhere, probably looking for food or clothing. I eventually came across a young girl lying dead in a large room with no roof. She was probably killed when the roof collapsed on her. She was covered in debris up to her torso and a thick layer of dust. In the moonlight, she looked almost like a statue. From the looks of her clothing, she was probably a Scavenger out foraging for food. Nobody should ever die that way.

I'll never forget her, and I want to try to find a way to end the Scavenger crisis. Finch told me that she has met many of them. She said that most of them are very good people, they're just misunderstood. Finch thinks if the

Scavengers had more women leaders, things would be a lot better."

Jim glanced around the opening.

"I guess you could say the same thing about where I come from," he mused. "Anyway, thank you again."

Jim turned and walked back to his cot as Isak and Atlas stared at each other.

Jim sat alone most of the day. While he was disappointed in Isak and Atlas, he understood their trepidation. Jim was also excited and eager to find his family. At dusk, he packed up his backpack. Atlas came over and handed him some food.

"Here," he said quietly. "Take this. You'll need to keep up your strength."

After carefully packing away the food, Jim put on his backpack as Isak slowly walked over.

"I'm going to miss you guys," said Jim.

"We'll miss you too," replied Atlas somberly.

Jim hugged Atlas. Sparkles from his focused energy lit up the entire enclosure. He then hugged Isak.

"Thanks for all the training," said Jim quietly. "Please promise me you'll be careful?"

"I Promise. And you do the same." Isak then smiled. "Remember, always —"

"Counterattack," interrupted Jim.

"That's right."

Jim walked to the blackened door at the edge of the enclosure. He waved one last time before heading down the hallway, the door slowly closing behind him.

Reaching the surface, he took a HorVert elevator to the main elevated walkway and headed toward the hyper speed railway.

Two levels above, three heavily armed Hologram soldiers were out on patrol. One of them noticed Jim walking alone. He activated the zoom feature on his night vision glasses and studied the subject intently before pushing a button on the left side of his glasses to capture images. The soldier quickly downloaded them onto his hand-held computer and compared them to the image of Jim Johnson on the missing person's message board. The screen quickly flashed a bright yellow message.

Identification match *probable* – 91.6 percent.

It's the missing alien, he thought. *I'm sure of it.*

He reached for his communications device and contacted the GDC. A Hologram technician tried to contact Markus. By mistake, he instead accessed Molly's communications device.

Molly was sitting in her living quarters with Susan who had just stopped in to check on her when the device beeped.

"Kind of late, isn't it?" Molly mused as she reached for it. She listened briefly before looking at Susan. "They're speaking Thraen," she said.

"Give it to me," instructed Susan. She listened intently, occasionally acknowledging in Thraen she understood. At the end, she thanked the technician. The device beeped again.

"Who was *that*?" asked Molly.

"A technician from the Global Defense Center," replied Susan. "He said there has just been a very credible sighting of Jim by a Hologram soldier. They said he was walking by himself on a main elevated walkway."

"What? *Where?*"

"A population center called Timad. I think it's about twenty minutes from here by hover craft, flying at full speed that is."

"Then let's go."

"It's late Molly. Locating soldiers to go with us on short notice at night is going to take a little time."

"*We don't have time.* Let's just go."

"Molly, the population centers can be very dangerous at night."

"That's even more reason to find him. He's walking out there defenseless all by himself."

Susan thought for a moment.

"OK, let's do it," she replied.

Molly and Susan rushed to the underground base. They quickly climbed into a medium sized military hover craft. After powering up the craft and entering the coordinates for Timad into the computer, Susan adjusted her night vision glasses.

"Here we go," she said.

Sixteen curved clear retractable overlapping roof sections closed tightly above them as the craft took off. They exited through an auxiliary tunnel into the darkness.

Twenty minutes later, Susan landed the hover craft in an open area at the direct center of Timad. After securing the craft, the two headed to the closest HorVert elevator and headed straight to the main elevated walkway. Stepping out of the elevator, Susan and Molly looked in both directions. The population center looked deserted.

"Let's try this way," pointed Molly.

Jim adjusted his backpack as he made his way along the elevated walkway. The structures on either side were becoming more numerous and irregular in shape. As he approached the corner of one unusually shaped structure, he froze. Off in the distance he noticed several figures standing on the walkway.

Scavengers. What are they doing up here? Jim thought as he continued to observe the group.

They're either looking for trouble or for Atlas, Isak and me. I wish there was a way I could warn them.

Jim then looked down the walkway behind him. He saw more figures headed his way.

I can't stay here, that's for sure.

He quickly turned and disappeared down a darkened narrow passageway.

Molly and Susan walked along the elevated walkway which became narrower as tall structures protruded on both sides. The women noticed dark and narrow passageways between some of the structures. Suddenly, several silhouettes stepped out of a passageway up ahead. Looking behind her, Susan noticed that several Scavengers were now following them.

"We've got company," said Susan apprehensively.

The women stopped walking as the first group of Scavengers walked toward them into the light, stopping just a few feet in front. An enormous Scavenger named Tiny Mountain stepped toward Susan. Without saying a word, he grabbed her by the shirt with his massive hand and tossed her to the ground and into the shadows next to a dark narrow passageway. He then reached for Molly.

"Don't you touch me," she shouted.

He grabbed her and tossed her into the shadows next to Susan.

Tiny Mountain stared down at them.

"You made a big mistake coming out here at night all by yourselves," he sneered. "You are going to pay for that mistake *with your lives.*"

By now, fifteen Scavengers had formed a semicircle around the two women. There was no escape.

"Molly I'm really scared," said Susan softly.

Once Jim's eyes grew accustomed to the darkness, he walked along the passageway which soon turned right. About three hundred yards beyond that, it intersected with another, even narrower, passageway.

Jim slowly stepped out and looked to his right. It was very dark.

Probably goes back to the walkway, he thought.

Looking to his left, Jim saw what appeared to be an opening to a well-lit area off in the distance.

Maybe I can find a way around the Scavengers going that way.

Jim suddenly heard muffled voices echo down the passageway on his right followed by a loud angry voice. By the sound of the voices, Jim sensed someone was in trouble and that the Scavengers were probably to blame. He glanced to his left one more time, looking at the well-lit opening.

As he was about to head toward the light, Jim remembered the young girl he found lying in the rubble.

I just can't walk away and let defenseless people die, he thought. *I won't be able to live with myself,* he sighed.

Jim dropped his backpack and ran up the darkened corridor toward the sound of the voices.

Tiny Mountain motioned one of his men forward who lifted a long fiberglass pole and prepared to strike Molly. Suddenly, Jim darted out of the dark passageway into the shadows, stopping directly in front of Susan and Molly. Without looking back, he barked instructions in Thraen. So focused on their safety, the women didn't recognize the sound of his voice.

"What did he say?" asked Molly nervously.

"He said to stay on the ground behind me," replied Susan. "And no matter what happens, *don't* move."

After a brief pause, the Scavenger lunged at Jim with his pole. Jim reached out with his graphene arm, stopping the pole in mid motion. He quickly yanked it out of the Scavenger's hands and swung it directly at attacker's mid-section, doubling him over. Jim swung the pole a second time, breaking it over his head. The Scavenger fell to the ground in an unconscious heap.

Tiny Mountain stared angrily at Jim for a long time. He then shined a small light toward him. Tiny Mountain's face suddenly brightened as he recognized Jim.

"I know you," he bellowed. "You're with Atlas and Isak aren't you?"

Jim didn't respond.

"Well, they aren't here to help you, are they?"

Jim silently adjusted his stance, readying for an attack.

"We *hate* your kind," continued Tiny Mountain, "even more so than the surface dwellers. Living underground, you are supposed to be one of us. But instead, you attack, injure and *kill* us. You helped kill Big Kelan. And because of that, not to mention all the misery you have caused *us*, tonight you are going to die!"

Tiny Mountain motioned three Scavengers forward. The first Scavenger lunged at Jim swinging his high strength fiberglass pole. Jim raised his graphene arm to block the blow, causing the pole to shatter into several pieces on impact. He then punched the startled Scavenger in the face several times with his open palm. The bloodied attacker crumpled to the ground next to the first one.

Jim then pivoted and blocked two punches from the second Scavenger before counterattacking by gouging his eyes. The Scavenger shrieked in pain. His screams quickly attracted another group patrolling nearby. With a chop to the neck, Jim silenced the Scavenger; the nauseating sound of his neck breaking caused Molly to cover her mouth. Given an opening, the third Scavenger hit Jim firmly above his left eye, opening a bloody gash. The Scavenger swiftly struck Jim a second time in his right eye, causing him to stagger backward. The force of the blow shattered the orbital bones around the eye, permanently blinding him on that side. Jim grunted under the excruciating pain. Regaining his footing, he quickly counterattacked, punching the Scavenger repeatedly in the face, dropping him to the ground unconscious.

By now, the other group had joined the semicircle.

Stay calm, thought Jim. *It's my only chance.*

Tiny Mountain motioned five Scavengers at Jim, who immediately positioned himself with his left side forward to maximize his remaining vision. The first Scavenger swung wildly at Jim, who easily dodged the blows by pivoting his torso. Before the second attacker could strike, Jim punched him in the face with his graphene arm, killing him instantly. He then grabbed the first Scavenger and stepping forward, shoved him into the third onrushing attacker. Swinging his high strength fiberglass pole, the fourth Scavenger inadvertently struck the third attacker in the head, rendering him unconscious. In all the turmoil, Jim grabbed and repeatedly struck the first attacker in the face with an open palm, knocking him lifeless to the ground.

The fourth Scavenger swung his pole again as he lunged at Jim, who reached out and grabbed it with his graphene arm. He yanked it out of the attacker's hands and stepping forward, hit the Scavenger in the neck with a sickening crack. Jim stepped around the crumpled Scavenger and swung the pole back and forth, hitting the fifth attacker, shattering the pole. He then tossed the remaining pole into the darkness as the fifth Scavenger slumped to the ground.

Growing impatient, Tiny Mountain motioned five more Scavengers at Jim who quickly dropped the first one before being grabbed by the second. He used his graphene arm to easily break the grip before punching him squarely in the nose. The Scavenger's eyes rolled back into his head as he fell to the ground just as the third Scavenger grabbed Jim. While raising his arm along his body to contain the attacker, the fourth Scavenger swung a metal pole hitting Jim squarely in his normal arm. The force of the blow splintered both the ulna and radius bones below his elbow. Jim breathed rapidly as he tried to maintain both his focus and balance. With his grapheme arm, he broke the third attacker's grip and in a single motion, punched him squarely in the face, killing him. The fourth Scavenger stepped back and swung the pole at Jim again, shattering his shoulder socket and upper arm. Jim groaned in anguish. As the Scavenger swung the pole a third time, Jim pivoted and grabbed it with his graphene arm, twisting it out of the attacker's hands. He then swung the pole down low with all his might, breaking both Scavenger's legs with a nauseating *cracking* noise.

The fifth Scavenger punched Jim in the face repeatedly causing the vision in his remaining eye to blur temporarily. Jim shook off the blows and kicked the attacker in the groin, dropping him to the ground. As the Scavenger lie withering in pain, yet another Scavenger lunged forward, swinging a metal pole at Jim's right leg. Seeing the pole at the last second, Jim tried to step aside, but it was too late. The forceful blow shattered his leg above the knee. The Scavenger quickly swung the pole again, striking Jim in the ankle. Jim dropped to his knees in agonizing pain. Looking down, he saw that his leg and ankle were both a twisted mess, blood seeping through his pants.

Don't . . . give . . . up, Jim thought.

Tiny Mountain stepped forward and yanked the metal pole away from the Scavenger. He cautiously approached Jim, gripping the pole tightly with both hands.

"I'm going to kill you myself," he shouted.

Jim desperately tried to push himself up to a standing position with his graphene arm but couldn't.

Get up. Get up, Jim exhorted his body. His heart and mind were racing. Jim tried to push himself up one last time, but it was no use. His body was broken and simply could not comply.

I just can't, Jim thought. His spirit, struggling with the excruciating pain inflicted upon his body, finally gave up. Jim slumped to the ground.

Oh god, he thought. *I'll never see my family again. I'm sorry Molly . . . I tried my best to do the right thing. I love you and I'm so sorry . . .*

Tiny Mountain raised the pole high into the air as he prepared to strike Jim squarely over the head.

Looking up, Jim raised his graphene arm to protect his head. He then grimaced as he waited for the oncoming blow. Tiny Mountain swung the pole down at Jim with all his might.

A few seconds earlier, Isak had darted out of the darkened passageway, his eyes flashing metallic green. He leaped forward and grabbed Tiny Mountain's pole in mid motion. Isak then yanked the shaft from the huge Scavenger leader's hands and in a single fluid motion, swung the metal object at Tiny Mountain's torso. In self-defense, the huge man tried unsuccessfully to extend his left arm. The force of the blow shattered his ribs in several places. Without hesitating, Isak pivoted around and swung the pole in the opposite direction, shattering Tiny Mountain's right arm. The huge Scavenger screamed in pain. Isak quickly stepped forward and punched the leader in the face as hard as he could, killing him instantly. The huge Scavenger fell to the ground with a loud thud.

As Isak stood over Tiny Mountain, the growing crowd of Scavengers stared at him in stunned disbelief. In their anger, three attackers rushed Isak. He swung the pole at each Scavenger with lethal precision. A fourth, and then a fifth attacker, raced forward.

The results were the same.

As several more Scavengers prepared to rush Isak, Atlas appeared from out of the darkness with a loud shriek.

The attacking Scavengers momentarily froze. Atlas stopped and quickly glanced down at Jim.

"Don't worry James, we'll take it from here. Please hang in there for us, OK?" he said softly.

Jim shook his head and spit out blood.

Atlas then floated over to Isak.

"Are you ready?" asked Isak.

"*Yes,*" replied Atlas resolutely, "*most definitely.*"

As the large group of Scavengers rushed forward, Atlas and Isak stepped toward them side by side. They grabbed, beat and tossed the attackers in all directions like rag dolls. By now, more patrolling groups of Scavengers had rushed to the scene to join in on the attack. As the skirmish raged on, the Scavenger's screams and shouts could be heard blocks away.

High above, three patrolling hologram soldiers were drawn toward all the noise. Looking down, they saw the attack unfolding. As they floated down to the walkway, they quickly drew their electro laser long guns.

Recognizing Atlas and Isak, they opened fire on the large contingent of attacking Scavengers. Several attackers fell to the ground in all directions, including several group leaders. Once the attackers realized their groups were being systematically slaughtered, the large Scavenger contingent turned and ran off, disappearing into the darkness.

The soldiers lowered their weapons and surveyed the scene. Scavengers lay dead and dying everywhere, smoke slowly drifting into the air from some of their torsos. After confirming the area was secure, the soldiers approached Atlas and Isak.

"Are you guys, OK?" the first soldier asked.

"Yes, and thank you," nodded Isak.

"You're most welcome," replied a second soldier. "We recognized both of you right away. It's an honor to finally meet you."

Isak and Atlas smiled modestly.

"Unfortunately, some of the Scavenger groups have gotten out of control," continued the soldier. "They're taking advantage of all the chaos brought on by the Mitel attacks. They no longer show any regard for innocent civilians and are starting to go out of their way to harm them. It's gotten to a point where it's beginning to shed a bad light on the Scavenger population as a whole."

"That seems to be the trend," acknowledged Isak. He then quickly turned his attention to Jim still kneeling on the ground, bloodied and silently clutching his badly mangled arm.

Isak knelt down next to Jim.

"Are you OK James?" he asked quietly.

"I think I'm going to need more graphene appendages," grunted Jim. "I also can't see out of my right eye."

"We'll arrange for all of that, don't worry."

"OK," muttered Jim. He then looked up at Isak. "You came for me. *Why*?"

"Because you're our friend . . ."

Jim gritted his teeth and attempted to stand up. Isak helped him to his feet.

"Does that mean you're going to come with me now?" asked Jim hopefully.

"Yes," Isak grinned. "Yes, it does . . ."

"This man requires *urgent* medical attention," said Atlas. "He needs to be taken to Pisco to see surgeon Evan Lennac right away."

"Understood," replied the first soldier who quickly called for a medical hover craft.

Seconds later, Janus, Ard and Zan came running down the walkway followed closely by Markus, Chad, and several hologram soldiers. A half hour earlier, Arius had finally reached Markus. After realizing Molly and Susan had left for Timad by themselves, he then contacted Janus who scrambled three military hover craft and raced to the population center.

As Janus approached, he couldn't believe his eyes. Recognizing Janus, Isak's eyes flashed metallic green. He motioned two hologram soldiers to come over and help Jim before walking toward Janus.

"I thought you were dead," said Janus incredulously.

"We thought the same of you Zebulon," replied Isak. "Why are you now going by the name *Janus Stone*?"

"It was my birth name," he replied. "I guess I finally decided to stop running from my past."

"Wait," said Atlas. "Are you telling us you're from the old wealthy, powerful and controversial Stone family?"

"Yes," replied Janus. "And speaking of the past, I'm so sorry for not helping both of you clear your names so long ago. Years later, after I found out that Isak was family, it made me even more ashamed. I searched and searched, but both of you had vanished. I'll do whatever it takes to make it up to you, *I promise*."

"What do you mean *family*?" asked Atlas curiously.

"Isak, Isak Stone," replied Janus. "He's my great-great-grandfather."

"You're *not* Isak *Sone*?" laughed Atlas. "After all this time . . . you have a different last name, and a famous one at that."

Janus stepped forward and hugged Isak tightly.

"Welcome back," he said quietly.

"This is indeed quite a surprise," smiled Isak, "and a very pleasant one at that."

By now Molly and Susan had gotten back on their feet and had slowly walked over to Janus and the group.

"Molly, Susan," said Janus. "We are all so relieved that both of you are OK."

Chad quickly floated over to Molly and gave her a long hug. Sparkles from his focused energy lit up the entire walkway. She then walked slowly toward Janus.

"A man," muttered Molly. "He came out of nowhere. He fought for us. He saved our lives . . ."

Janus translated what Molly had said to Isak.

"Wait," said Isak. "She's *Molly Johnson?*"

He then paused.

"Tell her that the man who saved her isn't just any man. He's quite special in many ways," he said.

Isak then stepped aside to reveal a man standing, aided by two hologram soldiers. His leg was bloodied and crumpled, and he was clinging to his badly broken arm. By now, he was being brightly illuminated by the soldiers' focused energy. His hair was matted with sweat and blood and his right eye bloodied and badly swollen.

Molly stopped in her tracks and stared. She raised her hands to her mouth.

Could it be? She thought. *Is it possible?*

Molly cautiously stepped forward, keenly studying the badly injured man standing before her.

Struggling with his pain and balance, Jim now sensed he was being watched. Looking over, he immediately recognized Molly.

"Hi honey," he grunted with a slight grin.

Molly couldn't believe what she was seeing. Her face lit up like a bright star at night as she rushed forward and hugged Jim with everything she had.

CHAPTER THIRTY-TWO – ONE LAST CHANCE

Adrian and Lex walked across the Leadership Complex followed by a contingent of Special Forces personnel. They came across a commander leading a dozen rebellion soldiers across the grounds. Hovering next to them was a small military hover-tran typically used to carry food and other supplies. Adrian noticed that it was covered with empty body bags.

"Where are you men headed?" he asked.

"We're retrieving bodies across the way, Sir," pointed the commander.

"I see," replied Adrian. "When you're done there, I'd like you to proceed to the Leadership Building. Several bodies need to be collected from the second floor Forum Hall including the *now former* Leadership members and Lon Rexx. I want the bodies of the Leadership members brought to the medical facility for a detailed autopsy."

"What about Rexx's body?"

"Burn it," replied Adrian.

"Yes, Sir."

In the Leadership Building's Forum Hall, Lon's body lie motionless on the floor behind the curving stone bench. His eyes were still open, although the blood had ceased oozing out his mouth. Smoke from the several laser blasts had all but stopped rising from the back of his torso.

Having slowly regained consciousness, Lon blinked, and slowly raised his head.

My graphene body armor underneath my uniform saved my life, he concluded.

Lon slowly sat up, wiped the saliva and blood from his mouth and rubbed his torso. Sitting there, his thoughts drifted back to what Zan had told him about his father, a Mitel Resistance commander who was killed by Mitel Embedded Special Forces when he was 4 years old. He then recalled the day his mother was killed by a suicide bomb at a produce market when he was 12.

"*Trust no one*," he muttered to himself. "It has gotten me this far."

His body now stiff and sore, Lon slowly reached for the top surface of the stone bench. He grabbed hold of its rear edge and with a tired groan, pulled himself up to a standing position.

ABOUT THE AUTHOR

With a graduate degree in thermo-fluids engineering, a financial MBA, and now a practicing lawyer, Keith has always had a thirst for learning, adventure, and trying new things. He has always had a creative side – drawing his first cartoon called *Bill Liss* at age 11 – and an imagination that knows no limits. His love of science fiction and the possibilities of the Universe led him to write this action packed and thought-provoking science fiction novel. Keith loves to be outdoors and is an avid stone wall builder, collector of marble patterned ocean rocks, and science enthusiast.

Also by Keith Michon, *The Last Immortal*.